BARBARA REBELL

BARBARA REBELL

MARIE BELLOC LOWNDES

ISBN: 978-93-90215-18-8

Published: 1907

LECTOR HOUSE LLP
E-MAIL: lectorpublishing@gmail.com

BARBARA REBELL

BARBARA REBELL

BY

MRS. BELLOC-LOWNDES
Author of "The Heart of Penelope"

FRONTISPIECE BY
GILBERT WHITE

AUTHORIZED EDITION

1907

CONTENTS

PROLOGUE.

"Have regard to thy name; for that shall continue with thee above a thousand great treasures of gold."

ECCLESIASTICUS xl. 12.

BARBARA REBELL'S tenth birthday,—that is the ninth of June, 1870,—was destined to be long remembered by her as a day of days; both as having seen the first meeting with one who, though unknown till then, had occupied a great place in her imagination, if only because the name of this lady, her godmother, had been associated every night and morning with that of her father and mother in her prayers, and as having witnessed the greatest of her childish disappointments.

Certain dates to most of us become in time retrospectively memorable, and doubtless this sunny, fragrant June day would in any case have been remembered by Barbara as the last of a long series of high days and holidays spent by her in her French home during the first few years of her life. Barbara Rebell left St. Germains two months after her tenth birthday; but the town which has seen so few changes in its stately, ordered beauty, since it afforded a magnificent hospitality to the last Stuart King and Queen of England, always remained to her "home," in the dear and intimate sense of the word, and that for many years after everything save the actual roof and walls of the villa where Mr. and Mrs. Rebell had lived such long, and on the whole such peaceful years, had been destroyed—overwhelmed with locust-like destruction—by the passage of an alien soldiery.

But early in the June of 1870 there was nothing to show what July and August were to bring to France, and the various incidents which so much impressed the child's imagination, and made the day memorable, were almost wholly connected with that solitary inner life which is yet so curiously affected by material occurrences.

Barbara's birthday began very differently from what she had thought it would do. The little girl had pleasant recollections of the fashion in which her last fête day, "la Sainte Barbe," had been celebrated. She remembered vividly the white bouquets brought by the tradespeople, the cakes and gifts offered by her little French friends, they who dwelt in Legitimist seclusion in the old town—for St. Germains was at that time a Royalist stronghold—far from the supposed malign influence of the high forest trees, and broad, wind-swept Terrace, which had first attracted Barbara's parents, and caused them to choose St. Germains as their place of retreat.

And so Barbara had looked forward very eagerly to her tenth birthday, but by eleven o'clock what, so far, had it brought her? No bouquets, no cakes, no trifling gifts of the kind she loved! As she sat out in her little chair on the balcony of which the gilt balustrade was now concealed by festoons of green leaves and white roses, and from which opened the windows of her mother's drawing-room, the child's conscience pricked her somewhat. Had not her parents early called her into their room and presented her with a beautiful little gold watch—a gift, too, brought specially from London by Mr. Daman, a Queen's Messenger, who was one of her father's oldest friends, and one of the very few English-speaking folk who ever sought out Mr. and Mrs. Rebell in their seclusion?

"You may wear it all to-day," her mother had said with some solemnity, "but after to-night I will put it away until you are old enough to take care of a watch." In time the little watch became a cherished possession, a dear familiar friend, but on this first day of ownership Barbara took small pleasure in her gift.

The child had not liked to ask if any further birthday treat was in contemplation. She stood in great awe of her quiet-mannered, preoccupied father: and, while loving her gentle, kind mother with all her eager passionate little heart, she did not at that time understand how tenderly she herself was loved in return by the fragile, pensive looking woman, who seemed to those about her absorbed rather in her husband than in her daughter.

And so, after having been dismissed rather curtly by her father, Barbara had made her way disconsolately out to the balcony which was in a sense her playroom, for there she spent many of her solitary hours. Sitting in her own little wicker chair, with *The Fairchild Family* lying on the osier table by her side, and *Les Malheurs de Sophie* on her lap, she wondered rather wistfully what the day to which she had so much looked forward was likely to bring forth.

Dressed in a white India muslin frock, her long dark hair curled, as was the fashion in those days, and tied neatly out of the way with a pale blue ribbon, her unseeing eyes gazing at one of the most beautiful views in the world, little Barbara Rebell, not for the first time, fell to wondering why her life was so different from that of the English children of whom she read in the books her mother had lately sent for from the home of her own childhood. Even the Fairchilds were a family, not a solitary little girl; each of the French children she knew had at least one brother or sister apiece to bear them company, and all through her thoughts—her disconnected, discontented birthday thoughts—there ran a thread of uneasy wonder as to why she and her parents were living here in France instead of in far away England.

Barbara had of late become dimly aware that her mother made no effort to enter into the eager, cheerful life about her; even after many years spent entirely in France Mrs. Rebell still spoke French with a certain difficulty, and she had tacitly refused to form any tie but one of courteous acquaintance with the few French families with whom—entirely for the sake of her child, but Barbara did not know that—she had entered into social relation, using a Protestant banker as a connecting link.

The summer before her tenth birthday Barbara had overheard some fragments of a conversation held between two mothers of some of her little French friends; and the few words, so carelessly uttered, had roused a passion of emotion in the innocent eavesdropper: the feeling which most predominated being the unreasoning, pathetic surprise felt by a childish mind when brought suddenly across anything in the nature of a masked attack.

"Enfin qu'est que ce Monsieur Rebell a bien pu faire de si terrible? Pour moi il a un air sinistre, cet homme-là!"

"Peut-être a-t-il tué quelqu'un en duel! Il parait qu'en Angleterre on est devenu féroce sur ce châpitre-là."

"En tous cas, cette pauvre Madame Rebell est bien jolie, et bien à plaindre!"

The effect of these few carelessly uttered words had been to transform the listener from a happy baby into a thoughtful, over-sensitive little girl. Barbara had felt a wild revolt and indignation in the knowledge that her parents were being thus discussed—that her father should be described as "sinister," her mother pitied. Again and again she repeated to herself the words that she had heard: their meaning had stamped itself on her mind. Could her father have indeed killed a man in a duel? To Barbara the thought was at once horrible and fascinating, and she brooded over it, turning the idea this way and that: the constant companionship of her mother—for Mrs. Rebell rarely left her alone with their French servants—having unconsciously taught her a deep and almost secretive reserve.

Were her father guilty of what these French ladies suspected, then—or so thought Barbara—his subdued, melancholy air was indeed natural, as also his apparent dislike of meeting fellow countrymen and countrywomen, for he and his wife always markedly avoided any English visitors to St. Germains. Now and again Mr. Rebell would spend a long day in Paris, returning laden with a large parcel of books, the latest English novels for his wife, more serious volumes for his own perusal; but both Mrs. Rebell and Barbara had learnt to dread these expeditions, for they brought with them sad after-days of silent depression and restlessness which left their effect on the wife long after the traveller himself had regained his usual sombre quietude of manner.

Barbara was secretly proud of the fact that her father was so extremely unlike, both in manner and in appearance, the Frenchmen who now formed his only acquaintances. This was perhaps owing in a measure to the periodical visit of his London tailor, for Richard Rebell had retained amid his misfortunes—and he was fond of telling himself that no living man had been so unfortunate—the one-time dandy's fastidiousness about his dress. The foreigners with whom he was unwillingly brought in contact sometimes speculated as to the mysterious Englishman's probable age; his hair was already grey, his pale, coldly impassive face had none of the healthy tints of youth, yet he was still upright and vigorous, and possessed to a singular degree what the French value above all things, distinction of appearance. As a matter of fact Mr. Rebell was only some twelve years older than his still girlish-looking wife; but certain terrible events seemed to have had a petrifying effect both on his mind and on his appearance, intensified by the fact that both he and Mrs. Rebell tacitly chose to live as if in a world of half-lights and neutral tints, rarely indeed alluding to the past, instinctively avoiding any topic which could cause them emotion.

Every age,—it might be said with truth every decade,—has its ideal of feminine beauty; and the man who had been the Richard Rebell of the London 'fifties would instinctively have chosen and been chosen by the loveliest girl in the brilliant world in which they both then moved and had their being. Adela Oglander, the youngest child of a Hampshire squire, had indeed been very lovely, satisfying in every point the ideal of her day, of her race, and of her generation: slender and yet not over tall: golden-haired and blue-eyed: with delicate regular features, and rounded cheeks in which the colour soon came and went uncertainly when Richard Rebell began to haunt the Mayfair ball-rooms where he knew he would meet her and her placid, rather foolish mother. The girl's sunny beauty and artless charm of manner had delighted the social arbiters of the hour. She became, in the sense which was then possible, the fashion, and her engagement to Richard Rebell, finally arranged at the royal garden party which in those days took place each season in the old-world gardens of Chiswick House, had been to themselves as well as to their friends a happy, nine days' wonder.

Richard Rebell had been long regarded as a bachelor of bachelors, a man whose means did not permit of such a luxury as marriage to ill-dowered beauty. But his friends reminded themselves that he was in a sense heir to a fine property, now in the actual ownership of his cousin, a certain Madame Sampiero, a beautiful childless woman separated from the Corsican adventurer whom she had married in one of those moments of amazing, destructive folly which occasionally overwhelm a certain type of clever and high-spirited Englishwoman. Still, if there were some who shook their heads over the imprudence of such a marriage as that of Richard Rebell and Adela Oglander, all the world loves a lover, and every man who had obtained the privilege of an introduction to Miss Oglander envied Rebell his good fortune, for his betrothed was as good and as blithesome as she was pretty.

Later, when recalling that enchanted time, and the five happy years which had followed, Mrs. Rebell told herself that there had then been meted out to her full measure of life's happiness: she might, alas! have added that since that time Providence had dealt out to her, as completely, full measure of pain and suffering. For what was hidden from the little circle of kindly French gossips at St. Germains had been indeed a very tragic thing.

After those first cloudless years of happy, nay triumphant, married life, the popular, much-envied man-about-town, the proud husband of one of the loveliest and most considered of younger London hostesses, had gradually become aware that he was being looked at askance and shunned by those great folk to whose liking he attached perhaps undue importance.

Then had followed a period of angry, incredulous amazement, till a well-meaning friend found courage to tell him the truth. It had come to be thought that he "sometimes" cheated at cards—more, it was whispered that he had actually been caught red-handed in the house of a friend who had spared him exposure in deference to what were then still the English laws of hospitality. His chief accuser, the man to whom Rebell, once on his track, again and again traced the fatal rumour, was, as so often happens in such cases, himself quite unimportant till he became the man of straw round whom raged one of the most painful and protracted libel suits fought in nineteenth century England.

At first public opinion, or rather the opinion of those whom Rebell regarded as important, ranged itself on his side, and there were many who considered that he had been ill-advised to take any notice of the matter. But when it became known, and that in the pitiless, clear publicity afforded by a court of law, that the plaintiff's private means were very small, much smaller than had been suspected even by those who thought themselves his intimates, that he was noted for his high play, and, most damaging fact of all, that he had been instrumental in forming a new and very select club of which the stated object was play, and nothing but play, feeling veered sharply round. Richard Rebell admitted—and among his backers it was pointed out that such an admission made for innocence—that a not unimportant portion of his income had for some time past consisted of his card winnings. That this should be even said outraged those respectable folk who like to think that gambling and ruin are synonymous terms. Yet, had they looked but a little below the surface, where could they have found so striking a confirmation of their view as in this very case?

To cut the story short, the lawsuit ended in a virtual triumph for the man whose malicious dislike and envy of the plaintiff had had to himself so unexpected a result. Richard Rebell was awarded only nominal damages. The old adage, "The greater the truth the greater the libel," was freely quoted, and the one-time man of fashion and his wife disappeared with dramatic suddenness from the world in which they had both been once so welcome. Apart from every other reason, Mr. and Mrs. Rebell would have been compelled, by their financial circumstances, to alter what had been their way of life. All that remained to them after the heavy costs of the lawsuit were paid was the income of Mrs. Rebell's marriage settlement, and then it was that Richard Rebell's cousin, the Madame Sampiero to whom reference has already been made, arranged to give her cousin—who was, as she eagerly reminded him, her natural heir—an allowance which practically trebled his small income. Thanks to her generosity Mr. and Mrs. Rebell and their only child, born three years after their marriage, had been able to live in considerable comfort and state in the French town finally chosen by them as their home of exile, where they had been fortunate in finding, close to the Forest and the Terrace, a house which had belonged to one of the great Napoleon's generals. The hero's descendants were in high favour at the Tuileries and had no love for quiet St. Germains: they had accordingly been overjoyed to find an English tenant for the stately villa which contained many relics of their famous forbear, and of which the furnishings, while pleasing the fine taste of Richard Rebell, seemed to them hopelessly rococo and out of date.

As time went on, Adela Rebell suffered more rather than less. She would have preferred the humblest lodging in the quietest of English hamlets to the charming villa which was still full of mementoes of the soldier who had found a glorious death at Waterloo. Sometimes she would tell herself that all might yet go well with her, and her beloved, her noble, her ill-used Richard—for so she ever thought of him—were it not for their child. The knowledge that Barbara would never enjoy the happy and lightsome youth which had been her own portion was bitter indeed: the conviction that her daughter must be cut off from all the pleasant girlish joys and privileges of her English contemporaries brought deep pain.

Let us now return to Barbara and to the birthday which was to prove eventful. The little girl was still hesitating between her French and her English storybook when the door of the drawing-room opened, and she saw her mother's slight figure advancing languidly across the shining floor to the deep chair where she always sat. A moment later Barbara's father came into the room: he held a newspaper in his hand, and instinctively the child knew that he was both annoyed and angered.

"Adela," he said, in the formal and rather cold accent which both his wife and child had come to associate with something painful or unpleasant, "I should like you to read this,"—then he added: "Well, no, I think I will ask you to listen, while I translate it," and slowly he read, choosing his words with some care, anxious to render every shade of meaning, the following sentences, composing one of the happily-named "Echoes" printed on the front page of the *Figaro*, the then newly-established, brilliant journal which had become the most widely read paper in French society:—

"Her Majesty the Empress to-day received in private audience Madame Sampiero, *née* Rebell, one of the most sympathetic and distinguished of English great ladies, and this in spite of the fact that the name of Sampiero is full of glorious memories to those who know and care—and what good Frenchman does not do so?—for the noble traditions of Corsican history. Mylady Sampiero"—here Barbara's father suddenly lowered the paper and, glancing at his wife, gave a queer sardonic laugh—"was presented subsequently to his Majesty the Emperor by the noted English statesman, Mylord Bosworth, who, it will be remembered, was on terms of intimacy with our Sovereign when he, as Prince Louis Napoleon, was living a life of exile in London. Indeed, it was Mylord who first gratified the London world with the news that the prisoner of Ham had escaped."

There was a slight pause: Mr. Rebell laid the *Figaro* down on a gilt-rimmed table which stood close to his wife's chair.

"Well?" he said, "what do you think of that? You'll see it dished up, and who can wonder at it, in next week's *Vanity Fair*!"

The child, sitting out on the balcony, saw her mother's pale face become gradually suffused with colour, and she heard the almost whispered words, "Yes, most unfortunate! But, my dear, how could poor Bar have foreseen such a thing?"

"Of course Bar did not foresee this, but equally of course Bosworth must have supplied the *Figaro* with the main facts—how else could this absurdly worded note have been written?" He added slowly, "This is obviously Bosworth's idea of a rebuff to the Embassy—Ah well! I didn't mean to tell you, but I had it from Daman yesterday that Barbara, immediately on her arrival in Paris, had been sent word that she must not expect, this time, to be received at the Embassy."

As he spoke Richard Rebell walked up and down the room with quick, rather mincing steps: again he came and stood before his wife: "Our name dragged in!" he exclaimed, "apropos of nothing!" a note of sharp chagrin and disgust piercing in his quiet voice. "And this ridiculous, this farcical reference to that adventurer, if indeed Sampiero is the man's real name, of which I always had my doubts!"

The colour faded from Mrs. Rebell's cheek; she put her hand with an instinctive movement to her side: "Richard," she said, her voice faltering, in spite of herself, "the letter I received to-day was from Barbara Sampiero. She is staying, as you know, at Meurice's, and—and—pray do not be angry, my love, but she proposes to come out and see us here, to-day!"

Her husband made no answer. He stood speechlessly looking down at her, and when the silence became intolerable Mrs. Rebell again spoke, but in a firmer, less apologetic tone. "And oh! Richard, I shall be so glad to see her—I can never never forget how good she was to me years ago—how nobly generous she has been to us all, since that time."

Richard Rebell turned abruptly away. He walked to the open window, and little Barbara, glancing up, noticed with surprise that her father looked very hot, that even his forehead had reddened. Standing there, staring out with unseeing eyes at the wonderful view unrolled below, he closed and opened his right hand with a nervous gesture, as he at last answered, "Of course, I also shall be glad to see her. Though, mind you, Adela, I think that during all these long years she might have found time to come before." Turning round, he added, "Surely you are not afraid that I shall insult my kinswoman in what is, after all, my own house?" and then, as his wife made no answer, he said with sudden suspicion, "Of course, she is coming alone? She would not have dared to propose anything else?"

Mrs. Rebell rose from her chair. She came and stood by her husband, and for the first time became aware of her little daughter's presence on the balcony. She had, however, said too much to retreat, and perhaps she felt that the child, sitting out there, would make her difficult task easier.

"No, Richard, unfortunately she does not propose to come alone. It seems that Lord Bosworth has been given the use of one of the Imperial carriages, and he proposes to drive her here, the whole way from Paris. He is staying, it appears, at the Bristol."

And then, turning away, she burst into sudden stormy tears, covering her face with her hands, swaying from head to foot with suppressed sobs.

Barbara watched the scene with bewildered surprise and terror. It is good when a child's ideal of married life is founded on that of her own father and mother. Richard Rebell was often impatient and irritable, but the little girl had never seen the shadow of anything resembling a dissension between her parents. What then did this mean, what did her mother's tears portend? But already Mrs. Rebell was making a determined effort to command herself. Her husband put his arm, not untenderly, round her shoulder, and, with his face set in stern lines, led her back to her seat. Then Barbara suddenly darted into the room, and flung herself on her mother, putting her slender arms round that dear mother's neck, and so making, all unconsciously, a welcome diversion. Mrs. Rebell even laughed a little. "Dear child—my little Barbara—you didn't know that grown-up people ever cried!"

But Barbara was already retreating to the balcony, and she heard her father say in a low voice, as if for the first time he realised that his words might be overheard: "I am sure you do not seriously contemplate our receiving Bar and—and Bosworth, together? The idea is monstrous! Whatever has come and gone, however degraded I may have become among my fellows, I still have the right to protect my wife from insult, and to expect her to obey me in such a matter as this."

But Mrs. Rebell clasped her hands together and looked up in the troubled face of the man opposite her with a look at once appealing and unsubmissive. "Richard!" she cried, "oh Richard! I always *do* obey you. When have you ever known me go against your wish, or even desire to do so?"

He shook his head impatiently, and she added urgently, "But in this one matter—oh, my dear love—pray try and look at it from my point of view! It is Barbara I wish to receive—Barbara who is of consequence to us. I know well all you would say," the speaker gave a sudden imperceptible look towards the open window, "but you would not put so cruel an affront on that noble, generous creature! Ah, yes, Richard, she *is* noble, she *is* generous."

"Her generosity shall cease to-morrow—nay, to-day," he said grimly.

"Do not say so!" she cried, starting up; and her little daughter, gazing fascinated, thought she had never till to-day seen her mother look really alive, alive as other women are. Mrs. Rebell had pushed her fair hair off her forehead, and her cheeks were red, her blue eyes bright, with excitement.

"Ah no, Richard, I was not thinking of *that*—not of such generosity as can be made to cease to-morrow or to-day; but of Barbara's long goodness to us both, nay, if you like to put it so, of her goodness to me, who am in no way related to her! Could any sister have been kinder than she has been? Were any of my own sisters as kind? True, we did not choose to avail ourselves of her hospitality."

"I think that now, even you, Adela, must see that I was right in that matter." Richard Rebell spoke rather drily.

"I never questioned it," she said, sharply; "you know, Richard, I never questioned your decision!"

There was a pause. The memories of both husband and wife were busy with the past, with an offer which had been made to them by Richard Rebell's kinswoman, the offer of a home in England, and of a chance, or so the wife had thought at the time, of ultimate rehabilitation for one whom many even then thought completely innocent of the charge brought against him.

Adela Rebell was a woman of high honesty, and so, "That is not quite true," she said reluctantly, "I *did* question your decision in my heart, and I see now that you were right. And yet perhaps, my dear, if we had been there——?"

Richard Rebell got up. He went and deliberately closed the window, making a temporary prisoner of the little girl: then he came back, and answered, very composedly, the meaning of the half-question which his wife's shrinking delicacy had prevented her putting into words. "Our being there, Adela, would not have made the slightest difference," he gave her a peculiar, not unkindly look, "for as a matter of fact I was then aware of what you apparently only began to suspect long after; and I think that you will admit that the state of things would have made our position at Chancton intolerable. We should very naturally have been expected to shut our eyes—to pander——"

"Yes—yes indeed!" his wife shrank back. "But you never told me this before——Why did you not tell me at the time?"

"My dear," he answered, very quietly, "that is not the sort of thing a man cares to tell, even his wife, when the heroine of the tale is his own cousin. And Barbara, as you have reminded me to-day, had behaved, and was behaving, very generously to us both."

"But if—if you felt like that, why——"

Mrs. Rebell looked up imploringly; she knew what this conversation meant in pain and retrospective anguish to them both. But again Richard Rebell answered, very patiently, his wife's unspoken question, "Well, I admit that I am perhaps illogical. But what happened two years ago, I mean the birth of Barbara's child—has made a difference to my feeling. I don't think"—he spoke questioningly as if to himself, "I hope to God I don't feel as I do owing to any ignoble disappointment?"

"No, no, indeed not!" There was an accent of eager protest in Adela Rebell's voice: "Besides, she wrote and said—she has said again and again—that it will make no difference."

"In any case," he spoke rather coldly, "Barbara Sampiero is certain to outlive me, and I do not think anything would make her unjust to our girl. But to return to what I was saying, and then, if you do not mind, Adela, we will not refer to the subject again——The birth of the child, I say, has altered my feeling, much as it seems to have done, from what I gather from Daman, that of the rest of the world."

"I always so disliked Mr. Daman," his wife said irrelevantly.

"No doubt, no doubt—I grant you that he's not a very nice fellow, but he's always been fond of her, and after all he has always stuck to us. There's no doubt as to what he says being the truth——"

"But Richard—is not that very unfair?" Mrs. Rebell spoke with a fire that surprised herself: "if, as you tell me now, you always knew the truth concerning Bar and Lord Bosworth, should what happened two years ago make such a difference?"

"Till two years ago,"—he spoke as if he had not heard her words,—"Barbara held her own completely; so much is quite clear, and that, mind you, with all the world, even including the strait-laced folk about Chancton. I suppose people were sorry for her—for them both, if it comes to that——Besides, it was nobody's business but their own. Now——" he hesitated: "Daman tells me that she's absolutely solitary, I mean of course as regards the women." He added musingly, as if to himself, "She's acted with extraordinary, with criminal folly over this matter."

"Then she is being treated as we should have been treated,—indeed as we were, by most people, during the short time we stayed in England eight years ago?"

"I do not think," Mr. Rebell spoke very coldly, "that your comparison, Adela, holds good. But now, to-day, the point is this: am I to be compelled to receive, and indeed to countenance, Barbara Sampiero and her lover? and further, am I to allow my wife to do so? Do you suppose"—he spoke with a sudden fierceness,—"that either Barbara or Bosworth would have ever thought of doing what you tell me they have actually written and proposed doing, to-day, had our own circumstances been different? Barbara may be—nay she is, as you very properly point out—a noble and generous creature, but in this matter, my dear Adela, she's behaving ungenerously; she's exacting a price, and a heavy price, for her past kindness. But it is one which after to-day I shall take care she shall not be in a position to exact.

"Yes," he went on slowly, "we shall of course have to give up this house," his eyes glanced with a certain affection round the room which had always pleased his taste. "Our requirements," he concluded, "have become very simple. We might travel, and show our child something of the world."

A light leapt into his wife's eyes; oh! what joy it would be to leave St. Germains, to become for a while nomadic, but with a sigh she returned to the present. "And to-day, what is to happen to-day, Richard? There is no time to stop them—they will be here in two or three hours."

Mr. Rebell remained silent for some moments, and then: "Not even to please you," he said, "can I bring myself to receive them. But I admit the force of what you said just now. Therefore, if you care to do so, stay—stay and make what excuse for my absence seems good to you. Bosworth will know the reason well enough, unless he's more lost to a sense of decency than I take him to be. But Bar—poor dear Bar," a note of unwilling tenderness crept into his cold voice, "will doubtless believe you if you tell her, what indeed is true enough, that I have an important engagement to-day with Daman, and that, if she cares to see me, I will come and see her before she leaves Paris——"

The speaker went to the window and opened it. He bent down and touched Barbara's forehead with his dry lips. "I trust," he said in his thin voice, "that you will have a pleasant birthday. I will bring you back a box of chocolates from Marquis'," and then, without waiting to hear the child's murmured thanks, he turned on his heel and was gone. Barbara did not see her father again till the next morning.

It was early afternoon, and the fair-haired Englishwoman and her little dark, eager-eyed daughter were sitting out on the rose-wreathed balcony of the Villa d'Arcole. Mrs. Rebell was very silent. She was longing for, and yet dreading, the coming meeting with one she had not seen since they had parted, with tears, at Dover, eight long years before. Her restlessness affected the child, the more so that Barbara knew that her marraine, that is to say in English, her godmother, the source of many beautiful gifts, was at last coming to see them, and in her short life the rare coming of a visitor had always been an event.

Below the balcony, across the tiny formal garden now bright with flowers, the broad sanded roadway stretching between the Villa d'Arcole and the high cool screen formed by the forest trees, was flecked with gay groups of children and their be-ribboned nurses. St. Germains was beginning to awake from its noonday torpor, and leisurely walkers, elegant women whose crinolines produced a curious giant blossom-like effect, elderly bourgeois dressed in rather fantastic summer garb, officers in brilliant uniforms—for in those days Imperial France was a land of brilliancy and of uniforms—were already making their way to the Terrace, ever the centre of the town's life and gossip.

Suddenly there came on Barbara's listening ears a sound of wheels, of sharply ringing hoofs, of musical jingling of harness bells. Several of the strollers below stayed their footsteps, and a moment later Mrs. Rebell became aware that before the iron-wrought gilt gates of the villa there had drawn up the prettiest and most fantastic of equipages, while to the child's eager eyes it seemed as if Cinderella's fairy chariot stood below!

Had Richard Rebell been standing by his wife, he would doubtless have seen something slightly absurd, and in any case undignified, in the sight presented by the low, pale blue victoria, drawn by four white horses ridden by postillions, two of whom now stood, impassive as statues, each at one of the leaders' heads. But to Richard Rebell's little daughter the pretty sight brought with it nothing but pure delight; and for a few moments she was scarcely aware of the two figures who sat back on the white leather cushions. And yet one of these figures, that of the woman, was quite as worthy of attention as the equipage which served to frame her peculiar and striking beauty, and so evidently thought the small crowd which had quickly gathered to gaze at what had been at once recognised as a carriage from the Imperial stables.

Dowered, perhaps to her own misfortune, with a keen dramatic instinct, and a rather riotous love of colour, Barbara Sampiero had chosen to dress, as it were, for the part. Her costume, a deep purple muslin gown, flounced, as was the fashion that spring, from hem to waist, her cross-over puffed bodice, and short-frilled sleeves, the broad Leghorn hat draped with a scarf of old lace fastened down with amethyst bees, and the pale blue parasol matching exactly in tint the colour of the carriage in which she was sitting, recalled a splendid tropical flower.

A certain type of feminine beauty has about it a luminous quality; such was that of Barbara Sampiero, now in full and glowing perfection: some of its radiance due to the fact that as yet Time—she was not far from forty—had spared her any trace of his swift passage. The involuntary homage of those about her proved that she was still as attractive as she had been as a younger woman; her beauty had become to her an all-important asset, and she guarded and tended it most jealously.

Her companion was also, though in a very different way, well worthy of attention. Before stepping out of the carriage he stood up for a moment, and, as he looked about him with amused and leisurely curiosity, the spectators at once recognised in him a typical Englishman of the ruling class. Every detail of his dress, the very cut of his grizzled hair and carefully trimmed whiskers, aroused the envy of those Frenchmen among the crowd who judged themselves to be of much his own age. He had not retained, as had done his contemporary and one-time friend, Richard Rebell, the figure of his youth, but he was still a fine, vigorous-looking man, with a bearing full of dignity and ease.

As his eyes quickly noted the unchanged aspect of the place where he found himself, he reminded himself, with some quickening of his pulses, that no Englishman living had a right to feel in closer touch with the romance of this French town. In the great grim castle—so unlike the usual smiling château—which rose to the right behind the Villa d'Arcole, his own Stuart forbears had spent their dignified exile. More, he himself had deliberately chosen to associate the most romantic and enchanting episode of a life which had not been lacking in enchanting and romantic episodes, with this same place, with St. Germains. He and Madame Sampiero had good reason to gaze as they were both doing at that famous hostelry, the Pavillon Henri IV., of which they could see, embowered in trees, the picturesque buildings overhanging the precipitous slopes.

Julian Fitzjames Berwick, Lord Bosworth of Leicester, had always made it his business to extract the utmost out of life. He had early promised himself that, whoever else were debarred from looking over the hedge, he would belong to the fortunate few who are privileged to walk through the gate. So far he had been wonderfully successful in attaining the various goals he had set himself to attain. This had been true even of his public life, for he had known how to limit his ambitions to what was easily possible, never taking undue risks, and ever keeping himself free from any connection with forlorn hopes. This perhaps was why this fortunate man was one of the very few statesmen in whom his fellow countrymen felt a comfortable confidence. All parties were apt to express regret when he was out of office, and though he was no longer in any sense a young man, it was believed that he had a future or several futures before him.

Many of Lord Bosworth's contemporaries and friends would have shrunk from taking part in such an expedition as that of to-day, but the intelligent epicurean had so arranged every detail of this visit to Richard Rebell and his wife, that it must bring, at any rate to himself, more pleasure than annoyance. Still, he was not sorry to stand for a moment enjoying the pretty, bright scene, the wonderful view, and his own and his beautiful companion's sentimental memories, before going in to face, as he fully believed he was about to do, the man who was at once Barbara Sampiero's unfortunate kinsman and his own former intimate.

Meanwhile Mrs. Rebell had made her way swiftly down the house: hurriedly she herself opened the front door, waving back the French servant: then, when she saw the little crowd gathered round the gate, she retreated nervously, leaving her two guests to make their way alone up the geranium-bordered path. But once they had passed through into the cool dim hall, once the light and brightness were shut out, then with a cry of welcome Adela Rebell put her arms round the other woman's neck, and with a certain shy cordiality gave her hand to the man whose coming to-day had caused Richard Rebell to be absent from this meeting, and this although, Mrs. Rebell eagerly reminded herself, Lord Bosworth also had been true and kind during that bitter time eight years ago.

At last all four, for little Barbara was clinging to her mother's skirts, made their way up the narrow turning staircase, and so into the long, sparsely furnished drawing-room, full of grateful quiet and coolness to the two who had just enjoyed a hot if a triumphal drive from Paris.

At once Madame Sampiero sat down and drew the child to her knee: "And so," she said, in a deep melodious voice, "this is little Barbara Rebell? my god-daughter and namesake! For do you know, my child, that I also am a Barbara Rebell? One always keeps, it seems, a right to one's name, and lately—yes really, Adela, I have sometimes thought of going back to mine!" Then, with a quick change of voice, her eyes sweeping the room and the broad balcony, "But where is Richard?" she asked. "Surely you received my letter? You knew that I was coming, to-day?"

But she accepted with great good humour Mrs. Rebell's faltered explanation, perhaps secretly relieved that there need be no meeting with the cousin who owed her so much, and who yet, she had reason to believe, judged with rather pitiless severity the way she had chosen to fashion her life.

Meanwhile, Lord Bosworth and little Barbara had gone out on the balcony, and there, with the tact for which he had long been famed, and which had contributed not a little to his successes when Foreign Minister, he soon made friends with the shy, reserved child.

But Madame Sampiero took no advantage of the *tête-à-tête* so thoughtfully arranged by her friend; instead, but looking intently the while into Adela Rebell's sensitive face, she dwelt wholly on the immediate present; telling of her stay in Paris, the first for many years; of her visit to St. Cloud—in a few satirical sentences she described to her silent listener the interview with the Empress Eugénie amid the almost theatrical splendour of the summer palace. But the gay voice altered in quality as she asked the quick question, "I suppose Richard reads the *Figaro*? Did he tell you of that reference to—to my visit to St. Cloud?" As her companion bent her head, she added: "It has annoyed us so very much! I am sorry that Richard saw it—I cannot imagine how they became aware of my maiden name, or why they brought in that reference to Corsica!"

Mrs. Rebell, the kindest, least critical of women, yet felt a certain doubt as to whether in this matter her cousin was speaking the truth, but Madame Sampiero had already dismissed the subject with an impatient sigh. She rose from her chair, and walked to and fro, examining with apparent interest the fine pieces of First Empire furniture at that time so completely out of fashion as to appear curiosities. Then she said suddenly, "Surely we might go out of doors. May little Barbara take Julian to the church where James II. is buried? He is anxious to see the inscription the Queen has had placed there. Meanwhile you and I might wait for them on the Terrace; I seem to have so much to tell you, and you know we cannot stay much more than an hour," and, as she noted remorsefully Mrs. Rebell's flush of keen disappointment, she added, "Did I not tell you in my letter that Julian was anxious to see the little place near here belonging to James Berwick, I mean the hunting lodge bought years ago by Julian's brother? However, there may be no time for that, as we are going on to St. Cloud, and also— — But I will ask you about that later."

Once out of doors, leaning over the parapet of the Terrace, gazing down on the wide plain below, and following abstractedly the ribbon-like windings of the river, Madame Sampiero at last touched on more intimate matters, on that which had been in both her own and her companion's minds ever since Mrs. Rebell had drawn her, with such eager hands, into the hall of the villa.

"If Richard had been here," she said, "I could not have spoken to you of my child—of my darling Julia. And though I'm sorry not to see him, I'm glad to have this opportunity of telling you, Adela, that I regret nothing, and that I do not feel that I have any reason to be ashamed." As the other looked at her with deeply troubled eyes, she continued: "Of course I know you think I have acted very wrongly. But in these matters every woman must judge for her own self. After all, that man over there,"—she waved her hand vaguely as if indicating some far distant spot, and Mrs. Rebell, slight though was her sense of humour, felt a flash of melancholy amusement as she realised that the place so indicated meant the Corsican village where Napoleone Sampiero was leading a most agreeable life on the income which he wrested only too easily from his English wife,—"That man, I say, has no claim on me! If there came any change in the French divorce laws he could easily be brought to do what I wish— —Oh Adela, if you only knew what a difference my child has made to me,—and in every way!"

For a few moments there was silence between them. Adela Rebell opened her lips—but no words would come, and so at last, timidly and tenderly she laid her hand on the other woman's, and Barbara again spoke. "I used to feel—who would not have done so in my position?—how little real part I played in Julian's life. The knowledge that Arabella and James Berwick were to him almost like his own children was, I confess, painful to me, but now that he knows what it is to have a child of his own—ah, Adela, I wish you could see them together! Only to-day he said to me: 'I love you, Barbara, but I adore our Julia!' I used to think he would never care to spend much of the year in the country; but now, since the child came, he seems quite content to stay for long weeks together at Fletchings."

"And I suppose," said Mrs. Rebell,—she did not know how to bring herself to speak of little Julia—"I suppose that James and Arabella—how well I remember them as small children—are a great deal with him?"

"Well, no," for the first time during the conversation Madame Sampiero reddened deeply. "Arabella has been taken possession of by her mother's people. They have not been quite kind about—about the whole matter—and I think at first Julian felt it a good deal. But after all it would have been rather awkward for him to have charge of a niece of eighteen. As to James Berwick, of course he comes and goes, and I'm told he's prodigiously clever. He doesn't grow better-looking as he grows older. Sometimes I find it difficult to believe that the ugly little fellow is Julian's nephew!"

"And Jane Turke?"

"Oh! I've left her and Alick McKirdy at Chancton, in charge of Julia, of course."

"Will you remember me to him—I mean to Doctor McKirdy,—you know I always liked him in old days."

"Yes, a very good fellow! Of course I'll tell him. He'll feel very flattered, I'm sure, that you remember him."

"And the Priory—I wish stones could feel! For then, Bar, I should ask you to give my love to the Priory—I do so cherish that place! Sometimes I dream that we, Richard and I, are there, as we used to be long ago——" Mrs. Rebell's voice broke.

Madame Sampiero put her hand through her companion's arm, and slowly they began to pace up and down. "As I told you," she said, rather suddenly, "we cannot stay long, for we are driving round by St. Cloud, and—and, Adela, I have a great favour to ask of you"—there came an eager, coaxing note into the low, full voice. "May I take little Barbara too? I mean with us to St. Cloud? The Prince Imperial is giving a children's party. Look, I have brought her a special invitation all to herself!" and from her pocket—for those were the days of voluminous pockets—the speaker drew a small card on which was written in gold letters, "Le Prince Impérial a l'honneur d'inviter Mademoiselle Barbara Rebell à gouter. St. Cloud, 9 Juin, 1870." "I told the Empress," she added eagerly, "that I should like to bring my god-daughter and namesake, and she made the boy—he is such a well-mannered little fellow—write Barbara's name on the card."

"Dear Bar, it was more than kind of you. But I fear—I know, that Richard would not allow it!"

"But Adela—if I take all the blame! Surely you would not wish the child to miss such a delightful experience?" Madame Sampiero spoke in a mortified tone, but Adela Rebell scarcely heard the words; to her the proposal did not even admit of discussion. "I cannot allow what Richard would certainly disapprove," she said; and then, with the eager wish of softening her refusal, "You do not realise, Barbara, my poor Richard's state of mind. We go nowhere, we know nobody; it was with the greatest difficulty I persuaded him to allow the Protestant banker to bring me in touch with a few people who have children of our child's own age. More than once we have been offered introductions which would have brought us in contact with the Tuileries and with St. Cloud, but Richard feels that in the circumstances we cannot live too quietly. And on the whole," she hastened to add, "I agree with him."

Before another word could be uttered on either side, the two oddly contrasted figures of Lord Bosworth and his small companion were seen hastening towards them. The man and the child had already become good friends, and, as they drew near to Madame Sampiero and Mrs. Rebell, little Barbara, a charming figure in her white muslin frock, blue sash and large frilled hat, ran forward with what was for her most unusual eagerness and animation.

"Oh mamma," she cried, "have you heard? The Prince Imperial has invited me to his *gouter*, and my marraine and this gentleman are going to take me to St. Cloud! There is a little seat in the carriage which can be let down." Her voice wavered; perhaps she had already become aware of her mother's look of utter dismay, "You know that Marthe Pollain went last year, and the little Prince danced with her—I do wonder if he will dance with me!"

She stopped, a little out of breath, and Madame Sampiero turned with a half-humorous, half-deprecating look at her cousin, "Come, Adela," she said, "surely you would never have the heart to refuse those pleading eyes?"

But the words seemed to nerve Mrs. Rebell to instant decision. "No, Barbara," she said, in a very low tone. "My poor little girl—I cannot allow you to accept this invitation. It would make your father very very angry." And then, as the child, submitting at once, to Bosworth's admiring surprise, turned away, the tears running down her cheeks, the mother added, even more really distressed than was the nervous, excited little girl herself: "I am so very sorry, Barbara, but we will try to think of something to do to-morrow which you will like almost as well."

Madame Sampiero bent towards the child. "Never mind, little Barbara," she said, her voice trembling a little, "only wait till you see me again, I will bring you the sweetest of playfellows! And some day I will myself persuade your father to let me take you to a real ball, at the Tuileries!" Turning to Mrs. Rebell, she added: "Julian and I both agree that in time, say in six or eight years, I should do very well to take some small château near Paris, and spend there part of each year. Julia will then be old enough to have masters, and I am sure, indeed we both think,"—she turned to the impassive man now walking slowly by her side,—"that I had better really try and make a half Frenchwoman of her, and perhaps ultimately, who knows, settle her in France!"

Mrs. Rebell suddenly laughed. "Oh Barbara," she said, "how fond you have always been of making plans, of looking forward! Surely this is rather premature?"

Madame Sampiero smiled. "English people," she said, quickly, "don't give half enough thought to the future. But, Adela, I was not only thinking of my Julia, but also of your little Barbara. Richard cannot mean her always to lead a cloistered life. In eight years she will be grown-up, eager to see something of the world. Where could she make her début so delightfully as at the Tuileries? Well, little Barbara"—and again she bent over the child—"look forward to the time when I shall be quite ready to play my *rôle* of fairy godmother, and so introduce you to the most beautiful, the most brilliant, the most delightful Court in the world!"

The group of walkers turned, and slowly they made their way back to the Villa d'Arcole. Then, after long clinging leave-taking, Mrs. Rebell and Barbara, both with bitter tears in their eyes, watched the fairy-like equipage disappear down the sanded road leading to the Grande Place, and so towards the broad highway which would bring it ultimately to St. Cloud.

When the carriage was clear of the town, Bosworth, laying his large powerful hand on that of his companion, as if to deaden the full meaning of his words, said suddenly, "I suppose, Barbara, that you never had the slightest doubt as to Richard Rebell's complete innocence?"

"Never!" she said sharply. "Never the slightest doubt! In fact I would far rather believe myself guilty of cheating at cards than I would Richard. I think it was an infamous accusation! Why, surely you, Julian, felt and feel the same?" She looked at him with real distress and anger in her blue eyes.

"Oh yes," he said slowly, "I certainly felt the same at the time. Still, his present way of going on looks very odd. It doesn't seem to me that of an innocent man. Why should he compel his wife to lead such a life as that she evidently does lead at St. Germains?"

"But how young she still looks," said Madame Sampiero eagerly. "I really think she's as pretty as ever!"

"H'm!" he said. "Rather faded—at least so I thought. And then,—another notion of Richard's no doubt,—there seemed something wrong about her dress."

Barbara Sampiero laughed. "You are quite right," she said, "but how odd that you should have noticed it! Richard won't allow her to wear a crinoline! Isn't he absurd? But she hasn't changed a bit. She loves him as much as ever—nay, more than ever, and that, Julian,"—again their hands clasped,—"is, you must admit, very rare and touching after all that has come and gone."

But each of the speakers felt that this visit to St. Germains had been vaguely disappointing, that it had not yielded all they had hoped it would do.

Barbara Sampiero made up her mind that before leaving Paris she would come again, and come alone. She did not carry out her good resolution, and many long years were to pass by before she and her god-daughter met again. And to both, by the time of that second meeting, St. Germains had become a place peopled with sad ghosts and poignant memories which both strove rather to forget than to remember.

END OF THE PROLOGUE.

CHAPTER I.

"Mon pauvre cœur maladroit, mon cœur plein de révolte et d'espérance...."

"The past is death's, the future is thine own."

SHELLEY.

FIFTEEN years had gone by since the eventful birthday and meeting at St. Germains.

As Barbara Rebell, still Barbara Rebell, though she had been a wife, a most unhappy wife, for six years, stepped from the small dark vestibule into the dimly-lighted hall of Chancton Priory, her foot slipped on the floor; and she would have fallen had not a man's hand, small but curiously bony and fleshless, grasped her right arm, while, at the same moment, a deep voice from out the darkness exclaimed, "A good omen! So stumbled the Conqueror!"

The accent in which the odd words were uttered would have told a tale as to the speaker's hard-bitten nationality to most English-speaking folk: not so to the woman to whom they were addressed. Yet they smote on her ear as though laden with welcome, for they recalled the voice of a certain Andrew Johnstone, the Scotch Governor of the West Indian island of Santa Maria, whose brotherly kindness and unobtrusive sympathy had been more comfortable to her, in a moment of great humiliation and distress, than his English wife's more openly expressed concern and more eagerly offered friendship.

And then, as the stranger advanced, hesitatingly, into the hall, she found herself confronted by an odd, indeed an amazing figure, which yet also brought a quick sense of being at last in a dear familiar place offering both welcome and shelter. For she was at once aware that this must be the notable Jane Turke, Madame Sampiero's housekeeper, one to whom Barbara's own mother had often referred when telling her little daughter of the delights of Chancton Priory—of the Sussex country house to which, when dying, the thoughts of Richard Rebell's wife seemed ever turning with sick longing and regret.

Mrs. Turke wore a travesty of the conventional housekeeper's costume. There, to be sure, were the black apron and lace cap and the bunch of jingling keys, but the watered silk of which the gown was made was of bright yellow, and across its wearer's ample bosom was spread an elaborate parure of topazes set in filigree gold, a barbaric ornament which, however, did not seem out of place on the remarkable-looking old lady. Two earrings, evidently belonging to the same set, had been mounted as pins, and gleamed on the black lace partly covering Mrs. Turke's grey hair, which was cut in a straight fringe above the shrewd, twinkling eyes, Roman nose, and firm, well-shaped mouth and chin.

For a few moments the housekeeper held, as it were, the field to herself: she curtsied twice, but there was nothing servile or menial about the salutation, and each time the yellow gown swept the stone-flagged floor she uttered the words, "Welcome, Ma'am, to Chancton," running her eyes quickly the while over the slender stranger whose coming might bring such amazing changes to the Priory.

Then, as Mrs. Rebell, half smiling, put out her hand, the old woman—for, in spite of her look of massive strength Mrs. Turke was by now an old woman—said more naturally, "You don't remember Jane Turke, Ma'am, but Jane Turke remembers you, when you was little Missy, and your dear Mamma used to bring you here as a babby."

Mrs. Turke's voice was quite amazingly unlike that which had uttered, close to the door, the few words of what Barbara had felt to be a far sincerer welcome. It was essentially a made-up, artificial voice,—one to which only the old-fashioned but expressive word "genteel" could possibly apply: an intelligent listener could not but feel certain that Mrs. Turke would be bound to speak, if under stress of emotion, in quite other accents.

A muttered exclamation, a growl from that other presence who still stood apart, hidden in the deep shadows cast by the music gallery which stretched across the hall just above the head of the little group, seemed to nerve the housekeeper to a fresh effort: "This gentleman, Ma'am," she cried, waving a fat be-ringed hand towards the darkness, "is Doctor McKirdy. He also knew your dear Mamma, and is very pleased to see you once more at Chancton Priory."

From behind Barbara Rebell lumbered forth into the light another strange figure, a man this time, clad in evening dress. But he also seemed oddly familiar, and Mrs. Rebell knew him for a certain Alexander McKirdy, of whom, again, she had often heard from her mother. "I'll just thank ye," he said harshly, "to let me utter my own welcome to this lady. My words, no doubt, will be poor things, Mrs. Turke, compared to yours, but they will have the advantage of being my own!"

Alexander McKirdy was singularly ugly,—so much had to be conceded to his enemies and critics, and at Chancton there were many who felt themselves at enmity with him, and few who were capable of realising either the Scotchman's intellectual ability or his entire disinterestedness. Of fair height, he yet gave the impression of being short and ungainly, owing to the huge size of his head and the disproportionate breadth of his shoulders. His features were rough-hewn and irregular, only redeemed by a delicate, well-shaped mouth, and penetrating, not unkindly pale blue eyes. His hair, once bright red, now sandy grey streaked with white, was always kept short, bristling round a high intelligent forehead, and he was supposed to gratify Scotch economy by cutting it himself. He was clean-shaven, and his dress was habitually that of a man quite indifferent to his outward appearance; like most ugly and eccentric-looking men, Doctor McKirdy appeared at his best on the rare occasions when he was compelled to wear his ancient dress clothes.

Such was the man who now turned and cast a long searching look at Barbara Rebell. "I shall know if you are welcome—welcome to me, that is—better an hour hence than now, and better still to-morrow than to-day"—but a twinkle in his small bright eyes softened the ungraciousness of his words: "Now," he said, "be off, Mrs. Turke! You've had your innings, and said your say, and now comes my turn."

"You're never going to take Mrs. Rebell up to Madam now,—this very minute?—before she has taken off her bonnet?—or seen her room?—or had her dinner?" but the man whom she addressed with such fussy zeal made no reply. Instead, he jerked his right shoulder, that as to which Barbara wondered if it could be higher than the other, towards the shadows from which he had himself emerged, and Mrs. Turke meekly turned away, her yellow silk gown rustling, and her barbaric ornaments jingling, as she passed through the swing door which shut off the hall, where they had all three been standing, from the commons of the Priory.

Doctor McKirdy lifted one of the high lamps, which seemed to make the darkness of the hall more visible, in his strong, steady hands. Then he turned abruptly to Mrs. Rebell. "Now," said he, "just a word with you, in your private ear."

Without waiting for an answer, he started walking down the hall, Barbara following obediently, while yet finding time to gaze, half fearfully, as she went, at the quivering grotesque shadows flung by herself and her companion across the bare spaces of flagged floor, and over the high-backed armchairs, the Chinese screen, and the Indian cabinets which lined the walls on either side of the huge fire-place.

At last they stopped before a closed door—one curiously ornate, and heavy with gilding. Doctor McKirdy motioned to his companion to open it, and as she did so they passed through into what was evidently the rarely-used drawing-room of the Priory.

Then, putting the lamp down on the top of a china cabinet, the Scotchman turned and faced his companion, and with a certain surprise Mrs. Rebell realised that he was much taller than herself, and that as he spoke she had to look up into his face.

"I should tell you," he said, with no preamble, "that it was I who wrote you the letter bidding you come."

Barbara shrank back: of course she had been aware,—painfully aware,—that the letter which had indeed bidden her, not unkindly, to leave the West Indian island where she had spent her wretched married life, and make Chancton Priory her home, had not been written by her godmother's own hand. The knowledge had troubled her, for it implied that her letter of appeal, that to which this was an answer, had also been read by alien eyes.

"Yes," the doctor repeated, as though unwilling to spare her, "I wrote it—of course at Madam's dictation: but it was my notion that when going through London you should see Goodchild. He's an honest man,—that is, honest as lawyers go! I thought may-be he might explain how matters are here—Well, did you see him?"

"Yes, I went there this morning. Mr. Goodchild told me that my godmother was paralysed,—but that, of course, I knew already. Perhaps you have forgotten that you yourself long ago wrote and told me of her illness? Mr. Goodchild also explained to me that Madame Sampiero sees very few people. He seemed to doubt"—Barbara's soft, steady voice suddenly trembled—"whether she would consent to see me; but I do hope"—she fixed her dark eyes on his face with a rather piteous expression—"I do hope, Doctor McKirdy, that she will see me?"

"Don't fash yourself! She *is* going to see you,—that is, if I just wish it!"

He looked down at the delicate, sensitive face of the young woman standing before him, with an intent, scrutinising gaze, allowed it to travel slowly downwards till it seemed wholly to envelop her, and yet Barbara felt no offence: she realised that this strange being only so far examined her outward shape, inasmuch as he believed it would help him to probe her character and nature.

In very truth the doctor's mind was filled at the present moment with the thought of one in every way differing from Mrs. Rebell. How would this still young creature—Barbara's look of fragility and youth gave him something of a shock—affect Madame Sampiero? That was the question he had set himself to solve in the next few moments.

"Are you one of those," he said suddenly, and rather hoarsely, "who shrink from the sight of suffering?—who abhor distortion?—who only sympathise with pain when they themselves are in the way to require sympathy?"

Barbara hesitated. His questions, flung at her with quick short words, compelled true answers.

"No," she said, looking at him with steady eyes, "I have not—I have never had—the feelings you describe. I believe many people shrink from seeing suffering, and that it is not to their discredit that they do so shrink——" There was a defiant note in her voice, and quickly her companion registered the challenge, but he knew that this was no time to wage battle.

Mrs. Rebell continued: "I have never felt any horror of the sick and maimed, and I am not given to notice, with any repugnance, physical deformity." Then she stopped, for the strong lined face of her companion had become, as it were, convulsed with some deep feeling, to which she had no clue.

"Perhaps I will just tell you," he said, "why I believe Madame Sampiero may see you, apart from the fact that she desires to do so. Mrs. Turke was quite right," he went on with apparent irrelevancy, "I *did* know your mother. I had a sincere respect for her, and——" Again his thoughts seemed to take an abrupt turn. "I suppose you realise that I am Madame Sampiero's medical attendant,—I have no other standing in this house,—oh no, none in the world!"

Barbara divined the feeling which had prompted the last words to be bitter, bitter.

"I know," she said gently, "that you have been here a long time, and that my mother"—a very charming smile lighted up her sad face—"fully returned the feeling you seem to have had for her."

But Doctor McKirdy hardly seemed to hear the words, for he hurried on,

"One day, many years ago—I think before you were born—your mother and I went for a walk. It was about this time of the year—that is the time when keepers and vermin are busy. We were walking, I say, and I—young fool!—was full of pride, for it was the first walk a lady had ever deigned to take with me. I was uglier, yes, and I think even more repulsive-looking than I am now!" he gave Barbara a quick glance from under his shaggy eyebrows, but she made no sign of dissent, and he smiled, wryly.

"Well, as I say, I was pleased and proud, for I thought even more ill of women than I think now; but Mrs. Richard,—that's what we call her here, you know,—was so beautiful, such a contrast to myself: just a pretty doll, I took her to be, and as thoughts are free, looking at her there walking along, I was glad to know that I had all the sweets of her company and none of the bitter!"

And still Barbara Rebell, staring at him, astonished at his words, felt no offence.

"At last," he went on, "we reached the edge of the first down. I'll take you there some day. And we heard suddenly a piteous squeal: it was a puppy, a miserable little beastie, caught in a rabbit trap. You've never seen such a thing? Ay, that's well, I hope you never will: since that day you run no risk of doing so in Chancton Woods! 'Twas a sickening sight, one of the doggie's paws nearly off, and I felt sick—wanted to get away, to fetch someone along from the village. But Mrs. Richard—she was the tenderest creature alive, remember—never flinched. Those were not the days of gun ladies, but there, with me standing by, foolish, helpless, she put an end to the poor beastie—she put it out of its misery—with my knife too. Now that deserved the Humane Society's medal, eh? I never go by there without thinking of it. It's a pity," he said, in abrupt irrelevant conclusion, "that you're not more like her. I mean, as regards the outer woman"—he added hastily—"you are dark, like your father. Well now, I'll be calling Mrs. Turke, and she shall show you your rooms. We thought you would like those Mrs. Richard used to have when she came here. She preferred them to those below, to those grander apartments on Madam's floor."

"And when shall I see my godmother?"

Doctor McKirdy looked at her consideringly:

"Time enough when you've had a rest and a good supper. Never fear, she's as eager to see you as you are to see her," then, as he watched her walking back into the hall, he muttered under his breath, "There's something of Mrs. Richard there after all!"

A few moments later Barbara was following the stout housekeeper up the small winding stair which occupied, opposite the porch and vestibule, one of the four corners of the great hall, for those who had designed and built the newer portion of Chancton Priory had had no wish to sacrifice any portion of the space at their disposal to the exigencies of a grand staircase.

Mrs. Turke, on the first landing, called a halt, and Barbara looked about her with languid curiosity. To the right stretched a dark recess, evidently the music gallery which overlooked the hall; to the left a broad well-lighted corridor led, as Mrs. Rebell at once divined, if only because of the sudden silence which had fallen on her companion, to the apartments of the paralysed mistress of the Priory, to those of her godmother, Madame Sampiero.

Then Mrs. Turke, her loquacity stilled, laboured on up more narrow winding stairs till they reached the third storey, and, groping her way down many winding turnings, she finally ushered Mrs. Rebell with some ceremony—for every incident connected with daily life was to Mrs. Turke a matter of ritual—into a suite of low-ceilinged, plainly furnished rooms, of which the windows opened on to the Tudor stone balcony which was so distinctive and so beautiful a feature of the great house, as seen from the spreading lawns below.

Till Barbara found herself left solitary—she had declared herself well able, nay, desirous to unpack and dress alone—all that had taken place during the last hour had seemed hardly real.

It is said that the first feeling of those who, after being buffeted in the storm, tossed to and fro by the waves, are finally cast up on dry land, is not always one of relief. Barbara was no longer struggling in deep water, but she still felt terribly bruised and sore, and the smart of the injuries which had befallen her was still with her. Standing there, in the peaceful rooms which had been those of her own mother, a keen, almost a physical, longing for that same dear tender mother came suddenly over her.

Slowly she put on her one evening dress, a white gown which had been hurriedly made during the hours which had elapsed between the arrival of the Johnstones' invitation to Government House, and the leaving by her of her husband's plantation. Then she looked at herself in the glass, rather pitifully anxious to make a good impression on her godmother—on this paralysed woman, who, if the London lawyer said truly, was yet mentally so intensely and vividly alive.

To give herself courage, Barbara tried to remember that her hostess was not only of her own blood, but that she had been the one dear, intimate, and loyal friend of her mother—the only human being whom Richard Rebell's wife had refused to give up at his bidding, and even after Madame Sampiero and her kinsman had broken off all epistolary relationship. Why had they done so? Out of the past came the memory of sharp bitter words uttered by Barbara's father concerning Madame Sampiero and a certain Lord Bosworth. Then, more recently, when she was perhaps about thirteen, had come news of a child's death—the child had been called Julia—and Barbara's mother had wept long and bitterly, though admitting, in answer to her young daughter's frightened questions, that she had not known the little Julia.

Mrs. Rebell wrapped a shawl, one of Grace Johnstone's many thoughtful gifts, round her white gown, and so stepped through her window on to the stone balcony. Standing there, looking down on the great dark spaces below, she suddenly felt, for the first time, a deep sense of peace and of protection from past sorrows and indignities. For the first time also she felt that she had been justified in coming, and in leaving the man who,—alas! that it should be so, he being kinsman as well as husband,—had treated her so ill.

During the long, solitary journey home—if, indeed, England was home—there had been time for deep misgiving, for that quick examination of conscience which, in a sensitive, over-wrought nature, leads to self-accusation, to a fear of duty neglected. Barbara Rebell was but now emerging from what had been, and that over years, the imprisonment of both body and soul. Physically she had become free, but mentally she still had often during the last five weeks felt herself to be a bondswoman. During the voyage—aye, even during the two days spent by her in London—she had seemed to suffer more sentiently than when actually crushed under the heel of Pedro Rebell, the half-Spanish planter whose name seemed the only English thing about him. Since she had escaped from him, Barbara had felt increasingly the degradation of her hasty marriage to one whose kinship to herself, distant though it was, had seemed to her girlish inexperience an ample guarantee. That she had once loved the man,—if, indeed, the romantic, high-strung fancy which had swept over the newly-orphaned girl could be dignified by the name of love,—served but to increase her feeling of shame.

To-night, leaning over the stone balcony of Chancton Priory, Barbara remembered an incident which had of late receded in her mind: once more she seemed to feel the thrill of indignation and impotent anger which had overwhelmed her when she had found out, a few weeks after her wedding day, that the sum of money paid yearly by Madame Sampiero to Richard Rebell's account, and untouched by him for some ten years before his death, had been discovered and appropriated by her bridegroom, with, if she remembered rightly, the scornful assent of Madame Sampiero.

Again she turned hot, as though the episode had happened but yesterday instead of six long years before; and she asked herself, with sudden misgiving, how she had ever found the courage to petition her godmother for the shelter of her roof. She could never have brought herself to do so but for the kindly letter, accompanied by a gift of a hundred pounds, which had reached her once a year ever since her ill-fated marriage. These letters seemed to tell her that the old link which had bound her mother and Barbara Sampiero so closely had not snapped with death, with absence, or even, on the part of the writer of them, with physical disablement.

At last Barbara turned back into the room, and, taking up a candle, made her way slowly and noiselessly down the old house.

CHAPTER II.

"Et voilà que vieillie et qu'infirme avant l'heure
Ta main tremble à jamais qui n'a jamais tremblé,
Voilà qu'encore plus haute et que toujours meilleure
L'âme seule est debout dans ton être accablé...."

P. D.

"Who ever rigged fair ships to lie in harbours?"

Donne.

Mrs. Rebell was surprised to note the state and decorum with which the meal to which she sat down in the dining-room was served. She looked with some curiosity at the elderly impassive butler and the young footman—where had they been at the moment of her arrival?

Barbara had yet to learn that implicit obedience to the wills of Doctor McKirdy and of Mrs. Turke was the rule of life in Chancton Priory, but that even they, who when apart were formidable, and when united irresistible, had to give way when any of their fancies controverted a desire, however lightly expressed, of their mistress.

Doctor McKirdy would long ago have abolished the office of butler, and even more that of footman; it irked him that two human beings,—even though one, that selected by himself, was a Scotchman,—should be eating almost incessantly the bread of idleness. But Madame Sampiero had made it clear that she wished the entertainment of her infrequent guests to be carried on exactly as if she herself were still coming and going with fleet, graceful steps about the house of which she had been for so many years the proud and happy mistress. She liked to feel that she was still dispensing hospitality in the stately dining-room, from the walls of which looked down an odd collection of family portraits, belonging to every period of English history and of English art; some, indeed the majority, so little worthy from the artistic point of view, that they had been considered unfit to take their places on the cedarwood panels of the great reception rooms.

Barbara found the doctor waiting for her in the hall, walking impatiently up and down, his big head thrust forward, his hands clasped behind his back. He was in high good humour, well pleased with the new inmate of the Priory, and impressed more than he knew by Barbara's fragile beauty and air of high breeding. In theory no living man was less amenable to the influence of feminine charm or of outward appearance, but in actual day-to-day life Alexander McKirdy, doubtless owing to the old law of opposites, had a keen feeling for physical perfection, and all unconsciously he abhorred ugliness.

As Mrs. Rebell came silently towards him from behind the Chinese screen which concealed the door leading from the great hall to the dining-room, he shot but at her a quick approving glance. Her white gown, made more plainly than was the fashion of that hour, fell in austere folds about her upright slender figure; the knowledge that she was about to see Madame Sampiero had brought a flush to her pale cheeks and a light to her dark eyes. Without a word the doctor turned and led the way up the winding stair with which Barbara was already feeling a pleasant sense of familiarity; an old staircase is the last of household strongholds which surrenders to a stranger.

When they reached the landing opposite the music gallery, the doctor turned down the wide corridor, and Barbara, with a sudden feeling of surprise, realised that this upper floor had become the real centre,—the heart, as it were,—of Chancton Priory. The great hall, the drawing-room in which she had received Doctor McKirdy's odd confidences, even the dining-room where a huge fire blazed in her honour, had about them a strangely unlived-in and deserted air; but up here were light and brightness, indeed, even some of the modern prettinesses of life,—huge pots of fragrant hothouse flowers, soft rugs under-foot.

When opposite to the high door with which the corridor terminated, Doctor McKirdy turned and looked for a moment at his companion; and, as he did so, it seemed to Barbara that he was deliberately smoothing out the deep lines carved by ever-present watchfulness and anxiety on the rugged surface of his face. Then he knocked twice, sharp quick knocks, signal-like in their precision; and, scarcely waiting for an answer, he walked straight through, saying as he did so, "Just wait here a moment—I will make you a sign when to come forward."

And then, standing just within the door, and gazing with almost painful eagerness before her, Mrs. Rebell saw as in a vision that which recalled, and to a startling degree, a great Roman lying-in-state to which she had been taken, as a very young girl, during a winter spent by her with her parents in Italy.

Between the door and the four curtainless windows, through one of which now gleamed the young October moon, Barbara became aware that on a long narrow couch, placed catafalque fashion, in the centre of the room, an absolutely immobile figure lay stretched out. The light shed from candles set in branching candlesticks about the room threw every detail of the still figure, and especially of the head supported on high pillows, into prominent relief.

From the black satin cushion on which rested two upright slippered feet, the gazer's fascinated eyes travelled up—past the purple velvet gown arranged straightly and stiffly from waist to hem, past the cross-over lace shawl which almost wholly concealed the velvet bodice, and so to the still beautiful oval face, and the elaborately dressed, thickly powdered hair. On the mittened hands, stiffly folded together, gleamed a diamond and a ruby. There was present no distortion—the whole figure, only looking unnaturally long, was simply set in trembling immobility.

Madame Sampiero—the Barbara Rebell of another day—was still made up for the part she chose to play to the restricted audience which represented the great band of former adorers and friends, some of whom would fain have been about her still had she been willing to admit them to her presence in this, her time of humiliation.

As the door had opened, her large, wide open deep blue eyes, still full of the pride of life, and capable of expressing an extraordinary amount of feeling, turned with a flash of inquiry to the left, and a touch of real colour—a sign of how deeply she was moved—came into the delicately moulded, slightly rouged cheeks. The maid who stood by,—a gaunt Scotchwoman who, by dint of Doctor McKirdy's fierceness of manner, and the foreknowledge of constantly increased wages, had been turned into little more than a trained automaton,—retreated noiselessly through a door giving access to a room beyond, leaving the doctor, his patient, and Mrs. Rebell alone.

Tears started to Barbara's eyes, but they were brought there, not so much by the sight she saw before her, as by the sudden change which that same sight seemed to produce in the elderly man who now stood by her. Doctor McKirdy's whole manner had altered. He had become quite gentle, and his face was even twisted into a wry smile as he put his small strong hands over the trembling fingers of Madame Sampiero.

"Well, here's Mrs. Barbara Rebell at last!" he said, "and I'm minded to think that Chancton Priory will find her a decided acquisition!"

Barbara was amazed, indescribably moved and touched, to see the light which came over the stiff face, as the dark blue eyes met and became fixed on her own. Words, nay, not words, but strange sounds signifying—what did they signify?—came from the trembling lips. Mrs. Rebell herself soon learned to interpret Madame Sampiero's muffled utterances, but on this first occasion she thought Doctor McKirdy's quick understanding and translating of her godmother's meaning almost uncanny.

"Madam trusts you enjoyed a good journey," he said; and then, after apparently listening intently for a moment to the hoarse muttered sounds, "Ay, I've told her that already,—Madam wants you to understand that the rooms prepared for you were those preferred by Mrs. Richard." He bent forward, and put his hand to his ear, for even he had difficulty in understanding the now whispered mutterings, "Ay, ay, I will tell her, never fear—Madam wishes you to understand that there are some letters of your mother's,—she thinks you would like to see them and she will give them to you to-morrow. And now if you please she will say good-night."

Following a sudden impulse, Mrs. Rebell bent down and kissed the trembling mittened hands. "I do thank you," she said, almost inaudibly, "very very gratefully for having allowed me to come here."

The words seemed, to the woman who uttered them, poor and inadequate, for her heart was very full, but Doctor McKirdy, glancing sharply at their still listener, saw that Madame Sampiero was content, and that his experiment—for so the old Scotchman regarded the coming of Barbara Rebell to Chancton—was likely to be successful.

Had Mrs. Rebell, as child and girl, lived the ordinary life of a young Englishwoman, she would have realised, from the first moment of her arrival at Chancton Priory, how strange, how abnormal were the conditions of existence there; but the quiet solitude brooding over the great house suited her mood, and soothed her sore humiliation of spirit.

As she moved about, that first morning, making acquaintance with each of the stately deserted rooms lying to the right and left of the great hall, and seeking to find likenesses to her father—ay, even to herself—in the portraits of those dead and gone men and women whose eyes seemed to follow her as she came and went among them, she felt a deep voiceless regret in the knowledge that, but for so slight a chain of accidents, here she might have come six years ago.

In fancy she saw herself, as in that case she would have been by now, a woman perhaps in years—for Barbara, brought up entirely on the Continent, thought girlhood ended at twenty—but a joyous single-hearted creature, her only past a not unhappy girlhood, and six long peaceful years spent in this beautiful place, well spent too in tending the stricken woman to whom she already felt so close a tie of inherited love and duty.

Ah! how much more vividly that which might have been came before her when she heard the words with which Mrs. Turke greeted her—Mrs. Turke resplendent in a black satin gown, much flounced and gathered, trimmed with bright red bows, and set off by a coral necklace.

"I do hope and trust, Miss Barbara"——and then she stopped, laughing shrilly at herself, "What am I saying?—well to be sure!—I *am* a silly old woman, but it's Madam's fault,—she's said it to me and the doctor a dozen times this fortnight, 'When Miss Barbara's come home so-and-so will have to be done,'—And now that you are come home, Ma'am (don't you be afraid that I'll be 'Missing' you again), I'll have the holland covers taken off the furniture!"

For they were standing in the first of the two great drawing-rooms, and Mrs. Turke looked round her ruefully: "I did want to have it done yesterday, but the doctor he said, 'Let them be.' Of course I know there'll be company kept now, and a good thing too! If it wasn't for the coming here so constant of my own young gentleman—of Mr. James Berwick, I mean—we would be perished with dulness. 'The more the merrier'—you'll hardly believe, Ma'am, that such was used to be the motto of Chancton Priory. That was long ago, in the days of Madam's good father, and of her lady mother. I can remember them merry times well enough, for I was born here, dear only daughter to the butler and to Lady Barbara's own woman—that's what they called ladies' maids in those days. Folk were born, married, and died in the same service."

"Then I suppose you have never left Chancton Priory?" Mrs. Rebell was looking at the old woman with some curiosity.

"Oh! Lord bless you *yes*, Ma'am! I've seen a deal of the world. There was an interlude, a most romantic affair, Miss Barbara—there I go again—well, Ma'am,

I'll tell you all about it some day. It's quite as interesting as any printed tale. In fact there's one story that reminds me very much indeed of my own romantic affair,—no doubt you've read it,—Mr. James Berwick, he knows it quite well,—that of the Primrose family. Olivia her name was, and she was deceived just as I was,—but there, I made the best of it, and it all came to pass most providentially. Why, they would never have reared Mr. Berwick if it hadn't been for me and my being able to suckle the dear lamb, and *there* would have been a misfortune for our dear country!"

A half shuffling step coming across the hall checked, as if by magic, Mrs. Turke's flow of reminiscence. She looked deprecatingly into Barbara's face. "You won't be mentioning what I've been telling you to the doctor, will you, Ma'am? He hates anything romantic, that he do, and as for love and poetry,—well, he don't even know the meaning of those expressions! I've often had to say that right out to his face!"

"And then what does he say?"

"It just depends on the mood he's in: sometimes—I'm sorry to say it of him, that I am—he uses most coarse expressions,—quite rude ones! Only yesterday, he said to me, 'If you will talk about spades, Mrs. Turke, then talk about spades, don't call them silver spoons,'—as if I would do such a silly thing! But there, he do lead such a horrid life, all alone in that little house of his, it's small wonder he don't quite know how to converse with a refined person. But he's wonderfully educated—Madam's always thought a deal of him."

As Doctor McKirdy opened the door Mrs. Turke slipped quickly past him, and silently he watched her go, with no jibe ready. He was looking straight at Mrs. Rebell, hesitating, even reddening dully, an odd expression in his light eyes.

Barbara's heart sank,—what was he going to tell her?—what painful thing had he to say? Then he came close to her, and thrust a large open envelope into her hand. "Madam bid me give you these," he said; "when you are wanting anything, just send one or more along by post,—duly registered, of course,"—and under her hand Barbara felt the crinkle of bank notes. "She would like you to get your things, your clothes and a' that, from Paris. Old Léonie, Madam's French maid,—I don't think you've seen her yet,—will give you the addresses. Madam likes those about her to look well. I'm the only one that has any licence that way—oh! and something considerably more valuable she has also sent you," he fumbled in his pocket and held out a small gilt key. "Madam desires you to take her writing-table, here, for your own use. Inside you'll find the letters she spoke of yesterday night—those written by Mrs. Richard,—the other packets, you will please, she says, not disturb."

He waited a moment, then walked across to the Louis XV. escritoire which was so placed at right angles to one of the windows that it commanded the whole wide view of woods, sea, and sky. "Now," he said, "be pleased to place that envelope in there, and turn the key yourself." As Barbara obeyed him, her hand fumbling with the lock, he added with a look of relief, "After business, let's come to pleasure. Would you be feeling inclined for a walk? Madam will be expecting you to tell her what you think of the place. She's interested in every little thing about it."

Doctor McKirdy hurried her through into the hall, and Barbara was grateful indeed that he took no notice and seemed oblivious of the tears—tears of oppressed, moved gratitude—which were trickling slowly down her cheeks. "Don't go upstairs to your room,—no bonneting is wanted here!" he said quickly, "just put this on." He brought her the long white yachting cloak, yet another gift, this time disguised as a loan, of Grace Johnstone, and after he had folded it round her with kindly clumsy hands, and when she had drawn the white hood over her dark hair,—"You look very well in that," he observed, in the tone in which he might have spoken to a pretty child, "I'm minded to take you up to Madam and let her see you so—and yet—no, we've not so long a time before your dinner will be coming," and so they passed through the porch into the open air.

Alexander McKirdy had come to have something of the pride of ownership in Chancton Priory, and as he walked his companion quickly this way and that,—making no attempt to suit his pace to hers,—he told her much that she remembered afterwards, and which amused and interested her at the time, of the people who had lived in the splendid old house. The life-stories of some of Barbara's forbears had struck the Scotchman's whimsical fancy, and he had burrowed much in the muniment room where were kept many curious manuscripts, for the Rebells had ever been cultivated beyond the usual degree of Sussex squiredom.

When they had skirted the wide lawns, the doctor hurried her through a small plantation of high elms to the stables. In this large quadrangular building of red brick, wholly encompassed by trees, reigned a great air of desolation: there were three horses stabled where there had once been forty, and as they passed out from the courtyard where grass grew between each stone, Barbara asked rather timidly, for her liking for the doctor was still tempered by something very like fear, "Why are there no flowers? I thought in England there were always flowers."

Now Doctor McKirdy was unaccustomed to hear even the smallest word of criticism of Chancton Priory. "What do ye want flowers for?" he growled out, "grass and trees are much less perishable. Is not this prospect more grand and more permanently pleasing than that which would be produced by flowers? Besides, you've got the borders close to the house."

He had brought her to an opening in the high trees which formed a rampart to the lawn in front of the Priory, and, with his lean arm stretched out, he was pointing down a broad grass drive, now flecked with long shafts of golden October sunlight. On one side of this grassy way rose a holly hedge, and on the other, under the trees, was a drift of beech leaves.

Turning round, Barbara suddenly gave a cry of delight; set in an arch, cut out of the dense wall of holly, was a small iron gate, and through the aperture so made could be seen a rose garden, the ancient rosery of Chancton Priory, now a tangle of exquisite colouring, a spot evidently jealously guarded and hidden away even from those few to whom the familiar beauties of the place were free.

Doctor McKirdy followed her gaze with softened melancholy eyes. He had not meant to bring Mrs. Rebell to this spot, but silently he opened the little iron gate, and stood holding it back for her to pass through into the narrow rose-bordered way.

Surrounded by beech trees and high hedges, the rosery had evidently been designed long before the days of scientific gardening, but in the shadowed enclosure many of the summer roses were still blooming. And yet a feeling of oppression came over Barbara as she walked slowly down the mossy path: this lovely garden, whose very formality of arrangement was an added grace, looked not so much neglected as abandoned, uncared for.

As the two walked slowly on side by side, they came at last to a fantastic fountain, set in the centre of the rosery, stone cupids shaking slender jets of water from rose-laden cornucopias, and so to the very end of the garden—that furthest from the Priory. It was bounded by a high red brick wall, probably all that remained of some building older than the rosery, for it had been cleverly utilised to serve as a background and shelter to the earliest spring roses, and was now bare of blossom, almost of leaves. In the centre of this wall, built into the old brick surface, was an elaborate black and white marble tablet or monument, on which was engraved the following inscription:—

> "Hic, ubi ludebas vagula olim et blandula virgo,
> Julia, defendunt membra foventque rosæ.
> Laetius ah quid te tenuit, quid purius, orbis?—
> Nunc solum mater quod fueris meminit"

"What is it? What is written there?" Barbara asked with some eagerness. "How strange a thing to find in a rose garden!"

She had turned to her companion, but for a while he made no answer. Then at last, speaking with an even stronger burr than usual, Doctor McKirdy translated, in a quiet emotionless voice, the inscription which had been composed by Lord Bosworth, at the bidding of Madame Sampiero, to the memory of their beloved child.

> "Here, where thou wert wont once to play, a little sweet wandering maid, Julia, the roses protect and cherish thy limbs. Ah, what happier or purer thing than thee did the world contain?"

"Do ye wish to hear the rest?" he said, rather sharply, "'Twas put in against my will and conscience, for 'tis false—false!"

She bent her head, and he read on,

> "Now, only thy mother remembers that thou wast."

Barbara looked up, questions trembling on her lips, but her eyes dropped as they met his. "Madam would have her put here," he said; "Julia's garden,—that's what we used to call it, and that is what it still is, for here she lies,—coffinless."

Again he pointed to the last line, "Madam ought not to have had that added when there's not a man or woman about the place who's forgotten the child! But beyond the walls,—ah! well, who knows what is remembered beyond the walls?"

"What do you mean?" asked Barbara in a low tone; out of the past she was remembering a June day at St. Germains. What had she been promised?—ah, yes! "the sweetest of playfellows."

"Well, I was just meaning that Madam, when she made us put in those words, was thinking may-be of some who do not belong to the Priory, who live beyond the walls. I make no doubt that those folk have no time to cast their minds back so far as to remember little Julia."

He turned sharply round and walked as if in haste through the garden, his head thrust forward, his hands clasped behind his back, in what Barbara already knew to be his favourite attitude.

Once outside the gate, Doctor McKirdy looked long, first towards the Priory, then down the broad grass drive. "And now," he said briskly, "let's get away to the downs,—there's more air out there than here!"

The road leading from the Priory gates to the open downs lay along a western curve of country-side, and was over-arched by great elms. To the west Mrs. Rebell caught glimpses of a wide plain verging towards the sea, and in the clear autumn air every tree and bush flamed with glory of gold and russet.

As they walked along the white chalky ridged cart track, the doctor looked kindly enough at the woman by his side. She was not beautiful as had been her mother, and yet he saw that her features were very perfect, and that health,—perfect recovery from what had evidently been a bad illness,—might give her the bloom, the radiance, which were now lacking. The old Scotchman also told himself with satisfaction that she was intelligent—probably cultivated. With the one supreme exception of Madame Sampiero, Doctor McKirdy had had very little to do with intelligent women; but Barbara, from her way of listening to his stories of Chancton Priory, from her questions and her answers, had proved—or so thought the doctor—that she was one of the very few members of her sex who take the trouble to think for themselves.

"I suppose Mr. Sampiero is dead?"

Never was man more unpleasantly roused from an agreeable train of thought.

"He was dead last time we heard of him, but that happened once before, and then he came to life again—and most inopportunely."

There was a pause, and Doctor McKirdy added, in a tone which from him was new to Barbara, "I wonder if you are one to take offence, even if the offensive thing be said for your own exclusive benefit?" He did not wait for her reply, "I think you should just be informed that the man—that individual to whom you referred—is never to be mentioned. Here at Chancton he is forgotten, completely obliterated—wiped out." He made a fierce gesture as though his strong hands were destroying, crushing the life out of, some vile thing.

"Since I came here, thirty years ago, no one has dared to speak of him to me, and the only time that Madam had to communicate with me about him she wrote what she had to say—I, making answer to her, followed the same course. I thought, may-be, I'd better let you know how he is felt about in this place."

"I am sorry," faltered Barbara. "I did not know—My father and mother told me so little——"

"They're a fearsome gossiping lot in Chancton," Doctor McKirdy was still speaking in an angry ruffled voice; "I don't suppose you'll have much call to see any of them, but Madam may just mean you to do so, and you may as well be put on your guard. And then you'll be having your own friends here, I'm thinking"—he shot a quick look at her—"Madam bid me tell you that she has no idea of your shutting yourself up, and having no company but Mrs. Turke and,"—he turned and made her an odd, ungainly little bow—"your most humble servant here!"

"I have no friends," said Barbara, in a very low tone. "Nay, I should not say that, for I have two very good friends, a Mr. Johnstone, the Governor of Santa Maria, and his wife—also, since yesterday, a third,—if he will take me on trust for my mother's sake." She smiled on her companion with a touch of very innocent coquetry. Doctor McKirdy's good humour came back.

"Ay," he said, "there's no doubt about that *third* friend," but his brow clouded as Barbara added, "There is one person in Chancton I'm very anxious to see,—a Mrs. Boringdon. She is the mother of my friend Mrs. Johnstone."

The mention of this lady's name found Doctor McKirdy quite prepared, and ready with an answer. "Well, I'm not saying you'll like her, and I'm not saying you'll dislike her."

"If she's at all like her daughter I know I shall like her."

"May-be you will prefer the son, Mr. Oliver Boringdon—I do so myself, though I've no love to waste on him."

How the doctor longed to tell Mrs. Rebell what he really thought of this Mrs. Boringdon, the mother of Madame Sampiero's estate agent, and of how badly from his point of view this same young gentleman, Oliver Boringdon, sometimes behaved to him! But native caution, a shrewd knowledge that such warnings often bring about the exact opposite to what is intended by those who utter them, kept him silent.

Barbara's next words annoyed him keenly.

"Oliver!" she cried, "of course I shall like him!"

"Oliver? Then you're already acquainted with him?" The doctor felt beside himself with vexation. He was a man of feuds, and to him the land agent, all the more so that he was a highly educated man, who had been a civil servant, and later, for a brief period of glory, a member of Parliament, was a very real thorn in the flesh.

But Barbara was laughing, really laughing, and for the first time since her arrival at Chancton. "If I were acquainted with him," she cried, "surely I should not be calling him by his Christian name! But of course his sister, Mrs. Johnstone, has talked to me of him: he is her only brother, and she thinks him quite perfect."

"It's well there are two to think him so! I refer, o' course, Ma'am, to the youth himself, and to this lady who is a friend of yours."

"Is he conceited? Oh! what a pity!"

"Conceited?" Doctor McKirdy prided himself on his sense of strict justice and probity: "Nay, nay, that's no' the word for it. Mr. Oliver Boringdon just considers that he is always right, and that such a good thinker as himself can never be wrong. He's encouraged in his ideas by the silly women about here."

"Does my godmother like him?—he's her land-agent, isn't he?"

"Madam!" cried Doctor McKirdy indignantly, "Madam has never wasted a thought upon him,—why should she?"

He looked quite angrily at his companion. Barbara was still smiling: a delicate colour, the effect of walking against the wind, had come into her face.

"They're all alike," growled the doctor to himself, "just mention a young man to a young woman and smiling begins," but the harsh judgment, like most harsh judgments, was singularly at fault. Poor Barbara was waking up to life again, ready to take pleasure in the slightest matter which touched her sense of humour. The doctor, however, had become seriously uneasy. Why this strange interest in the Boringdons? Mrs. Rebell now belonged to the Priory, and so was surely bound to adopt without question all his, Alexander McKirdy's, views and prejudices. Her next words fortunately gave him the opening he sought.

"I suppose there are many young ladies at Chancton?"

"There is just one," he said, brightening, "a fine upstanding lass. The father of her is General Thomas Kemp. May-be you've heard of him, for he's quite a hero, Victoria Cross and a' that, though the fools about here don't recognise him as such."

"No," said Barbara, "I never heard of the heroic General Kemp."

Her eyes were brimming over with soft laughter. Living with her parents first in one and then in another continental town, she had had as a young girl many long solitary hours at her disposal, and she had then read, with keen zest, numberless old-fashioned novels of English life. This talk seemed to bring back to her mind many a favourite story, out of which she had tried in the long ago to reconstruct the England she had then so longed to know. Ah! now she must begin novel-reading again! And so she said, "I suppose that Oliver Boringdon is in love with the General's daughter."

Doctor McKirdy turned and looked at her, amazed and rather suspicious; "you show great prescience—really remarkable prescience, Ma'am. I was just about explaining to you that there is no doubt something like a kindness betwixt them. There's another one likes her, a Captain Laxton, but they say she won't have aught to say to him."

"Oh no! she must be true to Mr. Boringdon, and then, after a long engagement,—oh! how wise to have a long engagement,"—Barbara sighed instinctively—"they will be married in the little church which I look down upon from my stone balcony? and then—why then they will live happy ever after!"

"No, no, I cannot promise you that," said Doctor McKirdy gruffly, "that would be forecasting a great deal too much!"

Even as he spoke the deeply rutted path was emerging abruptly on a vast expanse of rolling uplands. They were now on the open down; Barbara laid a detaining hand on the old Scotchman's arm, and looked about her with enraptured eyes. Before her, to the east, lay a dark oasis, a black-green stretch of fir plantation, redeemed a hundred years ago from the close cropped turf, and a large white house looked out from thence up the distant sea. To the north, some three miles away, rose the high sky-line. A dense wood, said to be part of the primeval forest, crept upwards on a parallel line. There, so says tradition, Boadicea made her last stand, and across this down a Roman road still asserts the final supremacy of the imperial force.

A sound of voices, of steady tramping feet, broke the exquisite stillness. Towards them, on the path which at a certain point sharply converged from that on which Doctor McKirdy and Barbara stood, advanced Fate, coming in the shape of two men who were in sharp contrast the one to the other.

Oliver Boringdon—dark, upright, steady-eyed—had still something of the Londoner and of the Government official about his appearance. His dark, close-cropped hair was covered by a neat cap which matched his serge coat and knickerbockers. His companion, James Berwick, looked—as indeed he was—far more a citizen of the world. He was bare-headed, his fair hair ruffled and lifted from his lined forehead by the wind; his shooting clothes, of rough tweed and ugly yellow check colouring, were more or less out of shape. He was smoking a huge pipe, and as he walked along, with rather ungainly steps—the gait of a man more at home in the saddle than on foot—he swung an oak stick this way and that, now and again throwing it in the air and catching it again—a trick which sorely tried the patience of his staider companion.

When they reached the nearest point to Doctor McKirdy and Mrs. Rebell, the one took off his cap and the other waved his stick vigorously by way of greeting. Indeed Berwick, as Doctor McKirdy very well saw, would have soon lessened the ten yards space between the two groups, but Boringdon, looking before him rather more straightly than before, was already walking on.

"Well," said the doctor, "you have now had your wish, Ma'am: that was Mr. Oliver Boringdon, and the other is his fidus Achates, Mr. James Berwick: *he's* a conceited loon if you like. But then he's more reason to be so! Now what d'ye think they reminded me of as they walked along there?"

"I don't know," faltered Barbara. She was still feeling as if a sudden blast of wind had beaten across her face—such had been the effect of the piercing, measuring glance of the man whom she took to be Oliver Boringdon. No doubt the over-bold look was excused by the fact that he recognised in her his sister's friend. Barbara flushed deeply; she was wondering, with acute discomfort, what account of her, and of her affairs, Grace Johnstone—impetuous, indiscreet Grace—had written to her mother and brother? Oh! surely she could be trusted to have kept secret certain things she knew—things which had been discovered by the Johnstones, and admitted by Barbara in her first moments of agonised relief from Pedro

Rebell's half-crazy ill-usage.

"Well, I'll tell you what the sight of the two of them suggested to me," went on Doctor McKirdy, "and in fact what they exactly appeared like, just now,— —" he hesitated a moment, and then with manifest enjoyment added, "The policeman and the poacher! That's what any stranger might well ha' taken them for, eh?" But Barbara had given no heed to the bold gazer's more drab companion.

CHAPTER III.

"Mates are chosen marketwise
Coolest bargainer best buys,
Leap not, nor let leap the heart;
Trot your track and drag your cart,
So your end may be in wool
Honoured and with manger full."

George Meredith.

Mrs. Boringdon, sitting in the drawing-room at Chancton Cottage, looked, in spite of her handsome dress and her manner and appearance of refinement, strangely unsuited to the place in which she found herself. Even the Indian tea-table—one of the few pieces of furniture added to the room by its present occupant, and now laden with substantial silver tea-pot, cream-jug, and sugar-basin burnished to their highest point of brilliancy—was out of keeping with its fragile charm. The room, indeed, had been scarcely altered since it had been furnished, some sixty years before, as a maiden retreat for one of Madame Sampiero's aunts, the Miss Lavinia Rebell of whom tradition still lingered in the village, and whose lover had been killed in the Peninsular War.

On her arrival at Chancton Mrs. Boringdon would have dearly liked to consign the shabby old furniture, the faded water-colours and colour prints, to some unhonoured lumber-room of the Priory, but even had such desecration been otherwise possible, the new mistress of Chancton Cottage was only too well aware that she lacked the means to make the old-fashioned house what she would have considered habitable. Indeed, she had been thankful to learn that the estate agency offered to her son through the intermediary of his friend, James Berwick, carried with it the use of a fully furnished house of any sort.

Whenever Mrs. Boringdon felt more than usually dissatisfied and critical of the furnishings of the rooms where she was fated to spend so much of her time—for she had no love of the open air—she tried to remind herself that this phase of her life was only temporary; that soon—her son thought in two or three years, but Berwick laughed at so prudent a forecast—the present Government would go out, and then "something" must surely be found for her clever Oliver.

To-day, her son had brought his friend back to lunch, and the two young men had stayed on in the dining-room and in the little smoking-room beyond, talking eagerly the one with the other. As the mother sat in her drawing-room patiently longing for her cup of tea, but content to wait Oliver's good pleasure—or rather that of James Berwick—she could hear the voices rising and falling, and she rejoiced to think of the intimacy which those sounds betokened.

Mrs. Boringdon was one of the many in whom the mere possession of wealth in others excites an almost hypnotic feeling of interest and goodwill. When in his presence—nay, when simply even in his neighbourhood—she never forgot that her son's intimate friend and one-time chief, James Berwick, was an enormously rich man. That fact impressed her far more, and was ever more present to her mind, than the considerable political position which his personality and his wealth together had known how to win for him. When with Berwick Mrs. Boringdon was never wholly at ease, never entirely her cool, collected self. And now this afternoon, sitting there waiting for them to come in and join her, she wondered for the thousandth time why Oliver was not more amenable to his important friend—why he had not known how to make himself indispensable to James Berwick. Had there only been about him something of the sycophant—but Mrs. Boringdon did not use the ugly word—he would never have been allowed to slip into this backwater. She was one of the few remaining human beings who believe that everything is done by "influence," and she had never credited her son's assurance that no "job" was in the least likely to be found for him.

His mother's love for Oliver was tempered by fear; she was keenly desirous of keeping his good opinion, but of late, seeing how almost intolerable to him was the position he had accepted, she had been sorely tempted to speak—to point out to him that men in the position of James Berwick come to expect from those about them something like subserviency, and that then they often repay in lavish measure those who yield it them.

At last the dining-room door opened and the two men came in.

"Well," cried Berwick, "we've thrashed out the whole plan of campaign! There's never anything like a good talk with Oliver to confirm me in my own opinion! It's really absurd he should stick on here looking after the Chancton cabbages, dead and alive—but he's positively incorruptible! I'm thinking of starting a newspaper, Mrs. Boringdon, and to coax him into approval—also, I must say, to secure him a little freedom—I offered him the editorship, but he won't hear of it."

Berwick had thrown himself as he spoke into a low chair, which creaked ominously under his weight. How indignant would Mrs. Boringdon have felt had any other young man, looking as James Berwick now looked, his fair hair tossed and rumpled with the constant ruffling of his fingers, come and thrown himself down in this free and easy attitude on one of the few comfortable chairs in Chancton Cottage! But his hostess smiled at him very indulgently, and turned a look of gentle reproach at her son's stern dark face.

"An editorship," she said, vaguely, "that sounds very nice. I suppose it would mean going and living in London?" Her quick mind, darting this way and that, saw herself settled in a small house in Mayfair, entertaining important people, acting perhaps as hostess to Berwick's friends and supporters! She had once been able to render him a slight service—in fact, on two occasions he had been able to meet a friend, a lady, in her drawing-room. In doing what she had done Mrs.

Boringdon had lowered herself in her own eyes, and she had had the uncomfortable sensation that she had lost in his some of the prestige naturally attaching to his friend's mother, and yet, for all she knew, these interviews might have been of a political nature. Women now played a great part in politics. Mrs. Boringdon preferred to think that the fair stranger, concerning whose coming to her house there had been so much mystery, had been one of these.

Her son's next words rudely interrupted her pleasant dream.

"The ownership of a newspaper," Oliver was saying abruptly, "has never yet been of any use to a politician or statesman, and has certainly prevented some from getting into the Cabinet," and he named two well-known members of Parliament who were believed to be financially interested in certain important journals. "It isn't as if you wanted what the Americans call a platform," he went on. "No man is more sure of a hearing than you are yourself. But just now, the less you say the more you will be listened to when the moment comes for saying it!"

The speaker was walking up and down the narrow room, looking restless and impatient, with Berwick smiling lazily up at him, though evidently rather nettled at the frank, unasked-for advice.

Mrs. Boringdon judged the moment had come to intervene. "I hear that Lord Bosworth and your sister are back at Fletchings, and that they are expecting a good many people down—" She added, in a tone of apology, "Chancton, as you know, has half-a-dozen Court newsmen of its own."

"To me"—Berwick had jumped up and was helping himself to sugar, to cake, with the eager insouciance of an intimate—"to me Chancton always has been, what it is now more than ever, the most delightful spot on earth! I know that Oliver doesn't agree with me, but even he, Mrs. Boringdon, ought to enjoy the humours of the place. What other village can offer such a range of odd-come-shorts, of eccentrics? Where else in these prosaic days can one see gathered together in one spot our McKirdys, our Vipens— —"

"Our Mrs. Turkes," said Oliver slily. He came forward smiling, good humour restored, and took his share of the good things his mother had provided.

"Oh! yes," said Berwick, rather hastily, "of course we must throw in my foster-mother—in fact, I'm sure she would be deeply offended at being left out! And then, there's another thing I think I can claim for Chancton. Here one may always expect to come across the unexpected! To-day whom should we meet, Mrs. Boringdon, but McKirdy, wrapped in his historic plaid and snuff-coloured hat, and accompanied by a nymph, and an uncommonly attractive nymph too!"

Mrs. Boringdon looked gently bewildered. "A nymph!" she exclaimed, "do you mean a lady? What an extraordinary thing!"

Berwick looked across at his hostess and grinned. Now and again Oliver's mother actually reminded this whimsical young man of Mistress Quickly, and it was an added delight to picture to himself her surprise and horror if only she had known what was in his mind.

But Boringdon was frowning. "Nonsense!" he said, irritably, "From what I could see, she was simply a very oddly dressed young woman! McKirdy has always been fond of making friends with the summer visitors, and he always prefers strangers to acquaintances. I must say the doctor is one of the Chancton characters with whom I, for one, could well dispense! He was really insolent to me yesterday, but there is no redress possible with an old man like that. His latest notion is that I must only communicate with Madame Sampiero through him!"

James Berwick turned round, and Mrs. Boringdon thought he looked annoyed; he always chose to regard everything and everybody connected with the Priory as his very particular concern. "I must be off now," he said, "Arabella has several people arriving this afternoon, and I ought to be there to look after them. Walk with me as far as the great gates, old fellow?"

But Boringdon shook his head. "Sorry I can't," he said, shortly, "but I'm expecting one of the village boys to come in any minute. Kemp promised me to talk to him, to try and persuade him to enlist, and he's coming up to tell me the result."

"Then you're not returning to the Priory to-night, Mr. Berwick?" a note of delicate reserve had come into Mrs. Boringdon's voice; she never, if she could help it, referred to the Priory or to the Priory's mistress.

"No, I'm still at Chillingworth. But I expect to be over just for the night to-morrow. Then I'm off for a month's yachting."

Oliver came back from the hall door and sat down. His mother saw with a pang how tired and how discouraged he looked. "I think," she said, "that you might have done, dear, what Mr. Berwick asked you to do—I mean, as to seeing him back part of the way to Fletchings. That village lad could have waited for you—and—I suppose it was all a joke about the new paper and the editorship?"

"Oh! no, he's thinking of it," he said. "I suppose, mother, you never heard of the *Craftsman*, the paper in which the great Duke of Berwick's friend, Lord Bolingbroke, wrote. Some fellow has been talking to him about it, and now he thinks he would like to resuscitate it. Incredible that so shrewd a man should sometimes choose to do such foolish things, actuated, too, by the silliest of sentimental motives! If I were he, I should feel anything but proud of my descent from the Stuarts. However, I hope I've choked him off the whole idea."

As he caught her look of fresh disappointment, he added, with a certain effort, "I'm afraid, mother, that you've as little reason to like Chancton as I have. Sometimes I wonder if we shouldn't do better to throw it all up and go to London. I certainly don't want to edit any paper for Berwick, but I dare say I could get work, literary work of sorts; and, after all, I should be far more in touch there with the things I really care about."

His tone of dejection went to her heart, but she answered, not the last, but the first sentence he had uttered. "You are right," she said, rather slowly, "I do not like Chancton any better than you do, but I shall always be glad we came here, if only because it has brought us in contact with the Kemps—or perhaps I should say with their daughter."

Oliver looked up at his mother uneasily; he was aware that with her a confidence was rarely spontaneous.

"I wonder," she said, and turning she fixed her eyes on the fire, away from his face, "I have often been tempted to wonder lately, my dear boy, what you really think of Lucy—how you regard her? Pray do not answer me if you would rather not do so."

Boringdon hesitated. His mother's words, her extreme frankness, took him completely by surprise; for a moment he felt nearer to her than he had done for years. Still, he was glad that she went on staring into the fire, and that he was safe from meeting the acute, probing glance he knew so well.

"You've asked me a very difficult question," he said at last—"one I find almost impossible to answer truly."

Mrs. Boringdon's hands trembled. She also felt unwontedly moved. She had not expected so honest a confession.

But Oliver was again speaking, in a low, preoccupied voice. "Perhaps we have not been wise, you and I, in having so—so"—his lips sought to frame suitable words—"so charming a girl," he said at last, "constantly about the house. I have certainly become fond of Lucy—in fact, I think I may acknowledge to you, mother, that she is my ideal of what a girl should be." How odd, how inadequate, how priggish his words sounded to himself! Still he went on, with gathering courage, "But no one knows better than you do how I am situated. For what I am pleased to call my political ambitions, you have already made sacrifices. If I am to do what I wish with my life, such a marriage—indeed, any marriage, for years to come—would be for me quite out of the question. It would mean the condemnation of myself to such a life as that I am now leading, and I do not feel—perhaps I ought to be ashamed of not feeling—that my attraction to Miss Kemp is so strong as to make me desirous of giving up all I have striven for."

Mrs. Boringdon made no reply. She still stared on into the fire; a curious look, one of perplexity and hesitation, had come over her face.

"Mother!" he cried, and the tone forced her to look round at him, "surely you don't think—it is not your impression that Lucy——"

"I think she has become very fond of you," said Mrs. Boringdon deliberately. "But I confess that I have sometimes thought that she seemed fonder of me than of you." She smiled as she spoke, but to Boringdon this was no smiling matter—indeed, it was one which to his mind could scarcely be discussed with decency by himself and his mother. Then a vision of Lucy Kemp, steady, clear-eyed Lucy, almost too sensible—so the people at Chancton, he knew, regarded her to be—came to his help. "No, no," he said, with a sudden sense of relief, "I'm quite sure, mother, that any feeling—I mean the kind of feeling of which we are speaking—has been entirely on my side! We will be more careful. I am willing to admit that I have been foolish."

But Mrs. Boringdon scarcely heard what he was saying. She who so seldom doubted as to her course of action, was now weighing the pros and cons of what had become to her a matter for immediate decision. Unfortunately her son's next words seemed to give her the opening she sought.

"Sometimes I am tempted to think"—Oliver had got up, he was leaning against the mantel-piece, looking down into his mother's face—"Sometimes, I say, I am tempted to think that after all money is the one important thing in life! When I look back to how I regarded James Berwick's marriage—he once accused me of condemning what he did, and I could not deny that I had done so—I see how much more wise he was than I. Why, to him that marriage which so shocked me was the turning point—ay, more, that money, together, perhaps, with his wife's death, steadied him—amazingly—I refer of course to his intellectual standpoint, and to his outlook on life! And you, mother—you've always thought more of money than I've ever done. But even you once thought that it could be too dearly purchased."

Mrs. Boringdon reddened. Her son's words gratified her. She was aware that he was alluding to an offer of marriage which she herself had unhesitatingly rejected at a time when her daughter was still in the schoolroom, and her son at Charterhouse. Her middle-aged wooer had been a man of some commercial standing and much wealth, but "not a gentleman," so the two pitiless young people had decided, and Mrs. Boringdon, her children believed, had not hesitated for a moment between a life of poor gentility and one of rather vulgar plenty.

"Oh! yes," she said slowly, "money can certainly be too dearly purchased. But still, you on your side, you and your sister Grace, have always thought far too little of it. Of late I have sometimes wondered, Oliver, if you knew—whether you are aware"—for the life of her she could not help the sudden alteration in her measured voice—"that our dear little friend, Lucy Kemp, is something of an heiress—that in four years time, when she is five-and-twenty, that is, there will be handed over to her £25,000?"

And then, while her son listened to her in complete silence, giving no clue as to how he regarded the information, she explained her knowledge as having come to her from an absolutely sure source, from a certain Miss Vipen, the chartered gossip of Chancton, whose information could be trusted when actual facts were in question.

Even after Mrs. Boringdon had done speaking, Oliver still sat on, resting his head on his hands. "I wonder if Laxton knows of this?" he said at last. "What a brute I should think him if he does!" and Mrs. Boringdon felt keenly, perhaps not unreasonably, irritated. Her son's words also took her by surprise—complete silence would have satisfied her, but this odd comment on the fact she had chosen to reveal was very different from what she had expected.

But when, some three hours later, the mother and son had finished their simple dinner, and Oliver announced to his mother that he must now go down to the Grange for half an hour in order to consult General Kemp over that village lad whose conduct was giving Oliver so much trouble, Mrs. Boringdon smiled. Her son caught the smile and it angered him. How utterly his mother misunderstood him, how curiously little they were in sympathy the one with the other!

As he left the house she heard the door bang, and sitting in the drawing-room knitting him a pair of silk socks, she allowed her smile to broaden till it transformed her face almost to that likeness which Berwick sometimes saw in her, to that of a prim Mistress Quickly.

Boringdon did not go straight down to the Grange. Instead, after having groped his way through the laurel hedges and so into the moonlit road, he turned to the left, and struck out, making a long round before seeking the house for which he was bound.

Both his long talk with Berwick, and the short, strange conversation with his mother, had disturbed and excited him, bringing on a sudden nostalgia for the life he had left, and to which he longed so much to get back. During his eager discussion with the man whom he regarded as being at once his political chief and his political pupil, Chancton and its petty affairs had been forgotten, and yet now, to-night, he told himself with something like dismay that even when talking to Berwick he had more than once thought of Lucy Kemp. The girl had become his friend, his only confidante: into her eager ears he had poured out his views, his aspirations, his hopes, his ambitions, sure always of sympathy, if not of complete understanding. A bitter smile came over his face—no wonder Mrs. Boringdon had so often left them together! Her attitude was now explained.

Boringdon had no wish to pose, even to himself, as a Don Quixote, but, in his views as to the fitting relationship of the sexes, he was most punctilious and old-fashioned, perhaps lacking the essential nobility which would have been required in such a man as himself to accept a fortune, even from a beloved hand. What, take Lucy's £20,000—or was it £25,000—in order to start his bark once more on the perilous political sea? How little his mother understood him if she seriously thought he could bring himself to do such a thing, and in cold blood!

As he strode along in the darkness, there came back to his mind the circumstances connected with an experience in his life which he had striven not unsuccessfully to forget,—the passion of feeling he had wasted, when little more than a boy, on James Berwick's sister.

Those men and women who jeer at first love have surely never felt its potent spell. Twelve years had gone by since Boringdon had dreamed the dream which had to a certain extent embittered and injured the whole of his youth. What a fool he had been! But, on the other hand, so he remembered now, how little he had thought—if indeed he had thought at all—as to any question connected with Arabella Berwick's fortune or lack of it!

Miss Berwick had been mistress of her uncle's house, that Lord Bosworth who was a noted statesman as well as a man of rank: of course she must have money, so Boringdon in his young simplicity had thought, and certainly that belief had been no bar to what he had brought himself tremblingly to believe might come to pass. The beautiful girl, secure in her superior altitude of twenty-five years of life, and an already considerable knowledge of the world, had taken up the clever boy, her brother's Oxford friend, with pretty enthusiasm. She had liked him quite well enough to accept smilingly his adoration, to allow that he should amuse her (so he had realised ever since) in the intervals of a more serious love affair. Well, as he reminded himself to-night, they had been quits! Small wonder indeed that even now, after twelve years had gone by, the recollection of certain bitter moments caused Boringdon to quicken his footsteps!

To-night it all came back to him, in a flood of intolerable memories. It had been late in the season, on the eve—or so he had thought—of his dream's fruition, during the last days of his first spring and summer in London after he had gone down from Oxford. Some merciful angel or some malicious devil—he had never quite known which—had caused him, one Sunday afternoon, while actually on the way to Bosworth House, to turn into Kensington Gardens.

There, in a lonely grassy by-way among the trees, where he had turned aside to think in solitude of his beautiful lady, he had suddenly come on her face to face,—on Arabella Berwick, on his goddess, on the woman whose every glance and careless word had been weighed by him with anxious thought,—finding her in such a guise that for a moment he had believed that his mind, his eyes, were playing him some evil trick.

Miss Berwick, her eyes streaming with tears, was clinging to a man's arm; and, what made the scene the more unreal, the more incredible, to the amazed onlooker, Boringdon knew the man quite well, and had often, in his young importance, looked down on him as being so much less intimate at Bosworth House than he was himself. The man into whose plain, powerful face Arabella Berwick was gazing with such agonised intensity was Daniel O'Flaherty, an Irish barrister, but lately come to practise at the English Bar, a Paddy whose brogue—so Berwick had assured his friend Boringdon—you could cut with a knife, but who was, he had added good-naturedly, said by many people to be a clever fellow!

And now Oliver was walking straight upon them,—on O'Flaherty and Arabella Berwick. He stopped short, staring with fascinated, horror-stricken eyes, making no effort to pass by, to show the decent hypocrisy he should have shown; and what he heard made it only too easy to reconstitute the story. Miss Berwick had also dreamed her dream, and she was now engaged in deliberately putting it from her.

At last the man had cut the painful scene short, but not before Boringdon had seen the woman, whom he had himself set on so high a pedestal, fling her arms round her companion's neck in one last agonised attempt to say good-bye. It was the Irishman, of whom Boringdon had made such small account in his own mind, who at last—with the measured dignity born of measureless grief and loss—led her towards the spectator whom he vaguely recognised as one of James Berwick's younger friends. "Perhaps you will kindly take Miss Berwick home?" and then he had turned and gone, and she who had renounced him, taking no heed of Boringdon, had stood and gazed after him as long as he remained in sight.

During the walk back to Bosworth House it had been Boringdon's lot to listen while his companion told him, with a sort of bald simplicity, the truth.

"I love him, Mr. Boringdon, with all my heart—with all my body—with all my soul! But certain things are impossible in this world,—apart from everything else, there is the fact that for the present we are both penniless. He admits that often years go by before a man situated as he is makes any real way at the Bar. I ought not to have allowed it to come to this! I have been a fool,—a fool!" She had tried to smile at him. "Take example by me, Mr. Boringdon, never allow yourself to really care. It's not worth it!"

She had gone on, taking very little notice of him, talking as if to herself—"Of course I shall never marry, why should I? I have James,—till now I have never cared for anything but James." Then at last had come a word he had felt sorely. Arabella Berwick had looked at him with something like fear in her eyes,—"You will not say anything of this to my brother, Mr. Boringdon? I trust to your honour,"—much as she might have spoken to a schoolboy, instead of to a man—a man, as he angrily reminded himself, of one-and-twenty!

How well he remembered it all still, and yet what a long time ago all that happened! He himself had altered, incredibly, in these short years. O'Flaherty was no longer an unknown, uncouth Irishman: he had won a place even in the Berwicks' high little world: steady, moderate adherence to his country's unpopular cause had made him something of a personage even in the House of Commons, and he was known to be now earning a large,—nay, a huge,—income at the Bar. Of the two men who at one and the same moment had loved Arabella Berwick, it was he who had forged ahead, Oliver Boringdon who had lagged behind.

And the heroine of the adventure? She was still what all those about her, with the possible exception of these two men, had always thought her to be—the accomplished, rather cold, brilliant woman of the world, content to subordinate exceptional intellectual gifts to the exigencies of her position as mistress of her uncle's house; bending her fine mind to the problem of how to stretch Lord Bosworth's always uncertain and encumbered income to its furthest possible limit, for one of Miss Berwick's virtues had always been a great horror of debt. More, she had so fashioned her life during the last ten years that she was regarded by many shrewd observers as being quite as remarkable a person as her brother—in fact, where he was concerned, the power behind the throne. She loved, too, to exercise her power, to obtain good places for her favourites, to cause some humble climber of the ladder of fame to leap at one bound several of the hard intervening bars. It was admitted that the only strong feeling finding place in her heart was love of her brother, James Berwick, and for him, in a worldly sense, she had indeed done well.

Since that afternoon, twelve years before, Miss Berwick and Oliver Boringdon had never been on really cordial terms. She had at first tried, foolishly, to make a friend of him, a confidant, but he had not been possessed of the requisite amount of philosophy, and she had drawn back mortified at the condemnation, even at the dislike, which she had read in his eyes.

Very early Berwick had said to his friend, "I don't know what has happened to my sister and yourself, old fellow, but it will not make any difference to us, will it?" But, as Boringdon was well aware, it had made a difference. The sister's influence was on the whole always thrown in against that of the friend. It had certainly not been with Miss Berwick's goodwill that Boringdon had been offered, through her brother's intermediary, work which would bring him within two miles of Lord Bosworth's country house; but Oliver Boringdon was very rarely at Fletchings, and never without a direct invitation from its mistress.

As so often happens, the stirring of heart depths brings up to the surface of the mind more than one emotion. Had it not been for his mother's smile, Boringdon would not now have turned into the Grange gate, but it was his great wish that what had been said this day should make no difference to his relations with the Kemps—save, of course, that of making him personally more prudent in the one matter of his indulging in Lucy's society.

Alas for Boringdon's good resolutions! He had meant that this evening call at the Grange should be of a purely business character, and at the door he asked only for General Kemp.

"The master's upstairs with Mrs. Kemp. She's got a chill, but I'll tell him you're here, sir," and Oliver had been shown as a matter of course into the panelled parlour where Lucy sat reading alone. The very sight of the girl seemed to bring with it peace—restored in subtle measure the young man's good opinion of himself. And then she seemed so simply, so unaffectedly glad to see him! Within the next hour, he was gradually brought to tell her, both of the long talk with Berwick—Lucy had proved an apt student of political economy within the last year—even of the proposed newspaper and the editorship, of which the offer, coming from anyone else, would, he said, "have tempted me."

"Ah! but you think Mr. Berwick ought not to start such a paper—that it might do him harm?" Lucy looked up with quick intelligent eyes.

Boringdon had scarcely said so,—in so many words,—yet, yet—certainly yes, that was what he had meant, and so, "Exactly!" he exclaimed; "and if I don't join in, the scheme will probably come to nothing." Lucy allowed her softened gaze to linger on the face of the man who had gradually made his way into her steadfast heart. How good, how noble he was, she thought, and, how unconscious of his own goodness and nobility!

The girl was in that stage of her mental development when the creature worshipped must necessarily appear heroic. Two men now fulfilled Lucy's ideal—the one was her father, the other Oliver Boringdon. Poor Laxton, with his humble passion for herself, his half-pretended indifference to the pleasures and duties of the British officer's life in time of profound peace, his love of hunting and rough out-door games,—all seemed to make him most unheroic in Lucy's eyes. She was dimly aware that Captain Laxton's love for her was instinctive, that he was attracted in spite of himself; and the knowledge perplexed and angered her. She knew well, or thought she knew well, the sort of woman with whom the young soldier ought to have fallen in love,—the well-dressed, amusing, "smart" (odious word, just then coming into fashion!) type of girl, whom he undoubtedly, even as it was, much admired. But Oliver Boringdon—oh! how different would be the natural ideal of such a man.

Lucy was only now beginning to see into her own heart, and she still believed that her regard for Boringdon was "friendship." Who could hesitate as to which was the better part—friendship with Boringdon, or marriage with Laxton?

"I—I want to ask you something." Lucy's heart was beating fast.

"Yes, what is it?" He turned sharply round.

"I've been reading the life of Edmund Burke."

He bent forward eagerly. "It's interesting, isn't it?"

"Yes, yes, indeed it is! But I want to ask you why a hundred years have made such a change? Why it is that now a young man who has every aptitude for political life— —" Lucy hesitated, the words were not really her own, they had been suggested—almost put into her mouth—by Oliver's mother.

"Yes?" he said again, as if to encourage her.

"Why such a person cannot now accept money from—from—a friend, if it will help him to be useful to his country?"

"You mean"—he went straight to the point—"why cannot I take money from James Berwick?" He was looking at her rather grimly. He had not thought that Mrs. Boringdon would find the girl so apt a pupil.

Poor Lucy shrank back. "Forgive me," she said, in a low tone, "I should not have asked you such a question."

"You have every right," he said, impulsively. "Are we not friends, you and I? Perhaps you did not know that this was an old quarrel between my mother and myself. Berwick did once make me such an offer, but I think you will see—that you will feel—with me that I could not have accepted it."

General Kemp, coming down half an hour later, found them still eagerly discussing Edmund Burke, and so finding, told himself, and a little later told his wife, that the world had indeed changed in the last thirty years, and that he, for his part, thought the old ways of love were better than the new.

CHAPTER IV.

"Il est plus aisé d'être sage pour les autres que de l'être pour soi-même."

LA ROCHEFOUCAULD.

CHANCTON PRIORY had been, from his earliest boyhood, even more James Berwick's home than was his uncle's house over at Fletchings, and it was incomparably dearer to him in every sense than Chillingworth, which came to him from his dead wife, together with the huge fortune which gave him such value in Mrs. Boringdon's eyes. The mistress of the Priory had always lavished on Lord Bosworth's nephew a measure of warm affection which she might just as reasonably have bestowed on his only sister, but Miss Berwick was not loved at Chancton Priory, and, being well aware that this was so, she rarely came there. Indeed, her brother's real love for the place, and for Madame Sampiero, was to her somewhat inexplicable: she knew that at the Priory he felt far more at home than he was at Fletchings, and the knowledge irked her.

In truth, to James Berwick one of the greatest charms of Chancton Priory had come to be the fact that when there he was able almost to forget the wealth which had come to him with such romantic fulness when he was only four-and-twenty. Madame Sampiero, Doctor McKirdy, and Mrs. Turke never seemed to remember that he was one of the richest men in the kingdom, and this made his commerce with them singularly agreeable.

Certain men and women have a curious power of visualising that fifth dimension which lies so near and yet so far from this corporeal world. For these favoured few, unseen presences sometimes seem to cast visible shadows—their intuition may now and then be at fault, but on the other hand, invisible guides will sometimes lead them into beautiful secret pastures, of which the boundaries are closely hidden from those of their fellows who only cultivate the obvious. It was so with James Berwick, and, as again so often happens, this odd power—not so much of second sight as of divination—was quite compatible with much that was positive, prosaic, and even of the earth earthy, in his nature and character. He attributed his undoubted gift to his Stuart blood, and was fond of reminding himself that the Old Pretender was said always to recognise a traitor when approached by one in the guise of a loyal servant and friend.

On the afternoon following that spent by him at the Boringdons', Berwick walked across to Chancton from Fletchings. He came the short way through the Priory park—that which finally emerged by a broad grass path into the lawn spreading before the Elizabethan front of the great mass of buildings. As he moved across, towards the porch, he thought the fine old house looked more alive and less deserted than usual, and having passed through the vestibule, and so into the vast hall, he became at once aware of some influence new to the place.

He looked about him with an eager, keen glance. A large log fire was burning in the cavernous chimney, but then he knew himself to be expected: to that same cause he attributed the rather unusual sight of a china bowl full of autumn flowers reflected in the polished mahogany round table, on which, as he drew near, he saw three letters, addressed in McKirdy's stiff clear handwriting, lying ready for the post. Berwick, hardly aware of what he was doing, glanced idly down at them: then, as he moved rather hastily away, he lifted his eyebrows in surprise—one was addressed to his sister, Miss Arabella Berwick, at Fletchings; yet another, with every possible formality of address, to the Duchess of Appleby and Kendal, at Halnakeham Castle; while the third bore the name of another great lady living some ten miles from Chancton, and to whom—Berwick would have been ready to lay any wager—no communication had been sent from the Priory for some twenty odd years, though both she and the kindly Duchess had in the long ago been intimate with Madame Sampiero.

Once more Berwick looked round the hall, and then, abruptly, went out again into the open air, and so made his way across at right angles to a glass door giving direct access to a small room hung with sporting prints and caricatures, unaltered since the time it had been the estate room of Madame Sampiero's father. Here, at least, Berwick felt with satisfaction, everything was absolutely as usual. He went through into a narrow passage, up a short steep staircase to the upper floor, and so to the old-fashioned bedroom and dressing-room which no one but he ever occupied, and which were both still filled with his schoolboy and undergraduate treasures. There was a third room on each of the floors composing the two-storied building which had been added to the Priory some fifty years before, and these extra rooms—two downstairs, one upstairs—were sacred to Mrs. Turke.

There, as Berwick well knew, she cherished the mahogany cradle in which she had so often rocked him to sleep: there were photographs of himself at every age, to which, of late years political caricatures had been added, and there also were garnered the endless gifts he had made and was always making to his old nurse. James Berwick had been sadly spoilt by the good things life had heaped on him in almost oppressive lavishness, but no thought of personal convenience would have made him give up, when at the Priory, these two rooms—this proximity to the elderly woman to whom he was so dear, and who had tended him so devotedly through a delicate and fretful childhood.

As he walked about his bedroom, he looked round him well pleased. A good fire was burning in the grate, still compassed about with a nursery fender, and his evening clothes, an old suit always kept by him at Chancton, were already laid out on the four-post bed. Everything was exactly as he would have wished to find it; and so seeing, he suddenly frowned, most unreasonably. Why was it, he asked himself, that only here, only at the Priory, were things done for him as he would have always wished them to be—that is, noiselessly, invisibly? His own servants over at Chillingworth never made him so comfortable! But then, as he was fond of reminding himself, he was one of those men who dislike to be dependent on others. A nice regard, perhaps, for his own dignity had always caused him to dispense with the services of the one dependant to whom, we are told, his master can never hope to be a hero.

There came a knock, a loud quavering tap-tap on the door. Berwick walked forward and opened it himself, then put his arms round Mrs. Turke's fat neck, and kissed her on each red cheek. The mauve and white striped gown was new to him, but each piece of handsome jewellery set about the substantial form had been his gift. "Well, Turke! well, old Turkey! it's an age since I've seen you all! I was in the village for a moment yesterday— —"

"For a moment? Fie, Mr. James, I know all about it, sir! You was at the Cottage for hours!"

"Well, I really hadn't a minute to come over here! But make me welcome now that I am come, eh Turkey?"

"Welcome? Why, bless you, sir, you know well enough that you're as welcome as flowers in May! We *have* missed you dreadful all this summer! I can't think why gentlemen should want to go to such outlandish spots: I looked out the place in 'Peter Parley,' that I did, and I used to shake in my bed when I thought of all you must be going through, when you might be at home, here, with everything nice and comfortable about you."

"I'll tell you what we'll do, Turkey—you can tell McGregor to lay dinner in the business room to-night, and you shall have it with me."

As if struck by a sudden idea, he added, "And we'll have beans and bacon!"

Mrs. Turke went off into a fit of laughter. "In October!" she cried. "Why, my lamb, where's all your fine learning gone to? Not but what, thanks to glass and the stoves, the fruits of the earth do appear at queer times nowadays, but it would be a sin to waste glass and stoves on beans!"

Berwick was not one whit abashed, "If we can't have broad beans, we can have toasted cheese. My sister has got a French chef at Fletchings, and luncheon to-day was—well, you know, Turkey!"

"I know, sir, just kickshaws! Taking the bread out of honest Englishwomen's mouths. I'd chef him!" and Berwick realised from the expression of her face that Mrs. Turke thought to chef was French for to cook.

But there was a more important matter now in hand to be discussed, and she said slily, "You'll have better company than me to-night, Mr. James,—you'll have to put on your company manners, sir, for there's a lady staying here now, you know."

"A lady?" he cried, "the devil there is!"

"You remember Mr. and Mrs. Richard Rebell, surelye? They were here constant,—now let me see, a matter of twenty-five years ago and more, when you, Mr. James, were ten years old, my dear."

"What?" he said, his tone suddenly altering, "do you mean—surely you cannot mean that poor Richard Rebell's daughter is staying here—in the Priory?—now?"

"Yes, that's just what she is doing—staying."

"Oh!" he said, in an altered voice, "perhaps after all I had better go back to Chillingworth to-night." He added abruptly, "She married (her name is Barbara, isn't it?) one of the West Indian Rebells. Is he here too?"

Mrs. Turke folded her hands together, and shook her head sadly, but with manifest enjoyment. It was well that Mr. James knew nothing, and that it had been her part to tell the great news. "Oh no, we never mention him; his name is never heard! From what I can make out from the doctor,—but you know, Mr. James, what he's like,—the poor young lady, I mean Mrs. Rebell, has been most unlucky, matrimonially speaking; just like—*you know who*, sir——"

"Oh! she's left her husband, has she? It seems to run in the family. Has she been here long, Turkey?"

"Only since the day before yesterday. But Madam has already took to her wonderful: she does the morning reading now."

"I should think that would be a great improvement on McKirdy's. But, by the way, isn't McKirdy jealous?"

Mrs. Turke shook her finger at the speaker. "That's only your fun now, Mr. James! What call would the doctor have to be such a thing as jealous? Fie! Besides, he's quite taken to her himself."

"Why then, the girl we saw with McKirdy yesterday must have been Mrs. Rebell! A tall, dark, slim creature, eh, Turkey? Very oddly dressed?" He turned and looked hard at his old nurse; she, in return, gave her nurseling a quick shrewd glance from out of her bright little eyes.

"She's not what I call dressed at all," she said, "I never did see a young lady so shabby, but there, out in those hot climates——" she paused tolerantly. "Never mind; we'll soon make that all right. Madam set Léonie to work at once. As for looks," Mrs. Turke bridled, "Mrs. Rebell favours her poor papa more than she does her poor mamma," she said, primly, "but she's a very pleasant-spoken young lady. I do think you'll like her, Mr. James; and if I was you, sir, I would make up my mind to stay to-night and to be kind to her. I don't think you'll want much pressing——"

Again she gave him that quick shrewd look which seemed to say so much more than her lips uttered. Sometimes Berwick felt an uncomfortable conviction that very little he thought and did remained hidden from his old nurse. To-night, as Mrs. Turke had felt quite sure he would do, he made up his mind to remain at Chancton Priory and to follow, in this matter of Mrs. Rebell, the advice given him.

Meanwhile, the subject of their discussion was sitting on a stool at the foot of her godmother's couch. It was strange how two days of constant communion with this stricken woman had impressed Barbara Rebell with a sense of Madame Sampiero's power of protecting and sheltering those over whom was thrown the mantle of her affection. The whole of Barbara's past life, her quiet childhood, her lonely girlhood, even the years she had spent with Pedro Rebell, had accustomed her to regard solitude as a normal state, and she now looked forward eagerly to what so many would have considered the long dull stretch of days spread out before her.

All she desired, but that most ardently, was to become dear,—she would whisper to herself, perhaps necessary,—to Madame Sampiero. The physical state others might have regarded with repugnance and horror produced no such effect on Barbara's mind and imagination. All the tenderness of a heart long starved, and thrown back on itself and on the past, was now beginning to be lavished on this paralysed woman who had made her so generously welcome, and who, she intuitively felt, was making so great and so gallant a stand against evil fortune.

Even to-night Mrs. Rebell, coming into the room, had been struck by the mingled severity and splendour of Madame Sampiero's appearance. The white velvet gown, the black lace cross-over, and the delicate tracery of the black coif heightened the beauty of the delicate features,—intensified the fire in the blue eyes, as a brighter scheme of colouring had not known how to do.

Léonie—the lean, clever-looking, deft-fingered French maid who had grown old in the service of her mistress—stood by the couch looking down at her handiwork with an air of pride: "Madame a voulu faire un petit bout de toilette pour Monsieur Berwick," she explained importantly. Poor Barbara was by now rather nervously aware that there was something about her own appearance to-night which did not please her godmother. Indeed, sitting there, in this lofty room full of beautiful and extremely ornate pieces of furniture and rich hangings, she felt acutely conscious that she was, as it were, out of the picture. Words were not needed to tell her that, for some mysterious reason, her godmother wished her to look well before this Mr. James Berwick, who, if Mrs. Turke was to be believed, seemed to come and go so often at the Priory, but regarding whom, she, Barbara, felt as yet no interest.

Almost involuntarily she answered the critical expression which rested on the clear-cut face. "I care so little how I look,—after all what does it matter?"

But more quickly than usual she realised the significance of the murmured words, "Nonsense, child, it does matter, very much!" and she divined the phrase, "A woman should always try to look her best." Barbara smiled as Léonie joined in with "Une jolie femme doît sa beauté à elle-même," adding, in response to another of those muffled questioning murmurs, "Mais oui, Madame, Monsieur Boringdon a dû venir avec Monsieur Berwick."

Mrs. Rebell looked up rather eagerly; if Oliver Boringdon were to be there this evening, and if outward appearance were of such consequence as these kind people, Madame Sampiero and the old Frenchwoman, seemed to think, then it was a pity that one of the only two people whom she had wished to impress favourably at Chancton should see her at a disadvantage.

Again came low murmurs of which the significance entirely escaped Barbara, but which Léonie had heard and understood: quickly the maid went across the great room, and in a moment her brown hands had pulled open a deep drawer in the Buhl wardrobe which had once adorned the bed chamber of the last Queen of France. Now Léonie was coming back towards her mistress' couch, towards Barbara, her arms laden with a delicate foam of old lace.

A few minutes of hard work with a needle and white thread, much eager chatter of French, and Barbara's thin white silk gown had been transformed from a straight and, according to the fashion of that day, shapeless gown, into a beautiful and poetic garment.

A gleam of amused pleasure flashed across Madame Sampiero's trembling lips and wide open blue eyes: she realised that a little thought, a little trouble, would transform her god-daughter, if not into a beauty, then into a singularly distinguished and attractive-looking young woman.

Like most beautiful people, Barbara Sampiero had always been generous in her appreciation of the beauty of others, and she would have been pleased indeed had Richard Rebell's daughter turned out as lovely as had been her mother,—lovely with that English beauty of golden hair and perfect colouring. But Barbara's charm, so far at least, seemed of the soul rather than of the body, and, recognising this fact, Madame Sampiero had at first felt disappointed, for her own experience—and in these matters a woman can only be guided by her own personal experience—was that in this world beauty of body counts very much more in obtaining for those who possess it their heart's desire than does beauty of soul.

The mistress of Chancton Priory had hesitated painfully before allowing Doctor McKirdy to write the letter which had bidden Barbara Rebell come to England. The old Scotchman, who to her surprise had urged Madame Sampiero to send for her god-daughter, regarded the coming of Barbara as a matter of comparatively small moment. If the experiment was not successful, well then Mrs. Rebell could be sent away again; but the mistress of the Priory knew that to herself the coming of Richard Rebell's daughter must either bring something like happiness, and the companionship for which she sometimes craved with so desperate a longing, or the destruction of the dignified peace in which she had known how to enfold herself as in a mantle.

For a few days, Barbara's fate had indeed hung in the balance, and could money have taken the place of the shelter asked for, it would have been sent in ample measure. At last what had turned the balance and weighed down the scale had been a mere word said by Mrs. Turke—a word referring incautiously to James Berwick as the probable future owner of Chancton Priory.

Hearing that word, the present owner's trembling lips had closed tightly together. So that was what they were all planning? That the Priory should be, in the fulness of time, handed over to James Berwick, to be added to the many possessions he had acquired by the sale of himself—Madame Sampiero, discussing the matter in the watches of her long night, did not choose and pick her words—by that of his young manhood, and of his already growing political reputation, to a sickly woman, older than himself, whose death had been the crowning boon she had bestowed on her husband.

And so Chancton, which Madame Sampiero loved with so passionate an affection, was meant to take its place, as if by chance, at the end of the long list of Berwick's properties—that list which all who ran might read in those books of reference where the mightiness of Lord Bosworth's nephew was set forth—after Chillingworth, after the town house, after Churm Paddox, Newmarket, even after the property he had inherited from his own father in France. The thought whipped her as if with scorpions—perhaps the more so that for one moment, in the long ago, at a time when Barbara Sampiero wished to share everything with the man she loved, and before little Julia, that *enfant de miracle*, was born, she had seriously thought of making Lord Bosworth's nephew her heir. But his marriage had revolted her profoundly, and had, of course, made the questions of his future and his career, which had at one time been a matter for anxious thought on the part of his uncle and political godfather, more than secure. Well, indeed, had he, or rather his sister Arabella, feathered James Berwick's nest!

Like most lonely wealthy women, Madame Sampiero had made and destroyed many wills in the course of her life, but since the death of her child she had made no new disposition of her property. Let the place go to any Rebell who could establish his or her claim to it—such had been her feeling. But while Barbara's short, pitiful, and yet dignified letter still remained unanswered, and while Mrs. Turke's incautious word still sounded in her ears, she had sent for her lawyer, and, after making a will which surprised him, had dictated to Doctor McKirdy the letter bidding Mrs. Rebell come and take up her permanent home at Chancton.

And now—ah! even after only very few hours of Barbara's company, Madame Sampiero lay and trembled to think how nearly she had let this good thing which had suddenly come into her shadowed life slip by. All her life through she had acted on impulse, and often she had lived to regret what she had done, but this time, acting on what was to be, so she had assured herself, the last memorable impulse of her life, her instinct had guided her aright.

What Barbara had felt, on the first morning when she wandered about the beautiful old house, her god-mother had since also experienced, with increasing regret and self-reproach. Why had she not sent for the girl immediately after Richard Rebell's death? Why had she allowed the terrible grief and physical distress which then oppressed her to prevent the accomplishment of that act of humanity and mercy? True, poor Barbara had already met the man whom she had married almost immediately afterwards, but had she, Madame Sampiero, done her duty by her god-daughter, the girl might have been saved from the saddest because the least remediable fate which can befall a woman, that of an unhappy uncongenial marriage—how unhappy, how uncongenial Madame Sampiero did not yet fully know.

But now it was no use to waste time in lamenting the irreparable, and the paralysed woman set her clear mind to do all that could be done to make the life of her young kinswoman as much as might be honoured and happy. Those old friends and neighbours whose disapproval and reprobation the owner of Chancton Priory had endured during many years with easy philosophy, and whose later pity and proffered sympathy she had so fiercely rejected when her awful loss and subsequent physical disability had made them willing to surround her once more with love, with sympathy, ay and almost with the respect she had forfeited, should now be asked to show kindness to Richard Rebell's daughter. Hence the letters dictated to Doctor McKirdy which Berwick had seen lying ready for post in the hall.

Other epistles, of scarcely less moment from the point of view of Madame Sampiero, had also been despatched from the Priory during the last two days. Barbara must be made fit in every way for the place which she was to take now, and in the future, at Chancton Priory. In material matters, money can do so much! Madame Sampiero knew exactly how much—and alas! how little—money can do. Her wealth could not restore poor Barbara's girlhood, could not obliterate the fact that far away, in a West Indian island, there lived a man who might some day make Barbara as wretched as she herself had been made by Napoleone Sampiero. But there remained the power of so acting that Barbara should be armed *cap-à-pie* for any worldly warfare that might come—the power of surrounding her with that outward appearance of importance and prosperity which, as Madame Sampiero well knew, means much in this world.

Hence milliners and dressmakers were told to hie them to Chancton, from Bond Street, and, better still, from the Rue de la Paix. Doctor McKirdy was amused, bewildered, touched to the heart, as he bent his red-grey head over the notepaper, and drew heavy cheques "all for the covering of one poor perishable body." So much fling he allowed himself, and then suddenly "Madam" had said something,—now what had she said? The doctor was completely nonplussed, angry with himself—he, whose mind always leapt to hers! Again and again the long sentence was murmured forth—it must be something of the utmost importance—luckily Mrs. Turke just then bustled into the room, and with startling clearness had come the words, "You tell him, Turkey!" Again the muttered incomprehensible murmur, and Mrs. Turke's instant comprehension, "Why, of course, Madam reminds you, doctor, that

"The very sheep and silkworms wore
The selfsame clothing long before!"

Well, well, as long as it all added a moment of cheerfulness, of forgetfulness of the bitter past to his patient, what did anything matter? Doctor McKirdy told himself rather ruefully that Madam had always been fond of fine raiment: for his part, he thought Mrs. Rebell looked very well as she was, especially when wearing that long white cloak of hers, but if it pleased Madam to dress her up like a doll, why, of course, they must all give in with a good grace.

Meanwhile, oh! yes, he quite understood that she was not to be shown overmuch to the critical eyes of the village—there was to be no going to church, for instance, till the fine feathers were come which were to transform the gentle modest dove-like creature into a bird of paradise.

To-day, for the first time for many years, Madame Sampiero could have dispensed with the presence of James Berwick at the Priory. Of all men he was the most fastidious in the matter of women's looks. A first impression, so Barbara's godmother reminded herself, counts so much with a man, and what James thought now of Barbara Rebell would be sure to be reported at once at Fletchings.

Fletchings, never long out of Madame Sampiero's thoughts, yet rarely mentioned to those about her—Fletchings the charming, rather small manor-house originally bought by Lord Bosworth in order that he might be close—and yet not too close, in the eyes of a censorious world—to Chancton Priory. This had been some thirty years ago, long before the memorable later period when both of them became entirely indifferent to what that same world might think.

And now James Berwick had come to be the only link between Fletchings and the Priory. It had been Madame Sampiero's will, ruthlessly carried out, that all relationship between herself and Lord Bosworth should cease—that they should no longer meet, even to mourn together their child Julia. She wished to be remembered as she had been, not as she now was, a living corpse, an object of repulsion—so she told herself with grim frankness—to any sanely constituted man.

The mistress of Chancton Priory never allowed herself to regret her decision, but still there were times when James Berwick's prolonged absences saddened her and seemed to make the lamp of her life burn very low. From him alone she chose to learn what her old friend was thinking and doing, and how he regarded those struggles in the political arena of which she was still almost as interested a spectator as he was himself. Through Berwick, she was thus able to follow each phase of the pleasant life Lord Bosworth had made for himself, in this, the evening of his days.

Madame Sampiero, during the long hour just before the dawn, had debated keenly within herself as to whether it would be well for Barbara to go to Fletchings. Certainly, yes, if the so doing would add to her happiness or consolidate her position, but then Arabella Berwick must be won over and propitiated, made to understand that Mrs. Rebell was destined to become a person of importance. What Arabella should be brought to think rested with James Berwick. For the first time for years, Madame Sampiero would have given much to be downstairs, to-night, to see what was going on in the great Blue drawing-room which lay just below her own room.

CHAPTER V.

"So every sweet with sour is tempered still,
That maketh it be coveted the more;
For easy things that may be got at will
Most sorts of men do set but little store."

SPENSER.

BERWICK walked up and down the hall waiting for Mrs. Rebell. Not only Mrs. Turke's ambiguous utterances, but his own knowledge of her parents, made him look forward with a certain curiosity to seeing her.

The story of Richard Rebell, the one-time brilliant and popular man about town, who, not long after his marriage to a reigning beauty, had been overwhelmed by the shameful accusation of cheating at cards; the subsequent libel case which had developed into a mid-Victorian *cause célèbre*; the award of nominal damages; and Mr. and Mrs. Richard Rebell's ultimate retreat, for ever, to the Continent—it was all well known to James Berwick.

Still, he would rather have met this Mrs. Rebell anywhere else than at Chancton Priory. Her presence here could not but destroy, for himself, the peculiar charm of the place.

How unpunctual she was! Why was it that women—with the one exception of his sister Arabella—were always either too early or too late?

McGregor's voice broke across the ungallant thought, "Mrs. Rebell, sir, is in the Blue drawing-room. She has been down some time."

The words gave Berwick a disagreeable shock. The Blue drawing-room? Years had gone by since the two charming rooms taking up the whole west side of the Priory had been in familiar use. He remembered very well the last time he had seen them filled with a feminine presence. It had been just after his first term at Oxford, when he still felt something of the schoolboy: Madame Sampiero, beautiful and gracious as she only knew how to be, had received him with great kindness, striving to put him completely at his ease. There had been there also his uncle, Lord Bosworth, and a certain Septimus Daman, an old friend and habitué of the Priory in those later days of Lord Bosworth and Madame Sampiero's intimacy, when no woman ever crossed its stately threshold.

Just before the little party of four, the three men and their hostess, had gone in to dinner, a radiant apparition had danced into the room, little fair-haired Julia, the incarnation of happy childhood. Her mother had placed her, laughing, beside the rather fantastic portrait which was then being painted of the child by an Italian artist, and which now hung in Lord Bosworth's study at Fletchings, bearing silent witness to many past events.

With the memory of this scene singularly vivid, it shocked Berwick that now, even after the lapse of so many years, another woman should be installed as mistress of the room towards which he was bending his steps. So feeling, he hesitated, and waited for a moment, a frown on his face, before turning the handle of the door.

James Berwick cultivated in himself a sense of the unusual and the picturesque; especially was he ever consciously seeking to find these qualities in those women with whom chance brought him into temporary contact. As he passed through into the Blue drawing-room, he became at once aware that the former ordered beauty of the apartment had been restored, and that the tall white figure standing by the fire harmonised, in some subtle fashion, with the old French furniture covered in the rather bright blue silk which gave its name to the room.

Barbara Rebell was gazing down into the wood fire, one slender hand and arm resting on the rose marble mantel-piece. She looked singularly young and forlorn, and yet, as she turned towards him, he saw that her whole bearing was instinct with a rather desperate dignity. She was not at all what the man advancing towards her had thought to find—above all she now looked curiously unlike the clear-eyed vigorous creature she had appeared when walking by McKirdy's side along the open down.

As James Berwick came into the circle of light thrown by the tall shaded lamps, she turned and directly faced him,—the expression of her face that of a shrinking and proud embarrassment. Then she spoke, the words she uttered bringing to her hearer discomfiture and rather piqued surprise.

"I have been wishing so much to see you, Mr. Boringdon, and also your mother. I think your sister must have written and told you of her kindness to me—though indeed I do not suppose for a moment she can have made you understand how very very good she and Mr. Johnstone both were. I am the bearer of several things from Grace. Also"—her low grave voice faltered—"I wish to ask if you will be so kind as to arrange for the sending back to your brother-in-law of some money he lent me." She held out as she spoke an envelope, "It is fifty pounds, and I do not know how to convey it to him."

Berwick felt keenly annoyed,—there is always something lowering to one's self-esteem in being taken for another person, and especially in receiving in that character anything savouring of a confidential communication.

"You are making a mistake," he said, rather sharply; "my name is Berwick—James Berwick. Oliver Boringdon, Mrs. Johnstone's brother, lives at Chancton Cottage. You will certainly meet him in the course of the next day or two."

Mrs. Rebell looked for a moment extremely disconcerted: a flood of bright colour swept over her face, but Berwick, now considering her closely, saw that, if confused, she was also most certainly relieved. Her manner altered,—she became, in a gentle and rather abstracted way, at ease. The man now standing close to her suddenly felt as if in the presence of a shy and yet confiding creature—one only half tame, ready to spring away at any rough unmannerly approach. He caught himself wondering how it was that she had already made friends with McKirdy, and he told himself that there was about this woman something at once delicately charming and at the same time disarming—he no longer grudged her presence at the Priory.

On their way to the dining-room, during their progress through the hall, Berwick looked down at the fingers resting on his arm. They were childishly small and delicate. She must have, he thought, a singularly pretty foot: yes, there was certainly something of the nymph about her,—his first instinct had not been at fault, after all.

Mrs. Rebell walked to the further side of the large round table, evidently regarding her companion as her guest, and from that moment onwards, James Berwick never disputed Barbara Rebell's sovereignty of Chancton Priory. Indeed, soon he was glad that she had chosen so to place herself that, whenever he looked up, he saw her small head—the ivory tinted face so curiously framed by short curling dark hair, and the rather widely set apart, heavy-lidded eyes—sharply outlined against the curtainless oriel window, of which the outer side was swept by the branches of a cedar of Lebanon.

Berwick felt himself in an approving mood. His old nurse had been right; Mrs. Rebell would add to, not detract from, the charm of the Priory. Many trifling matters ministered to his fancy. The dining-table was bare of flowers and of ornament: McGregor, it was clear, had lost touch with the outside world. Berwick was glad too that Mrs. Rebell wore no jewels,—not even, to his surprise, a wedding ring. She must be even more out of touch with her contemporaries than McGregor! And yet her dress,—yes, there could be no doubt about it—had an air of magnificence, in spite of its extreme plainness. Now that he came to think of it, her white lace gown, vaporous and mysterious, resembled, quite curiously so, that of a bride.

So, doubtless, sitting there, as they were sitting now, more than one Rebell bride and bridegroom had sat in this old dining-room, at this very round table, in those days when men brought their newly-wedded wives straight home. The last Rebells to have done so must have been Madame Sampiero's grandfather and grandmother, her own and her god-daughter's common ancestors. Berwick wondered swiftly if it was from that bride of a hundred years ago that Barbara had taken her eyes—those singularly desolate eyes which alone in her face implied experience.

He looked across the table with a whimsical, considering look. A stranger passing by outside that window would take them for husband and wife. So do folk judge by mere appearance! The fact that for himself as well as for her marriage was out of the region of practical possibilities made amusing,—gave something of piquancy to this little scene of pseudo-domesticity.

Barbara also looked up and across at him. She saw clearly, for the first time, for the lamps in the Blue drawing-room gave but a quavering light, the tanned and tense-looking face, of which perhaps the most arresting features were the penetrating bright blue eyes. The strong jaw—not a handsome feature, this—was partly concealed by a ragged straw-coloured moustache, many shades lighter than the hair brushed straight across the already seamed forehead. She smiled, a delicate heart-whole smile, softening and brightening, altering incredibly the rather austere lines of her face.

"I'm thinking," she said, "of Mrs. Turke. I was in her sitting-room to-day, and she showed me the many portraits she has there of you; that being so, I certainly ought not to have mistaken you, even for a moment, for Mr. Boringdon!"

But with the mention of the name the smile faded, and a look of oppression came over her face.

"Grace Johnstone," Berwick's sudden utterance of the name was an experiment: he waited: ah! yes, that was it! The painful association was with Mrs. Johnstone, not with Oliver Boringdon or his mother.

"Grace Johnstone," he repeated, "is a very old friend of mine, Mrs. Rebell, and it is always a pleasure to me to have news of her."

Barbara was opening and shutting her ringless left hand with a nervous gesture: she began crumbling the bread by her plate.

"I have not known her very long," she said, "but nothing could have exceeded her kindness to me. I was very ill, and Mrs. Johnstone took me into her own house and nursed me well again. It seemed so very strange a coincidence that her mother and brother should be living at Chancton, so near to my godmother." But Berwick realised that the coincidence was not regarded by the speaker as a happy one.

"Mrs. Boringdon," he said slowly, "is quite unlike her daughter. I should think there was very little confidence between them. If you will allow me to be rather impertinent, to take advantage of our relationship—you know my great-grandfather very wisely married your great-grandmother's sister—I should like to give you a piece of advice— —"

Barbara looked at him anxiously—the youthfulness which had so disarmed him again became manifest in her face.

"My advice is that you write a note to the Johnstones, and then confide it to my care to send off with the fifty pounds you are returning to them. I will see that they receive it safely." Some instinct—the outcome, perhaps, of many money dealings with pretty women—made him add, with a touch of reserve, "But perhaps Mrs. Johnstone did not know of this loan?"

"Oh! yes, of course she did! Indeed it was she who suggested it. But for that I could not have come home." Barbara was blushing, and Berwick saw tears shining in her eyes. He felt oddly moved. He had often heard of, but he had never seen, the shedding of tears of gratitude.

"Yes," he said hastily, "I felt sure that was the case. But I do not think Mrs. Boringdon need be informed of the fact."

Mrs. Rebell had risen. A sudden fear that she might be going upstairs, that he would not see her again that night, came over Berwick.

"Do go into the drawing-room and write that note to the Johnstones, and I will join you there in a few moments. I am going over to my own quarters to fetch something which will, I think, interest you."

Berwick held open the door, waited till the echo of her footsteps had gone, then quickly lighted a pipe, and walking across the dining-room pushed open one of the sections of the high oriel window. Then he made his way round, almost stealthily, to the stretch of lawn on which opened the French windows of the two drawing-rooms. The curtains were not drawn: McGregor, and his satellite, the village lad who was being transformed into a footman, had certainly grown careless,—and yet it would have been a pity to shut out the moon, and it was not at all cold.

Pacing up and down, Berwick, every few moments, saw, set as in a frame, the whole interior of the Blue drawing-room, forming a background to Barbara Rebell. Indeed, she was quite near the window, sitting—an hour ago the fact would have shocked him—at Madame Sampiero's own writing-table, at that exquisite Louis XV. escritoire which had been discovered by Lord Bosworth in a Provençal château, and given by him, now many a long year ago, to the mistress of Chancton Priory.

Barbara had lighted the two green candles which her unseen watcher could remember as having been there so long that their colour had almost faded. She was bending over the notepaper, her slight supple figure thrown forward in a curiously graceful attitude. Again and again Berwick, walking and smoking outside, stopped and looked critically at the little scene. It is seldom that a man can so look consideringly at a woman, save perhaps at a place of public amusement, or in a church.

At last, slightly ashamed of himself, he turned round for the last time, and plunged into the moonlit darkness lying the other side of the house. In his room was a graceful sketch of Mrs. Richard Rebell, Barbara's lovely mother. He felt certain that the daughter would greatly value it. How surely his instinct had guided him he himself hardly knew. Barbara had loved her mother passionately, and after this evening she never glanced at the early presentment of that same beloved mother without a kind thought for the giver of it.

A curious hour followed: spent by Berwick and Mrs. Rebell one on each side of Madame Sampiero's couch—Barbara listening, quite silently, while Berwick, never seen to more advantage than when exerting himself to please and interest the stricken mistress of Chancton Priory, told news of that absorbing world of high politics which to Madame Sampiero had long been the only one which counted, and in which much of her past life had been spent.

So listening, Barbara felt herself pitifully ignorant. Pedro Rebell, proud as he had been of his British name and ancestry, made no attempt to keep in touch with England. True, certain names, mentioned so familiarly before her, were remembered as having been spoken by her father, but this evening, seeing how much this question—this mysterious question of the Ins and the Outs—meant to Madame Sampiero, Barbara made up her mind, rather light-heartedly considering the magnitude of the task, to lose no time in mastering the political problems of her country.

It must be admitted that Berwick's eager out-pouring—though it included what one of his listeners knew was a masterly forecast of the fate he hoped was about to overwhelm the Government which had already earned the nickname of "The Long Parliament"—did not add much to Mrs. Rebell's knowledge of contemporary statecraft. Still, her attention never flagged, and the speaker, noting her absorption, thought he had never had so agreeable an audience, or one which showed more whole-heartedly its sympathy with Her Majesty's Opposition.

The entrance of Doctor McKirdy into the room proved a harsh interruption.

"Be off!" he cried unceremoniously. "Madam won't be having a glint of sleep this night!" and then as Madame Sampiero spoke, her speech sadly involved, "Ay, ay, I've no doubt that all this company and talking has made ye feel more alive, but we don't want you to be feeling dead to-morrow, Madam—eh, what? That wouldn't matter? It would indeed matter, to those who had your death on their consciences!"

But already Berwick and Mrs. Rebell were in the corridor. "I hope I have not tired her?" he said ruefully.

"No—no, indeed! You heard what she said? You made her feel alive—no wonder she looks forward to your coming! Oh! I hope you will be here often."

Berwick looked at her oddly, almost doubtfully, for a moment. "I expect to be here a good deal this winter," he said slowly.

But if he thought that the evening, so well begun, was to be concluded in the Blue drawing-room downstairs, he was disappointed. Barbara turned and made him an old-fashioned curtsey—such an obeisance as French and Italian girls are taught to make to those of rank, and to the aged,—and then in a moment she was gone, up the winding staircase, leaving Berwick strangely subjugated and charmed.

He was turning slowly when there came the sound of shuffling feet. "Madam insists on your coming back just for a moment. Now don't go exciting of her or she'll never live to see you occupying that chair of little ease."

"What chair?" asked Berwick lazily: he was fond of McKirdy with an old fondness dating from his earliest childhood.

"The high seat, the gallows of fifty cubits set apart for the Prime Minister of this great country!"

"I'm afraid Madam will have to wait a long time before she sees me there!"

"Well, man, give her at least the chance of living to see that glorious day!"

But Madame Sampiero had, as it turned out, very little to say, and nothing of an exciting nature.

"Do I think Arabella will like her?" Berwick was rather taken aback and puzzled. He had not thought of his sister and Mrs. Rebell in conjunction, and the idea was not a particularly agreeable one. "Well, yes, why shouldn't she? They are absolutely unlike," a not unkindly smile came over his face. He added, "I am sure my uncle will be charmed with her," then bent forward to catch the faltering utterance, "Yes, I know Richard Rebell was a friend of his—but do I understand that you want Arabella to ask her to Fletchings?" There was a rather long pause—"Yes, yes, Arabella shall certainly call on Mrs. Rebell, and at once."

One fact necessarily dominated Berwick's relations with, and attitude towards, women. That he often forgot this fact, and would remain for long periods of time quite unaware that it lay in wait for him to catch him tripping, was certain. But even so, any little matter, such as a moment of sudden instinctive sympathy with some pretty creature standing on the threshold of life, was apt to bring back the knowledge, to make the Fact the one thing to be remembered.

Again, it was never forgotten—not for a moment—by the human being who had Berwick's interest most at heart, and who had played from his earliest boyhood a preponderant part in his life. Arabella Berwick always remembered that her brother's dead wife, behaving on this unique occasion as a man might have done, and as men have often done, had so left her vast fortune that even the life interest must pass away from him, and that irrevocably, in the event of his making a second marriage.

At the time of his wife's death, James Berwick had been annoyed—keenly so—by the comment this clause in her will had provoked—far more so indeed than by the clause itself. His brief experience of married life had not been such as to make him at all desirous of repeating the experiment; and what he saw of marriage about him did not incline him to envy the lot of the average married man. Accordingly, the condition of bachelorhood attaching to his present wealth pressed very lightly on him. It was, however, always present to Miss Berwick, and when her brother was staying at Fletchings—even more, when she was acting, as she sometimes did, as hostess to his friends—attractive girls were never included in the house party, and the agreeable, unattached widow, who has become a social institution, was rigorously avoided by her.

Unless the attraction is so strong as to cause him to overleap each of the many barriers erected by our rather elaborate civilisation, a man of the world—a man interested supremely in politics, considerably in sport, and in the hundred and one matters which occupy people of wealth and leisure—is generally apt to know, in an intimate social sense, only those women with whom he is brought in contact by his own womenfolk. Berwick went into many worlds to which his sister had no wish to have access, but both before his marriage and since he had become a widower, she had been careful to throw him, as far as lay in her power, with women who could in no way dispute her own position as his trusted counsellor and friend. This was made the more easy because James Berwick in all good faith disliked that feminine type which plays in politics the part of francs-tireurs—he called them by the less agreeable name of "stirabouts." Miss Berwick cultivated on her brother's behalf every type of pretty, amusing, and even clever married woman, but no worldly mother was ever more careful in keeping her daughter out of the way of detrimentals than was Arabella Berwick in avoiding for her brother dangerous proximities of an innocent kind.

Unfortunately Berwick was not always as grateful as he should have been to so kind and far-sighted a sister. He would suddenly take a fancy to the freshest and prettiest *débutante*, and for a while, perhaps from June to August, Arabella would tremble. On one occasion she had conveyed some idea of her brother's position to an astute lady who had regarded him as a prospective son-in-law, and when once the mother had thoroughly realised the dreadful truth concerning the tenure of his large income, the young beauty had been spirited away.

Then, again,—and this, it is to be feared, happened more frequently—Berwick would deliberately put himself in the way of some devastating charmer, who, even if technically "safe" from his sister's standpoint, belonged to the type which breeds mischief, and causes those involuntary appearances in the law courts of his country which stand so much in the way of the ambitious young statesman. Such ladies, as Miss Berwick well knew, have a disconcerting knack of getting rid of their legal impediment to re-marriage. Berwick had lately had a very narrow escape from such a one. In the sharp discussion between the brother and sister which had followed, he had exclaimed sardonically, "Really, Arabella, what you ought to look out for—I mean for me—is some poor pretty soul with a mad husband safe out of the way. You know lunatics live for ever." And Arabella, though she had smiled reprovingly, had been struck by the carelessly uttered words.

Miss Berwick's attitude to certain disagreeable and sordid facts of human life had been early fixed by herself as one of disdainful aloofness. She did not permit herself to judge those about her, and far preferred not to know of their transgressions. When such knowledge was thrust upon her—as had necessarily been the case with her uncle, Lord Bosworth, and Madame Sampiero—she judged narrowly and hardly the woman, contemptuously and leniently the man.

CHAPTER VI.

"Crois-tu donc que l'on peut commander à son cœur?
On aime malgré soi, car l'Amour est un hôte
Qui vient à son caprice, et toujours en vainqueur."

E. Augier.

During the ten days which followed that on which Mrs. Boringdon had held a certain conversation with her son, Lucy Kemp gradually became aware of two things. The first, which seemed to blot out and exclude everything else, was that she loved—in the old-fashioned pathetic sense of the abused word—Oliver Boringdon.

Hitherto she had been able to call the deep feeling which knit her to him "friendship," but that kindly hypocrisy would serve no longer: she was now aware what name to call it by. She had known it since the evening she had noticed that his manner had altered, that he had become more reserved, less really at ease. The second thing of which Lucy became aware, during those long dragging empty days, was the fact of her keen unhappiness, and of her determination to conceal it from those about her—especially from the father and mother who, she knew, were so strangely sensitive to all that concerned her.

Major-General and Mrs. Kemp had been settled at Chancton Grange for some years, and the Mutiny hero, the man whose gallant deed had once thrilled England, Mrs. Kemp, and their young daughter, had come to be regarded by the village folk with that kindly contempt which is bred, we are told, by familiarity.

The General's incisive, dry manner was rather resented by those of his neighbours who had hoped to make of him a local tea-party celebrity, and his constructive interest in local politics won him but tepid praise from the villagers, while the fact that Mrs. Kemp's large-minded charity and goodness of heart was tempered by a good deal of shrewd common-sense, did not make her the more loved by those, both gentle and simple, whom she was unwearying in helping in time of trouble.

The husband and wife were, however, rather grudgingly regarded as a model couple. It had soon been noticed that they actually appeared happier together than apart, and, surprising fact, that in the day-to-day life of walking and driving, ay and even of sitting still indoors, they apparently preferred each other's company to that of any of their neighbours!

Why one man succeeds, and another, apparently superior in every respect, fails in winning the prizes, the pleasant places, and the easy paths of life, is a mystery rather to their acquaintances than to their intimate friends—people who, according to the schoolboy's excellent definition, "know all about you, but like you all the same." Now the peculiarity about General Kemp was that he had neither succeeded nor failed, or rather he had been successful only up to a certain point. He had won his V.C. as a subaltern in the Mutiny, and promotion had naturally followed. But after he had attained to field rank, he saw his career broken off abruptly, and that for no shortcomings of his own, for nothing that he could have helped or altered in any way.

It was a prosaic misfortune enough, being simply the relentless knife of economy, wielded by a new and enthusiastic Secretary at War, which cut off at one sweep General Kemp and various of his contemporaries and comrades in arms. The right honourable gentleman, as he explained to an admiring House of Commons, was able to save the difference between the full pay and the retired pay of these officers—a substantial sum to be sure, but still not so much as was afterwards expended by the right honourable gentleman's successors in bringing the establishment of officers up to its proper strength again.

General Kemp was a deeply disappointed man, but he kept his feelings strictly to himself, and only his wife knew what compulsory retirement had meant to him, and, for the matter of that, to herself, for Mrs. Kemp, very early in life, had put all her eggs in Thomas Kemp's basket.

But in one matter there had been no disappointment. The fact that Lucy's childhood had been spent, though not unhappily, far from her parents, seemed to make her doubly dear to them: and then, to their fond eyes and hearts, their child was everything a girl should be. Unlike the girls of whom Mrs. Kemp sometimes heard so much, she showed no desire to leave her father and mother—no wish even to enjoy the gaieties which fell to the lot of her contemporaries who lived amid livelier scenes than those afforded by a remote Sussex village, and this though she was as fond of dancing and of play as other young creatures of her age.

Until a year ago,—nay, till six months back,—Mrs. Kemp would have disbelieved an angel, had so august a visitant foretold that there would soon arise, and that through no fault of hers or of the girl's, a cloud between her daughter, her darling Lucy, and herself; and yet this thing, this incredible thing, had come to pass.

The worst the mother had feared, and she had sometimes feared it greatly, was that her only daughter, following in this her own example, would marry to India, or, worse still, to some far-away colony. But, even so, Mrs. Kemp would have made the sacrifice, especially if Lucy's lover had in any way recalled the Tom Kemp of thirty years before.

However, as so generally happens, the danger the mother had dreaded passed by harmlessly: Lucy received and rejected the offer of a soldier, the son of one of the General's oldest friends; and her girlish heart had turned to something so utterly different, so entirely unexpected, that neither Mrs. Kemp nor Lucy's father had known how to deal with the situation which had come upon them with a suddenness which had amazed them both.

In spite of her look of unformed youth and gravely young manner, Lucy Kemp was in no sense a child. There are surely many women who at some stage of their life, paraphrasing the famous phrase, might well exclaim, "I think, therefore I am—a woman." But such a test would convict many women of eternal childhood.

Lucy, during the last year, had thought much—too much, perhaps, for her comfort. She had early made up her mind as to what she did not wish to do with her life. In no circumstances would she become the wife of Captain Laxton, but she had found it difficult to convince him of her resolution.

So it was that now, during those dreary days when the flow of constant communication between Oliver Boringdon and the Grange had ceased, as if by a stroke of malignant magic, poor Lucy had had more than time to examine her mind and heart, and to feel a dreadful terror lest what she found there should also be discovered by those about her, and especially by Oliver himself.

Mrs. Kemp was not well—so rare an occurrence as to alter all the usual habits of the Grange. The General wandered disconsolately about the garden, and through the lower rooms, reading, smoking, and gardening, but it always ended in his going up to his wife's room. Lucy, standing apart, was not too busy with her thoughts to realise, more than she had ever done before, the vitality, the compelling bondage, of such an attachment as that between her quiet, rather silent, father and her impulsive affectionate mother. Watching those two with a new, and an almost painful, interest, the girl told herself that, for a year of such happy bondage between herself and Oliver Boringdon, she would willingly give the rest of her life in exchange.

Looking back, especially on the last few months, Lucy was able to recall many moments, nay hours, when Oliver had undoubtedly regarded her as being in a very special sense his friend. Bending over her work, sitting silent by her mother's bedside, Lucy would suddenly remember, with a fluttering of the heart, certain kindly looks, certain frankly uttered confidences—and, remembering these things, she would regain some of the self-respect which sometimes seemed to have slipped away from her in a night. To Lucy Kemp the thought of seeking before being sought was profoundly repugnant, and she was deeply ashamed of the feeling which possessed her, and which alone seemed real in her daily life.

There had been no love-making on Oliver's part—no, indeed!—but the very phrase has acquired a vulgar significance. The girl thought she knew every way of love, and she shrank from being "made love to." Captain Laxton's eager desire to anticipate her every trifling wish, his awkward and most unprovoked compliments, the haunting of her when she would so much rather have been alone—ah! no, Oliver could never behave like that, in so absurd, so undignified a manner, to any woman. If Captain Laxton was a typical lover, then Lucy Kemp felt sure that Boringdon was incapable of being, in that sense, in love, and she thought all the better of him for it.

Nay, more,—the belief that Oliver was in this so different from other, more commonplace, men, brought infinite comfort. Lucy, compelled to admit that he had at no time shown any wish to make love to her, brought herself to think it possible that Boringdon was in very truth incapable of that peculiar jealous passionate feeling of which the girl now knew herself to be as much possessed as was Captain Laxton himself—that strange state of feeling so constantly described in those novels which she and her mother read, and of which her soldier lover, when in her company, seemed the living embodiment.

During the past ten days, Lucy had only twice seen Oliver, and this in village life must mean deliberate avoidance. So feeling, pride, and instinctive modesty, had kept her away from the Cottage, and Mrs. Boringdon—this was surely strange—had made no effort to see her. Once, in a by-way of Chancton, Lucy had met Oliver face to face,—he had stopped her, inquired eagerly concerning Mrs. Kemp, and seemed inclined, more than she had done at the moment, to talk in the old way, to linger—then with an odd, almost rude abruptness, he had turned and left her, and tears, of which she had been bitterly, agonisingly ashamed, had rushed into poor Lucy's brown eyes.

Their other meeting—one which was infinitely pleasanter to look back upon—had been at the Grange. Boringdon had come with a note from his mother to Mrs. Kemp; Lucy had taken it from him at the door, and unasked he had followed the girl through the hall out into the old-fashioned garden. There, after a word said by her as to the surprising result of an important by-election,—since she had known him Lucy had become very much of a politician,—Oliver had suddenly taken from his pocket a letter which concerned him nearly, and acting as if on an irresistible impulse, he had begged her to read it.

The letter was from a man who had been one of his principal constituents and supporters during his brief period of Parliamentary glory, and contained private information concerning the probable resignation of the member who had been Boringdon's successful rival at the last election—it of course amounted to an invitation to stand again.

For a moment standing, out there in the garden, Time seemed to have been put back: Oliver and she were talking in the old way—indeed, he was just telling her exactly what he meant to write in answer to this all-important letter, when, to Lucy's discomfiture and deep chagrin, General Kemp had suddenly appeared in the garden porch of the Grange and had put a quick sharp end to the discussion. "Your mother wants you, Lucy—will you please go up to her at once?" and the girl had obeyed without saying good-bye, for she felt sure—or perhaps, had hoped to ensure—that Boringdon would wait till she came down again. But alas! when she ran down, a few minutes later, the young man was gone, and her father answered her involuntary look of deep disappointment with one that made her hang her head and blush! The child in Lucy asked itself pitifully how father could have been so unkind.

General Kemp had indeed been angry—nay, more than angry. The showing of a letter by a man to a woman is an action which to an onlooker has about it something peculiarly significant and intimate. Standing just within the threshold of his house, seeing the two figures standing on the path close to one another, and so absorbed in what they were saying that some moments elapsed before they looked up and became aware of his presence, the father realised, more than he had done before, Lucy's odd relation to the young man. "What the devil"—so General Kemp asked himself with rising anger—"what the devil did Boringdon mean by all that sort of thing?"

"Il faut qu'une porte soît ouverte ou fermée!" The wise French saying which provided de Musset with a title for one of his most poignant tragi-comedies, was probably unknown to General Kemp, but it exactly expressed his feeling. The upright soldier had no liking for half-open doors—for ambiguous sentimental relations.

"I can't think what the man was thinking of—taking a letter out of his pocket, and showing it to her for all the world as if she were his wife! I wish, Mary, you'd say a word to Lucy."

"What word would you have me say, Tom?" Mrs. Kemp raised herself painfully in bed. She still felt in all her bones the violent chill she had caught, and the being compelled to lie aside had made her, what she so seldom was, really depressed. On this unfortunate afternoon she had followed with intuitive knowledge every act of the little drama enacted downstairs: she had heard the General's sharply uttered command; noted Lucy's breathless eager longing to be down again; and then she had heard the front door open and shut; and she had listened, almost as disappointedly as Lucy might have done, to Boringdon's firm steps hurrying up the road past her windows. If only she had not caught this stupid cold, all this might have been prevented! To-morrow she must really persuade the doctor to let her come down again.

"Surely, Mary, you don't need to be told what to say to the child! A mother should always know what to do and what to say in such a case. If we had a son and I thought him behaving badly to some girl, I should be at no loss to tell him what I thought of his conduct,—in fact, I should think it my duty as his father to do so." The General came and stood by his wife's bed. He glowered down at her with frowning, unhappy eyes.

"But that would be so different, Tom! I should be quite willing to speak to Lucy if I thought she were behaving badly—if she were to flirt, for instance, as I have seen horrid girls do! But this, you see, is so different—the poor child is doing nothing wrong: it is we who have been wrong to allow it to come to this."

The General walked up and down the room. Then he suddenly turned and spoke, "Well, I think something ought to be done. Get the matter settled one way or the other. I never heard of such a state of things! Lucy looks very far from well. Such a case never came my way before."

"Oh! Tom, is that quite true?"

"Certainly it is!"—he turned and faced her,—"quite true. Of course I've known men behave badly to women, very badly indeed, who hasn't? and women to men too, for the matter of that. But I've never come across such an odd fellow as Boringdon. Why, he scowled at me just now,—upon my word you might have thought I was the stranger and he her father! but I took the opportunity of being very short with him—very short indeed!" Then, as Mrs. Kemp sighed a long involuntary sigh, "No, Mary, in this matter, you must allow me to have my own way. I don't approve of that sort of conduct. It's always so with widows' sons—there are certain things only a man can knock into 'em! I wish I'd had that young fellow in the regiment for a bit. It would have done him a great deal more good than the House of Commons seems to have done. And then again I can't at all see what Lucy sees in him. He's such a dull dog! Now Laxton—I could understand any girl losing her heart to Laxton!" He walked to the window. "There's McKirdy coming in. I'll go down and have a talk with him. Meanwhile, you think over all I've been saying, Mary."

Poor Mrs. Kemp! as if she ever thought nowadays, in a serious sense, of anything else! But she was inclined, in her heart of hearts, to share Lucy's view of Boringdon's nature. Perhaps he was one of those men—she had known a few such—who are incapable of violent, determining feeling. If that were so, might not his evident liking for, and trust in, Lucy, develop into something quite sufficiently like love amply to satisfy the girl?

And Boringdon? Boringdon also was far from happy and satisfied during those days which had followed on his talk with his mother. The result of the conversation had been to make him deliberately avoid Lucy Kemp. But at once he had become aware that he missed the girl—missed, above all, the power of turning to her for sympathy, and even to a certain extent for counsel, more than he would have thought possible. He felt suddenly awakened to a danger he would rather not have seen,—why, oh! why, had not his mother left well alone? The state of things which had existed all that summer had exactly suited him. Looking back, Oliver felt sure that Lucy had not misunderstood the measure of affection and liking which he was willing, nay, eager, to bestow on her.

As the days went by, the young man wondered uneasily why his mother had suddenly left off asking the girl to lunch and to tea, as she had done, at one time, almost daily. He knew that Mrs. Boringdon rarely acted without a definite motive. Often her eyes would rest on his moody face with a questioning look. He longed to know why Lucy never came to the Cottage, but he was unwilling to give his mother the satisfaction of hearing him make such an inquiry. Then he reminded himself that, after all, Mrs. Kemp was really ill: the whole village watched with interest the daily visit to the Grange of the Halnakeham doctor. Perhaps Lucy found it difficult to leave home just now.

Even concerning his village worries—those connected with his work as land-agent to the Chancton estate—Boringdon had got into the way of turning to Lucy Kemp for comfort, and so he felt cut off from the only person to whom he could talk freely. Then had come that short meeting in the lane, and something timid, embarrassed in Lucy's manner had suddenly made him afraid, had put him on his guard—but afterwards he had been bitterly ashamed of the way in which he had behaved in leaving her so abruptly.

His heart grew very tender to her, and, had he not known that his mother was watching him, he would almost certainly have "made it up"—have given way—

and nature would have done the rest. But Oliver was aware that any sign of weakness on his part would be a triumph for Mrs. Boringdon—a proof that she had known how to shepherd him into a suitable engagement with a well-dowered girl: and so he had held out, knowing secretly that it only rested with him to restore his old relation with Lucy to its former footing.

At last, it had been Mrs. Boringdon who had asked him, in her most innocent and conventional voice, to take a note from her to Mrs. Kemp, and the accident that it had been Lucy who had opened the front door had been enough to shake his resolution, and to break down the barrier which he had put up between himself and her. At the time he had been carrying the letter concerning his old constituency about with him for two days, and the temptation to tell Lucy all about it proved too strong. Hence he had followed her through into the quiet fragrant garden which held for him so many pleasant associations of interesting, intimate talk with both the mother and the daughter.

Then, almost at once, had come the sharp, he told himself resentfully the utterly unwarrantable, interruption—more, there had been no mistaking General Kemp's manner—that of the man who cries "hands off!" from some cherished possession. Boringdon's guilty conscience—it was indeed hard that his conscience should feel guilty, for he was not aware of having done anything of which he should be ashamed—Boringdon's guilty conscience at once suggested the terrible thought that General Kemp doubtless regarded him as a fortune-hunter. When the front door of the Grange had closed on him he felt as if he could never come there again, and as if one of the pleasantest pages of his life had suddenly closed.

He determined to say nothing of the pregnant, even if almost wordless, little scene to his mother, and it was with a nervous dread of questions and cross questions that he entered the drawing-room of the Cottage with words concerning a very different person from Lucy Kemp on his lips. "Don't you think," he asked, "that the time has come when we ought to do something about Mrs. Rebell? She has been here, it seems, at least a week, and several people have already called on her."

Mrs. Boringdon looked at her son with some surprise, and he saw with satisfaction that his little ruse had been successful; the news he brought had made her forget, for the moment, the Grange and Lucy Kemp.

"Several people?" she repeated, "I think, my dear boy, you must be mistaken. No one *ever* calls at Chancton Priory. How could anyone—unless you mean Miss Vipen and the Rectory," she smiled slightingly—"have even been made aware of this Mrs. Rebell's arrival?"

"And yet there's no doubt about it," he said irritably, "I had the list from McKirdy, who seemed to take these calls as a personal compliment to himself! Miss Berwick drove over two or three days ago, and so did the Duchess of Appleby and Kendal." He waited a moment, feeling rather ashamed. He had known how to rouse his mother to considerable interest and excitement.

"The Duchess?" she echoed incredulously.—Most country districts in England have a duchess, and this district was no exception to the rule,—"what an extraordinary thing! I should have called on Mrs. Rebell, Grace's friend, before now, but it seemed so strange that she was not in church. It made me fear"—Mrs. Boringdon looked slightly shocked and genuinely grieved—"that she was going to follow the example of all the other people connected with the Priory."

"I don't know why you should say that, mother. It is quite impossible for Madame Sampiero to go to church, even if she wished to do so. As for McKirdy, I suppose he is a Presbyterian, but the Priory servants all go, don't they?"

"Yes," said Mrs. Boringdon, reluctantly, "the servants certainly do go,—that is, the lower servants. No one has ever seen the housekeeper at church, and, of course the state of things here must grieve Mr. Sampson very much."

Oliver smiled grimly. "If that is really so, Sampson doesn't know when he's well off. The sight of Mrs. Turke, resplendent in a new gown each Sunday, would certainly distract the congregation from his dull sermon!" But Mrs. Boringdon bent her head gravely, as if refusing to discuss so unsavoury and painful a subject.

"Have you seen her?" she asked with some natural curiosity. She added hastily, "I mean, of course, Mrs. Rebell."

"No," he said, "but I expect to do so in a few minutes. I saw McKirdy in the village just now, and profiting by his absence, I'm going to try and establish some kind of communication between Madame Sampiero and myself. There's a most urgent matter which ought to be settled at once, and McKirdy was so disagreeable the last time we met that I do not wish to bring him into it if I can possibly avoid it."

The Chancton estate, in addition to two villages, comprised many large farms stretching out on the fringe of the downs, and no day went by without the transaction by Boringdon of much complicated and tiresome business. In this, however, there would naturally have been much to interest such a man as himself, especially as he and Berwick had theories about agricultural problems and were eager to try experiments—in fact, Berwick was already doing so very successfully on his Sussex estate.

But for Boringdon, the new work to which he had set his hand had soon been poisoned, owing to the peculiar conditions under which he was compelled to do it. His immediate predecessor had been Doctor McKirdy, whose duties as medical attendant to Madame Sampiero had comprised for a while that of being her vice-regent as regarded estate matters. That arrangement had been anything but a success, hence the appointment, through Lord Bosworth's, or rather through James Berwick's, influence, of Oliver Boringdon. The change had been made the more easy because McKirdy, with an obstinacy worthy of a better cause, had always refused to accept any payment for this extra labour.

At first, the old Scotchman had been glad to give up the work he knew himself to have performed inadequately. Then, as time went on, he began to interfere, and Boringdon discovered, with anger and astonishment, that many matters were being gradually referred, both by the greater and the lesser tenants, directly to Madame Sampiero, or rather to the man who was still regarded, and with reason, as her vice-regent.

The doctor also insisted on being the sole means of communication between his patient and Boringdon. This was after he had found them speaking together,—or rather Boringdon speaking and Madame Sampiero listening,—concerning some public matter quite unconnected with Chancton. From that moment, Alexander McKirdy had set his very considerable wits to work against the younger man. He had informed him with sharp decision that his weekly audiences with his employer must cease: pointing out that almost everything that must be referred to her could be so done through him. Boringdon, for a while, had felt content that this should be so—he had always had a curious fear and repugnance of the still stiff figure, which seemed to be at once so physically dead and so mentally alive.

Then had come the gradual awakening, the realisation of his folly in consenting to an arrangement which destroyed his authority with those with whom he was brought into daily contact. Even the humblest cottager had soon discovered that the doctor, or "Kirdy," as he was unceremoniously styled amongst themselves, was once more the real over-lord of Chancton, and Boringdon found himself reduced to the disagreeable *rôle* of rent collector, his decisions concerning any important matter being constantly appealed from, and revoked by, the joint authority of Madame Sampiero and Doctor McKirdy.

The situation soon became almost intolerable to the high-spirited and sensitive young man: if it had not been for his mother, and for the fact that the very generous income allotted to him for the little he now did was of the utmost importance to her, he would ere this have resigned the land agency.

His pride prevented any mention of the odious position in which he found himself to Berwick, the more so that in theory he had all the power—it was to him, for instance, that Madame Sampiero's lawyers wrote when anything had to be settled or done. McKirdy also always allowed him to carry on any negotiations with neighbouring landowners. Boringdon had a free hand as regarded the keepers and the shooting—indeed, it was only with regard to the sporting amenities of the estate that he was really in the position of master rather than servant.

To his mother he always made light of his troubles, though he was well aware that he had her ardent sympathy, which took the, to him, disagreeable form of slight discourtesies to Doctor McKirdy—discourtesies which were returned with full interest by the old Scotchman. To Lucy and to Lucy's mother he had been more frank, and all she knew had not contributed to make Lucy feel kindly to Doctor McKirdy, though he was quite unconscious of how he was regarded by her.

To-day, matters had come, so felt Boringdon, to a head. On his way from the Cottage to the Grange, he had stopped for a moment at the estate office, and there had engaged in a sharp discussion with one of the more important Chancton farmers concerning a proposed remittance of rent. The man had brought his Michaelmas rent in notes and gold, the sum considerably short, according to Boringdon, of what should have been paid. The land-agent had refused to accept the money, and the farmer, naturally enough, had declared it to be his intention to make an appeal to Madame Sampiero through Doctor McKirdy.

It had been partly to turn his mind from the odious memory of this conversation that the young man had not been able to resist the temptation of following Lucy through into the garden with which he had so many pleasant memories, and once there, of showing her the letter which seemed to point to an ultimate escape from Chancton, and all that Chancton now represented of annoyance and humiliation.

Leaving the Grange, he had passed Doctor McKirdy, and had made up his mind to try and see Madame Sampiero within the next few hours. If it came to the point, he believed he could conquer, only, however, by calling to his aid the Bosworth faction, but the thought of an appeal to Berwick was still, nay, more than ever, disagreeable. At the same time this was a test case. He was sorry that his mother had not called on Mrs. Rebell, for he was dimly aware that the trifling lack of courtesy would give McKirdy a slight advantage, but during the last few days he had had other things to think of than his sister's unfortunate protégée, in whom, however, he unwillingly recognised another adherent to the McKirdy faction.

And yet the first meeting of Boringdon and Barbara Rebell fell out in such wise that it led to a curiously sudden intimacy, bred of something between pity and indignation on her side and gratitude on his.

CHAPTER VII.

"She whom I have praised so,
Yields delight for reason too:
Who could dote on thing so common
As mere outward-handsome woman?
Such half-beauties only win
Fools to let affection in."

WITHER.

MRS. REBELL was sitting by her god-mother's couch, pouring out tea. She had just come in from a walk on the downs, and as she sat there, her eyes shining, the colour coming and going in her cheeks, Madame Sampiero's gaze rested on her with critical pleasure and approval, lingering over every detail of the pretty brown cloth gown and neat plumed hat, both designed by a famous French arbiter of fashion who in the long ago had counted Madame Sampiero as among his earliest and most faithful patronesses.

The last few days had been to Mrs. Rebell days of conquest. She had conquered the right to come in and out of her god-mother's room without first asking formal leave of Doctor McKirdy, and he had given in with a good grace. She had won the heart of Mrs. Turke, and was now free of the old housekeeper's crowded sitting-room; and she had made friends also with all the dumb creatures about the place.

Then again, the pretty gowns, the many charming trifles which had come from Paris, and which she had been made to try on, one by one, in her god-mother's presence, contributed, though she felt rather ashamed of it, to her feeling of light-heartedness. Barbara Rebell, moving as one at home about the Priory, looked another creature from the shrinking sad-eyed woman who had arrived at Chancton a fortnight before, believing that youth, and all the glad things that youth represents, lay far behind her.

There came a knock, McGregor's discreet knock, at the door. Barbara sprang up, and a moment later came back with a letter, one which the bearer had apparently not dared to put by, as was the rule with such missives, and indeed with all letters addressed to the mistress of the Priory, till Doctor McKirdy was ready to read them, and to transmit such portions of their contents as he thought fit to his friend and patient.

"A note for you, Marraine!" The French equivalent for god-mother had always been used by Barbara Rebell both as child and girl in her letters to Madame Sampiero, and she had now discovered that it was preferred to its more formal English equivalent, or to the "Madam" which all those about her used. "Shall I read it to you?"

Barbara was looking down at the letter which she held in her hand with some surprise. The ink was not yet dry,—it must therefore have been written, in great haste, just now in the hall, and must call for an immediate answer. She waited for a sign of assent, and then opened the envelope:—

> "DEAR MADAME SAMPIERO,—I am sorry to trouble you, but I fear I must ask you to see me at your early convenience about a certain matter concerning which your personal opinion and decision are urgently required. Perhaps you will kindly send me word as to what time will suit you for me to come and see you.
>
> "Yours faithfully,
> "OLIVER BORINGDON."

Madame Sampiero's eyelids flickered, "Would you like to see him, child—our Chancton *jeune premier*?" and the ghost of a satirical smile hovered over the still face and quivering mouth.

"Yes, indeed, Marraine, if it would not tire you! You know it was his sister who was so kind to me in Santa Maria. May I send for him now? He evidently wants to see you about something very important—"

But McGregor, convinced that there would be no answer to the note he had most unwillingly conveyed upstairs, had not waited, as Barbara had expected to find, in the corridor. She hesitated a moment, then, gathering up her long brown skirts, ran down to the hall.

Boringdon was walking up and down, waiting with dogged patience for the message which might, after all, not be sent to him. "Will you kindly come up—now—to Madame Sampiero? She is quite ready to see you!" To the young man the low, very clear voice, seemed at that moment the sweetest in the world: he turned round quickly and looked at the messenger with a good deal of curiosity.

No thought that this elegant-looking girl could be Mrs. Rebell came to his mind. Doubtless she was one of the few people connected with Madame Sampiero's past life—perhaps one of the cousins who sometimes came to Chancton, and whom, occasionally, but very rarely as the years had gone on, the paralysed woman consented to receive.

Rather bewildered at the ease with which the fortress had been stormed and taken, he followed the unknown young lady upstairs. But once in the corridor, when close to Madame Sampiero's door, Barbara stopped, and with heightened colour she said, "I know that you are Grace Johnstone's brother, I have been hoping the last few days to go and see your mother. Will you please tell her how much I look forward to meeting her?" And before he could make any answer, she whom Boringdon now knew to be Mrs. Rebell had opened the door, and was motioning him to precede her into the room into which he had not been allowed to come for two months.

A moment later he stood at the foot of Madame Sampiero's couch, feeling the place in which he found himself curiously transformed, the atmosphere about him more human, less frigid than in those days when his weekly conferences with the owner of Chancton had been regarded by him with such discomfort and dread.

The presence of the low table on which now lay a tea-tray and a bowl of freshly-gathered roses affected him agreeably, though he still quailed inwardly when his eyes met those of the paralysed woman stretched out before him: Boringdon was not imaginative, and yet these wide open blue eyes had often haunted him—to-day they rested on him kindly, and then looked beyond him, softening as they met those of her god-daughter.

Before he was allowed to begin on what he felt to be such disagreeable business, Mrs. Rebell—the woman whom he now knew to be his sister's friend, and regarding whom he was being compelled to alter, moment by moment, all his preconceived notions—had poured him out a cup of tea, and had installed him by her side. Later, when she made a movement as if to leave him alone with Madame Sampiero, she was stopped with a look, and Boringdon, far from feeling the presence of a third person as disagreeable and as unwarranted as he had always felt that of McKirdy or of Mrs. Turke, was glad that Mrs. Rebell had been made to stay, and aware, in some odd way, that in her he would have an ally and not, as had always been the case with McKirdy, a critic, if not an enemy.

After a short discussion, he was allowed to go with the point settled to his satisfaction. Madame Sampiero had retained all her shrewdness, and all her essential justness of character; moreover, his case, presented partly through the medium of Barbara's voice, had seemed quite other than what it would have done explained inimically by Alexander McKirdy. Indeed, during the discussion Boringdon had the curious feeling that this soft-voiced stranger, who, after all, was in no position to judge between himself and the peccant farmer, was being made to give the ultimate decision. It was Barbara also who had to repeat, to make clear to him, reddening and smiling as she did so, her god-mother's last words, "If you're not busy, you might take Mrs. Rebell down to the Beeches. The trees won't look as well as they are doing now in a week's time;" and while murmuring the words Madame Sampiero's eyes had turned with indefinable longing towards the high windows which commanded the wide view she loved and knew so well, but which from where she lay only showed the sky.

A rude awakening awaited both Barbara and Boringdon in the hall below; and a feeling of guilt,—an absurd unwarrantable feeling, so he told himself again and again when he thought over the scene later,—swept over the young man when he saw Doctor McKirdy pacing, with quick angry steps, that very stretch of flagstones where he himself had walked up and down so impatiently half an hour before.

"So you've been up to see her? Against my very strict orders—orders, mind ye, given as Madam's medical man! Well, well! All I can say is, that I'm not responsible for what the consequences may be. Madam's not fit to be worried o'er business—not fit at all!" The words came out in sharp jerky sentences, and as he spoke Doctor McKirdy scowled at the young man, twisting his hands together, a trick he had when violently disturbed.

As the two culprits came towards him he broke out again, almost turning his back on them as he spoke, "I cannot think what possessed the man McGregor! He will have to be dismissed, not a doubt about it! He has the strictest, the very strictest orders—he must have been daft before he could take up a stranger to Madam's room!" There was a world of scorn in the way in which McKirdy pronounced the word "stranger."

Angry as Boringdon had now become, indignant with the old man for so attacking him in the presence of one who was, as Oliver did not fail to remind himself, the real stranger to all their concerns, he yet felt that to a certain extent the doctor's anger and indignation were justified. Boringdon knew well enough that, but for McKirdy's absence from the Priory that afternoon, he could never have penetrated into Madame Sampiero's presence. He had also been aware that McGregor was acting in direct contravention of the doctor's orders, and that nothing but his own grim determination to be obeyed had made the man take his note upstairs. All this being so, he was about to say something of a conciliatory nature, when suddenly Mrs. Rebell came forward—

"It is I," she said—and Boringdon saw that she showed no sign of quailing before Doctor McKirdy's furious looks—"who asked my god-mother to see Mr. Boringdon, and so it is I alone, Doctor McKirdy, who should be blamed for what has happened. Madame Sampiero asked my advice as to whether she should see him, and as the matter seemed urgent, I decided that she had better do so at once, instead of waiting, as I should perhaps have done, to ask you if she was fit to do so."

She looked inquiringly from one man to the other—at the old Scotchman whose face still twitched with rage, and whose look of aversion at herself she felt to be cruelly unjust, almost, she would have said, had she not become really fond of him, impertinent; and at Boringdon, who also looked angry, but not as surprised as she would have expected him to be before so strange an outburst.

There was a moment of tense silence, and then, suddenly, Barbara herself caught fire. Like most gentle, self-restrained natures, she was capable of feeling deep instant gusts of anger, and one of these now swept over her.

"If you will go up and see Madame Sampiero," she spoke very coldly, "I think you will admit, Doctor McKirdy, that my god-mother has not been in any way injured by seeing Mr. Boringdon." She turned, rather imperiously, to the young man. "I think," she said, "that now we had better go out. I suppose it will take at least half an hour to walk round by the Beeches, and later my god-mother will be expecting me back to read to her."

Without again glancing at Doctor McKirdy, Mrs. Rebell walked across to the vestibule, and so out into the open air, Boringdon following her rather shamefacedly, and in silence they struck off down the path which led round the great meadow-like enclosure to the broad belt of beeches which were the glory of

Chancton Priory.

Then, somewhat to his own surprise, Boringdon found himself making excuses for the old Scotchman, while explaining to Mrs. Rebell the odd position in which he often found himself. The conversation which followed caused strides, which might otherwise have taken weeks or even months to achieve, in his own and Barbara's intimacy.

Very little was said of Grace Johnstone and of Santa Maria; it was of the Priory, and of its stricken mistress, of Chancton and of Doctor McKirdy, that they talked, and it was pleasant to Boringdon to hear his own part being taken to himself, to hear McKirdy severely censured in the grave low voice whose accents had sounded so sweetly in his ears when it had come to call him to Madame Sampiero's presence.

So eager was their talk, so absorbed were they in what they were saying, that neither had eyes for the noble trees arching overhead; and when at last they came out, from the twilight of the beeches, into the open air, Barbara felt respect and liking for the young man.

When they were once more close to the house, she put up her hand with a quick gesture. "Don't come up with me to the porch," she said, "I am sure you had better not meet Doctor McKirdy—I mean for the present." He obeyed her silently, though for the moment he felt not unkindly towards the old man he had conquered in what, he confessed to himself, had been unfair fight. With Mrs. Rebell on his side he could afford to smile at McKirdy's queer susceptibilities and jealousies. He must come and see her to-morrow; there seemed so much more to say, to ask too, about Grace—dear Grace, who had written with such warm-hearted feeling of this charming, interesting woman who ought to be, so Boringdon told himself, a most agreeable and softening influence at the Priory.

That same evening, Mrs. Boringdon, after much hesitation and searching of heart, ventured to ask her son a question.

"How did you find them all at the Grange? It seems a long time since I have seen Lucy."

Oliver's face clouded over, but he was surprised at his own calmness, his absence of annoyance; that disagreeable episode at the Grange now seemed to have happened long ago.

"Everything was as usual," he answered hesitatingly; "—at least, no, I should not say that, for General Kemp's manner to me was far from being usual. I cannot help thinking, mother, that you made a mistake the other day—I mean as regards Lucy;"—a note of reserve and discomfort crept into his voice as he pronounced her name,—"The General's manner was unmistakable, he all but showed me the door! I think it would be as well, both for you and for me, if we were to put all thought of her from our minds, and to see, in the future, less of her."

Boringdon found it less easy to answer his mother's next question, "And Madame Sampiero,—I suppose you did not see her to-day? I wonder if she sees anything of Mrs. Rebell?"

"Yes," he said, rather reluctantly, "McKirdy was out, and I had, on the whole, a satisfactory interview with Madame Sampiero, owing it, in a measure, to Mrs. Rebell. Madame Sampiero is evidently very fond of her. By the way, she—I mean Mrs. Rebell—sent you a nice message about Grace."

"Oh! then she's a pleasant woman—I'm so glad! Everything makes a difference in a little place like Chancton. I suppose," Mrs. Boringdon spoke absently, but her son knew that she would require an answer, "that Mrs. Rebell did not mention Miss Berwick, or the Duchess?"

"Oh! no, mother," Oliver answered rather drily, "Why should she have done so—to me?"

"Oh! well—as a kind of hint that I ought to have called. I hope you explained the matter to her? I mean to go there to-morrow."

Boringdon made no remark. He had no intention, nay, he had an instinctive dislike to the idea, of discussing Mrs. Rebell with his mother, and he vaguely hoped that they would never become intimate.

Arabella Berwick was sitting in the little room, originally a powder closet, which was set aside for her use at Fletchings. It was well out of the way, on the first floor of the old manor-house, tucked away between the drawing-room, which was very little used except in the evening, and the long music gallery, and it was characteristic of Miss Berwick that very few among the many who came and went each summer and autumn to Fletchings were aware of the existence of this, her favourite retreat.

In the Powdering Room, as it was still called, Lord Bosworth's niece wrote her letters, scrutinised with severely just eyes the various household accounts, and sometimes allowed herself an hour of complete relaxation and rest. The panelled walls, painted a pale blue, were hung with a few fine engravings of the more famous Stuart portraits, including two of that Arabella Stuart after whom Miss Berwick had been herself named. There was also, on the old-fashioned davenport at which she wrote her letters, a clever etching of her brother, done when James Berwick was at Oxford.

The mistress of such a house has a well-filled, and indeed often a tiring, life, unless she be blessed with a highly paid, and what is not always the same thing, a highly competent, housekeeper and factotum, to take the material cares off her shoulders. Lord Bosworth was nothing if not hospitable. There was a constant coming and going of agreeable men and women in whatever place he happened to find himself. He disliked solitude, and in the long years Miss Berwick had kept her uncle's house, she could scarcely remember a day in which they had been absolutely alone together.

As a high-spirited, clever girl, brought suddenly from the companionship of an austere aunt and chaperon, she had found the life a very agreeable one, and she had set her whole mind to making it successful. Even now, she had pleasant, nay delightful, moments, but as she grew older, and above all, as Lord Bosworth grew older, much in the life weighed upon her, and any added trouble or anxiety was apt to prove almost unbearable.

To-day, she had received a letter from her brother which had caused her acute annoyance. James Berwick was coming back, a full fortnight before she had expected him,—his excuse, that of wishing to be present at the coming-of-age festivities of Lord Pendragon, the Duke of Appleby and Kendal's only son, which were shortly to take place at Halnakeham Castle. He had always had,—so his sister reminded herself with curling lip,—a curious attachment to this neighbourhood, a great desire to play a part in all local matters; this was the more strange as the Berwicks' only connection with Sussex had been the purchase of Fletchings by their uncle, and James Berwick's own inheritance from his wife of Chillingworth, the huge place, full of a rather banal grandeur, where its present possessor spent but little of his time.

There were three reasons why Miss Berwick would have much preferred that her brother should carry out his original plan. The first, and from her point of view the most important, concerned, as did most important matters to Arabella, Berwick himself. She had just learned, from one of the guests who had arrived at Fletchings the day before, that the woman whom, on the whole, she regarded as having most imperilled her brother, would almost certainly be one of the ducal house-party at Halnakeham. This lady, a certain Mrs. Marshall, was now a widow, and the sister feared her with a great fear.

The second reason was one more personal to herself. Miss Berwick was trying to make up her mind about a certain matter, and she felt that her brother's presence—nay, even the mere fact of his being in the neighbourhood—would make it more difficult for her to do so. She knew herself to be on the eve of receiving a very desirable offer of marriage. Its acceptance by her would be, in a sense, the crowning act of her successful life. The man was an ambassador, one of the most distinguished of her uncle's friends, a childless widower, who, as she had long known, both liked and respected her. In a few days he would be at Fletchings, and she knew that the time had come when she must make up her mind to say yes or to say no.

The third complication, from the thought of which Miss Berwick shrank with a pain which surprised herself, was the fact that both Lord Bosworth, and now her brother in this letter which lay before her, had requested her to write and ask Daniel O'Flaherty—the man whom she had once loved—to come and spend a few days at Fletchings. They had met many times since that decisive interview in Kensington Gardens which had been so strangely interrupted by Oliver Boringdon—for such meetings are the unforeseen penalties attendant on such conduct as had been that of Arabella—but both had hitherto contrived to avoid staying under the same roof. Now, however, she felt she could no longer put off giving this invitation, the more so that it was for her brother's sake that Lord Bosworth wished O'Flaherty to be asked to Fletchings.

Miss Berwick had early found it advisable, when something painful had to be done, to "rush her fences." She took up her pen and wrote, in her fine, characteristic hand-writing, the words, "Dear Mr. O'Flaherty."

Then she laid the pen down, lay back in her chair, and closed her eyes. Even after so long a time had gone by, the memory of what had passed between Daniel O'Flaherty and herself was intolerably bitter. Arabella even now never thought of him without asking herself how it happened that she had not realised what manner of man he really was, and why she had not foreseen how sure he was to make his way. She never saw his name printed, never heard it uttered, without this feeling of shamed surprise and acute self-reproach coming over her.

The strong attraction she had felt for the then untried Irishman had in a sense blinded her—made her distrustful of his real power. Her uncle, Lord Bosworth, had been more clear-sighted, in those far-off days when he had encouraged the unknown barrister to come about Bosworth House, just before she herself so ruthlessly sent him away.

And now she found the wording, as well as the writing, of her letter difficult: she wished to leave the matter of Daniel O'Flaherty's coming to Fletchings, or his staying away, entirely to his own sense of what was fitting. He had become, as she had reason to know, a man much sought after: perhaps the dates which she was able to offer him would all be filled up.

There came a slight sound; Miss Berwick opened her eyes, she sat up, an alert look on her face, ready to repel the intruder whoever he might be. Lord Bosworth, introducing his ample person through the narrow door of the tiny room, was struck by the look of age and fatigue which had come over—it seemed to him only since yesterday—his niece's delicate clear-cut features and shadowed fairness. Arabella Berwick had always been a good-looking replica of her remarkable-looking brother, but youth, which remains so long with many women, had gone from her. She often looked older than thirty-eight, and her deep-set compelling bright blue eyes, of which the moral expression was so different from that produced by those of James Berwick, gave an impression of singular disenchantment.

"Am I disturbing you?"—Lord Bosworth spoke very courteously—"if so, I will speak to you some other time." Arabella at once hid the great surprise she felt at seeing him here, for this was, as far as she could remember, her uncle's first visit to the Powdering Room: "Oh! no," she said, "I was only writing to Mr. O'Flaherty. You would like him to come soon, wouldn't you?"

"Yes, certainly! I am told he will have to be Attorney-General. He is the sort of man James ought to have got hold of long ago. We seem to have lost sight of him. I know I went to some trouble for him years ago—and then somehow he disappeared. Perhaps it was my fault—in that case I ought to write him a line myself."

Then he became silent, looking at his niece with a curious persistent gaze which embarrassed her. There had never been any real intimacy between the uncle and niece, and the thought that Lord Bosworth had suspected anything concerning what had occurred between herself and O'Flaherty would have been intensely disagreeable to Arabella. She felt herself flushing, but met his look with steady eyes, comforted by the knowledge that, whatever he knew or suspected, he would most certainly say nothing.

"I see," he said, "that you guess what I have come to tell you. I have had a letter from Umfraville—you know he comes to-morrow? It is a very good letter, a better letter than I should have thought he could have written on such a subject, but it amounts to this: before offering himself, he wishes to be sure of what your answer will be, and he wants you to make up your mind within the next few days,—in fact before he leaves us. It would be a great position, my dear, and one which you would fill admirably."

As he spoke the colour had faded from Miss Berwick's face. She felt relieved and rather touched. "But what would *you* do?" she said involuntarily.

Lord Bosworth made none of the answers which might have been expected from him. He said no word as to his niece's happiness being of more consequence than his own comfort, and if he had done so, Miss Berwick would not have believed him.

"I do not suppose that you are aware,"—he put his strong hands on the table before him, and looked at her with a sudden pleading look which sat oddly on his shrewd, powerful face—"I do not suppose, Arabella, that you are aware that I made Madame Sampiero an offer of marriage some six or seven years ago, not long after the death of—of Sampiero. I believe her answer was contained in one of the very last letters she ever wrote with her own hand. Well, now—in fact for a long time past—I have been contemplating a renewal of that offer. Nay more, should she again refuse, which I know well to be more than probable, I cannot see why, at our time of life, especially in view of her present state, we should even so not be together."

His niece looked at him in frank incredulous astonishment. She felt mortified to think how little she had known this man with whom she had lived for so long.

"Surely," she said, "surely you would find such an existence absolutely intolerable?"

"I do not know what I have done that you should judge me so severely."—Lord Bosworth's answer was made in a very low tone. "You are a clever woman, Arabella, and I have always done full justice to your powers, but, believe me, there are certain things undreamt of in your philosophy, and I do not think"—he stopped abruptly, and finished the sentence to himself, "I do not think Umfraville is likely to bring them any nearer to you."

He got up. "I thought I ought to tell you," he said, with a complete change of tone, "because my intention may influence your decision. Otherwise, I should not have troubled you with the matter." Then his heart softened to her: he suddenly remembered her long and loyal, if loveless, service. "Quite apart from any question of our immediate future, you must remember, my dear, that I'm an old man. I cannot help thinking that your life alone would be very dreary, and, much as you care for James, I cannot see either of you making in a permanent sense any kind of life with the other. In your place—and I have thought much about it—I should accept Umfraville. The doing so would enable you to lead the same life that you have led for the last twenty years, with certain great added advantages. Then Umfraville, after all, is a very good fellow,—good yet not too good, clever and yet not too clever!"

She smiled at him an answering but rather wavering smile, and he went out, closing the door behind him, leaving her alone with her thoughts, and with her scarcely begun letter to O'Flaherty lying before her.

CHAPTER VIII.

"I beg to hint to all Equestrian Misses
That horses' backs are not their proper place;
A woman's forte is music—love—or kisses,
Not leaping gates, or galloping a race;
I sometimes used to ride with them of yore,
And always found them an infernal bore."

Ascribed to Lord Byron.

It was the morning of the first meet of the South Sussex Hunt, and in spite of the humble status of that same hunt among sporting folk, the whole neighbourhood was in an agreeable state of excitement.

Even in a country district where hunting plays a subordinate part in the local life, the first meet of the season is always made the occasion for a great gathering. There had been a time when it had taken place on the lawn of Chancton Priory, and the open-handed hospitality of that Squire Rebell who had been Madame Sampiero's father was still regretfully remembered by the older members of the S.S.H.

Nowadays the first meet was held at a place known locally as Whiteways, which, though close to no hospitable house, had the advantage of proximity to the town of Halnakeham, being situated just outside the furthest gate of the park stretching behind Halnakeham Castle.

Whiteways was a singularly beautiful and desolate spot, forming the apex of a three-sided hill commanding an amazing view of uplands and lowlands, and reached by various steep ways, cut through the chalk, which gave the place its name, and which circled ribbon-wise round the crest of the down, the highest of the long range which there guards the coasts of Sussex.

General Kemp had taken to hunting in his old age, and though in theory he disapproved of hunting women, in practice he often allowed his daughter many a happy hour with the hounds, although she had to be contented with the sturdy pony, "warranted safe to ride and drive," a gift from Captain Laxton to Mrs. Kemp.

At the Grange breakfast was just over. The General looking his best—so Mrs. Kemp assured herself with wifely pride—in his white riding breeches and grey coat, stood by the window of the pretty room opening out on to the lawn.

"I think it's time you went up and dressed, Lucy. You know it's a good way to

Whiteways, and we don't want the horses blown."

Lucy looked up obediently from a letter she was reading, "Yes, father, I'll go up at once. It won't take me long to dress."

The girl would have given much to have been allowed to stay at home. But she knew that her doing so would probably mean the giving up on the part of her mother of one of the few local festivities which Mrs. Kemp heartily enjoyed. Even more, Lucy feared her father's certain surprise and disappointment, followed, after the first expression of these feelings, by one of those ominous silences, those tender questioning glances she had come to look for and to dread.

General Kemp was treating his daughter with a consideration and gentleness which were growing daily more bitter to Lucy. The poor child wondered uneasily what she could have done to make her father see so clearly into her heart. She would have given much to hear him utter one of his old sharp jokes at her expense.

Nothing was outwardly changed in the daily life of the village, Chancton had been rather duller than usual. Mrs. Rebell's back had been seen at church in the Priory pew, but she had gone out, as she had come in, by the private door leading into the park. Mrs. Boringdon had been away for nearly a fortnight, staying with an invalid sister, and so there had been very little coming and going between the Cottage and the Grange, although the Kemps and Oliver had met more than once on neutral ground.

To-day, as Lucy well knew, was bound to be almost an exact replica of that first day out last autumn. Then, as now, it had been arranged that Mrs. Boringdon should drive Mrs. Kemp to Whiteways; then, as now, Lucy and her father were to ride there together, perhaps picking up Captain Laxton on the way. But, a year ago, Oliver Boringdon had ridden to the meet in their company, while this time nothing had been said as to whether he was even going to be there. A year ago, the day had been one full of happy enchantment to Lucy: for her father had allowed her to follow the hounds for over an hour, with Boringdon as pilot, and he,—or so it seemed to the happy girl,—had had no eyes, no thought for anyone else! The knowledge that to-day would be so like, and yet, as a subtle instinct warned her, so unlike, was curiously painful.

Still, no thought of trying to escape from the ordeal entered Lucy's mind. But mothers—such mothers as Mrs. Kemp—often have a sixth sense placed at their disposal by Providence, and the girl's mother divined something of what Lucy was thinking and feeling.

"I wonder," she said, "if you would rather stop at home? You look tired, child, and you know it is a long way to Whiteways, and a rather tiring experience altogether! Of course I should go just the same."

General Kemp turned to his wife inquiringly, as if asking for a lead, and Lucy intercepted the look which passed between them. "Why, mother," she cried, "I shouldn't think of doing such a thing! I've been looking forward to to-day for ever so long! I know what you are thinking"—she flushed vividly, "but I'm sure Captain Laxton is much too old a friend to bear me a grudge, or to feel any annoyance as to meeting me. After all, he need not have come back— —" and without giving either of her parents time to answer, she ran out of the room.

General Kemp was much taken aback. This was the first time he had heard Lucy allude to Captain Laxton's affection for herself, or to the offer which she had rejected. To his mind such an allusion savoured almost of indelicacy. He did not like to think his daughter guilty of over-frankness, even to her father and mother.

"Can it be, Mary," he said, puzzled, "that she's thinking of Laxton after all?"

Mrs. Kemp shook her head. She knew very well why Lucy had mentioned her lover—that his image had been evoked in order to form as it were a screen between herself and what she had divined to be her mother's motive in suggesting that she should stay at home, but it would be hopeless to try and indicate such feminine subtleties to Lucy's father.

In the country, as in life, there are always many ways of reaching the same place. The pleasantest carriage road to Whiteways lay partly through the Priory park, and it was that which was chosen by Mrs. Boringdon and Mrs. Kemp. Lucy and her father preferred a less frequented and lonelier path, one which skirted for part of the way the high wall of James Berwick's property, Chillingworth.

They had now left this place far behind, and were riding slowly by the side of a curving down: Captain Laxton had evidently gone on before, or deliberately chosen to linger behind, and the father and daughter were alone. Soon they left the road for the short turf, broken here and there with hawthorn bushes; and Lucy, cheered by the keen upland air, was making a gallant effort to bear herself as she had always done on what had been such happy hunting days last winter. Already she could see, far away to her left, a broad shining white road, dotted with carriages, horsemen and horsewomen, and groups of walkers all making their way up towards the castellated gate-way which frowned on the summit of the hill above them.

When the father and daughter reached the large circular space, sheltered on one side by two wind-blown fir-trees, they found that they were rather late, and so had missed the pretty sight of the coming of the huntsman and his hounds over the brow of the down. Lucy made her way at once through the crowd close to where Mrs. Boringdon's low pony-carriage was drawn up just beneath the high stone gate-way, next to that of Mrs. Sampson, the Chancton rector's wife, who had weakly consented to bring Miss Vipen. Even Doctor McKirdy had vouchsafed to grace the pretty scene, and he was sitting straightly and lankily on the rough old pony he always rode, which now turned surprised and patient eyes this way and that, for the doctor had never before attended a meet of the S.S.H.

As yet Lucy could see nothing of Captain Laxton or of Boringdon, and she felt at once relieved and disappointed. Perhaps Oliver was too busy to give up a whole day to this kind of thing, and yet she knew he always enjoyed a day with the hounds, and that he had theories concerning the value of sport in such a neighbourhood as this. She reminded herself that if he had not been really very busy, more so than usual, he would certainly have found time to come to the Grange during his mother's absence from Chancton.

As these thoughts were coming and going through her mind in between the many greetings, the exchange of heavy banter such an occasion always seems to provoke, she suddenly heard Boringdon's voice, and realised that he was trying to attract her attention. Lucy's pony, feeling the agitation his young mistress was quite successfully concealing from the people around her, began to quiver and gave a sudden half-leap in the air.

"What has come over sober Robin?"—Boringdon was smiling; he looked in a good-tempered, happy mood—"I did so hope you would be here! I looked out for you on the road for I wanted to introduce——"

There was a sudden babel of voices; an old gentleman and his two talkative daughters, all three on foot, were actually pulling Lucy's habit to make her attend to what they were saying. Oliver shook his head, shrugged his shoulders, and to Lucy's bitter, at the moment almost intolerable disappointment, turned his horse through the crowd towards the fir-trees close to which were drawn up several carriages, including the Fletchings phaeton, driven, so the girl observed, by Miss Berwick, by whose side an elderly man was looking about him with amused indulgent eyes.

Still, the day was turning out pretty well. Oliver would surely come back soon,—doubtless with whoever it was he wished to introduce to her. It was always a great pleasure to Lucy to meet any of Boringdon's old political acquaintances. Such men were often at Fletchings. Of course Lucy Kemp knew Miss Berwick, but by no means well,—besides, an instinct had told her long ago that Oliver had no liking for his friend's sister.

There was a pause. Then Lucy saw that Oliver was riding towards her, and that he was accompanied by a lady, doubtless one of the Fletchings party, for she was mounted on a fine hunter, a certain Saucebox, locally famous, which belonged to James Berwick, and which was often ridden by his sister.

The unknown horsewoman was habited, booted, and hatted, in a far more *cap-à-pie* manner than was usual with the fair followers of the South Sussex Hunt, and she and her mount together, made, from the sportsman's point of view, a very perfect and pretty picture, though she was too pale, too slight, perhaps a thought too serious, to be considered pretty in the ordinary sense.

Still, both horse and rider were being looked at by many with eyes that were at first critical but soon became undisguisedly admiring, and the Master, old Squire Laxton, was noticed to cut short a confidential conversation with the huntsman in order to give the stranger an elaborate salutation.

Even Mrs. Kemp felt a slight touch of curiosity. "Who is that with whom your son is riding?" she inquired of Mrs. Boringdon.

"I don't know—perhaps one of the Halnakeham party. The Duke always makes a point of being here to-day."

Mrs. Boringdon's eyes rested appreciatively on the group formed by her son and the unknown horsewoman; they took in every detail of the severely plain black habit, the stiff collar, neat tie, and top hat. Oliver seemed to be on very good terms with his companion—doubtless she was one of his old London acquaintances. What a pity, thought Mrs. Boringdon with genuine regret, that he saw so few of that sort of people now—prosperous, well-dressed, well-bred women of the world, who can be so useful to the young men they like!

Lucy, also becoming conscious of the nearness of Oliver and his companion, looked at the well-appointed horsewoman with less kindly eyes than the two older ladies sitting in the pony carriage had done. The girl told herself that such perfection of attire, worn at such a meet as this of Whiteways, was almost an affectation on the part of the lady towards whom Oliver was bending with so pleased and absorbed a glance. A moment later the two had ridden up close to her, and Boringdon was saying, "Miss Kemp——Mrs. Rebell, may I introduce to you Miss Lucy Kemp?"

Barbara's eyes rested very kindly on the girl. She remembered what Doctor McKirdy had told her, during that walk that he and she had taken together on the downs on the morning of her first day at Chancton. It was nice of Oliver Boringdon to have brought her up at once, like this, to the young lady whom he admired, but who was not,—so Barbara thought she remembered McKirdy saying,—as yet his *fiancée*.

Mrs. Rebell had lately seen a great deal of Grace Johnstone's brother, in fact he was constantly at the Priory and always very much at her service; they had become quite good friends, and since she had "made it up" with the old doctor, she had taken pains to show both him and Madame Sampiero that Oliver Boringdon had a right to more consideration than they seemed willing to give him.

Then Lucy's steady gaze rather disconcerted her; she became aware of the girl's scanty riding habit—General Kemp's favourite form of safety skirt—of the loose well-worn covert coat, and the small bowler hat resting on her bright brown hair.

"I feel rather absurdly dressed"—Lucy was struck by Barbara's soft full voice—"but my god-mother, Madame Sampiero, ordained that I should look like this. My last riding habit was made of khaki!"

The note of appeal in Mrs. Rebell's accent touched Lucy at once. "Why, of course you look absolutely right! My father often says what a pity it is that so many women have given up wearing plain habits and top hats," Lucy spoke with pretty sincere eagerness——

"She is a really nice girl," decided Barbara to herself; and Oliver also looked at his old friend Lucy very cordially. To his mind both young women looked exactly right, that is, exactly as he liked each of them to look—Lucy Kemp perhaps standing for the good serviceable homespuns of life, Barbara Rebell for those more exquisite, more thrilling moments with which he had, as yet unconsciously, come to associate her.

"Of course," he said, a little quickly, "this is Mrs. Rebell's first experience of hunting, though she has ridden a great deal,—in fact, all her life. Otherwise Madame Sampiero would hardly have suggested sending over to Chillingworth for

Saucebox. Hullo, Laxton!"—his voice became perceptibly colder, but Lucy noticed with some surprise that Mrs. Rebell bowed and smiled at the newcomer, but Boringdon gave her no time to speak to him—"You had better come over here," he said urgently, "we shall be getting to work soon," and in a moment, or so it seemed to Lucy, he and the lady whom she knew now to be Mrs. Rebell had become merged in the crowd, leaving Captain Laxton by her side looking down on her with the half bold, half fearful look she knew so well.

Boringdon had taken Barbara to the further side of the great stone gateway, and she was enjoying every moment of the time which seemed to many of those about her so tedious. She was even amused at listening to the quaint talk going on round her. "Scent going to be good to-day?" "Well, they *say* there's always a scent some time of the day, and if you can find the fox *then*, why you're all right!"—and the boastful tone of a keen weather-beaten elderly man, "I never want a warranty,—why should a man expect to find a perfect horse?—he don't look for perfection when he's seeking a wife, eh?" "Oh! but there's two wanted to complete that deal. The old lady 'as not come up to the scratch yet, 'as she, John?" "Well, when she does, I shan't ask for any warranty, and I bet you I'll not come out any worse than other folk do!"—and then the old joke, one of Solomon's wise sayings, uttered by an old gentleman to a nervous girl, "Their strength shall be in sitting still!"

Mrs. Rebell looked straight before her. Of all the cheerful folk gathered together near her, none seemed to have eyes for the beauty, the amazing beauty of the surrounding country. To the right of the kind of platform upon which the field was now gathered together, the hill dropped abruptly into a dark wood, a corner of the ancient forest of Anderida, that crossed by Cæsar when he came from Gaul—a forest stretching from end to end of the South Downs, broken by swift rivers running down to the sea. It was here—but Barbara, gazing with delighted eyes down over the treetops, did not know this—it was here, in this patch of primeval woodland, that the first fox of the season was always sought for and often found.

Yet another "white way" wound down towards the red-roofed farmhouses which lined the banks of the tidal stream glistening in the vale below; and opposite, in front, a gleaming cart-track led up to a strip of fine short grass, differing in quality and even in colour from the turf about it, and marking the place where, according to tradition, Boadicea made her last stand. From thence, by climbing up the low bank on which a hedge was now set, the lover of the downs looked upon one of the grandest views in the South of England—that bounded on one side by the sea, on the other, beyond the unrolled map-like plain, by the long blue barrier of the Surrey hills.

Barbara's eyes dilated with pleasure. The fresh autumn wind brought a faint colour to her cheeks. She felt a kind of rapture at the beauty of the sight before her. It was amazing to her that these people could be talking so eagerly to one another, gazing so critically at the huntsman and at the hounds gathered on their haunches, while this marvellous sight lay spread out around and before them.

Mrs. Kemp, sitting by the side of Mrs. Boringdon in the pony-carriage, had something of the same feeling. She turned—foolishly, as she somewhat ruefully admitted to herself a moment later—to her companion and contemporary for sympathy—"I never saw Whiteways looking so beautiful as it does to-day!"

Mrs. Boringdon looked deliberately away from the sight which lay before her, and gazed thoughtfully at the sham Norman gateway. "Yes," she said, "very pretty indeed! Such a charming background to the men's red coats and to the dogs! Still, I wonder the Duke allows so many poor and dirty people to come streaming through the park. It rather spoils the look of the meet, doesn't it? If I were he, I should close the gates on this one day of the year at any rate."

Mrs. Kemp made no answer, but she bethought herself it was surely impossible that Lucy should be happy, in any permanent sense, if made to live in close proximity to Oliver Boringdon's mother.

Time was going on. The walkers and those who had driven to Whiteways were asking one another uneasily what the Master was waiting for. Miss Vipen, sitting bolt upright by Mrs. Sampson's side, addressing now and again a sharp word of reproof to the two young Sampsons sitting opposite to her, alone divined the cause of the delay. The Master of the South Sussex Hunt, that is, Tom Laxton—she had known him all her life, and even as a boy he had been afraid of her—was, of course, waiting for the Duke, for the Duke and the Halnakeham party! It was too bad to keep the whole field waiting like this, and probably the fault of the Duchess, who was always late at all local functions. Miss Vipen told Mrs. Sampson her opinion of the Duke, of the Duchess, and last but not least of the Master, whose subserviences to the great she thoroughly despised.

All at once there was a stir round the gate-way: "The Duke at last!" looking for all the world, so Miss Vipen observed to Mrs. Sampson, like an old fat farmer, and apparently quite pleased at having kept everybody waiting. As for Lord Pendragon, he was evidently very much the fine gentleman—or, stay, the weedy scholar from Oxford who despised the humble sports of a dull neighbourhood. But the time would come—Miss Vipen nodded her head triumphantly—when he, Lord Pendragon, would become very fat, like his mother, who, it was well known, was now too stout to ride. "They say," whispered Miss Vipen in Mrs. Sampson's unwilling ear, "that he is in love with a clergyman's daughter, and that the Duke won't hear of it! If they made her father a Bishop, I suppose it would be less objectionable— Ah! there's the Duchess. They say her carriages are always built just about a foot broader than anybody else's in order that her size may not show so much."

A move was now made for Whitecombe wood, and the Master trotted down towards a point from which on many a former occasion he had viewed a fox break away in the direction of the open down, and had been able to get a good start before he could be overtaken by what he used to call "all these confounded holiday jostlers."

While all this was going on, Captain Laxton had not stirred from Lucy's side, and together they rode over up towards Boadicea's camp. "If they find soon, which I think very doubtful," he said quietly, "and if, what is even less likely, the fox breaks, he is sure to head this way"—he pointed to the left—"because of the wind."

Lucy looked at him with a certain respect: she herself would never have thought of that! Captain Laxton, in the past, had often surprised her by his odd little bits of knowledge. She suddenly felt glad that he was there, and that apparently he bore her no grudge. More, she reminded herself that during the whole of the past summer she had missed his good-natured presence—that they had all missed him, her mother even more than herself. If he had not come to Whiteways to-day, she would now be by herself, down among those foolish people who were riding quickly and aimlessly up and down the steep roads near the wood, her father throwing her a word now and then no doubt, but Oliver giving her neither look, word, nor thought.

Lucy had become aware that Boringdon and Mrs. Rebell had chosen, as she and Laxton had done, a point of vantage away from the rest of the field, and that Oliver, with eager glowing face, was explaining the whole theory of hunting to his companion—further, that she was hanging on his words with great interest.

Meanwhile, Captain Laxton was looking at Lucy Kemp no less ardently than Boringdon was gazing at Barbara Rebell. The young man had come out to-day with the definite intention of saying something to the girl, and now he wished to get this something said and over as quickly as possible.

"I hope that what happened last time I saw you won't make any difference, Lucy—I mean as to our being friends, and my coming to the Grange?"

He had always called her Lucy—always, that is, since her parents had come home from India when she was twelve years old. Now it is difficult, or so at least thought Lucy Kemp, to cherish any thought of romance in connection with a man who has called you by your Christian name ever since you were a little girl!

She hesitated. To her mind what had happened when they had last met ought to make a difference. She remembered how wretched his evident disappointment and unhappiness had made her at the time, and how kindly, since that time, had been her thoughts of him, how pained her father and mother had been. And now? Even after so short a time as three months, here he was, looking as cheerful and as good-tempered as ever! It was clear he had not cared as much as she had thought, and yet, according to her mother, he had wanted to speak to her nearly two years ago, and had been asked to bide his time. It was the knowledge of this constancy on his part which had made Lucy very tender to him in her thoughts.

Laxton misunderstood her silence: "You need not be afraid, Lucy, that—that I will bother you again in the same way. But honestly, you don't know how I have missed you all, how awfully lonely I've felt sometimes."

Lucy became aware that he was looking at her with a troubled, insistent face, and she suddenly remembered how much he used to be with them, making the Grange his home when she was still a very young girl, though he was more than welcome at another house in the neighbourhood. As for old Squire Laxton, Lucy knew only too well why he now always looked at her so disagreeably; the coming and going of this young soldier cousin to Laxgrove had been the old sporting bachelor's great pleasure, apart of course from hunting, and he had missed him sorely that summer.

Why should not everything go on as it had done before, if Captain Laxton really wished it to do so? And so she said in a low tone, "Of course we have missed you too, all of us, very much."

"Oh! well then, that's all right! I will come over to the Grange to-morrow—I suppose you would all be tired out this evening? I've been at Laxgrove nearly a week already, and I must be back at Canterbury on Monday, worse luck! I say, Lucy— —"

"Yes?" Lucy smiled up at him quite brightly, but her mind was absorbed in the scene below her: the Duke, the great potentate of the neighbourhood, had come up to Mrs. Rebell—she was now following him towards the victoria in which sat the ample Duchess, and Boringdon had ridden off, galloping his mare down the steep rough road where the Master, with anxious eyes, was watching the hounds slipping in and out of the wood. Lucy was rather puzzled. How was it that this strange lady, who had only arrived at the Priory some three weeks ago, and who never came into the village—she had been out driving when Mrs. Boringdon had called on her—knew everybody? She said suddenly, "I did not know that you knew Mrs. Rebell: we have none of us seen her excepting in church."

"I can't say I know her, but old Cousin Tom has made great friends with her. You know she's been riding Saucebox every morning, and they, she and Boringdon, always go past Laxgrove about twelve o'clock. The first morning there was quite a scene. The mare didn't quite understand Mrs. Rebell, I suppose, for a steam roller came up, and in a minute she was all over the place. Mrs. Rebell sat tight, but it gave her rather a turn, and Tom made her come into the house. Then yesterday—you know what a down-pour there was—well, she and Boringdon came in again. I was rather glad to see them, for he and Tom have had rather an unpleasantness over the Laxgrove shooting. However, now, thanks to this Mrs. Rebell, they've quite made it up. She's a nice-looking woman, isn't she?—quite the kind of figure for a showy beast like Saucebox!"

But Lucy made no answer: could it be, so thought Laxton uneasily, that she did not like to hear another woman praised? To some girls, the young man would never have said anything complimentary concerning another lady, but Lucy Kemp was different; that was the delightful thing about Lucy,—both about the girl and her mother.

Old Tom, sitting over the smoking-room fire the evening before, had told his young kinsman to give up all thought of Lucy Kemp. "Whoever you marry now, it will be all the same about ten years hence!" so the cynical bachelor had observed, but then, what did Tom Laxton know about it? The younger man was well aware, in a general sense, that this was true of many men and their wives. It would probably be true of him were he to choose, and to be chosen, from among the group of pleasant girls with whom he had flirted, danced, and played games during the last few months. But with Lucy, ah! no,—Lucy Kemp had become a part of his life, and he could not imagine existence without her somewhere in the background.

Of course, to his old cousin, to Tom Laxton, Miss Kemp was simply a quiet rather dull girl who could not even ride really well—ride as women ought to ride if they hunted at all. The old sportsman had only two feminine ideals,—that of the loud, jolly, hail-fellow-well-met sort of girl, or else the stand-offish, delicate, high-bred sort of woman, like this Mrs. Rebell.

Lucy was looking straight before her, seeing nothing, thinking much. Oliver's absence from the Grange was now explained: he had been riding every morning with Mrs. Rebell, putting off the dull hours which he had to spend in the estate office till the afternoons. The girl thought it quite reasonable that Boringdon should ride with Madame Sampiero's guest, in fact, that sort of thing was one of those nondescript duties of which he had sometimes complained to her as having been more than he had bargained for. But how strange that he had not asked her, Lucy Kemp, to come too! When a certain girl cousin of Oliver's was at the Cottage, the three young people often enjoyed delightful riding expeditions,—in fact, that was how Lucy had first come to know Oliver so well.

"They've found at last! This way, Lucy!—"

Lucy woke up as if from a dream. The sharp unmistakable cry of Bluebell, one of the oldest hounds in the pack, broke on her ears. She and Laxton galloped down to the left—then waited—Laxton smiling broadly as the whole field swept past them just below, the men jostling one another in their eagerness to get first to a gate giving access to a large meadow which enclosed a stretch of down.

Rather on one side Lucy saw Mrs. Rebell and Boringdon, and Oliver—quiet, prudent Oliver—was actually giving Saucebox a lead over a low hedge! A group of town-folk from Halnakeham clapped their hands on seeing the lady clear the obstacle. Laxton laughed. "Miss Vipen would talk about circus performances, eh! Lucy?" He had never liked Boringdon, the two men had nothing in common. "But, of course, Mrs. Rebell may have told him she wanted to jump. They were doing that sort of thing yesterday down at Laxgrove, and I must say I thought it very sensible of Boringdon."

But in point of fact the hounds had not found. They had struck a strong drag in the lower end of the cover, but, after running for only thirty or forty yards, scent had quickly failed, and a few minutes afterwards the majority of the field had reappeared near the old gate on the crest of the hill.

"Well, it's not been much use so far, has it? I see that Mrs. Boringdon and your mother have gone home"—General Kemp seemed in high good humour. "And now that the Duchess is off, too, we shall be able to try the Bramber wood." The speaker's eyes twinkled; the Duchess of Appleby and Kendal had been a keen sportswoman in her day, and it had been hoped that the hounds would find in the ducal covers. "Would you like to go on, child?" He thought Lucy had been quite long enough with Laxton—that is, if, as his wife assured him, she had not changed her mind about the young man whom he himself liked so cordially.

"I think, father, if you don't mind, I'd rather go home." The General's face fell—it seemed such a pity to turn back now, just when the real work of the day was to begin. He had heard the Master's dry words:—"The Duchess is gone, isn't she? Then let's make for Highcombe without losing a minute." But Laxton was interposing eagerly—"May I take Lucy home, sir? I will look after her all right, and perhaps Mrs. Kemp will give me a little lunch."

The General looked doubtfully at the two young people. They had remained close to one another during the last hour—what did it all mean? He wished his wife were there to give him a word, a glance, of advice.

"All right!" he said, "but in that case, I should advise you to go back over the downs. It's a pleasanter way, and you'll be at Chancton twice as quickly."

Lucy looked gratefully at the young man: it was really nice of him to do this—to give up his afternoon to her, and to brave, as he was certainly about to do, old Squire Laxton's anger: the Master of the S.S.H. had never understood his favourite kinsman's attitude to the noblest sport ever devised by man. And so she assented eagerly to the proposal that they should ride back over the downs.

"But wouldn't you rather stay?"

"I'm really glad of the excuse to get away!"—he smiled down on her—"I've been simply longing to see your mother!"

Slowly they made their way over the brow of the hill, and then down the wide grassy slopes skirting the high wall which shut off Chillingworth from the rest of the world.

Lucy was very subdued, and very gentle. It was a relief to be with someone who did not suspect, as her parents seemed to do, the truth as to her feeling for Oliver Boringdon. Soon she and her companion were talking quite happily together, he asking her about all sorts of familiar matters. Again she bethought herself that she really had missed him, and that it was nice to have him back again.

Then there was a pause—Laxton had felt the kindness, the confidence of her manner. Suddenly bending down, he saw that the tears were in her eyes—that her lips were trembling. Could it be—? Oh! God, was it possible that she relented—that his intense feeling had at last roused an answering chord? A flood of deep colour swept over his fair sunburnt face. "Lucy!" he said hoarsely, "Lucy!" She looked up at him with sudden mute appeal, but alas! he misunderstood the meaning of the look. "If it is ever any good—any good now, my asking you again, you will let me know—you will be kind?" Poor, inadequate words, so he felt them to be, but enough, more than enough, if he had interpreted aright the look he had surprised.

But Lucy shook her head, "It is no good, I only wish it were—though I don't know why you should care so much."

They rode on into the village, and Laxton showed the good stuff he was made of by coming, as he had said he would, to the Grange, where Mrs. Kemp, after glancing at Lucy, entertained him with a pitying and heavy heart.

CHAPTER IX.

"Falling in love is the one illogical adventure, the one thing of which we are tempted to think as supernatural, in our trite and reasonable world."

R. L. S.

Love has been described, by one who had a singularly intuitive knowledge of men's hearts, as a vital malady, and in one essential matter the similitude holds good—namely, in the amazing suddenness with which the divine fever will sometimes, nay often, seize upon its victim, driving out for the time being all other and allied ills, leaving room only for the one all-consuming passion.

James Berwick was one of those men—more rarely found perhaps in England than on the Continent, and less often now than in the leisurely days of the past—who can tell themselves that they are pastmasters in the art of love. Two things in life were to him of absorbing interest—politics and women, and he found, as have done so many of his fellows, that the two were seldom in material conflict. His sister, Miss Berwick, did not agree in this finding, but she kept her views and her occasional misgivings to herself.

Women had always played a great part in James Berwick's life, and that, as is generally true of the typical lover, in a very wide sense, as often as not "en tout bien tout honneur." He thought no hour wasted which was spent in feminine company: he was tender to the pruderies, submissive to the caprices, and very grateful for the affection often lavished on him by good and kindly women, to whom the thought of any closer tie than that of friendship would have been an outrage.

More than once he had been very near, or so he had thought at the time, to the finding of his secret ideal,—of that woman who should be at once lover and friend. But some element, generally that of the selfless tenderness for which his heart craved, was lacking in the unlawful loves to which he considered himself compelled to confine his quest.

He based his ideal on the tie which had bound his uncle, Lord Bosworth, to Madame Sampiero, and of which he had become aware at a moment when his youth had made him peculiarly susceptible to what was fine and moving in their strange, ardent romance.

To his ideal,—so he could still tell himself when on one of those lamentable return journeys from some experimental excursion in that most debatable land, le pays du tendre,—he could and would remain faithful, however faithless he might become to the actual woman who, at the moment, had fallen short of that same ideal.

Berwick constantly made the mistake of consciously seeking love, and so of allowing nothing for that element of fantasy and surprise which has always played so great a part in spontaneous affairs of the heart.

He asked too much, not so much of love, as of life—intellect, passion, tenderness, fidelity, all these to be merged together in one who could only hope to be linked with her beloved in unlawful, and therefore, so whispered experience, in but temporary bonds.

During the last ten years—Berwick was now thirty-five, and, while his brief married life lasted, he had been absolutely faithful to the poor sickly woman whose love for him had fallen short of the noblest of all—he had found some of the qualities he regarded as essential to a great and steadfast passion, first in one, and then in another, but never had he found them all united, as his uncle had done, in one woman.

Mrs. Marshall, of whom his sister was still so afraid had first attracted him as a successful example of that type of woman to whom beauty, and the brilliant exercise of her feminine instincts, stand in lieu of mind and heart, and whose whole life is absorbed in the effort to excite feelings which she is determined neither to share nor to gratify. To vivify this lovely statue, to revenge, may-be, the wrongs of many of his sex, had been for Berwick an amusing diversion, a game of skill in which both combatants were to play with buttoned foils.

But Mrs. Marshall, caught up at last into the flames in which she had seen so many burn—holocausts to her vanity and intense egotism—suddenly began to love Berwick with that dry, speechless form of passion which sears both the lover and the beloved, and which seems to strip the woman of self-respect, the man of that tenderness which should drape even spurious passion.

The death of the lady's husband had occurred most inopportunely, and had been followed, after what had seemed to Berwick—now wholly disillusioned—a shockingly short interval, by one of those scenes of horror which sometimes occur in the lives of men and women and which each participant would give much to blot out from memory. During the interview he shuddered to remember, Berwick had been brought to say, "My freedom is dearer to me, far more so, than life itself! If I had to choose between marriage and death, I should choose death!"

Arabella need not have been afraid. Louise Marshall's very name had become hateful to him, and the fact that she was still always trying to throw herself across his path had been one reason why he had spent the whole summer far from England.

It was in this mood, being at the moment out of love with love, that Berwick had come back this autumn to Sussex and to Chancton Priory. It was in this same mood that he had first met Barbara Rebell, and had spent with her the evening of which he was afterwards to try and reconstitute every moment, to recall every word uttered by either. He had been interested, attracted, perhaps most of all relieved, to find a woman so different from the type which had caused him so much distress, shame, and—what was perhaps, to a man of his temperament, worse—annoyance.

Then, after that short sojourn at the Priory, he had gone away, and thought of Barbara not at all. Certain matters had caused him to come back to Chillingworth before going on to Halnakeham Castle, and during those days, with a suddenness which had left him defenceless, had come a passion of deep feeling—none of those about them ventured to give that feeling its true name—for the desolate-eyed, confiding creature, who, if now thrown defenceless in his way as no woman had ever yet been, was yet instinct with some quality which seemed to act as a shield between himself and the tremulous, tender heart he knew was there, if only because of the love Barbara lavished on Madame Sampiero.

During those early days, and for the first time in Berwick's experience, humility walked hand in hand with love, and the lover for a while found himself in that most happy state when passion seems intensified by respect. James Berwick had hitherto been always able to analyse every stage of his feeling in regard to the woman who at the moment occupied his imagination, but with regard to Mrs. Rebell he shrank from such introspection.

Yet another feeling, and one oddly new, assailed him during those long hours which were spent in Barbara's company—now in the quiet stately downstair rooms of the Priory, now out of doors, ay, and even by Madame Sampiero's couch, for there Barbara, as if vaguely conscious of pursuit, would often take refuge. Jealousy, actual and retrospective jealousy, sharpened the edge of Berwick's feeling,—jealousy of Boringdon, of whom he gathered Barbara had lately seen so much, and with whom, as he could himself see, she must be on terms of pleasant comradeship—jealousy, far more poignant and searching, of Pedro Rebell, and of that past which the woman Berwick was beginning to regard as wholly his, had spent with him.

Mrs. Rebell never made the slightest allusion to her husband, and yet for six long years—those formative years between nineteen and five-and-twenty—Pedro Rebell must have been, and in a sense rarely allowed to civilised man, the master of this delicate, sensitive woman, and, when he so pleased, her lover. Who else save the half-Spanish West Indian planter could have brought that shadow of fear into Barbara's eyes, and have made her regard the passion of love, as Berwick had very soon divined she did regard it, as something which shames rather than exalts human nature?

From one and another, going even to Chancton Cottage, and questioning Mrs. Boringdon in his desire to know what Barbara he knew well would never tell him, Berwick had so far pieced together her past history as to come somewhere near the truth of what her life had been. He could picture Barbara's quiet childhood at St. Germains: could follow her girlhood—spent partly in France, partly in Italy—to which, as she grew to know him better, she often referred, and which had given her a kind of mental cultivation which, to such a man as himself, was peculiarly agreeable. Then, lastly, and most often, he would recall her long sojourn in the lonely West Indian plantation. There, if Grace Johnstone was to be believed, she had at times suffered actual physical ill-treatment from the man whom she had married because he had come across her path at a moment when she had been left utterly alone; and also because—so Berwick, as he grew to understand her, truly divined—Pedro Rebell bore her father's name, and shared the nationality of which those English men and women who are condemned to exile are so pathetically proud.

Mrs. Turke, Doctor McKirdy, and Madame Sampiero all watched with varying feelings the little drama which was being enacted before their eyes.

Of the three, Mrs. Turke had the longest refused to believe the evidence afforded by her very shrewd senses. The old housekeeper took a frankly material view of life, and Doctor McKirdy had not been far wrong when he had once offended her by observing, "I should describe you, woman, as a grand old pagan!" There were few things she would not have done to pleasure James Berwick; and that he should enjoy a passing flirtation with Mrs. Rebell would have been quite within his old nurse's view of what should be—nay more, Mrs. Turke would have visited with condemnation any lady who had shown herself foolishly coy in accepting the attentions of such a gentleman.

But when the old woman realised, as she soon came to do, that Berwick's feeling for Madame Sampiero's kinswoman was of a very different quality from that with which she had at first credited him, then Mrs. Turke felt full of vague alarm, and she liked to remind herself that Mrs. Rebell was a wife, and, from certain indications, a good and even a religious woman in the old-fashioned sense of the word.

These stormy November days, so rough without, so peaceful within, each big with the presage of coming winter, reminded Mrs. Turke of another autumn at Chancton, and of other lovers who had found the atmosphere of the Priory strangely conducive to such a state of feeling as that which seemed to be brooding over James Berwick and Barbara Rebell.

True, Madame Sampiero and Lord Bosworth had been far more equally matched in the duel which had ended in the defeat of both: but the woman, in that conflict, had been troubled with fewer scruples. They also had begun by playing at friendship—they also had thought it within their power to absorb only the sweet, and to reject the bitter, of the feast spread out before them. In those far away days Mrs. Turke had been, to a certain limited extent, the confidante of her mistress, and now she felt angered at the knowledge that her foster-son was becoming impatiently aware of her watching eyes, and nervously afraid of any word, even said by his old nurse in joke, concerning his growing intimacy with Mrs. Rebell.

To Madame Sampiero, the present also brought back the past, and that, ah! yes, most poignantly. As she lay in her beautiful room, her solitude only broken by those two whom she had begun to watch so painfully, or by Doctor McKirdy who gave her news of them, she felt like the wounded warrior to whom heralds bring at intervals news of the conflict raging without. A word had been said by Mrs. Turke soon after Berwick's return, but the housekeeper had been rebuked by her paralysed mistress with sharp decision.

The thought that the creature who was beginning not to take, so much as to share, in her heart the place of her dead child, could be caught in the net out of which she herself had not even yet cut herself free, was intolerable—the more so that she had been amused, rather cynically amused, at the effect her god-daughter had produced on the austere Boringdon. To see them together, to see his growing infatuation, and Barbara's utter unconsciousness of the feeling which, after the first memorable interview, brought him daily to the Priory, had been to Barbara's god-mother a delicious comedy. The woman in her delighted in the easy triumph of this other woman, more particularly because at first she had not credited Barbara Rebell with the possession of feminine charm.

In this matter Boringdon showed Madame Sampiero how wrong she had been, and not he only, but many others also had at once come under her spell. And then, as is nearly always the way with those women who inspire sudden passions, Mrs. Rebell's charm was not, in its essence, one of sex. The grim, silent Scottish woman, Madame Sampiero's night attendant, smiled when Barbara came into the room, and Léonie, the French maid, had very early informed her mistress, "Je sens que je vais adorer cette Madame Rebell!" while as for James Berwick, his attitude the more moved and interested Madame Sampiero, because she had never seen him in any relation save in that of her own kind, cool, and attentive guest.

Every nature betrays feeling in a manner peculiarly its own. Berwick would have been surprised indeed had he realised his constant betrayal of a passion so instinctive as to be as yet only partially revealed to his innermost self. For the first time in his experience he loved nobly—that is, with tenderness and abnegation. To be constantly with Barbara, to talk to her with that entire intimacy made possible by the solitary circumstances of her life, was all he asked as yet. Barbara Rebell, during those same short weeks, was also happy, and wholly content with the life she saw spread out before her—looking back to the six years spent with Pedro Rebell as to a terrible ordeal lying safely far behind her, so deep, so racial had been, after the first few weeks of their married life, the antagonism between them.

Feeling her physical helplessness more than she had ever done, Madame Sampiero asked herself, with a foreboding which deepened into pain, whether certain passages in her own life were now about to be enacted over again in that of her own cousin? Lying there, her mind alone free, she told herself that while regretting nothing that had been, she yet would do all in her power to prevent one she loved from going through what she had endured—the more so that, to her mind, James Berwick was not comparable to the man for whom she had herself sacrificed everything. Lord Bosworth's only desire, and that over long years, had been to make the woman he loved his wife. She knew well that the nephew had a more ingenious and a less simple nature—that the two men looked at life from a very different standpoint.

Madame Sampiero also realised to the full what Berwick's great wealth had meant and did mean to him, and how different a man he would have been without it. Had Barbara Rebell been free, so the paralysed woman now told herself, James

Berwick would have fled from the neighbourhood of the Priory at the first dawn of his attraction.

Barbara's god-mother would have given much to know what neither her own observation nor Doctor McKirdy's could tell her—namely, how Berwick's undisguised passion was affecting the object of it. Every day the older woman looked for some sign, for some conscious look, but Barbara remained in this one matter an enigma to those about her. Madame Sampiero knew—as every woman who has gone through certain experiences is bound to know—the deep secrecy, the deeper self-repression, which human beings, under certain conditions, can exercise when the question involved is one of feeling, and so sometimes, but never when Mrs. Rebell was actually with her, she wondered whether the attitude of Barbara to Berwick hid responsive emotion, which, when the two were alone together, knew how to show itself articulate.

One thing soon became clear. Barbara much preferred to see either Boringdon or Berwick alone; she avoided their joint company; and that, so the three who so closely observed her were inclined to think, might be taken as a sign that she knew most surely how it was with them, if still ignoring how it was with herself.

Concerning love—that mysterious passion which Plotinus so well describes as part god part devil—Doctor McKirdy was an absolute fatalist. He regarded the attraction of man to woman as inevitable in its manifestations as are any of the other maleficent forces of nature, and for this view—not to go further than his own case—he had good reason. Till he was nearly thirty, he had himself experienced, not only a distaste but a positive contempt for what those about him described as love.

However much the fact was disguised by soft phrases, he, the young Alexander McKirdy, knew full well that the passion was wholly base and devilish—playing sometimes impish, more often terrible, tricks on those it lured within its labyrinth; causing men to deviate almost unconsciously from the paths lying straight before them; generally injuring their careers, and invariably—and this, to such a nature as his own, seemed the most tragic thing of all—making, while the spell was upon the victims, utter fools of them. Above all had he condemned, with deepest scorn and intolerance—this, doubtless, owing in a measure to his early religious training—that man who allowed himself to feel the slightest attraction for a married woman; indeed, for such a one, he felt nothing but scathing contempt. The whole subject of man's relation to woman was one on which the doctor had been, even as a very raw and shy youth, always ready to hold forth, warning and admonishing those about him, especially his own sentimental countrymen cast up on the lonely and yet siren-haunted sea of London life.

Then, holding these views more than ever, though perhaps less eager to discuss them, a chance had brought him to Chancton, there to fall himself in the same snare which he believed in all good faith so easy to avoid. After one determined effort to shake himself free, he had bowed his neck to the yoke, gradually sacrificing all that he had once thought made life alone worth living to a feeling which he had known to be unrequited, and which for a time he had believed to be unsuspected by the object of it.

Who was he, Alexander McKirdy, so he asked himself during those days when he watched with very mingled feelings Berwick and Barbara—who was he to jeer, to find fault, even to feel surprised at what had now befallen James Berwick and Barbara Rebell? And yet, as was still apt to be his wont, the old Scotchman blamed the woman far more than the man—for even now, to his mind, man was the victim, woman the Circe leading him astray. This view angered the mistress of the Priory, but not even to please Madame Sampiero would the doctor pretend that he thought otherwise than he did.

"Is this, think you, the first time she soweth destruction?" he once asked rather sternly. "I tell ye, Madam, she cannot be so simple as ye take her to be! I grant her Jamie"—falling back in the eagerness of the discussion on what had been his name for Berwick as a child—"we all know he's a charmer! But how about that poor stiff loon, Oliver Boringdon? would you say that there she has not been to blame?"

But the answering murmur was very decided, "I am sure it is the first time she has sowed destruction, as you call it."

"Well then, she has been lacking the opportunities God gives most women! If she has not sowed, it has not been for lack of the seed: she has a very persuasive manner—very persuasive indeed! That first night before she stumbled into this house, I was only half minded that she should see you, and she just wheedled me into allowing her to do so—oh! in a very dignified way, that I will admit. Now as women sow so shall they reap."

"That," muttered Madame Sampiero, "is quite true;" and the doctor had pursued, rather ruthlessly, his advantage. "Can you tell me in all honesty," he asked, peering forward at her, meeting with softened gaze the wide open blue eyes, "if you yourself sowed destruction innocently-like, that is without knowing it? Was there ever a time when you were not aware of what you were doing?"

For a moment the paralysed woman had made no answer, and then her face quivered, and he knew that the sounds which issued from between her trembling lips signified, "Yes, McKirdy, I always did know it! But Barbara is a better woman than I ever was——"

"Ay, and not one half so beautiful as you ever were!" The doctor had remained very loyal to his own especial Circe.

It now wanted but a week to Lord Pendragon's coming-of-age ball, and Chancton Priory shared in the general excitement. Madame Sampiero was well aware that this would be her god-daughter's real introduction to the neighbourhood, and she was most anxious that the first impression should be wholly favourable. As regarded what Barbara was to wear, success could certainly be achieved; but in whose company she should make her first appearance at Halnakeham Castle was more difficult to arrange, for it had come to Doctor McKirdy's knowledge that James Berwick intended that he and Mrs. Rebell should share the long drive from Chancton to the Castle.

This the mistress of the Priory was determined to prevent, and that without signifying her sense of its indecorum. The way out of the difficulty seemed simple. Madame Sampiero intimated her wish that Doctor McKirdy should be the third occupant of the Priory carriage, and that with this strange-looking cavalier, Barbara should make her appearance at the Castle: in that matter she thought she could trust to Berwick's instinct of what was becoming, and further, she had little fear that he would wish to attract the attention of the Duchess of Appleby and Kendal to his friendship with Mrs. Rebell. But, to Madame Sampiero's astonishment and chagrin, Doctor McKirdy refused to lend himself to the plan.

"Nay," he said, "I've been thinking the matter over, and I cannot make up my mind to oblige ye. Your wit will have to find out another way." There had been a pause, and he added, with one of his curious twisted smiles, "It's not such as I who would dare to intervene at 'the canny hour at e'en'!"

"Then I must tell James it cannot be!" Madame Sampiero spoke the words with the odd muffled distinctness which sometimes came over her utterance. But Doctor McKirdy had been thinking carefully over the situation: "Why not ask Mrs. Boringdon?" he growled out. "The woman does little enough for the good living she gets here!"

Madame Sampiero looked at her faithful old friend with real gratitude. How foolish she had been not to have thought of that most natural solution! But to her, Oliver Boringdon's mother was the merest shadow, scarcely a name.

And so it was that James Berwick's plan was defeated, while Barbara Rebell, who had not as yet become as intimate with Grace Johnstone's mother as she hoped to do, was made, somewhat against her will, to write and invite Mrs. Boringdon and her son to share with her the Priory carriage.

CHAPTER X.

"Never, my dear, was honour yet undone
By love, but by indiscretion!"

COWLEY.

It was the second day of the three which were being devoted to the coming-of-age festivities of Lord Pendragon, and Miss Berwick had asked herself to lunch at Halnakeham Castle. Because of the great ball which was to take place that evening, this day was regarded by the Duchess and the more sober of her guests as an off-day—one in which there was to be a lull in the many old-fashioned jollifications and junketings which were being given in honour of the son of the house.

The Duchess of Appleby and Kendal had been a very good friend to Arabella and to her brother, and that over long years. Owing to a certain inter-marriage between her own family and that of the Berwicks, she chose to consider them as relations, and as such had consistently treated them. She was fond of James, and believed in his political future. Arabella she respected and admired: both respect and admiration having sure foundations in a fact which had come to the Duchess's knowledge in the days when she was still young, still slender, and still, so she sometimes told herself with a sigh, enthusiastic! This fact had been the sacrifice by Arabella Berwick of the small fortune left her by her parents, in order that some debts of her brother's might be paid.

At the present moment James Berwick was actually staying at the Castle, and his sister had asked herself to lunch in order, if possible to see, and if not, to hear, on what terms he found himself with that one of his fellow guests whom his hostess, knowing what she did know of Arabella's fears, should not have allowed him to meet under her roof.

To Miss Berwick's discomfiture, Louise Marshall was at lunch, more tragic, more mysterious in her manner, alas! more lovely, in her very modified widow's dress, than ever; but Arabella's brother, so her host informed her when they were actually seated at table, had gone over for the day to Chillingworth! This meant that the sister had had a four-mile drive for nothing—a drive, too, which was to be repeated that same evening, for the whole of the Fletchings party, even Lord Bosworth, were coming to the ball.

One of the most curious of human phenomena met with by the kindly and good-hearted who are placed by Providence in positions of importance and responsibility, is the extreme willingness shown by those about them to profit by that same kindliness and good-heartedness—joined to a keen disapproval when those same qualities are exercised on behalf of others than themselves!

There had been a time when the Duchess's rather culpable good-nature, strengthened by her real affection for the two young people concerned, had been of the utmost service to Arabella Berwick—when, indeed, without the potent help of Halnakeham Castle, Miss Berwick would have been unable to achieve what had then been, not only the dearest wish of her heart, but one of the utmost material moment—the marriage of her brother to the great heiress whose family had hoped better things for her than a union with Lord Bosworth's embarrassed though brilliant nephew and heir.

But the kind Duchess's services on that occasion were now forgotten in Arabella's extreme anger and indignation at the weak folly which had led to Mrs. Marshall's being asked to meet Berwick. The sister had come over to Halnakeham determined to say nothing of what she thought, for she was one of those rare women who never cry over spilt milk,—the harm, if harm there were, was already done. But the old habit of confidence between the two women, only separated by some ten years in age, had proved too strong, especially as the opportunity was almost thrust upon the younger of the two by her affectionate and apologetic hostess.

"Qui s'excuse s'accuse"; the Duchess, sitting alone after lunch with her dear Arabella, should surely have remembered the wise French proverb, the more so as she had not made up her mind how much she meant to say, and how much to leave unsaid, concerning James Berwick's strange behaviour during the few days he had been sleeping,—but by no means living,—at the Castle.

"Well, my dear, we need not have been afraid about your brother and poor Louise Marshall—from what I can make out, he has hardly said a word to her since he has been here! In fact, he has hardly been here at all. He goes off in the morning and comes back late in the afternoon. He did stay and help yesterday, and made, by the way, a most charming little speech,—but then he took his evening off! I've been wondering whether there can be any counter attraction in the neighbourhood of Chillingworth—?"

The speaker looked rather significantly at her guest. She had been at some trouble to find out what that attraction could be which took Berwick daily to Chancton, and as her own confidential maid was Mrs. Turke's niece, and a Chancton woman, she had come to a pretty shrewd idea of the truth.

But Miss Berwick was absorbed in her grievance. "No," she said sharply, "certainly not! James hasn't ever been over to Fletchings, and we have no one staying there whom he could want to see. I suppose the truth is he wisely tries to escape from Mrs. Marshall. Knowing all you know, Albinia, and all I said to you last year, how *could* you have the woman here? I was really aghast when I heard that she was coming, and that James was hurrying back to see her—of course everyone must be putting two and two together, and he will find himself at last in a really bad scrape!"

The Duchess began to look very uncomfortable. "The poor soul wrote and asked if she might come," she said feebly; "I do think that you are rather hard-hearted. It would melt your heart if you were to hear her talking about him to me. She has paid a woman—some poor Irish lady recommended to her—to look up all his old speeches, and she devotes an hour every day to reading them over, and that although she doesn't understand a word of what she's reading! It's really rather touching, and I do think he owes her something. Of course you know what she would like, what she is hoping for against hope—old Mr. Marshall was a very rich man— —"

Miss Berwick knew very well, but she thought the question an outrage—so foolish and so shocking that it was not worth an answer. Indeed, she shrugged her shoulders, a slight but very decided shrug, more eloquent than any words could have been from such a woman.

The Duchess, kind as she was, and with a power of sympathetic insight which often made her unhappy, felt suddenly angered. She took up a book. It had a mark in it. "Reading this sentence," she said rather nervously, "I could not help thinking of your brother."

Miss Berwick held out a languid hand. She thought this rather a mean way of avoiding a discussion. Then she read aloud the sentence—

"It is the punishment of Don Juanism to create continually false positions, relations in life which are false in themselves, and which it is equally wrong to break or to perpetuate."

There was a pause. Arabella put the book down, and pushed it from her with an almost violent gesture. "I cannot understand," she cried, "how this can in any way have suggested James! I never met a man who was less of a Don Juan. If he was so he would be happier, and so should I. Imagine Don Juan and Louise Marshall—why, he would have made mincemeat of such a woman; she would have been a mere episode!"

"And what more has poor Louise been? No woman likes to be a mere episode! I do not say"—the Duchess spoke slowly; she knew she had gone a little too far, and wished to justify herself, also to find out, for the knowledge had made her very indignant, if Arabella was aware of how her brother was now spending his time,—"I do not say by any means that your brother is a Don Juan in the low and mean sense of the term, but circumstances and you—yes, you, in a measure—have made his relations to women essentially false and unnatural. Yes, my dear girl, that sort of thing *is* against nature! You are amazed and indignant when I speak of it as being possible that he should marry Louise Marshall, and yet I am quite sure that James is a man far more constituted for normal than for abnormal conditions, and that he would be happier, and more successful in the things that you consider important for him if, like other men, he realised that—that— —"

The Duchess stole a look at her guest's rigid face, then went on with dogged courage—

"Well, that a certain kind of behaviour nearly always leads to a man's having to take a woman—generally the wrong woman, too—to church, that is, if he is, in the ordinary sense, an honourable man! I fear," concluded the Duchess dolefully, "that you think me very coarse. But James and Louise between them have made me quite wretched the last few days, so you must forgive me, and really I don't think you have anything to fear—Louise is leaving the day after to-morrow."

The speaker got up; why, oh! why, had she allowed herself to be lured into this odious discussion?

Arabella had also risen, and for a moment the two women, perfectly contrasted types of what centuries have combined to make the modern Englishwoman of the upper class, faced one another.

The Duchess was essentially maternal and large-hearted in her outlook on life. She was eager to compass the happiness of those round her, and thanked God daily for having given her so good a husband and such perfect children—unconscious that she had herself made them to a great extent what they were. Particular to niceness as to her own conduct, and that of her daughters, she was yet the pitying friend of all black sheep whose blackness was due to softness of heart rather than hardness of head. On the whole, a very happy woman—one who would meet even those natural griefs which come to us all with soft tears of submission, but who would know how to avert unnatural disaster.

To her alone had been confided the story of Miss Berwick's love passages with Daniel O'Flaherty. To-day, looking at the still youthful figure and proud reserved face of her friend, she marvelled at the strength of character, the mingled cruelty and firmness, Arabella had shown, and she wondered, not for the first time, whether the agony endured had been in any sense justified by its results. Then she reminded herself that as Mrs. O'Flaherty the sister could hardly have brought about, as Miss Berwick had known how to do, her brother's marriage to one of the wealthiest unmarried women of her day.

"I think we ought to be going downstairs: and—and—please forgive me for speaking as I did just now—you know I am simply tired out!"

And indeed the Duchess had endured that which had gone far to spoil her innocent happiness in her son's coming-of-age festivities. After each long day of what was on her part real hard work, the poor lady, whom all about her envied, would call on her only confidant, the Duke, to scourge her for the folly to which her kindness of heart and platonic sympathy with the tender passion had led her; and husband-wise he would by turns comfort and scold her, saying very uncomplimentary things of both the sinners now in full enjoyment of his hospitality. Berwick, generally the most agreeable and serviceable of guests, was moody, ill at ease, and often absent for long hours—behaving indeed in a fashion which only his hosts' long kindness to him could, in any way, excuse or authorise.

As to Mrs. Marshall, she made no effort to disguise her state of mind. She gloried in her unfortunate and unrequited passion, and made the object of it appear—what he flattered himself he had never yet been—absurd. She made confidences to the women and entertained the men with eulogies of Berwick. Now, to-day, she was looking forward, as her hostess well knew, to the evening. At the ball it would surely be impossible for her lover to escape her, though her anxiety—and this, the Duchess's fatal knowledge of human nature also made clear to her—was somewhat tempered by the fact that on this occasion, in honour, as she plaintively explained, of dear Pendragon, and in order to cast no gloom over the festivity, she would once more appear in a dress showing the lovely shoulders which had once been described as "marmorean"—the word had greatly gratified her—by a Royal connoisseur of feminine beauty.

The fact that the whole affair much enlivened the party and gave an extraordinary "montant" to what would otherwise have been rather a prosy gathering,—that her guests so much enjoyed an item which had no place in the long programme of entertainments arranged by the Duke and herself—was no consolation to the Duchess.

"One moment, Albinia!"

The younger woman had turned very pale. The Duchess's words concerning Berwick and his sentimental adventures had cut her to the quick. Heavens! was this the way people were talking of her brother? The words, "an honourable man," sounded in her ears. How cruelly, how harshly, men and women judged each other!

"Of course, what you said just now concerning James and his love affairs,—if one may call them so,—impressed me. How could it be otherwise? As you know, I have no sympathy, I might almost say no understanding, of his attitude in these matters. There is a whole side of life to which I feel," her voice dropped, "the utmost repugnance. I have never allowed anyone to make me those confidences which seem so usual nowadays, nay, more, I have never even glanced at the details of any divorce case. I once dismissed a very good maid—you remember Bennett?—because I found her reading something of the kind in my room. I could not have borne to have about me a woman who I knew delighted in such literature——"

"But my dear Arabella——"

"Let me speak! Bear with me a moment longer! Now, about James. Of course I know he's in a difficult position—one that is, as you say, unnatural. But, after all, many men remain unmarried from choice, ay, and even free from foolish intrigues—to me such episodes are not love affairs. If there is any fear of such folly leading to marriage, well then, for my brother the matter becomes one of terrible moment——"

"You mean because of the money?" The Duchess had sunk down again into a chair—she was looking up at her friend, full of remorse at having seemed to put Arabella on her defence.

"Yes, Albinia, because of the money. You do not know—you have never known—what it is to lack money. I have never wanted it for myself, but I have longed for it, Heaven alone knows how keenly, simply to be relieved from constant care and wearing anxieties. I seem to be the first Berwick who has learnt how *not* to spend! As for James, it is impossible to imagine him again a poor man."

"And yet he is not extravagant."

Miss Berwick looked pityingly at the Duchess. "What is extravagance? Perhaps in the common sense of the word James is not extravagant. But he cares supremely for those things which, in these ignoble times of ours, money alone ensures—Power—the power to be independent—the indefinite, but very real, prestige great wealth gives among those who despise the prestige of rank."

"But do those people matter?" asked the Duchess, rather superbly. "Snobbish radicals—I've met 'em!"

"But that is just what they are *not*!" cried Arabella feverishly. "They care nothing for rank, but they do care, terribly so, for money. The man who is known to have it—fluid at his disposal (that's how I heard one of James's friends once describe it)—at the disposal, if so it be needed, of the party, commands their allegiance and their respect, as no great noble, every penny of whose income is laid out beforehand, can hope to do. If James, instead of marrying as he did do, had gone on as he began, where would he be now? What position, think you, would he occupy? I will tell you, Albinia,—that of a Parliamentary free-lance, whose very abilities make him feared by the leaders of every party; that of a man whose necessities make him regard office as the one thing needful, who is, or may be, open to subtle forms of bribery, whose mouth may be suddenly closed on the bidding of—well, say, of his uncle, Lord Bosworth, because he gives him, at very long and uncertain intervals, such doles as may keep him out of the Bankruptcy Court. Can you wonder that I am anxious? To me he is everything in the world——"

She stopped abruptly, then began speaking again in far more bitter accents.

"Louise Marshall! You spoke just now of his possible marriage to that woman. She may be rich, but I tell you fairly that I would rather see James poor than rich through her. I cannot find words to express to you what I think of her. She sold herself, her youth, her great beauty, her name, and her family connections—you among them, Albinia—to that vulgar old man, and now that the whole price has been meted out to her, she wishes to re-invest it in a more pleasant fashion. She has sold and now she wishes to buy——"

"My dear Arabella!"

"Yes, it is I who am coarse,—horribly so! But I am determined that you shall hear my side of the case. You speak of my brother's honour. Do you know how Louise Marshall behaved last year? Do you know that, when that wretched old man lay dying, she came to Bosworth House—to *my* house—and insisted on seeing James, and—and"—the speaker's voice broke, the Duchess could see that she was trembling violently; "Why do you make me remember those things—those horrible things which I desire to forget?"

Emotion of any sort is apt to prove contagious. The Duchess was very sorry for her friend; but she had received, which Arabella had not, Mrs. Marshall's confidences, and then she knew, what Arabella evidently did not know, how James Berwick was now spending his time, and what had dislodged—or so she believed—Louise Marshall from his heart. And so—

"As you have spoken to me so frankly," she said, "I also owe you the truth. Perhaps I am not so really sorry for Louise as you seem to think me, but, during the last few days, a fact has come to my knowledge—I need hardly tell you that I have said nothing to Louise about it—which has made me, I must say, feel rather indignant. I asked you just now, Arabella, whether there could be any rival attraction at Chillingworth; that, I confess, was rather hypocritical on my part, for there *is* an attraction—at Chancton Priory."

"At Chancton Priory?" repeated Miss Berwick, "why there's absolutely no one at Chancton Priory! Who can you possibly mean?"

All sorts of angry, suspicious thoughts and fears swept through her mind. As is so often the case with women who keep themselves studiously aloof from any of the more unpleasant facts of real life, she was sometimes apt to suspect others of ideas which to them would have been unthinkable. She knew that her friend's maid was a niece of Madame Sampiero's housekeeper. Was it possible that there had been any gossip carried to and fro as to Berwick's attraction for some rustic beauty? Well, whatever was true of him, that would never be true. To him temptation did not lie that way.

But it was the Duchess's turn to look astonished. "Do you mean," she exclaimed, "that you have not seen and know nothing of Barbara Sampiero's cousin,—of this Mrs. Rebell, who has been at Chancton for the last six weeks, and whom, if I judge rightly from the very pathetic letter which poor dear Barbara Sampiero dictated for me to that old Scotch doctor of hers, she is thinking of making her heiress?"

"Mrs. Rebell?"—Miss Berwick's tone was full of incredulous relief—"My dear Albinia, what an extraordinary idea! Certainly, I have seen her. My uncle made me call the very moment she arrived, and I never met a more apathetic, miserable-looking woman, or one more *gauche* and ill at ease."

"She did not look *gauche* or ill at ease at the Whiteways meet."

"Mrs. Rebell was not at the meet," said Arabella positively. "If she had been, I should, of course, have seen her. Do you mean the woman who was riding Saucebox?—that was some friend of the Boringdons."

It was the Duchess's turn to shrug her shoulders: "But I spoke to her!" she cried. "I can't think where your eyes could have been. She's a strikingly attractive-looking woman, with—or so I thought, when I called on her some ten days after she arrived at Chancton—a particularly gentle and self-possessed manner."

"Oh! but you," said Miss Berwick, not very pleasantly, "always see strangers *en beau*. As to James, all I can say is that I only wish he did admire Mrs. Rebell—that, at any rate, would be quite safe, for she is very much married, and to a relation of Madame Sampiero."

"You would wish James to admire this Mrs. Rebell? Well, not so I! To my mind his doing so would be a most shocking thing, a gross abuse of hospitality"—and as she saw that Miss Berwick was still smiling slightly, for the suggestion that her brother was attracted to the quiet, oppressed-looking woman with whom she had spent so uncomfortable a ten minutes some weeks before, seemed really ludicrous—the Duchess got up with a sudden movement of anger. "Well, you will be able to see them together to-night, and I think you will change your opinion about Mrs. Rebell, and also agree with me that James should be off with the old love before he is on with the new!"

"Albinia"—Miss Berwick's voice altered, there came into it something shamed and tremulous in quality—"Sir John Umfraville has left us. When it came to the point—well, I found I couldn't do it."

CHAPTER XI.

"To the fair fields where loves eternal dwell
There's none that come, but first they fare through Hell."

BEAUMONT AND FLETCHER.

It is wonderful how few mistakes are made by those who have the sending out of invitations to a great country function. The wrong people are sometimes included, but it rarely happens that the right people are left out.

Halnakeham Castle was famed for its prodigal hospitality, and on such an occasion as the coming-of-age ball of the only son, the ducal invitations had been scattered broadcast, and not restricted, in any sense, to those for whom the word "dancing" was full of delightful significance. In Chancton village alone, Miss Vipen could show the Duchess's card, and so could Doctor McKirdy, while both the Cottage and the Vicarage had been bidden to bring a party.

This being the case, it was felt by Mrs. Kemp's neighbours to be very strange and untoward that no invitation had been received at Chancton Grange, but, as so often happens, those who were supposed to be the most disturbed were really the least so. General Kemp and his wife were not disposed to resent what Miss Vipen eagerly informed their daughter was a subtle affront, and a very short time after the amazing omission became known, Lucy Kemp received five invitations to join other people's parties for the ball, and declined them all.

Then came an especially urgent message from Mrs. Boringdon, brought by Oliver himself. "Of course you will come with us," he said insistently, "my mother is to have the Priory carriage, and," he added, smiling as if speaking in jest, "I will tell you one thing quite frankly—if you refuse to come, I shall stay at home!"

Lucy gave him a quick, rather painful glance. What could he mean by saying that to her?—but Mrs. Kemp, again dowered with that sixth sense sent as a warning to those mothers worthy of such aid, asked rather sharply, "Are you and Mrs. Boringdon then going alone, for Lucy's father would not wish her in any case to remain up very late?" and Oliver answered at once, "Oh! no, Mrs. Rebell will, of course, be with us—in fact, in one sense we are going as her guests. It is she who is so anxious that Lucy should come too, and you need have no fear as to our staying late, for we are going especially early in order to be home before one o'clock." And then, to Mrs. Kemp's surprise, Lucy suddenly declared that she would come after all, and that it was very kind of Mrs. Rebell to have asked her.

On the great day, but not till five o'clock, the belated invitation did at last arrive at the Grange, accompanied by a prettily worded sentence or two of apology and explanation as to a packet of unposted cards. The General and Mrs. Kemp, however, saw no reason to change the arrangement which had been made; more than once Mrs. Boringdon had chaperoned their daughter to local entertainments, and, most potent reason of all, every vehicle in the neighbourhood had been bespoken for something like a fortnight. If Lucy's father and mother wished to grace the ducal ball with their presence, they would have to drive there in their own dog-cart, and that neither of them felt inclined to do on a dark and stormy November night, though there were many to inform them that they would not in so doing find themselves alone!

Lucy Kemp had a strong wish, which she hardly acknowledged to herself, to see Mrs. Rebell and Oliver Boringdon together. The girl was well aware that Oliver's manner to her had first changed before the coming of this stranger to the Priory, but she could not help knowing that he now saw a great deal of Mrs. Rebell. She knew also that, thanks to that lady's influence, the young man was now free to see Madame Sampiero—that hidden mysterious presence who, if invisible, yet so completely dominated the village life of Chancton.

This, of course, was one reason why he was now so often at the Priory. Indeed, his mother complained to Lucy that it was so: "I suppose that, like most afflicted persons, Madame Sampiero is very capricious. As you know, in old days she would never see Oliver, and now she expects him to be always dancing attendance on her!"

Lucy implicitly accepted this explanation of the long mornings spent by her old friend at the Priory; but it may be doubted whether in giving it, Mrs. Boringdon had been quite honest. On making Mrs. Rebell's acquaintance, which she had not done till Barbara had been at Chancton for some little time, the mistress of the Cottage realised that the Priory now contained within its walls a singularly attractive woman.

The excuse which Boringdon made, first to himself, and then to his mother, concerning Madame Sampiero's renewed interest in village affairs, was one of those half-truths more easily believed by those who utter them than by those to whom they are uttered. During the fortnight Mrs. Boringdon was away, Oliver spent the greater part of each day in Mrs. Rebell's company; the after-knowledge of that fact, together with his avoidance of Lucy Kemp, made his mother vaguely suspicious. She also, therefore, was not sorry for the opportunity now presented to her of seeing her son and Mrs. Rebell together, but she would have liked on this occasion to be with them alone, and not in company with Lucy Kemp.

In this matter, however, her hand was forced. Boringdon, when bringing his mother's note to the Grange, told the truth, as indeed he always did; the taking of Lucy to Halnakeham Castle was Mrs. Rebell's own suggestion, and in making it Barbara honestly believed that she would give her good friend—for so she now regarded Oliver Boringdon—real pleasure. Also, she was by no means anxious for a drive spent in the solitary company of this same good friend and his mother—especially his mother. In Mrs. Boringdon, Barbara had met with her only disappointment at Chancton. There had arisen between the two women something very like antipathy, and more than once Mrs. Rebell had felt retrospectively grateful to James Berwick for having given her, as he had done the first evening they had spent together, a word of warning as to the mistress of the cottage.

Certain days, ay and certain hours, are apt to remain vividly marked, and that without any special reason to make them so, on the tablets of our memories.

Lucy Kemp always remembered, in this especially vivid sense, not only the coming-of-age ball of Lord Pendragon, but that drive of little more than half an hour, spent for the most part in complete silence by the occupants of the old-fashioned, roomy Priory carriage.

Lucy and Oliver, sitting with their backs to the horses, were in complete shadow, but the carriage lamps threw a strong, if wavering, light on Mrs. Boringdon and Barbara Rebell. For the first time the girl was able to gaze unobserved at the woman who—some instinct told her—had come, even if unknowingly, between herself and the man she loved.

Leaning back as far as was possible in the carriage, Barbara had a constrained and pre-occupied look. She dreaded the festivity before her, fearing that an accident might bring her across some of her unknown relations—some of the many men and women who had long ago broken off all connection with Richard Rebell and his belongings; for these people Richard Rebell's daughter felt a passion of dislike and distaste.

Barbara also shrank from meeting James Berwick in that world from which she herself had always lived apart, while belonging to it by birth and breeding; she found it painful to imagine him set against another background than that where she had hitherto seen him, and she felt as if their singular intimacy must suffer, when once the solitude with which it had become encompassed was destroyed.

That afternoon there had occurred in Mrs. Turke's sitting-room a curious little scene. Barbara and Berwick had gone in there after lunch, and Berwick had amused both Mrs. Rebell and his old nurse by telling them something of the elaborate preparations which were being made at Halnakeham Castle for the great ball. Suddenly the housekeeper had suggested, with one of her half-sly, half-jovial looks, that Mrs. Rebell should, there and then, go and put on her ball-dress—the beautiful gown which had arrived the day before from Paris, and which had already been tried on by her in Madame Sampiero's presence.

For a moment, Barbara had not wholly understood what was being required of her, and Mrs. Turke mistook the reason for her hesitation: "La, ma'am, you need not be afraid that your shoulders won't bear daylight—why, they're milky white, and as dimpled as a baby's, Mr. James!" And then, understanding at last the old woman's preposterous suggestion, and meeting the sudden flame in Berwick's half-abashed, wholly pleading eyes, Barbara had felt inexplicably humiliated—stripped of her feminine dignity. True, Berwick had at once altered his attitude and had affected to treat Mrs. Turke's notion as a poor joke, quickly speaking of some matter which he knew would be of absorbing interest to his old nurse.

But even so Mrs. Rebell, sitting there in the darkness, felt herself flush painfully as she remembered the old housekeeper's shrewd, appraising look, and as she again saw Berwick's ardent eyes meeting and falling before her own shrinking glance.

"I don't know that we shall have a really pleasant evening"—Mrs. Boringdon's gentle, smooth voice struck across the trend of Barbara's thoughts. "It is certain to be a terrible crush—the Duke and Duchess seem to have asked everybody. Even Doctor McKirdy is coming! I suppose he will drive over in solitary state in one of the other Priory carriages?"

Mrs. Rebell stiffened into attention: "No," she said, rather distantly, "Doctor McKirdy is going to the Castle with a certain Doctor Robertson who lives at Halnakeham." Here Oliver interposed—"Robertson is one of the Halnakeham doctors, and, like McKirdy himself, a bachelor and a Scotchman; he is, therefore, the only medical man hereabouts whom our friend honours with his intimate acquaintance."

And then again silence fell upon the group of ill-assorted fellow travellers.

One of the long low rooms on the ground floor of the Castle, a portion of the kitchens and commons in the old days when Halnakeham was a Saxon stronghold, was now turned into a cloak-room and dressing-room. There it was that Lucy and Mrs. Boringdon—animated by very different feelings—watched, with discreet curiosity, their companion emerging from the long black cloak which concealed her gown as effectually as if it had been a domino.

Some eyes, especially when they are gazing at a human being, only obtain a general agreeable or disagreeable impression, while others have a natural gift for detail. To Lucy Kemp, the sight of Mrs. Rebell, standing rather rigidly upright before a long mirror set into the stone wall, presented a quite unexpected vision of charm and feminine distinction. But, even after having seen Barbara for a whole evening, the girl could not have described in detail, as Mrs. Boringdon could have done after the first quick enveloping glance, the dress which certainly enhanced and intensified the wearer's rather fragile beauty. The older and keener eyes at once took note of the white silk skirt, draped with festoons of lace caught up at intervals with knots of dark green velvet and twists of black tulle—of the swathed bodice encrusted with sprays of green gems, from which emerged the white, dimpled shoulders which had been so much admired by Mrs. Turke, and which Barbara had inherited from her lovely mother.

Gazing at the figure before her with an appreciation of its singular charm far more envious than that bestowed on it by Lucy Kemp, Mrs. Boringdon was speculating as to the emeralds—might they not, after all, be only fine old paste?—which formed the *leit motif* of the costume.

"Paris?" Mrs. Boringdon's suave voice uttered the word—the question—with respect.

Barbara started: "Yes, Peters. My god-mother has gone to him for years. He once made her a gown very like this, in fact trimmed with this same lace,"—Mrs.

Rebell hesitated—"and of the same general colouring. I am so glad you like it: I do think it really very pretty!"

And then, suddenly looking up and seeing the vision of herself and her dress in the mirror, again the memory of that little scene in Mrs. Turke's sitting-room came over Barbara in a flash of humiliation. Now, in a moment, she would see Berwick—Berwick would see her, and a vivid blush covered her face and neck with flaming colour.

"I hope you don't think the bodice is—is—cut oddly off the shoulders?" she said, rather appealingly.

"Oh! no—quite in the French way, of course, but very becoming to you." Mrs. Boringdon spoke amiably, but her mind was condemning Madame Sampiero for lending fine old lace and priceless jewels to one so situated as was Barbara Rebell. It was such a mistake—such ill-judged kindness! No wonder the woman before her had reddened when admitting, as she had just tacitly done, that the splendid gems encrusted on her bodice were only borrowed plumes.

"You will have to be careful when dancing," she said, rather coldly, "or some of those beautiful stones may become loosened and drop out of their setting."

Barbara looked at her and answered quickly—"I do not mean to dance to-night,"—but she felt the touch of critical enmity in the older woman's voice, and it added to her depression. Instinctively she turned for a word of comfort to Lucy Kemp.

In her white tulle skirt and plain satin bodice, the girl looked very fresh and pretty: she was smiling—the very sight of the lovely frock before her had given her a joyous thrill of anticipation. Lucy had never been to a great ball, and she was beginning to look forward to the experience. "Oh! but you must dance to-night, mother says that at such a ball as this everybody dances!" The other shook her head, but it pleased her to think that she had been instrumental in bringing this pretty, kind young creature to a place which, whatever it had in store for her—Barbara—could only give Lucy unclouded delight.

Walking with stately steps up the great staircase of Halnakeham Castle, Mrs. Boringdon became at once conscious that her party had arrived most unfashionably early, and she felt annoyed with Mrs. Rebell for having brought about so regrettable a *contretemps*. While apparently gazing straight before her, she noticed that her present fellow-guests were in no sense representative of the county; they evidently consisted of folk, who, like Barbara, had known no better, and had taken the ducal invitation as literally meaning that the Duchess expected her guests to arrive at half-past nine!

Mrs. Boringdon accordingly made her progress as slow as she could, while Lucy, just behind her, looked about and enjoyed the animated scene. The girl felt happier than she had done for a long time; Oliver's manner had again become full of affectionate intimacy, and she had experienced an instinctive sense of relief in witnessing Mrs. Rebell's manner to him. A woman, even one so young as Lucy Kemp, does not mistake a rival's manner to the man she loves.

At last, thanks to a little manœuvre on the part of the older lady, she and Lucy, with, of course, her son, became separated from Mrs. Rebell. Barbara was soon well in front, speeding up the staircase with the light sliding gait Oliver so much admired, and forming part of, though in no sense merged in, the stream of rather awe-struck folk about her.

The kindly Duchess, standing a little in front of a brilliant, smiling group of men and women, stood receiving her guests on the landing which formed a vestibule to the long gallery leading to the ball-room. There came a moment when Barbara Rebell—so Boringdon felt—passed out of the orbit of those with whom she had just had the silent drive, and became absorbed into that stationary little island of people at the top of the staircase. More, as he and his mother shook hands with the Duchess, he saw that the woman who now filled his heart and mind to the exclusion of almost everything else, was standing rather in the background, between James Berwick and an old gentleman whom he, Oliver Boringdon, had long known and always disliked, a certain Septimus Daman who knew everyone and was asked everywhere.

Down on Mr. Daman—for he was very short and stout—Mrs. Rebell was now gazing with her whole soul in her eyes; and to-night old Septimus found that his one-time friendship with poor forgotten Richard Rebell conferred the pleasant privilege of soft looks and kindly words from one of the most attractive women present. To do him justice, virtue was in this case rewarded, for Septimus Daman had ever been one of the few who had remained actively faithful to the Rebells in their sad disgrace, and when Barbara was a little girl he had brought her many a pretty toy on his frequent visits to his friends in their exile.

But of all this Boringdon could know nothing, and, like most men, he felt unreasonably annoyed when the woman whom he found so charming charmed others beside himself. That Mrs. Rebell should exert her powers of pleasing on Madame Sampiero and on old Doctor McKirdy had seemed reasonable enough,—especially when she had done so on his behalf,—but here, at Halnakeham Castle, he could have wished her to be, as Lucy evidently was, rather over-awed by the occasion, and content to remain under his mother's wing. In his heart, he even found fault with Barbara's magnificent dress. It looked different, so he told himself, from those worn by the other women present: and as he walked down the long gallery—every step taking him, as he was acutely conscious it did, further away from her in whom he now found something to condemn—his eyes rested on Lucy's simple frock with gloomy approval.

"Mrs. Rebell's gown?" he said with a start, "no, I can't agree with you—Frankly, I don't like it! Oh! yes, it may have come from Paris, and I dare say it's very elaborate, but I never like anything that makes a lady look conspicuous!"

So, out of the soreness of his heart, Oliver instructed Lucy as to the whole duty of woman.

To the Duchess, this especial group of guests was full of interest, and—if only Mrs. Boringdon had known it—she felt quite grateful to them all for coming so early! On becoming aware of Mrs. Rebell's approach, she was woman enough to feel a moment's keen regret that Arabella Berwick was not there to see the person whom she had called *gauche* and insignificant, coming up the red-carpeted staircase. Even the Duke had been impressed and interested, but rather cross with himself for not knowing who it was, for he prided himself on knowing everybody in the neighbourhood.

"Who's this coming up alone?" he asked, touching his wife's elbow.

"Poor Richard Rebell's daughter—I told you all about her the other day. Barbara Sampiero seems to be going to adopt her; don't you see she's wearing the Rebell emeralds? Remember that you saw and spoke to her at Whiteways!"

"Bless me, so I did to be sure! She looked uncommonly well then, but nothing to what she does now, eh?"

And so it was that Barbara successfully ran the gauntlet of both kind and indifferent eyes, and finally found herself absorbed into the group of people standing behind her host and hostess.

Then the Duchess passed on to Mrs. Boringdon and her son, treating them with peculiar graciousness simply because for the moment she could not remember who they were or anything about them! She felt sure she had seen this tall dark man before—probably in London. He looked rather cross and very stiff. A civil word was said to Lucy and an apology tendered for the mistake made about the invitation. "Let me see," the speaker was thinking, "this pretty little girl is to marry Squire Laxton's soldier cousin, isn't she? Pen must be told to dance with her."

An hour later; not eleven o'clock, and yet, to the Duchess's infinite relief, every guest—with the important exception of the Fletchings party—had arrived. She was now free to rest her tired right hand, and to look after the pleasure of those among her guests who might feel shy or forlorn. But, as the kind hostess filled up one of the narrow side doors into the ball-room, she saw that everything seemed to be going well. Even Louise Marshall, to whom the Duchess had spoken very seriously just before dinner, appeared on the whole to be leaving James Berwick alone, and to have regained something of her power of judicious flirtation. She looked very lovely; it was pleasant to have something so decorative, even if so foolish, about! Too bad of Lord Bosworth to be so late, but then he was privileged, and a cordon of intelligent heralds had been established to announce his approach; once the Fletchings carriages drew up at the great doors, the Duchess would again take up her stand at the top of the staircase.

Lucy Kemp was thoroughly enjoying herself. Had she cared to do so she could have danced every dance twice over—in fact, she would willingly have spared some of the attention she received from the young men of the neighbourhood, the sons of the local squires and clergy, who all liked her, and were glad to dance with her.

Oliver seemed to have gone back to his old self. He and Lucy—though standing close to Mrs. Boringdon and an old lady with whom she had settled down for a long talk—were practically alone. Both felt as if they were meeting for the first time after a long accidental absence, and so had much to say to one another.

Mrs. Rebell's name was not once mentioned,—why indeed should it have been? so Lucy asked herself when, later, during the days that followed, she went over every word of that long, intermittent conversation. Their talk was all about Oliver's own affairs—especially they discussed in all its bearings that important by-election which was surely coming on.

Then something occurred which completed, and, as it were, rounded off Lucy's joy and contentment. James Berwick made his way across the vast room, now full of spinning couples, to the recess where they were both standing, and at once began talking earnestly to Oliver, tacitly including the girl by his side in the conversation. At the end of the eager, intimate discussion, he turned abruptly to Lucy and asked her to dance with him, and she, flushing with pleasure, perceived that Boringdon was greatly pleased and rather surprised by his friend's action. As for herself, she felt far more flattered than when the same civility—for so Lucy, in her humility, considered it—had been paid her earlier in the evening by the hero of the day, shy Lord Pendragon himself. That Berwick could not dance at all well made the compliment all the greater!

And Barbara Rebell? Barbara was not enjoying herself at all. It has become a truism to say that solitude in a crowd is the most trying of all ordeals. In one sense, Mrs. Rebell was not left a moment solitary, for both the Duke and the Duchess took especial pains to introduce her to those notabilities of the neighbourhood whom they knew Madame Sampiero was so eager, so pathetically anxious, that her god-daughter should know and impress favourably. But, as the evening went on, she felt more and more that she had no real link with these happy people about her. Even when listening, with moved heart, to old Mr. Daman's reminiscences of those far-off days at St. Germains, when his coming had meant a delightful holiday for the lonely little English girl to whom he was so kind, she felt curiously, nay horribly, alone.

With a feeling of bewildered pain, she gradually became aware that James Berwick, without appearing to do so, avoided finding himself in her company. She saw him talking eagerly, first to this woman, and then to that; at one moment bending over the armchair of an important dowager, and then dancing—yes, actually dancing—with Lucy Kemp. She also could not help observing that he was very often in the neighbourhood of the woman who, Barbara acknowledged to herself, was the beauty of the ball, a certain Mrs. Marshall, whose radiant fairness was enhanced by a black tulle and jet gown, and who was—so Mr. Daman informed her with a chuckle—but a newly-made widow. And in truth something seemed to hold Berwick, as if by magic, to the floor of the ball-room. He did not wander off, as did everybody else, either alone or in company, to any of the pretty side-rooms which had been arranged for sitting out, or into the long, book-lined gallery; and yet Mrs. Rebell had now and again caught his glance fixed on her, his eyes studiously emptied of expression. To avoid that strange alien gaze, she had retreated more than once into the gallery, but the ball-room seemed to draw her also, or else her companions—the shadow-like men and women who seemed to be brought up to her in an endless procession, and to whom she heard herself saying she hardly knew what—were in a conspiracy to force her back to where she could not help seeing Berwick.

Oh! how ardently Barbara wished that the evening would draw to a close. It was good to remember that Mrs. Boringdon and Lucy had both expressed a strong desire to leave early. Soon her martyrdom, for so in truth it was, would cease, and so also, with this experience—this sudden light thrown down into the depths of her own heart—would cease her intimacy with James Berwick.

The anguish she felt herself enduring frightened her. What right had this man, who was after all but a friend and a friend of short standing, to make her feel this intolerable pain, and, what was to such a nature as hers more bitter, such humiliation? There assailed her that instinct of self-preservation which makes itself felt in certain natures, even in the rarefied atmosphere of exalted passion. She must, after to-night, save herself from the possible repetition of such feelings as those which now possessed her. She told herself that those past afternoons and evenings of close, often wordless, communion and intimacy yet gave her no lien on James Berwick's heart, no right even to his attention.

Sitting there, with Mr. Daman babbling in her ear, mocking ghosts, evil memories, crowded round poor Barbara. She remembered the first time—the only time that really mattered—when she had been told, she herself would never have suspected or discovered it, of Pedro Rebell's infidelity, of his connection with one of their own coloured people, and the passion of outraged pride and disgust which had possessed her, wedded to a sense of awful loneliness. Even to herself it seemed amazing that she should be suffering now much as she had suffered during that short West Indian night five years ago. Nay, she was now suffering more, for then there had not been added to her other miseries that feeling of soreness and sense of personal loss.

"Are you enjoying yourself, Doctor McKirdy?" His hostess was smiling into the old Scotchman's face. She had seen with what troubled interest his eyes followed Mrs. Rebell and James Berwick—the Duchess would have given much to have been able to ask the doctor what he really thought about—well, about many things,—but her courage failed her. As he hesitated she bent forward and whispered, "Don't say that it's a splendid sight; you and I know what it is—a perfect *clanjamfray*! Confess that it is!" and as Doctor McKirdy's ugly face became filled with the spirit of laughter, the Duchess added, "You see I didn't have a Scotch mother for nothing!"

And Mrs. Boringdon, watching the little colloquy with a good deal of wonderment, marvelled that her Grace could demean herself to laugh and joke with such an insufferable nobody as she considered Doctor McKirdy to be!

CHAPTER XII.

"Que vous me coûtez cher, ô mon cœur, pour vos plaisirs!"

COMTESSE DIANE.

"WILL you please introduce me to the lady with whom Mr. Daman has been talking all the evening? I have something I very much want to ask her, and I don't wish to say it before that horrid old man, so will you take him aside while I speak to her?"

Louise Marshall was standing before James Berwick. She looked beautiful, animated, good-humoured as he had not seen her look for a very long time, and the plaintive, rather sulky tone in which she had lately always addressed him was gone. There are women on whom the presence of a crowd, the atmosphere of violent admiration, have an extraordinary tonic effect. To-night, for the first time since she had become a widow, Mrs. Marshall felt that life, even without James Berwick, might conceivably be worth living; but unfortunately for himself, the man to whom she had just addressed what he felt to be so disquieting a request, did not divine her thoughts. Instead, suspicions—each one more hateful than the other—darted through his mind, and so, for only answer to her words he looked at her uncertainly, saying at last, "You mean Mrs. Rebell?"

She bent her head; they were standing close to the band, and it was difficult to hear, but he realized that she had some purpose in her mind, and there shone the same eager good-tempered smile on the face which others thought so lovely.

"Very well," he said, "I will take you across to her," and slowly they skirted the walls of the great room, now filled with movement, music, and colour.

Up to the last moment, Berwick had seriously thought of escaping the ordeal of this evening. The mere presence of Louise Marshall in his neighbourhood induced in him a sense of repulsion and of self-reproach with which he hardly knew how to cope in his present state of body and mind. And now had come the last day. Escape was in sight; not with his good will would he ever again find himself under the same roof with her—indeed, in any case he was actually going back to Chillingworth that very night. Wisdom had counselled him to avoid the ball, but the knowledge that Mrs. Rebell would be there had made him throw wisdom to the winds. Why spend hours in solitude at Chillingworth while he might be looking at Barbara—talking to Barbara—listening to Barbara?

But when it came to the point Berwick found that he had over-estimated the robustness of his own conscience. From the moment he had seen Mrs. Rebell coming up the broad staircase of Halnakeham Castle, he had realised his folly in not following the first and wisest of his instincts. Although the two women were entirely different in colouring, in general expression, indeed in everything except in age, there seemed to-night, at least to his unhappy, memory-haunted eyes, something about Barbara which recalled Mrs. Marshall, while in Mrs. Marshall there seemed, now and again, something of Barbara. So strong was this impression that at last the resemblance became to Berwick an acute obsession—in each woman he saw the other, and as the evening went on, he avoided as far as possible the company of both.

Now it had become his hateful business to serve as a link between them.

For a moment Mrs. Marshall looked at Barbara, then smilingly shook her head. "A string band would have been so much nicer, don't you think so, but the Duke believes in encouraging local talent. I wonder if you would mind coming out here for a moment—it is so much quieter in there—and I want to ask you to do me such a favour!"

Even as she spoke, she led the way from the ball-room into one of the book-lined embrasures of the long, now almost deserted, gallery, and Barbara, wondering, followed her.

Louise Marshall put on her prettiest manner. "I do hope you won't think me rude," she said, "but I am so very anxious to know if your beautiful gown came from Adolphe Peters? I do not know if you have noticed it, but of course I saw it at once,—there's a certain family likeness between my frock and yours! They say, you know, that Peters can only think out one really good original design every season—but then, when he has thought it out, how good it is!"

Mrs. Marshall spoke with a kind of sacred enthusiasm. To her, dress had always been, everything considered, the greatest and most absorbing interest of life.

After having received the word of assent she sought, she hurried on, "Of course, I felt quite sure of it! It is easy to see that he has followed out the same general idea—la ligne, as he calls it—in my frock as in yours. Several times this evening, I couldn't help thinking how awful it would have been if our two gowns had been exactly alike! I am probably going to India very soon"—Mrs. Marshall lowered her voice, for she had no wish that Berwick, who was standing a few paces off, his miserable eyes fixed on the two women while he talked to Septimus Daman, should thus learn the great news,—"but I shall be in Paris for a few days, and I have been wondering if you would mind my asking Peters to make me a gown exactly like yours, only of grey silk instead of white, and with mauve velvet bows and white tulle instead of green and black—that mauve," she added eagerly, "which is almost pale blue, while yet quite mourning! Well, would you mind my telling him that I have seen your dress?"

"No, of course not," said Barbara with some wonderment. "But I think that you should say that the gown in question was that made to the order of Madame Sampiero; he won't remember my name."

"Thanks so much! Madame Sampiero? Oh! yes, I know—I quite understand.

Are you a niece of hers? Oh! only a god-daughter, that's a comfort, for then you need never be afraid of becoming like her,"—a look of very real fear came over the lovely, mindless face,—"I've often heard about her, and the awful state she's in! Isn't it a frightful thing? Do you think people are punished for the wicked things they do,—I mean, of course, in this life?"

Barbara stared at her, this time both amazed and angered. "Yes," she said, slowly, "I am afraid one cannot live long in this world and not believe that, but—but——"

Mrs. Marshall, however, gave her no time to speak, and indeed Barbara would have found it difficult to put into words what she wished to convey concerning the courage, aye, the essential nobility, of the poor paralysed woman whom she had come to love so dearly.

"I wish you had been staying here during the last few days, I'm sure we should have become great friends." The speaker took a last long considering look at Barbara's bodice. "Your black tulle is dodged in and out so cleverly," she said, with a touch of regret, "mine is not twisted half so well, it looks more lumpy"—without any change of tone she added, "Since you are Madame Sampiero's god-daughter, I suppose you have known James Berwick quite a long time, as he is Lord Bosworth's nephew."

"But I have never seen, and do not know, Lord Bosworth," Barbara spoke rather stiffly.

"How very strange! But you know he is expected here to-night. He's a dear, splendid old thing, always particularly nice to *me*. But there he is!—there they all are—the whole Fletchings party,—coming in now!"

Barbara turned eagerly round. She was intensely desirous of seeing Lord Bosworth, and she fixed her eyes, with ardent curiosity, on the group of figures slowly advancing down the gallery.

Slightly in front of the others came the Duchess, and by her side paced a tall, large-framed man; now he was bending towards his companion, listening to what she was telling him with amused interest. The Duke and Arabella Berwick walked just behind them, and some half-dozen men and women ended the little cortége.

Men wear Court dress with a difference. To Lord Bosworth, the velvet coat, the knee-breeches, and silk stockings, lent an almost majestic dignity of deportment. The short stout Duke, trotting just behind him, looked insignificant, over-shadowed by the larger figure—indeed, even the Garter gracing the ducal leg seemed of no account when seen in contrast with the red riband of the Bath crossing Lord Bosworth's stalwart chest.

As the procession came nearer, Barbara saw that the man in whom she took so great an interest still looked full of the pride of life, and just now his large powerful face was lighted up by a broad smile. His curling grey hair had receded, leaving a large expanse of broad forehead, and the shaggy eyebrows, which were darker than his hair, overhung two singularly shrewd grey eyes. Thanks to the many months of each year now spent by him in the country—thanks also to the excellent care taken of him by his niece—Lord Bosworth's face was ruddy with the glow so easily mistaken for that of health. Of the many who looked on him that night, marvelling at the old statesman's air of robust power, and inclined perhaps to criticise his long retirement from public affairs—for he had been one of the most successful, and therefore one of the most popular, Foreign Ministers of his generation—only two people—that is he himself and a certain famous doctor who had come to the ball as member of a house-party—were aware that Lord Bosworth would in all probability never see old age, in the sense that many of his Parliamentary contemporaries and former colleagues might hope to do.

And now, as Barbara Rebell saw him walking down the gallery, talking with mellow sonorous utterances, and now and again laughing heartily at the remarks of the Duchess, there swept over her a sudden rush of revolt and indignation. She contrasted the fine, vigorous figure, advancing towards her, with that of the paralysed woman, whom she had left to-night lying stretched out in that awful immobility; and she recalled Madame Sampiero's last muttered words to herself—"I think you will see Lord Bosworth to-night. I should like you to have word with him—you will tell me how he looks—how he seems——"

As the Duchess and her honoured guest drew close to the embrasure where Barbara and Mrs. Marshall were standing, Lord Bosworth's acute eyes—those eyes which had been early trained to allow nothing of interest, still less nothing of an agreeable nature, to escape them—became focussed on the charming group formed by the two women, the one as dark as the other was fair, who stood together against the soft deep background made by the backs of the Halnakeham Elzevirs.

Lord Bosworth bent his head, and asked the Duchess a question—then in a moment the whole expression of the powerful, still handsome face altered, the smile faded from his lips, and a look of extreme gravity, almost of suffering, came over the firm mouth and square chin. The Duchess stayed her steps, and Barbara heard distinctly the eager—"Certainly, I shall be delighted! I have been most anxious to meet her. Yes—once, when she was a child, long ago, in France."

A moment later the formal group had broken up; Barbara's name was uttered, she felt her right hand taken in a strong grasp, and unceremoniously Lord Bosworth turned away with her. Still holding her hand, he led her aside and, looking down at her with a moved expression on his face, "I have been wishing much to see you," he said, "but, as you perhaps may know, I am not allowed to come to Chancton. I was attached, most truly so, to both your parents." He hesitated, and added in a lower tone, "Barbara,—that is your name, is it not?—to me the most beautiful, the noblest of women's names!"

Meanwhile, much by-play was going on around them, but of it all Mrs. Rebell was quite unconscious. Even Berwick was for the moment forgotten, and she did not see Arabella's mingled look of quick interest and slowly gathering surprise as Miss Berwick realised with whom her uncle had turned aside.

Still less was Barbara aware that the Duchess was speaking rather urgently to Mrs. Marshall. "There is no one in my sitting-room," she was saying, "and you will never have such a good opportunity again to-night. Do take him there now! I am sure, Louise, you will be acting wisely as well as rightly, but do not be too long, for everyone wants to see you,—even in the last few moments several people have come up and asked who you were, and wanted to be introduced to you. I have never seen you looking better than you look to-night." There was a commanding as well as a caressing quality in the kind voice.

Then the Duchess looked round, and in answer to her glance, Berwick, ill at ease and looking haggard, came forward. He also had been watching his uncle and Mrs. Rebell, wondering what they could have to say to one another that seemed to move Barbara so much; but he was not given much time for that or any other thought. Timidly, with more grace of manner than she usually showed, Louise Marshall turned towards him. "The Duchess," she said, nervously, "wants us to go into her sitting-room—I have something to say to you there."

For a moment, the man addressed looked round, as if seeking a way of escape: then he realised that the moment he had so dreaded, and which he had up to the present instant so successfully evaded, had come, and must be both faced and endured. A feeling of rage came over him—a self-scourging for his own exceeding folly in being here to-night. But without making any answer, he followed her down the gallery, only Arabella Berwick and the Duchess having overheard Mrs. Marshall's words, and witnessed their result.

In matters of feeling and emotion, as in everything else, it is the unexpected which generally happens. When at last James Berwick found himself alone with Mrs. Marshall in the small, dimly-lighted room which had but a few hours before seen the interview between the Duchess and his sister, his companion's words—even her action, or lack of action—took him entirely by surprise. He had expected, and was ashamed for so expecting, that the woman who had compelled him to follow her to this solitary place, would turn and fling herself into his arms with a cry of "Jimmy!"—the name which she herself had invented for him, and which he had always thought grotesque—on her lips.

While walking quickly down the long corridors which led from the more modern side of the Castle to this older portion, he had strung himself up to meet any affectionate demonstration with good-humour and philosophy, for, whatever else was not sure, this he was determined should be the last meeting between them, even if he had to give up half his friends and all his acquaintances in consequence.

But Mrs. Marshall's behaviour was quite different from that which he had expected. After he had shut the door of the boudoir, she walked away from him, and sitting down began to play with the fringe of a table cover, while he stood moodily staring down at her.

"Must you stand?" she asked at last, in the plaintive tone which he so much disliked.

"Oh! no, not if you wish me to sit down," and he sat down, fiercely waiting till it should be her pleasure to begin.

How could he have allowed himself to be so entrapped? He had heard it asserted that women never stood by one another—well, in that case the Duchess was an exception! He ground his teeth with anger at the thought of the trick which had been played him. But stay—now, at last, Mrs. Marshall was speaking—

"Albinia has been talking to me. She has been telling me things which I did not really know before,—I mean about your position, and how important it is to you that you should remain free. You remember our talk last year?"

Berwick bent his head, but into his strained face there came no sign of the inward wincing which her words brought with them. Still, he began unconsciously to revise his opinion of the Duchess; she had meant well by him after all, but he wished she had kept out of his affairs, and left him to manage them himself—

Mrs. Marshall was again speaking: "I could not understand what you meant by what you said then, it seemed so unkind! But now, of course, I realise that you were right—in fact I've brought you here to-night to tell you that I do understand."

There was a long pause. Berwick was at an utter loss for words, and every moment he expected the woman before him to make some more direct allusion to the condition under which he held his fortune. He felt a kind of helpless rage to think of his affairs being thus discussed, even by one so good-natured and well-meaning as had evidently been, in this matter, the Duchess of Appleby and Kendal. But what did all this preamble signify?

"I am glad you do understand," he said at last in a hoarse voice which he scarcely recognised as his own. "I know I must have seemed a great brute."

"If you had only trusted me more," she said plaintively. "Of course I should have understood at once! I should have known that what I could offer was not enough—that there was no comparison——"

Berwick made a sudden movement. Was it really necessary that he should listen to this? Was it part of his punishment that he should endure such unforgettable abasement? But, alas for him! Louise Marshall was in a sense enjoying both the scene and the situation. While she was speaking, there came into the still air of the room the sound of distant melody, and she felt as if she were looking on at a touching last act in some sentimental play. Also there was, after all, something uplifting in the sensation—to her a novel one—of doing a noble action, for so had the Duchess, with innocent cunning, represented her renunciation of James Berwick.

This frivolous, egoistical woman, ever guided by her instincts, never by her heart or conscience, thoroughly understood, as many shrewd and clever women fail to do, the value of money. From the plane whence Mrs. Marshall took her survey of life, the gratification of that instinct which she called love had always been a luxury, and the possession of wealth with which to gratify all other instincts an absolute necessity of existence. The contempt which most women, even those themselves ignoble, naturally feel for a man whom they suspect of putting material possessions before the deepest feelings of the heart, would to her have savoured of gross hypocrisy.

The Duchess—clever woman as she was, and dealing, in this case, with one whose intellect she despised—would have been surprised indeed had she known that what had really impressed and influenced Louise Marshall during their painful talk that day, had been the short statement, thrown in as an after-thought, of Berwick's financial position and of what he would lose if he married again. That, so Mrs. Marshall at once told herself, made all the difference. To her mind it absolutely justified James Berwick in rejecting the offer practically made by her within a few weeks of her husband's death, for what were her few thousands a year compared to the huge income which he would lose on a second marriage? She was, however, inclined to consider that he had shown false delicacy in not at once telling her the circumstances of the case. Then, at any rate, they might have sorrowed together over the inscrutable dictates of Providence. But instead of taking that sincere and manly course, Berwick, during that interview which even she shrank from recalling, had actually implied that his distaste to her was personal, his horror of marriage a singular idiosyncracy! Now it behoved her to beat a dignified retreat. And so, "As things are——"

Berwick began to realise that the woman before him had prepared what she wished to say, nay more, that she had probably rehearsed the present scene—

"As things are, Jimmy, I think it will be best for us to part, and so I have made up my mind to go to India with the Thorntons." She hurried over the words, honestly afraid of provoking in herself emotion of a disfiguring nature, for the thought of her unselfishness naturally brought the tears to her eyes. "That's all," she said in abrupt conclusion, "and now I think we had better go back to the ball-room."

She gave Berwick a quick, furtive look, and suddenly felt sorry for him. How he must have cared after all! For, as he stood opening the door for her to pass through, his face had turned ashen, and his blue eyes were sunken. So might a man look who, suddenly relieved of an intolerable weight, is, for a moment, afraid to move or to speak, lest the burden should again descend upon his shrinking shoulders.

When once more in the ball-room, Berwick made his way straight to his sister. Even before he stood by her, the expression on his face had aroused her quick anxious attention. But Arabella had learnt to spare her brother feminine comment.

"Have you yet spoken to Mrs. Boringdon?" he asked her, rather sharply.

"No, I have not even seen her; do you wish me to speak to her? I think she must know many of the people here. Where is she?"

"Over there, sitting with that old lady. I should be glad if you would tell her that we—that is, that you—are going to drive Mrs. Rebell back to Chancton tonight. The Boringdons have to leave early, and it would of course be absurd for Mrs. Rebell to go away just when you have arrived, and when the Duke has arranged for her to sit at supper next to Monsieur Parisot."

Now Monsieur Parisot was the French Ambassador.

"Of course, if you really wish it, it can be managed." Miss Berwick spoke hesitatingly; in these little matters she did not like to have her hand forced. "But, James, it will not be very convenient." And she looked at her brother with puzzled eyes.

Was it possible, after all, that Albinia had been right and she wrong? If so, why that obedient following of Louise Marshall out of the gallery half an hour before, and why this strange look on his face now? Miss Berwick had just spoken to Barbara Rebell, but her eyes were still holden; indeed, her feeling as to Madame Sampiero's god-daughter, or rather as to her beautiful gown and superb jewels, had not been unlike that of Mrs. Boringdon, and would have translated itself into the homely phrase, "Fine feathers make fine birds." Arabella did not credit, for one moment, the Duchess's belief that the mistress of Chancton Priory intended to make the daughter of Richard Rebell her heiress. Miss Berwick had persuaded herself that Chancton would pass in due course into her brother's possession, and she knew that there had been some such proposal years before, in the heyday of Lord Bosworth's intimacy with Madame Sampiero. This being so, it surely seemed a pity that Mrs. Rebell should now be treated in a way that might ultimately cause disappointment.

"I do wish it, and it will be quite convenient!" Berwick's tone was very imperious. "I myself am going back to Chillingworth to-night. I offered long ago to leave here to-day, for they have every attic full. I have of course arranged for an extra carriage, so you will be put to no inconvenience,"—but his bright blue eyes, now full of strange fire, fell before his sister's challenging glance, and the altered accent with which she observed, "Oh! of course if you and Mrs. Rebell have arranged to go back together——"

Berwick's hand closed on his sister's arm and held it for a moment in a tight, to her a painful, grip.

"You have no right to say, or even to think, such a thing! The arrangement, such as it is, was made by me, Mrs. Rebell knows nothing of it; she is quite willing, and even eager, to go back now with the Boringdons. The other proposal must come from you——" he hesitated, then, more quietly, muttered, "I don't often ask you to oblige me."

Arabella gave in at once, but with a strange mingling of feelings,—relief that she had been wrong as to Louise Marshall's hold on her brother; a certain pique that in this matter the Duchess had understood James better than she had herself; and, above all, there was a sensation of bewildered surprise that such a man as Berwick, one so intelligent, so eagerly absorbed in public affairs, should require this—this—Arabella did not know how to qualify, how to describe, even to herself, her brother's passion for romance, his craving for sentimental adventure. Well, if it was so, better far that he should find what he sought, that he should follow his will-of-the-wisp in their own neighbourhood, and, for the moment, with so colourless—so the sister seeking for another word, could only find that of respectable—yes, so respectable a woman as was this Mrs. Rebell!

Miss Berwick, on her way to Mrs. Boringdon, allowed her eyes to sweep over the great ball-room. Barbara was standing talking to Mr. O'Flaherty whom Lord Bosworth had just introduced to her. "She certainly looks intelligent," said Arabella to herself, "and quite, yes quite, a lady. Perhaps my first impression of her was wrong after all. But how foolish, how wrong of poor Barbara Sampiero to let her wear those emeralds!" Yet perhaps the jewels played their part in modifying her view of Barbara Rebell. The wearing of fine gems is a great test of a woman's refinement.

Then Miss Berwick's gaze softened as it became fixed on Barbara's companion. Thank Heaven, all men were not like James, or all women like Louise Marshall. Daniel O'Flaherty had the steadfast, pre-occupied look which soon becomes the mark of those men who are architects of their own fortunes; such men can find time for a great passion, but none for what the French happily describe as *passionettes*. As for Barbara Rebell, there was a look of pride and reserve as well as of intelligence in her dark eyes and pale face. "If James likes to flirt with her, and Dan,"—her thought lingered over the homely name,—"likes to talk to her, we must see about having her to Fletchings!"

CHAPTER XIII.

"Friendship, I fancy, means one heart between two."

GEORGE MEREDITH.

"I will hold your hand so long as all may,
Or so very little longer."

ROBERT BROWNING.

BARBARA REBELL, wrapped in her black domino-like cloak, bent forward and looked out of the carriage window.

There was something fantastic, magnificent, almost unreal in the scene she saw. The brougham in which she sat by Berwick's side was gliding quietly and smoothly between pillars of fire. The glare lighted up the grey castle walls, and gave added depth to the forked shadows lying across the roadway. Already the loud shouts, the sound of wheels and trampling horses filling the courtyard, lay far behind. In a few moments they would be under the tower, through the iron gates, now opened wide to speed the parting guests, and driving down the steep streets of sleeping Halnakeham town—so into the still darkness of the country lanes.

Suddenly, to the left of the Gate Tower under which they were about to pass, there quickened into brightness a bengal light, making vividly green the stretch of grass, and lending spurious life to the fearsome dragons and stately peacocks which were the pride of the Halnakeham topiarist.

Barbara clasped her hands in almost childish pleasure.

"Oh! how beautiful!"—she turned, sure of sympathy, to the silent man by her side, and then reddened as she met his amused smile, and yet it was a very kind and even tender smile, for he also felt absurdly light-hearted and content.

Till the last moment, Berwick had trembled lest his scheme should miscarry. Well, Providence, recognising his excellent intentions, and realising how good an influence such a woman as Mrs. Rebell could not but exercise on such a man as himself, had been kind. He felt as exultant as does a schoolboy who has secured a longed-for treat, and it was a boy's expression which rose to his mind concerning his sister—"Arabella behaved like a brick!"

Looking back, he could still see the group of people standing in the square entrance hall of the castle, himself gradually marshalling Arabella's guests into the Fletchings omnibus and the Fletchings carriage. Again he felt the thrill with which at last he had heard his sister's clear voice say the words, "Now, Mrs. Rebell, will you please get in there, and kindly drop my brother at Chillingworth on your way back to Chancton?"

The whole thing had been over in a moment. He himself had placed Barbara, bewildered but submissive, in the little brougham which he had bought that last spring in Paris, and which was supposed to be the *dernier cri* in coachbuilding luxury; and then, taking the place beside her, had found himself at last alone with her.

The old Adam in Berwick also rejoiced in having, very literally, stolen a march on Madame Sampiero and Doctor McKirdy. These two good people had gone to some trouble to prevent his being with Mrs. Rebell on the way to the ball, but in the matter of her return they had proved powerless. And yet, now that he came to think of it, what right had they to interfere? Who could be more delicately careful of Barbara than he would ever be?—so Berwick, sitting there, feeling her dear nearness in each fibre of his being, asked himself with indignation. He had made every arrangement to prevent even the most harmless village gossip. Fools all of them, and evil-minded, not to divine the respect, the high honour in which he held the woman now by his side! But he meant to be with her every moment that was possible, and 'ware those who tried to thwart this wholly honourable intention!

Thinking these thoughts, and for the moment well satisfied, he turned his head and looked at Barbara Rebell. Her lips were smiling, and she looked absorbed in some happy vision. The long night had left no trace of fatigue on her flushed face and shining eyes. Berwick, with a pang of mingled pain and pleasure, realised how much younger she was than himself.

"You must be tired. Would you like to go to sleep?" his voice shook with tenderness, but he put a strong restraint on himself. He was bound by every code of honour to treat her to-night as he would have done any stranger confided by his sister to his care.

Barbara started slightly, and shook her head. She had been living again the last three hours of the ball. How delightful and how unexpected it had all been! She had enjoyed intensely her long talk with the French Ambassador. He also had spent his childhood, and part of his youth at St. Germains, the stately forest town where the brighter days of her parents' exile had been passed. It is well sometimes to meet with one who can say, "I too have been in Arcadia." Even Monsieur Parisot's little compliments on her good French had reminded Barbara of the sweet hypocrisies which make life in France so agreeable to the humble-minded, and especially to the very young.

Lord Bosworth had surely been the magician, for it was after his arrival that everything had changed from grey to rose-colour. It was then that James Berwick had again become to her what he always was in manner, and the uncle and nephew had vied with one another in amusing and interesting her. And then had come this delightful conclusion, the drive back in this fairy chariot!

"This is a very pretty, curious little carriage," her eyes met his frankly; "I feel like Cinderella going to, not coming back from, the ball!"

Berwick allowed himself to look his fill. The brougham was lined with some sort of white watered silk, and never would Barbara have a kinder background, or one which harmonised more exquisitely with her rather pale, dark beauty. Women were then wearing their hair cut straight across the forehead, and dressed in elaborate plaits about the nape of the neck; Barbara's short curls seemed to ally her with a more refined, a less sophisticated age,—one when innocence and archness were compatible with instinctive dignity.

And yet, such being the nature of man, Berwick would have been better pleased had she not been now so completely, so happily at her ease. He felt that between them there lay—not the drawn sword which played so strange and symbolical a part in mediæval marriage by procuration—but a sheaf of lilies. Berwick would have preferred the sword.

His had been the mood which seeks an extreme of purity in the woman beloved. Till now he had been glad to worship on his knees, and where she walked had been holy ground. But now he craved for some of the tenderness Barbara lavished on Madame Sampiero. Could she not even spare him the warmth of feeling shown by her when speaking of Grace and Andrew Johnstone? Since that last interview with Mrs. Marshall he had felt free—free as he had not felt for over a year. Was he to have no profit of his freedom?

"It is you who look tired, Mr. Berwick; I'm afraid you stayed on for my sake?"

Barbara was looking at him with real concern. How unlike himself he had been all that evening! Perhaps, when she had been stupidly annoyed at his supposed neglect of her, he had really been suffering. His face looked strained and thin in the bright light thrown by a cunning little arrangement of mirrors. She felt a pang of fear. How would she be able to bear it if he fell ill, away from her, in that large bare house which seemed so little his home?

It was well perhaps that Berwick could not see just then into her heart, and yet it was still an ignorant and innocent heart. The youngest girl present at the Halnakeham Castle ball could probably have taught Mrs. Rebell more than she now knew of the ways of men—almost, it might be said, of the ways of love. Her father had had the manhood crushed out of him by his great misfortune. Barbara, as child and girl, had reverenced—not the chill automaton, caring only for the English papers and a little mild play, which Richard Rebell had become in middle life,—but the attractive early image of him sedulously presented to her by her mother. She had had no brothers to bring young people to the many homes of her girlhood. Then, across her horizon, had come the baleful figure of Pedro Rebell, but at no time, after her marriage, had she made the mistake of regarding him as a normal man. No, her first real knowledge of the average Englishman had been during those weeks of convalescence, spent at the Government House of Santa Maria, when she had been slowly struggling back into a wish to live. There she had known, and had shrunk from the knowledge, that all those about her were aware of what sort of life she had been compelled to lead on her husband's plantation. Every step of Mr. Johnstone's negotiations with Pedro Rebell was followed by her new friends with intense sympathy, and when at last the planter had been half persuaded, half bribed into signing a document binding him not to molest his wife, her only longing had been to go away, and never to see any of the people connected with the island again.

What could Barbara Rebell know of men—of such men as James Berwick and Oliver Boringdon? She dowered them with virtues and qualities, with unselfish impulses and powers of self-restraint, which would have brought a Galahad to shame. She knew enough of a certain side of life to recognise and shrink from such coarseness as was not the saving grace of Mrs. Turke. She realised that that type of mind must see evil in even the most innocent tie between a man and a woman, but on such minds she preferred not to dwell. She knew how close had been the affection between her mother and Madame Sampiero. Why should not some such feeling, close and yet sexless, link her to James Berwick, to whom she had experienced,—so much she had perforce to acknowledge to herself,—a curious, intimate attraction from the first time they had met?

So it was that to-night she looked at him with concern, and spoke with a new note of anxiety in her voice, "I should have been quite content to go back with the Boringdons—I fear you stayed on for my sake."

"But I should not have been at all content if you had gone back with the Boringdons! Why should I not stay on for your sake?" he was smiling at her. She looked at him rather puzzled. When they were alone, they two, with no third influence between them, Barbara always felt completely happy and at ease. His presence brought security.

"Only if you were tired," she said rather lamely, and then again with that new anxiety, "Old Mr. Daman said to someone before me, 'James Berwick's looking rather fagged to-night'——"

"Let us talk of you, not of me," he said rather hastily. Heavens! what might she not have heard during this evening concerning him and his affairs? He lowered for a moment the window to his right and looked out into the starless moonless night, or rather early morning.

"We are now on the brow of Whiteways. I wish it were daylight, for then you would see the finest view in Sussex."

"But I have seen the view. I was at the meet, and thanks to your kindness, for I rode Saucebox. Mr. Berwick, I do not think I have ever thanked you sufficiently for Saucebox!"

He turned to her with a quick movement. "I do not think there should ever be a question of thanks between you and me. We are—at least I hope so—too good friends for that." And with a certain gravity he added, "Do you not believe friendship possible between a man and woman?" He waited a moment, then hurried on, "Listen! I offer you my friendship; I have never done so, in the sense I do now, to any other woman. Shall I tell you who has been my best, indeed my only, woman friend? only my sister, only Arabella. I owe her more than one debt of very sincere gratitude. You will not grudge her place in my—" again he hesitated,—"in my heart."

Barbara smiled tremulously. What a strange question to ask her! She felt a little afraid of Miss Berwick, and yet how friendly and gracious had been her manner to-night.

"Tell me," he said urgently, "you do not mind my saying this to you? I only wish to seal an existent compact. Ever since we met, have we not been close friends, you and I? I take it we are both singularly placed," he bent down and tried to look into her downcast eyes, "I am very solitary, and you have only Madame Sampiero—is not that so?"

Barbara bent her head. She felt that Berwick's low, ardent voice was slowly opening the gates of paradise, and drawing her through into that enchanted garden where every longing of the heart may be safely and innocently satisfied.

The carriage was going slowly down the steep hill leading from Whiteways to Chillingworth, and Berwick knew that he would soon have to leave her. His voice dropped to a lower key—he ventured, for a moment, to take her ringless left hand and hold it tightly: "I ask but little—nothing you do not think it right to give. But your friendship would mean much to me—would protect me from evil impulses of which, thank God, you can know nothing. Even to-night I suffered from misdeeds—to put it plainly, from past sins I should not have been even tempted to commit had I known you when I committed them."

His words—his confession—moved Barbara to the soul. "I am your friend," she spoke with a certain difficulty, and yet with solemnity. She looked up, and he saw that her eyes were full of tears.

The carriage stopped, and they both, or perhaps it was only Berwick, came down again to the everyday world where friendship between a man and a woman is regarded as so dangerous a thing by the prudent.

"Good-night! Thank you for bringing me." He added a word or two as to the carriage and the Priory stables—his coachman was a Chancton man—and then he was gone, leaving Barbara to go on alone, happy, content with life, as she had never thought it possible to be.

James Berwick, making his way quickly up the steep path leading from the wall built round Chillingworth Park to the high plateau on which stood the house, felt less content and very much less happy. Had he not been rather too quixotic in this matter of leaving Barbara to go on her way alone? Why should he not have prolonged those exquisite moments? What harm could it have done had he given himself the pleasure of accompanying his friend to the Priory, and then driving back to Chillingworth by himself? Perhaps there had been something pusillanimous in his fear of idle gossip. Oh! why had he behaved in this matter so much better than there was any occasion to do?

So our good deeds rise up and smite us, and seldom are we allowed the consolation of knowing what alternative action on our part might have brought about.

Thus it was an ill-satisfied and restless man who let himself in by a small side-door into the huge silent house. He had given orders that no one should sit up, and in such a matter disobedience on the part of a servant would have meant dismissal. Yet Berwick was an indulgent master, and when he walked into the comparatively small room which he always used when at Chillingworth, the only apartment in the house which in any way betrayed its owner's tastes and idiosyncrasies, he became aware that his comfort, or what it had been thought would be his comfort, had been studied; for a tray, laden with food and various decanters of wines and spirits, stood on a table, and the remains of what had been a large fire still burned in the grate.

He stifled an exclamation of disgust. How hot, how airless the room was! He walked over to the high window, pulled back the curtains and threw it open. It was still intensely dark, but along the horizon, above the place where he knew the sea to be, was a shaft of dim light—perhaps the first faint precursor of the dawn. Leaving the window open he came back to the fireplace and flung himself down in a chair, and there came over him a feeling of great depression and of peculiar loneliness.

Soon his longing for Barbara's soothing intimate presence became intolerably intense. For the first time since they had come to know one another well, Berwick deliberately tried to analyse his feeling towards her. He was not in love with Barbara Rebell—of that he assured himself with a certain fierceness. He thought of what he had said to her to-night. In a sense he had told her the exact truth. He had never offered any other women the friendship he had asked her to accept. He had always asked for less—or more—but then, looking back, he could tell himself that there was no one woman who had ever roused in him the peculiar sentiment that he felt for Mrs. Rebell. The feeling he now experienced was more akin, though far deeper and tenderer in texture, to the fleeting fancy he had had for that pretty *débutante* whom Arabella had so greatly feared. But, whereas he had borne the girl's defection, when it had come, with easy philosophy, he knew that his relation to Barbara was such that any defection there would rouse in him those primeval instincts which lead every day to such sordid tragedies in that class where the passion of love is often the only thing in life bringing hope of release and forgetfulness from ignoble and material cares.

Berwick had many faults, but personal vanity was not one of them. He considered Oliver Boringdon more a man to attract women than he was himself, and he had thought his friend lamentably backward in making use of his opportunities. Now, the knowledge that Boringdon was daily in Mrs. Rebell's company was distinctly disturbing. Was Barbara the type of woman—Berwick knew there were many such—who make a cult of sentimental friendships? Then he felt deeply ashamed of the thought, and in his heart he begged her forgiveness.

A Frenchman, once speaking to him of an acquaintance whose unhappy passion for a celebrated beauty was being much discussed, had observed, "Il l'a dans la peau! Dans ces cas-là il n'y a rien à faire!" He had thought the expression curiously apt, and he remembered it to-night. More than once during the last few days he had found himself planning his immediate future entirely by the light, as it were, of Chancton Priory. By every post he was refusing invitations, and avoiding coming political engagements. But there was one great exception. Even while speaking to Arabella at the ball, he had been wondering whether he could persuade her to secure Mrs. Rebell's inclusion in a very small and entirely political house-party in Scotland, the occasion of which was a series of important political meetings, and to which both brother and sister had been for some time pledged. It would be good to be away with Barbara, among strangers, far from Chancton and from Chillingworth.

Berwick hated Chillingworth. When there he felt himself to be the unwelcome guest of the man who had built the huge place, and whose personality it seemed to express and to perpetuate, as houses so often do the personality of their builders. The creator of Chillingworth had been an acute early Victorian manufacturer, a worthy man according to his lights, and a pillar of the Manchester School. He had taken fortune at the flood, and his late marriage to a woman of slightly better birth and breeding than his own had produced the sickly, refined daughter whom Berwick had married.

Chillingworth seemed plastered with money. Every room bore evidence of lavish expenditure; money spent on furniture, on pictures, on useless ornaments, during a period of our history when beauty seemed wholly in eclipse; and this was all the more pitiable because the house was gloriously placed on a spur of the down, and the views from its windows rivalled those of Chancton Priory.

Even had Berwick wished to do so, he could not have made any serious alterations to the place, for the trustees of his marriage settlement were the very people, distant relatives of his wife's, whose children would benefit were he to forfeit his life interest in her fortune. To these people Chillingworth spelt perfection, and was a treasure-house of beautiful, because costly, objects of art. Occasionally, perhaps once in two years, its present owner would fill the great mansion for a few weeks with men and women—political acquaintances and their wives—to whom an invitation to James Berwick's Sussex estate gave pleasure, but otherwise he was little there, and the neighbourhood had long since left off wondering and exclaiming at his preference for Chancton Priory.

"If Miss Berwick sends over for a carriage, the French brougham which was used last night is not to go."

"Very good, Sir." And then, after a short pause, "Anything wrong with the carriage, Sir?"

"No. By the way, it may be required at Chancton. I have told Madame Sampiero that she may have the use of it for the lady who is staying there. Where's Dean?"

Berwick, haggard-looking, and evidently in a mood which his servants knew and dreaded, was looking sharply round the stable yard. If he, the master, was up and about by nine o'clock, the morning after the Halnakeham Castle ball, then surely his coachman could be the same.

"Dean's in trouble, Sir. He will be sending to ask if you can spare him to-day. Wife was taken ill last night, babby dead."

The laconic words struck Berwick with a curious chill, and served to rouse him from his self-absorption. He was fond of Dean. The man had been with him for many years. They were the same age,—Berwick could remember him as a stolid Chancton child—and he had only been married about a year, after one of those long, faithful engagements common in those parts. Heavens! If Dean felt for his wife a tenth of what he, Berwick, felt for Barbara Rebell, what must not the man have gone through that night—that early morning?

Muttering some expression of concern, he turned and went off into the house, there to consult with the housekeeper as to the sending of practical relief to the stricken household, and to write a note telling Dean he could be absent for as long as he wished.

CHAPTER XIV.

"Men may have rounded Seraglio Point: they have not yet doubled Cape Turk."

GEORGE MEREDITH.

MISS VIPEN's cottage was exactly opposite the Chancton Post Office. Even in winter it was a pretty, cheerful-looking little house closely covered with evergreen creepers, the path up to the porch guarded by four lemon trees cut into fantastic shapes.

From her sitting-room window, the old lady could see all that went on in the main street of Chancton village, and take note of the coming and going both of familiars and of strangers, thus providing herself with the material whereby she wove the web of the destinies of those about her.

They who exist only to sow spite and malice should always live in the country. A town finds them at a disadvantage, for there those about them have too much to do to find more than a very passing amusement in their conversation. But in a country neighbourhood, such a woman as Miss Vipen is a godsend, partly because, in addition to being a centre of gossip, she is often the source of authentic news. People tell her things they would be ashamed to tell each other, and, with the strange lack of imagination or excess of vanity which afflicts most of us in certain circumstances, each member of the large circle formed about such a woman, and with whom she is often actually popular, believes himself or herself exempt from her biting tongue.

Here, in Chancton, each and all admired Miss Vipen's easy kindness,—a quality which so often accompanies evil speaking. Yet another thing was accounted to her for righteousness. She never mentioned the mistress of the Priory,—never spoke either good or evil of Madame Sampiero, of the one human being who had for long years provided even the staid and prudent with legitimate subjects of scandal and gossip.

As a matter of fact, Miss Vipen owed her cottage, her income, her very position in Chancton, to the mistress of the Priory. Her father had been land-agent to Madame Sampiero's father. The two women had been girls together, and when finally the arrangements had been made which provided for Miss Vipen's later life and for what she cared for so much more, the keeping up of her adequate position in the neighbourhood where she had spent her whole existence, her old friend had said to her: "I only ask one thing. I beg you, Martha, never to speak of me again, kindly or unkindly, in love or in anger!"—and Miss Vipen had faithfully kept her side of the bargain.

Only two people in Chancton had the moral courage steadily to avoid her dangerous company. The one was Doctor McKirdy, who, as a young man, and when still a stranger to the place, had extracted from her a written apology for something she had said of him which identified him too closely for his taste with the physiologists who were then beginning to be much discussed. The other was General Kemp. Making one day sudden irruption into her sitting-room, he had overheard a remark made by her concerning his own daughter and Captain Laxton; at once he had turned on his heel, and, after giving his wife a short sketch of what would have happened to Miss Vipen had she worn breeches instead of petticoats, he had declared it to be his intention never willingly to meet her again.

Malice, to be effective, however vulgar in its essence, should on the whole be refined in its expression. There were certain people, notably poor Mrs. Sampson, the rector's wife, to whom Miss Vipen felt she could say anything, sure of a fascinated, even if a fearful, listener. With others she was more careful, and to Mrs. Boringdon she had soon become a valuable ally, and a precious source of information.

This was the woman from whose company and conversation Oliver Boringdon, two days after the Halnakeham Castle ball, came straight down the village street to Chancton Grange. He had been to see Miss Vipen on a matter of business connected with a slight leakage in her roof, but the hawk-eyed old lady, as was her wont, had in a very few moments planted an envenomed dart in his mind and brain.

Partly perhaps because he knew her to be so intensely disliked by Doctor McKirdy, and partly because she was one of the very few people who never tried to extract from him information concerning Madame Sampiero and the Priory, Oliver actually liked Miss Vipen. She was an intelligent woman, and her kindnesses to the village people were intelligent kindnesses. She would lend books and papers to the sick and ailing, and more than once he had come across traces of her good deeds among the poor of the place,—men and women with whom she had life-long links of familiarity and interest. She was aware that Boringdon liked her, and she took trouble to keep his good opinion. So it was that to-day her few remarks—said more, or so it seemed, in pity than in anger, had been carefully chosen—and only amounted to the regrettable fact that James Berwick's frequent visits to the Priory, and the long hours he was said to spend alone with Mrs. Rebell, were causing unpleasant remark both in the village and in the neighbourhood.

Boringdon had listened in absolute silence, then, taking up his hat and stick, had gone, leaving his hostess rather uncomfortable. But Miss Vipen's words had met with unquestioning belief, and they had made her listener's smouldering jealousy and unhappiness—for in these days Oliver was very jealous and wretchedly unhappy—burst into flame.

Since the ball the young man had seen practically nothing of Barbara, although she had been present at each of his daily interviews with Madame Sampiero; and when one day, late in the afternoon, he had gone contrary to his custom, to the Priory, the admirably trained McGregor had informed him that Mrs. Rebell was "not at home," although Boringdon had seen her shadow and that of Berwick cast on the blind of the blue drawing-room.

James Berwick's attitude towards women had always been inexplicable to Oliver, for he was entirely out of sympathy with his friend's interest in Woman *qua* Woman. In no circumstances would the younger man have been capable of imagining the peculiar relationship which had sprung up between these two people, to each of whom—and it was an aggravating circumstance—he felt himself bound by so close a tie.

During the last two days his jealousy and suspicion of Berwick's motives had almost prompted him to say something to Mrs. Rebell, but there was that in Barbara which made it very difficult to approach such a subject with her. Also, even if lacking in a sense of humour, Boringdon was yet dimly aware that she might well retort with a *tu quoque* argument which he would find it difficult to meet. For there had been one fortnight in which, looking back, he was obliged to admit to himself that he had spent far more time in Mrs. Rebell's company than he could accuse Berwick of now doing. He and she had walked together, ridden together, and talked together of everything under heaven and earth. Even—fool that he had been—he had told her much of Berwick, and all to that dangerous sentimentalist's advantage.

Then there had come a sudden change over his own and Mrs. Rebell's pleasant and profitable relationship. Saucebox had kicked herself in the stable, and had gone back, in disgrace, to Chillingworth, so the rides had perforce come to an end. Little by little, or so it now seemed to Oliver, he had been shepherded into only going over to the Priory in the morning—made to feel that at other times he was not welcome.

The young man remembered well the first time he had come over to the Priory to find Berwick installed, almost as master, in the great hall, and Barbara listening to this new acquaintance as she had hitherto only listened to him, to Boringdon himself. And yet what was there to be done? Madame Sampiero's attitude filled him with indignation; surely it was her duty to save her god-daughter from the snares of such a fowler as she must know Berwick to be?

Boringdon had long been aware of the type of feminine companionship his friend was always seeking, and dimly he understood that hitherto the pursuit had been unavailing. But now?—Mrs. Rebell, so Boringdon, with something like agony, acknowledged to himself, fulfilled all the conditions of Berwick's ideal; and a nobler, more unselfish feeling than mere personal instinct stirred him to revolt, while he was also swayed by an anger born of keen jealousy, dignified by him with a hundred names, of which the most comfortable to his self-esteem and conscience was care for Mrs. Rebell's reputation.

At certain moments he reminded himself how much Berwick had been at the Priory before Mrs. Rebell's arrival, but even so, such a man's constant presence there was terribly dangerous! Some kind, wholly disinterested woman must tell

Barbara that in England Berwick's conduct would surely compromise her, whatever might be the case at Santa Maria or on the Continent.

Casting about in his mind, Boringdon could think of but one person in the neighbourhood who was fitted to undertake so delicate a task, and who would, so he told himself, understand his own personal share in the matter; this person was Mrs. Kemp. To the Grange he accordingly made his way, after having listened in silence to Miss Vipen's softly uttered remarks.

From the first fortune favoured him, for Mrs. Kemp was alone. The General and Lucy were gone to Halnakeham for the afternoon; and Boringdon, coming in out of the late November air full of suppressed excitement and ill at ease, felt soothed by the look of warmth and comfort with which Lucy's mother always managed to surround herself.

To Oliver's own mother, to Mrs. Boringdon, an appearance of comfort, even of luxury, was all-important when guests were expected at Chancton Cottage. Then everything was suitably lavish, and even luxurious. But when the young man and his mother were alone, fires were allowed to burn low, the food, poor in quality, was also limited as to quantity, and it was well for Oliver that he cared as little as on the whole he did for creature comforts. In Mrs. Boringdon's mind the page boy was set against the sweets at luncheon and the cakes at tea which Oliver would have enjoyed, but then in the country a man-servant was essential—an essential portion of her own and her son's dignity.

It was now four o'clock. At home Boringdon would have had to wait another hour for tea, and so would any passing guest who could be regarded as an intimate friend, but here, at the Grange, it appeared as if by magic a few minutes after the visitor had sat down opposite Mrs. Kemp, and Oliver soon felt heartened up to approach what even he felt to be a rather difficult subject.

The kind woman whose aid he was about to invoke made it easy for him to begin, for she was very cordial; thanks to Boringdon, Lucy had thoroughly enjoyed the ball at Halnakeham Castle, and the mother felt grateful for even this small mercy. During the last two days she had reminded herself more than once that affairs of the heart, when not interfered with unduly, have an odd way of coming right.

"I need not ask," he said, rather awkwardly, "if Lucy is no worse for the ball."

Mrs. Kemp was not sure whether she liked to hear Boringdon call her daughter Lucy; he had only begun doing so lately, and she had not thought it necessary to mention it to the General. There was still a certain coolness between Oliver and Lucy's father—they avoided each other's company.

He went on without waiting for an answer: "Mrs. Rebell seems to have found it a trying experience, and yet she did not dance at all. I went to the Priory this morning, and she was too tired to come down."

"But then she came back so much later than you all did. I understand that she stayed on with the Fletchings party, and I heard some of their carriages going through the village at four o'clock in the morning!"

Boringdon looked at her with quick suspicion. He had just learnt from Miss

Vipen of Berwick's solitary drive with Mrs. Rebell. But the remark Mrs. Kemp had just made was wholly innocent in intention; she never dealt in innuendoes.

"I wish," he said, impulsively, "that you would get to know Mrs. Rebell! Everyone else in the neighbourhood has called on her; have you any reason for not doing so?"

She hesitated, then said slowly, "No. No real reason, except, of course, that we have never received, during all the years we have been here, any mark of attention or civility from Madame Sampiero, whose tenants after all we are. Also I fancied, from something that Doctor McKirdy said, that Mrs. Rebell did not wish to make many acquaintances in the neighbourhood."

"It's a great pity, for she must feel very lonely, and I'm sure it would be much to her to have such friends as yourself, and as—as Lucy."

The mother's heart hardened; Mrs. Kemp was no gossip, but she knew how much time Oliver had spent at the Priory during the fortnight Mrs. Boringdon had been away.

"Yes, she must be rather lonely," and then she could not help adding, "but you are a great deal over there, are you not?"

His answer made her feel ashamed of what she had said. "I am over there most days, but she cannot make a companion, a friend, of a man, as she could of you or of Lucy." Now surely was his opportunity for saying what he had come to say, but he found the task he had set himself demanded a bluntness, a crudity of speech, that was almost intolerable to him.

"Mrs. Kemp, may I speak frankly to you?"

There was a strong note of appeal in the speaker's voice. Mrs. Kemp gave him a quick, anxious look, and took her knitting off the table. "Certainly, frankness is always best," she said, then wondered with beating heart what he was about to tell her. She had felt, during the last few minutes, that Boringdon was only marking time. He was once more on his old terms of friendship with Lucy, indeed, the girl had lunched at Chancton Cottage that very day. But his next words shattered Mrs. Kemp's dream, and that most rudely.

"I want you to call on Mrs. Rebell," he was saying in a low eager tone, "and to come really to know her, because—well, because I fear she is in some danger. It isn't a matter one wants to discuss, but James Berwick is constantly at the Priory, and his visits there are already being talked about in the neighbourhood. She is, as you know, a friend of my sister, and I feel a certain responsibility in the matter. Someone ought to put her on her guard."

Mrs. Kemp put down her work and looked at him with a steady, disconcerting look of surprise. He no longer felt sure, as he had done a moment ago, of her sympathy, but he met her glance with a dogged courage. He cared so little what she thought; the great point was to enlist her help. Boringdon had known her do really quixotic things with reference to certain village matters and scandals—and always with healing results.

It is fortunate that we cannot see into each other's minds. What would Oliver have felt had he become aware of the feeling, half of dislike, half of pity, with which he was being regarded at that moment by the woman to whom he had made his appeal? Mrs. Kemp withdrew her eyes from his face; it was possible,—just possible,—that it was as he said, and that he was animated by worthy and impersonal motives. Berwick was not a man with an absolutely good reputation as regarded women; his position, too, was a singular one,—of so much even Mrs. Kemp was aware.

"As you have spoken frankly to me, so will I speak frankly to you," she said. "I have never known any good come from interfering,—or rather I have never known any good come from speaking, in such a case, to the woman. The person to reach is Mr. Berwick. If he is indeed compromising Mrs. Rebell, he is doing a very wrong and treacherous thing, not only to her, but to Madame Sampiero, who has always been, so I understand, especially kind to him. Still, you must remember that, long before this lady came here, he was constantly at the Priory. Also, may I say that, if your information as to the gossip about them comes from Miss Vipen, its source is tainted? I never believe a word she says about anything or anybody!"

"Miss Vipen did certainly say something—she had heard——"

"What had she heard?"

"That Berwick drove back with her"—Mrs. Kemp noticed the use of the pronoun—"alone, the night of the ball, and that they sat up, talking, till morning, in the hall of the Priory. No wonder Mrs. Rebell still feels tired!" The speaker had gone grey in the lamplight.

"Well, that story is false, vilely false! I do not know how, or with whom, Mrs. Rebell came home; but by an odd chance I do happen to know that Mr. Berwick went straight from Halnakeham to Chillingworth, and that he was there in the morning. His coachman's wife, who is staying here in Chancton with her parents, was taken ill that night. I was there by six the next morning—perhaps you know that the poor baby died—and the man told me that he had driven his master home, and that he would send him over a message asking leave to stay with his wife. Mr. Berwick is a very good master, they seem all devoted to him——" Then, struck by his look, "Surely you believe me? Do you put Miss Vipen's piece of spiteful gossip against what I tell you?"

Boringdon hesitated. "I don't know what to believe," he said. "James Berwick, when conducting an intrigue, is capable of—of——"

"If you think so ill of Mrs. Rebell as that——!"

"But I don't!" he cried hastily, "indeed I don't! It is Berwick, only Berwick, that I blame in this matter. I think Mrs. Rebell is wholly innocent! I feel for her the greatest respect! She is incapable, I feel sure, of a wrong thought,"—he spoke with growing agitation. "But think of the whole circumstances—of Madame Sampiero's past life, of Mrs. Rebell's present position! Can you wonder that I feel sure your friendship, even your countenance, might make a great difference? But pray,"—he got up, and looked at Mrs. Kemp very earnestly,—"pray do not suppose I think ill of Mrs. Rebell! Were it so, should I suggest that you—that Lucy—should make a friend of her?" and wringing her hand he left the room, eager to escape before the return of General Kemp and his daughter.

There are times when the presence of even the best-loved and most trusted grown-up son or daughter could be well spared by father and mother. Mrs. Kemp, during the evening which followed Oliver's afternoon call, thought constantly of the conversation she had held with him, and she longed to tell her husband what had passed. Men were such strange, such inexplicable beings! Doubtless Tom would be able to reassure her as to Oliver Boringdon's interest in this Mrs. Rebell, whose charm had won over Lucy too, for the girl spoke with enthusiasm of the beauty and of the kindness of Madame Sampiero's god-daughter. But nothing could be said in the presence of Lucy, who had regained, during the last day or two, her old lightness of heart and manner, and who showed no wish to go early to bed.

At last Mrs. Kemp went up alone, and when, an hour later, the General followed her, and she had the longed-for opportunity of telling her tale, her listener proved most irritatingly quiescent. He went in and out of his dressing-room, saying "Yes," and "That's it, is it?" at suitable intervals. Still, when she stopped speaking, he would suddenly appear in some leisurely state of *déshabillé* and his wife would feel encouraged, to go on, and even to ask for his opinion and advice.

"And now, Tom, what do you *really* think of the whole matter?"

General Kemp came and stood before the fire. He wore his dressing-gown,—a sure sign that he was ready for discussion, if discussion should prove necessary.

"Well, Mary, what I *really* think can be put in a very few words." He advanced till he stood at the foot of the large four-poster, and, with a twinkle in his eye, declaimed the lines:—

"'And it was you, my *Berwick*, you!
The friend in whom my soul confided!
Who dared to gaze on her—to do,
I may say, much the same as I did!'"

"Oh! Tom, you should not make fun of such a serious matter," but Mrs. Kemp could not help smiling—the lines were indeed apt.

"Well, my dear, what else is there to say? I can't say I should be sorry if Boringdon were to burn his wings a bit! I hate your fellow who is always trying to set the world straight. To take his information from Miss Vipen too—!" The General had also heard of Oliver's renewed interest in the Priory, and his wife's talk had not surprised him quite as much as she, in the innocence of her heart, expected it to do. "Berwick, from what you tell me, and from what I hear," he added in a low voice, "knows what he's after, and that's more than your friend Boringdon seems to do! I hate a man who goes dangling after a woman for her good; that's what he told you, I take it?"

"Well, something rather like it; but I think better of him than you do, Tom."

"They generally get caught at last." General Kemp gave a quick, short sigh:

"and then comes—unless the chap's as clever as Boringdon doubtless means to be—pretty heavy punishment, eh, Mary?"

And he went off back into his dressing-room, and Mrs. Kemp, turning on her side, wet her pillow with sudden bitter tears.

Some days later Lucy and her mother called at the Priory, only to be informed that Mrs. Rebell was at Fletchings, staying there as the guest of Lord Bosworth and Miss Berwick till the following Saturday. This then,—so thought Mrs. Kemp with a quick revulsion of feeling,—was why Boringdon now found time hang so heavy on his hands, and why he had been, of late, so often at the Grange. Life, even at Chancton, was full of inexplicable cross currents,—of deep pools and eddies more likely to bring shipwreck than safe haven to the creature whom she loved so dearly, and for whom she felt that responsibility which only mothers know.

CHAPTER XV.

"But as we walked we turned aside
Into a narrow tortuous lane
Where baffling paths the roads divide
And jealous brambles prick to pain:
Then first I saw, with quick surprise,
The strange new look in friendship's eyes.

"And now, in one stupendous dream,
We wander through the purple glades,
Which love has tinted with the gleam
Of wonderful, enchanting shades:
But I—would give it all away
For those dear hours of friendship's day."

Eleanor Esher.

Mrs. Rebell had now been at Fletchings five days. It was Saturday night—in three days more she would be back at Chancton.

Standing before her dressing-table, she found herself counting the last hours of a holiday which had proved more enchanting than she had thought possible. How sorry she would be to leave the curious pretty room in which she found herself! This room, and that next door now turned into a dressing-room, had been fitted up when the wonders of China were first becoming known to the Western world. It was instinct with the strange charm so often found in those old English country houses where Christendom and Goblindom fight for mastery.

The greatest poet of his time had spent at Fletchings the honeymoon which formed a beginning to the most disastrous of marriage tragedies; and Septimus Daman, now Barbara's fellow guest, had managed to convey to her his belief that the rooms which she now occupied had been those set aside for the hapless pair. Was it here, so Barbara wondered—here, or perhaps sitting at the lacquer table in the dressing-room—that the bride had written the formal, yet wholly contented, letter to her parents, with its concluding sentence: "I cannot tell you any more for Lord Byron is looking over my shoulder!"—playful, intimate words, written by the proud, headstrong girl who was to lead a later life of such harsh bitterness.

Barbara felt a vague retrospective pity for the long-dead writer of these words. How far superior is friendship to what people call love! Every day she was proving the truth of this, her own, and—yes, her friend's—discovery.

After those five perfect days, it seemed strange to remember that she had wondered if she were acting rightly in accepting Miss Berwick's invitation. There had not been much time for thought. The note had come only two days after the ball at Halnakeham Castle, and, as she held it in her hand, before telling any of those about her of its contents, there had swept over Barbara Rebell a foreboding memory. Was she about to expose herself to a repetition of what she had gone through during those first hours at the ball? Was she to see Berwick avoiding her company,—gazing at her, when he looked her way, with alien eyes?

But then Berwick himself had come, full of eagerness, and with his abrupt first words—"Has Arabella written? That's right!—I think you will like it. My uncle wants me to be over there in order to see something of Daniel O'Flaherty, and we are also to have old Septimus Daman; he always spends part of November at Fletchings"—her fears, her scruples had vanished.

Just before leaving the Priory, Barbara's heart had again misgiven her. Madame Sampiero, looking at her with the wide-open, dark-blue eyes which could express so many shades of feeling, had murmured, "Do not be too long away, child. Remember what befell the poor Beast when Beauty stayed away too long!" How could she have had the heart to write, on the second day of her visit, "They want me to stay on till Tuesday"?

And now it was Saturday night. In a few days she would again take up the life which till so very lately had seemed to fulfil each aspiration, to content every longing of her heart. Now, she found herself dreading her god-mother's glances of uneasy, questioning tenderness; Mrs. Turke's eager interest in Berwick's comings and goings; most of all, and for reasons of which her mind avoided the analysis, Barbara shrank from the return to the long mornings—they had become very long of late—spent by Boringdon at the Priory.

In contrast to all that awaited Mrs. Rebell at Chancton, how happy these few days at Fletchings had been! With the possible exception of Daniel O'Flaherty—and, after all, both he and Arabella knew better—the six people gathered there under Lord Bosworth's roof, were linked in close bonds of old and new friendship, of old and new association.

Barbara could tell herself in all honesty that she did not seem to see very much of James Berwick, and yet, in truth, they were much together, he encompassing her with a depth of voiceless tenderness, and a devotion so unobtrusive that it seemed to lack every gross element of self. Then again, her host had been especially kind. To Lord Bosworth she had been "Barbara" from the first, and during that week he had talked much to her of that wide world in which he himself had played so noted and agreeable a part; of her own parents as they had been during the unshadowed years of their life; of present politics which he had soon discovered interested her in a singular degree. One day he had exclaimed—and had been surprised to see the vivid blush his words called forth—"Why, we shall make a politician of you yet!" During those days, however,—and the omission pained her,—Lord Bosworth made no allusion to Madame Sampiero.

Perhaps, of all those at Fletchings, the most contented of the party was Septimus Daman. Because he seemed to each of the others the odd man out, they were all particularly kind to him, and eager that he should not feel himself neglected. The old man did not, however, burden his fellow-guests with much on his company, for he was busily engaged in writing his recollections, and he rarely made his appearance downstairs before the afternoon.

To-day, quite suddenly and for no apparent reason, Berwick's mood had changed. Arabella was the first to become aware of it; she knew of old the danger signals. The day had been spent by him and by O'Flaherty at Laxgrove, where Squire Laxton was as proud of his coverts as of his hounds. The two men came in wet and tired, and Berwick, after a long fruitless search for his sister and Mrs. Rebell, at last found them sitting together where Arabella so seldom entertained a guest—in the powder closet.

"I have been looking for you everywhere!" he exclaimed. "Daman is wandering about downstairs, evidently afraid to pour himself out a cup of tea and O'Flaherty has disappeared,—tealess,—to his room!"

While he was speaking, gazing at his sister and her friend with an accusing glance, Barbara went out, and for a moment the other two stayed on alone together.

Arabella rose and faced her brother. Her own nerves were not wholly under control. Neither her conscience nor her heart was really at ease.

"I don't know, James, and I don't inquire, what your relations to Mrs. Rebell may be! But this I do know—you will not advance your friendship with her by being savage to me. Besides, it is so absurd! However delightful she finds your company, she may yet prefer to be occasionally with me. I have been doing—I am doing—all I can for you."

"What do you mean?"

Berwick's steady, angry gaze disconcerted his sister, but she was mentally adroit, and determined not to fear him in his present mood.

"You know best what I ought to mean!" she cried. "You apparently take pleasure in Mrs. Rebell's company, and it was to please you that I asked her to come here. I mean nothing else. But I should like to add that, now I know her, I have grown to like, and even to respect her." Berwick's face softened, but again he looked at her in the way she dreaded as she added, "I do not think you should act so as to make those about you aware that you so greatly prefer her company to that of our other guests. I am sure Mr. O'Flaherty has noticed it. Perhaps I ought to add that I am speaking entirely for her sake."

On leaving Miss Berwick and her brother, Mrs. Rebell went up to her room. There she sat down and fulfilled a neglected duty,—the writing of a long letter to Grace Johnstone. She did not find the task an easy one. She knew that her friend would expect to be told much of the occupants of Chancton Cottage, and especially of Oliver. The writer was well aware how letters were treasured at Santa Maria, and, till the last fortnight she had written to the woman who had been so good a friend to her by every mail. Suddenly she bethought herself of the ball. Why, here was a subject all ready to her pen! But Barbara was no polite letter-writer, and she found the description difficult; especially did her references to Oliver and to his mother seem hypocritical. During those hours at Halnakeham Castle she had been scarcely aware of the young man's existence, while Mrs. Boringdon she actually disliked.

One reason why Barbara had been glad to come to Fletchings had been that it meant escape from Boringdon's constant presence at the Priory, and the daily morning walk with him to the home farm. She had come to resent Oliver's assumption of—was it brotherly?—interest in what she did and left undone. The thought that in three days she would again be subject to his well-meant criticism and eager, intimate advice certainly added another and a curiously acute touch of discomfort to her return to Chancton.

For the first time since Mrs. Rebell's stay at Fletchings, dinner, served in a blue and white octagon room which seemed to have been designed to serve as background to Miss Berwick's fair, delicate type of beauty, passed almost silently and rather dully. Berwick and O'Flaherty, tired after their long day in the open air, scarcely spoke; Mr. Daman alone seemed entirely at ease, and he babbled away happily, trying to extract material for his recollections from Lord Bosworth's better garnished memory.

And so it was with a sense of relief that Barbara followed her hostess out of the room. During the last few days the two women had become, in a sense, intimate. Each liked the other better than either would have thought possible a week before. They had one subject in common of which neither ever tired, and yet how surprised they both would have been to learn how constantly their talk drifted to the political past, the uneventful present, the brilliant nebulous future, of James Berwick!

Arabella led the way up to the music gallery, and there, very soon, the two younger men joined them.

Miss Berwick was sitting at an inlaid spinet, playing an old-fashioned, jingling selection of Irish melodies, and O'Flaherty, taking up his stand by the fire-place, was able to look down at the player without seeming to do so.

Listening to the woman he had loved making music for him, Daniel O'Flaherty's mind went back, setting out on a sentimental excursion, dolorous as such are apt to be, into the past. No other woman's lips had touched his since their last interview, thirteen years before; and yet, standing there, his arm on the mantel-piece, his right hand concealing his large rather stern mouth, he told himself that his love for Arabella Berwick had burned itself out, and that he could now look at her quite dispassionately.

Still, love may go, and interest,—even a certain kind of sentiment,—may remain. What else had brought him to Fletchings? Above all, what else had made him stay on there, as he was now doing? O'Flaherty still felt an odd closeness of heart,—aye, even of body,—

Miss Berwick, to this woman whom others found so unapproachable. The years which had gone by, the long separation, had not made them strangers. After she had left him, as he thought so cruelly, he had made up his mind to put away all thought of her. He had believed it certain that she would marry—indeed, during that last interview she had told him that she intended to do so—and thinking of this, to a man so callous and incredible a statement, his heart had hardened, not only to her, but in a sense to all women.

Then time had gone on, and Lord Bosworth's niece had remained unmarried—wholly devoted, so said rumour, to her brother, but living with her uncle instead of with James Berwick because of her filial affection and gratitude to the older man. That O'Flaherty had known not to be true, for no special tie bound Arabella to her uncle. The arrangement was probably one of convenience on either side.

And now, during these last few days? O'Flaherty acknowledged that Miss Berwick's manner to him had been perfect—courteous and kind, nay, even deferential, and then sometimes a look, a word, would subtly acknowledge his claim on her special attention, while putting forward none of her own. How could he help being flattered? From where he now sat, he could see, without seeming to observe too closely, the delicate, cameo-like profile, the masses of flaxen hair, less bright in tint than when he had first admired what was still Arabella's greatest beauty.

The barrister was under no illusion as to why he had received this invitation to Lord Bosworth's country house. His present host, and of course his hostess, wished him not merely to be on James Berwick's side in the coming political struggle, for that he was already, but to ally himself in a special sense with this future Cabinet-Minister, and to join the inner circle of his friends and supporters. Neither of them yet understood that in politics all O'Flaherty cared for supremely was his own country, in spite of the fact that he had always sat for an English constituency, and had never identified himself, in any direct sense, with the Irish party. Whatever his future relations to Miss Berwick might be, his attitude to her brother must be influenced by Berwick's attitude to Ireland and Irish affairs. Perhaps it would be more honest, so he told himself to-night, to let Arabella know this fact, for during the last few days he had avoided any political discussion with his host or his hostess.

Daniel O'Flaherty had watched James Berwick's career with painful interest. During his brief, passionate intimacy with the sister, the young Irishman had disliked the brother intensely. He had despised him for squandering,—as for a while Berwick had seemed to do,—his many brilliant gifts. Perhaps O'Flaherty had also been jealous of those advantages which came to the younger man by the mere fact of his name, and of his relationship to Lord Bosworth.

Then, with the passing of years, the barrister had become, as the successful are apt to do, more indulgent, perhaps more understanding, in his view of the other's character and ambitions. Also nothing succeeds like success, and James Berwick had himself by no means lagged behind. To O'Flaherty there had been nothing untoward in Berwick's marriage. He had regarded it as one of those strokes of amazing luck which seem to pursue certain men; and though a trifling circumstance had made the barrister vividly aware of the young politician's conditional tenure of his dead wife's fortune, the man who had fought his way to eminence naturally regarded the other as belonging to that class which seems in this country sufficiently wealthy, with the garnered wealth of the past, to consider the possession of a larger or of a lesser income as of comparatively small account.

Daniel O'Flaherty was an Irishman, a lonely man, and a Roman Catholic—thus traditionally interested in romance. And so, during these days at Fletchings, he had become aware, almost in spite of himself, of Berwick's evident attraction to Mrs. Rebell—to the gentle, intelligent woman whom he, O'Flaherty, naturally regarded as Arabella's widowed friend. It amused him to see the course of true love running smooth. What amazing good fortune seemed to pursue James Berwick!

True, the shrewder half of O'Flaherty's mind warned him that Miss Berwick's action in deliberately throwing her brother with so charming a woman as Barbara was an odd, an almost unaccountable move on her part. But there was no getting over the fact that she was doing this, and most deliberately.

Well, all that money could do for Berwick had surely been accomplished. The barrister, watching the two—this man and woman wandering in a paradise of their own making—felt that Berwick was indeed to be envied, even if he was on the eve of forfeiting the huge income which had for so many years given him an almost unfair prestige and power among his fellows. Still, now and again,—to-night for instance, when he became aware that Berwick and Mrs. Rebell had retreated together to the further end of the long, bare room,—he wondered if Arabella was acting sentiently, if she really wished her brother to marry again.

Mrs. Rebell and the man she called her friend stood together, half concealed by the organ which gave the gallery its name. They were practically alone, for the long room was only lighted by the candles which threw a wavering light on Arabella's music-book. For the first time since she had arrived at Fletchings, Barbara felt ill at ease with her companion. Twice during dinner she had looked up and seen Berwick's eyes fixed on her, or so she thought, coldly and accusingly. What had she done? For what must she ask forgiveness?

"Where were you before dinner?" he said at last, in a low voice. "I looked for you everywhere. I found you, and then you disappeared—utterly! We were close to the Priory to-day, and I went in for a moment, thinking you would like to have news of Madame Sampiero. By the way, McGregor gave me some letters for you."

He put two envelopes down on the ledge of a prie-dieu behind which Barbara was standing, and which formed a slight barrier between them. She took the letters in her hand, and then, partly because of the dim light, put them back again on the prie-dieu. One note, unstamped, was from Oliver Boringdon,—she knew the handwriting, and so did Berwick. Barbara was to have gone back to-day; doubtless this note concerned some village matter which the writer was unwilling to mention to Doctor McKirdy. The other envelope bore the peculiar blue West Indian stamp. Why had not McGregor kept these letters till Tuesday? For the moment Barbara wanted to forget Boringdon and his rather morbid susceptibilities—to forget, till her next letter to the Johnstones, Santa Maria.

"Won't you read your letters?" Berwick was looking straight across at her with a singular expression—was it of appeal or of command?—in his eyes.

"Why should I—now?" But a moment later she changed her mind, "Yes, of course I will; Mr. Boringdon may have sent some message to my god-mother which ought to be seen to at once— —" She opened the note, glanced through it, then put it down on the ledge of the prie-dieu.

Berwick had turned away while she read Boringdon's note, but now he was again staring at her with those strange, appealing eyes which seemed to shine in the dim light.

Reluctantly, as if in spite of herself, Barbara stretched out her hand and took up the other letter. Yes, it was, as she thought, from Andrew Johnstone—a bare word of kindly acknowledgment for the return of the fifty pounds which he had lent her.

She looked round, still holding the letter in her hand, but they were far from the fire—

Berwick's face became set. Ah! no, that should not be.

"Mrs. Rebell—?"

He had not called her so, to herself, since the drive back from Halnakeham Castle, and she had not noticed his avoidance of her name; but now, the formal mode of address fell strangely on her ears.

"Yes?"

"May I read these two letters?" He added, almost inaudibly, "You cannot think more ill of me than I do of myself."

Barbara suddenly felt as if she were taking part in an unreal scene, a dream colloquy, and yet she knew this was no dream. What had happened, what evil magic had so transformed her friend? That maternal instinct which slumbers lightly in the depths of every woman's heart, woke into life; she did not stay to diagnose the disease of which this strange request was a symptom: "Do read them," she said, and tried to speak indifferently, "I do not think ill of you—far from it, as Doctor McKirdy would say."

She put Johnstone's letter down by the other, but Berwick left them lying there; he still looked at her with a probing, suspicious look, and she began to be desperately afraid. At Santa Maria she had once met a miserable white man, the overseer of a neighbouring plantation, who was said to have suddenly gone "fantee"—so had that man looked at her, as Berwick was doing now, dumbly. Was this what he had meant when he had spoken to her in the carriage of ungovernable impulses—of actions of which he had afterwards felt bitterly ashamed?

Very slowly, still looking at her, he at last took up the two letters. Then, with a sudden movement, and without having looked at it, he put Boringdon's back on the ledge of the prie-dieu. "No," he said roughly, "not that one—I do not think he ought to write to you, but no matter!" Barbara felt herself trembling. She was beginning to understand. Berwick's hands fingered nervously the West Indian letter;

at last he held it out to her, still folded, in his hand. "Here it is—take it—I won't read it!"

"Oh! but do," she said. "It is from Mr. Johnstone, saying that he has received the money you so kindly arranged to send back for me."

But Barbara's words came too late.

"Mr. Johnstone?" Berwick repeated the name, then laughed harshly. "Fool that I was not to think of him! But all to-day, since McGregor gave me that letter, I have been in hell. Of course you know what I believed"—Barbara's lips quivered, and her look of suffering ought to have disarmed the man who was staring at her so insistently, but he was still possessed by a jealous devil. "Tell me"—and, leaning over the prie-dieu, he grasped her hands—"We may as well have it out now. Do you hear from him—from your husband, I mean? Do you write to him—sometimes?"

She shook her head, and Berwick, at last free to see the agony and surrender in the face into which he was looking down, and to which he suddenly felt his lips so near, was swept by an irresistible rush and mingling of feelings—remorse and fierce relief, shame and exultant joy.

"I think we ought to go downstairs,"—Arabella's clear voice broke into and echoed through the silent room.

Berwick straightened himself slowly. Before releasing Barbara's hands he kissed first one and then the other. As he did so, passion seemed to melt into tenderness. How fragile, how childish he had thought the fingers resting on his arm that first evening of their acquaintance! He remembered also the fluttering, the trembling of her ringless left hand when for a moment he had covered it with his own during that drive from Halnakeham to Chillingworth, when he had made so much—or was it so little?—of his opportunity.

The two walked down the gallery, towards O'Flaherty, who was still standing by the wood fire, and Arabella, who was putting out the candles with the rather disdainful thoroughness and care she gave to small household matters. Lord Bosworth's servants were old, like himself, and grew unmindful of their duties.

Berwick suddenly left Mrs. Rebell's side, but not till he had reached the door did he turn round and say, "I am not coming down, for I have work to do, so good-night!" A moment after, he was gone, with no more formal leave-taking.

That night Barbara cried herself to sleep, but to her tears brought no relief—rather an added shame for the weakness which made them flow so bitterly. She felt overwhelmed by a great calamity—face to face with a situation out of which she must herself, unaided, find an issue.

She had asked so little of the shattered broken life which remained to her—only quietude and the placid enjoyment of a friendship which had come to her unsought, and in which there could be no danger, whatever Madame Sampiero or Mrs. Turke might think. Did not the feeling which bound her to James Berwick enjoy the tacit approval of such a woman as was Arabella Berwick? What else had made Miss Berwick say to her, as she had done, that her brother could never marry? Surely the words had been uttered with intention, to show Mrs. Rebell how desirable it was that he should have—friends?

Till to-night, love, to Barbara Rebell, had borne but two faces. The one, that of the radiant shadow-like figure, half cupid half angel, of her childhood and girlhood, was he who had played his happy part in the love affair of her father and mother, binding them the one to the other as she, Barbara, had seen them bound. It was this love—noble, selfless, unmaterial in its essence, or so she had thought—that lighted up Madame Sampiero's face when she spoke, as she sometimes did speak, in the same quivering breath, of Lord Bosworth and her little Julia.

Love's other face, that which she shuddered to know existed, had been revealed to her by Pedro Rebell. It was base, sensual, cunning, volatile, inconstant in its very essence, and yet, as Barbara knew, love after all—capable, for a fleeting moment, of ennobling those under its influence. Such, for instance, was love as understood by the coloured people, among whom she had spent these last years of her life, and with whose elementary joys and sorrows she had perforce sympathised.

Now, to-night, she realised that love could come in yet a third guise—nay, for the first time she saw that perhaps this was the only true love of them all, and that her first vision of the passion had been but its shadow. Some such feeling as that which now, she felt with terror, possessed her body as well as her soul, must have made her mother cling as she had clung, in no joyless way, to sombre, disgraced Richard Rebell.

Love again—warm, tender, passionate love—had linked together Lord Bosworth and Barbara Sampiero for so many years, and had found expression in their child. Thinking of those last two, Barbara lay and trembled. Bitter words of condemnation uttered by her father leapt from the storehouse of memory, as did the fact that her mother had once implied to her that but for Madame Sampiero, but for something—was it something wrong, or merely selfish and unwise which she had done?—Barbara's father might have returned in time to England and made some attempt to rehabilitate himself.

The maid who brought in her cup of tea in the morning laid a parcel down on Barbara's bed. It was a book wrapped in brown paper, and fully addressed to her with the superscription:—

> "Dear Mrs. Rebell,—Here is the book I promised to send you.
>
> "Yours truly,
> "James Berwick."

Some instinct made her wait till she was alone. Then, opening the parcel, she saw that, with the volume of Jacobite songs Berwick had indeed promised to give her, was a large envelope marked "private." From it she drew out slowly some twenty sheets or more, closely covered with the as yet unfamiliar writing of the man she loved. To the end of her life Barbara could have repeated portions of this, her first love letter, by heart, and yet, before going downstairs, she burnt each separate sheet.

Over the last she hesitated. Indeed, she cut out the three words, "my heart's darling." But the little gilt scissors had belonged to her mother—how would her mother have judged what she was now doing?—and the slip of paper went into the fire with the rest.

CHAPTER XVI.

"He smarteth most who hides his smart
And sues for no compassion."

RALEIGH.

"WOULD you mind taking me with you to church this morning? Miss Berwick tells me that her uncle won't be shocked."

When Mrs. Rebell made her request, Daniel O'Flaherty was walking up and down the small hall, waiting for the carriage in which he was to drive that Sunday morning to the nearest Roman Catholic chapel. He had shared with the two ladies a comparatively early breakfast, for the service he was to attend took place at ten.

"Yes, of course," he said, rather awkwardly, "I shall be very glad of your company, but I'm afraid you won't be comfortable, for Mass is said, it seems, in a little mission room." O'Flaherty had a vividly unpleasant recollection of the last time he had taken "a smart lady" to church. She had apparently expected to find a Notre Dame or Sistine Chapel in the wilds of Herefordshire, and she had been very much annoyed with the inartistic furnishings of the iron chapel. So it was that Mrs. Rebell's request fell disagreeably on his ear.

Barbara's whole soul was possessed with the desire of putting off the meeting with Berwick. How could she greet him before his sister? how could she behave as if last night—as if his soul-stirring, ardent letter, had not been? Berwick had written, among a hundred other contradictory things, "Everything shall go on as before. I will school myself to be content with the least you can give me." But even she knew that that was impossible, and she blessed the chance which had now come to her of escaping for a few hours the necessity of playing a part before Lord Bosworth and Arabella.

So absorbed was Barbara in her thoughts that she scarcely noticed Mr. Daman, when she crossed him on the broad staircase on her way to her room to get ready for her expedition. The old man, however, had seen the light from a large window beat straight on her absorbed face. For the first time Barbara reminded him of her father, of Richard Rebell, and the reminiscence was not pleasing. Pretty women, he said to himself rather crossly, should study their looks; they owed it to those about them. They ought not to get up too early in the morning and go racing upstairs! Why, it was now only half-past nine, and Mrs. Rebell had evidently already breakfasted. He himself was up at this unwonted hour because it was Sunday, and on Sunday everything should be done to spare the servants in a country house. Septimus Daman lived up to his own moral code much more completely than many of those who regarded him as a selfish old worldling could pretend to do. Still, he did not like to be baulked of innocent pleasures, and not least among them was that of having his tea poured out for him on Sunday morning by a pretty woman.

"Then you've breakfasted too?" Failing Barbara, Mr. Daman would have liked the company of Daniel O'Flaherty. "Oh, I forgot! of course you're going to your church"—a note of commiseration crept into the thin voice; the old Queen's Messenger belonged to a generation when an Irishman's religion was still the greatest of his disabilities.

"Yes, and I'm taking Mrs. Rebell with me." Septimus Daman's vested interest in Barbara amused the barrister.

"Are you indeed?" Old Septimus always went to church on Sunday, but he liked to have the duty sweetened by the presence of youth and beauty in the pew. "You never saw her mother, did you?"

"No. The Rebell Case took place some years before I came to London." It was not the first time Mr. Daman had asked the question, but O'Flaherty answered very patiently, and even added—also not for the first time—"She must have been an exceptionally beautiful and charming woman."

"Perfection, absolute perfection! Her daughter isn't a patch on her as to looks. I remember now the first time I saw Mrs. Richard Rebell I thought her the loveliest creature I'd ever set eyes upon. Her name was Adela Oglander, and people expected her to do uncommonly well for herself. Awful to think what she did do, eh? But Richard Rebell was a very taking fellow in those days. When I was a young man women were content to look—well, as Mrs. Richard Rebell looked! One doesn't see such pretty women now," Mr. Daman sighed, "I suppose our Mrs. Barbara lost her complexion in the West Indies. Those climates, so I've always understood, are damnation to the skin. Not that hers has roughened—eh, what? And she can still blush—a great thing that, almost a lost art!" he chuckled. "From what Bosworth tells me she had an awful time with the brute she married."

"Was he in the Army?"

O'Flaherty was vaguely interested. He and Mrs. Rebell had had a good deal of desultory talk, but she never alluded to her married life. Those years—he roughly guessed them to be from twenty to seven-and-twenty—seemed dropped out of her memory.

"Not that I ever heard of. He's always been a sugar planter, a descendant of a Rebell younger son who went out to the West Indies to make his fortune a hundred years ago. Poor Barbara Sampiero told me about it at the time of the marriage."

"And how long has Mrs. Rebell been a widow?"

"She's not a widow. Whatever gave you such an idea?" The old man shot a sudden shrewd look at the barrister; O'Flaherty's face expressed surprise, yes, and profound annoyance. Dear, dear, this was distinctly interesting!

Mr. Daman lowered his voice to a whisper, "Her husband's very much alive, but he's signed, so Bosworth tells me, some kind of document promising to leave her alone. Of course he keeps her fortune, such as it is, for she was married before this act which makes women, I understand, so very independent of their lords and masters. But that's rather a good thing, for it takes away his only reason for molesting her. Still, there'll be trouble with him, if, as I'm told, Madame Sampiero intends to leave her well off. Good Lord, what a business we all had with Napoleone Sampiero! He was a regular leech. Strange, isn't it, that both these poor dear women—each, observe, a Barbara Rebell—should make such a mess of their lives? However, in this case there's no *Bosworth* to complicate matters!"

O'Flaherty wheeled round, and looked hard at the old man, but Septimus Daman had spoken with no after-thought in his mind. He had come to the stage of life when old people are curiously unobservant, or perhaps it should be said, no longer capable of realising the proximity of passion.

Condemnation of James Berwick, who, it seemed to O'Flaherty, should remember the fact that he was under his sister's roof, and a certain pity for, and shrinking from Mrs. Rebell, the woman now sitting so silently by his side in the victoria, filled the barrister's mind. He was also aware of experiencing that species of bewilderment which brings with it the mortifying conviction that one has been excessively, inexcusably blind. O'Flaherty cast his mind back over the last week. That which he in his simplicity had taken for love,—love capable of inducing such a man as Berwick to make a great sacrifice,—was doubtless but the preliminary to one of those brief intrigues of which he heard so much in the world in which he now lived.

And Mrs. Rebell? He had really liked her—unconsciously thought the better of Arabella for having such a woman, one so gentle, kindly, unassuming, for her friend. He knew the tragic story of Richard Rebell, of his banishment from the pleasant world in which he had held so prominent a place; and Barbara had been the more interesting, the more worthy of respect in his eyes because she was in no sense ashamed of her parentage. Was it possible that she was one of those women—he had sometimes heard of them—who are said to possess every feminine virtue save that on which, as he, the Irish farmer's son, absolutely believed, all the others really depend?

O'Flaherty had seen a great deal of Mrs. Rebell; they had had more than one long talk together. Never had he met a woman who seemed to him more pure-minded in the very essence of her. And yet—well, the Irishman had seen—as indeed who could help seeing, save that self-centred and *naif* egoist, Septimus Daman?—that Barbara loved Berwick. The sight of these two, so absorbed in one another, had deeply moved the one who looked on, and quickened his own feeling for Arabella into life.

The barrister had envied Berwick the devotion of such a woman, thinking a fabulous fortune well forfeited in the winning of Barbara Rebell as companion on that mysterious, dangerous journey which men call life. Realising the kind of intimate sympathy which seemed to bind these two, O'Flaherty had recalled the phrase, "a marriage of true minds," and he had thought of all it would mean to

Berwick, even as regarded his public career, to have so conciliatory, so charming a creature by his side. Arabella Berwick, in spite of her many fine qualities and intellectual gifts, possessed neither the tact nor the self-effacement so essential to the fulfilment of the *rôle* of statesman's wife or sister.

And now O'Flaherty learned that all the time he had been thinking these things, Mrs. Rebell was well aware that there could be nothing permanent or avowable in her tie with Berwick; while Berwick, on his side, was playing the most delightful and absorbing of the great human games with dice so loaded that, come what might, he was bound to win. The barrister told himself that he had indeed been simple-minded to suppose that such a man as Arabella's brother would sacrifice to love the wealth which gave him an absolute and preeminent position among those he wished to lead. "A marriage of true minds?"—an ugly look came over the plain, strong face of the man sitting by Mrs. Rebell, and she, catching that look, wondered what hateful thought, or sudden physical discomfort, had brought it there.

But, when once he found himself kneeling in the humble little iron chapel, long habit acted on Daniel O'Flaherty's mind, cleared it of sordid images, made him think more charitable thoughts of the woman who crouched rather than knelt by his side, in what seemed a position of almost painful abasement. Poor Barbara Rebell! Mingling with the prayers he knew by heart, and which were, after all, one long supplication for mercy and forgiveness, came the slow conviction that she might not be deserving of so much condemnation as he had at first assumed. Perhaps she had come here, with him, to-day, to be out of the way of temptation, and not, as he had unkindly suspected, to satisfy an idle and not very healthy curiosity.

Busy as he had been last night in the music gallery with thoughts of his own self and Arabella, O'Flaherty had yet been aware that an eager colloquy was going on by the organ. He had heard Berwick's voice become urgent and imperious, and he had put down the other man's rather dramatic disappearance, and Mrs. Rebell's extreme quietude during the rest of the evening, to some lovers' quarrel between these two, who up to that time had required no such artificial stimulus to their passion. Perhaps what had taken place between them had been more tragic, for Mrs. Rebell looked to-day very unlike her gentle, composed self.

Barbara had risen from her knees, and sat apparently listening to the little sermon. The expression of her face suddenly recalled to Daniel O'Flaherty an evening in his life—that which had followed his parting from Arabella Berwick. He had been taken by friends to the play, and on leaving the theatre had found that his mind had retained absolutely nothing of what had gone on before him on the stage. Not to save his life could he have recalled a single scene, or even the most telling of the speeches to which he had been listening the last three hours. Doubtless he had then looked as Barbara looked now; and a feeling of great concern and infinite pity took the place of that which had filled his mind during the drive from Fletchings. But this new-born charity did not extend to Berwick; for him, O'Flaherty still felt nothing but condemnation.

They waited till the small congregation had streamed out, and then walked slowly down the little aisle. "You don't look fit to walk back. I expect I can easily get a carriage if you will wait a little while."

But Barbara answered with nervous decision, "I would much rather walk, in fact, I was about to ask you if you would mind going round by Chancton; it is scarcely out of our way, and I want to see Madame Sampiero."

"I beg you to send for me—to-day—home again. I am tired of being away from you! Oh! do not refuse, Marraine, to do as I ask——"

Barbara was kneeling by Madame Sampiero's couch, holding the stiff, trembling hands, gazing imploringly into the set face and the wide open eyes, now fixed on her with rather sad speculation and questioning.

"Why should I refuse? Have I not missed you? Ask McKirdy if we have not all missed you, child?"

The muffled tones were even less clear than usual, but Barbara gave a sigh, almost a sob, of relief. "You must insist on my coming back, at once,—at once, Marraine—or they will want to keep me! Some people are coming over to lunch to-morrow, and Miss Berwick will wish me to be there."

"Why go back at all?"

"I must go back. Someone is waiting for me outside." Madame Sampiero's eyelids flickered—"Oh, no, no! Marraine, not Mr. Berwick, but a Mr. O'Flaherty. Besides, they would all be so surprised if I were not to come back now. Send for me this afternoon."

She bent over and kissed her god-mother's hands. "How nice it is to be home again!" and her voice trembled, "What, darling Marraine? Was Lord Bosworth kind? Yes, indeed—more than good and kind! I have been very happy—very, very happy!" and then she turned away to hide the tears rushing to her eyes.

While waiting for Mrs. Rebell, Daniel O'Flaherty looked with great interest at the splendid old house before which he was pacing up and down. This, then, was Chancton Priory, the place belonging to the woman who some said had made, and others said had marred, Lord Bosworth's life.

The story had been widely known and discussed. Madame Sampiero had made a desperate and an unsuccessful effort to break her marriage to the Corsican adventurer whom she had married in a moment of headstrong, girlish folly; and the world, hers and Lord Bosworth's, had been loud in its sympathy. But for the fact that the ceremony had been solemnised according to French law, she would easily have obtained release.

For a while, all had gone fairly well. Each lived his and her own life; Madame Sampiero had acted as hostess to Lord Bosworth's friends, both at Chancton, and in her London house, for she was a wealthy woman, and all, save the very strait-laced, had condoned a situation which permitted the exercise of tolerant charity.

Then had come the sudden appearance on the scene of a child, of the little Julia concerning whose parentage scarcely any mystery was made, and the consequent withdrawal of that feminine countenance and support without which social life and influence are impossible in such a country as England.

O'Flaherty looked up at the mullioned windows sunk back in the grey stone; behind which of them lay the paralysed woman, now bereft of lover, of child, of the company of friends, of everything which made life worth living to such as she? Septimus Daman had talked of Madame Sampiero again and again during the last few days, and had apparently rejoiced in the thought that Mrs. Rebell was so devoted to the mistress of Chancton Priory. What a strange life the two women must lead here! The barrister looked round him consideringly. November is the sad month of our country year. Even the great cedars added to the stately melancholy of the deserted lawns, and leafless beeches.

Now, at last Mrs. Rebell was coming towards him from the porch; he saw that she looked, if not happier, more at peace than she had done before going into the Priory, yet her eyelids were swollen, and if victorious she seemed one whose victory has cost her dear.

As she led the way down the broad grass drive, she began to talk of indifferent matters, making what O'Flaherty felt was rather a pitiful, and yet a gallant attempt to speak of things which might interest him.

Suddenly they touched on politics, "My father," Barbara's face softened, became less mask-like, "cared so much about English politics. As a young man he actually stood for Parliament, for in those days Halnakeham had a member, but he was defeated. I have sometimes thought, since I have heard Mr. Berwick and Mr. Boringdon talk—I don't know if you have met Mr. Boringdon—how different everything might have been if my poor father had been elected. He only lost the seat by thirty votes."

When she mentioned Berwick, the colour had flooded her face, and O'Flaherty had looked away. "Oh yes, I've met Oliver Boringdon," he said quickly, and to give her time to recover herself he went on, "I remember him in the House. But I had the luck to get in again, and he was thrown out, at the last General Election. The two friends are an interesting contrast. I regard James Berwick as the typical Parliament man; not so Mr. Boringdon, who is much more the permanent official, the plodding civil servant—that was what he was originally, you know—and Berwick did him a bad turn in taking him away from that career and putting him into Parliament."

"But you do think well of Mr. Berwick? I mean, do you consider, as does his sister, that he has a great future before him?"

She looked at her companion in undisguised anxiety, and O'Flaherty felt rather touched by the confidence Barbara evidently reposed in his judgment.

"I think," he said—and he offered up a mental prayer that he might so speak as to help, not hinder, the woman by his side—"that James Berwick's future will depend on the way he shapes his life. Do not think me priggish—but the one thing that seems to me sure is that character still tells more than ability in English public life. Character and ability together are apt to prove irresistible."

"But what," asked Barbara in a low voice, "do you exactly mean by character?"

"I mean something which Oliver Boringdon possesses to a supreme degree—a number of qualities which together make it positively more difficult for a man to go wrong than to go right, especially in any matter affecting his honour or probity."

"Then—surely you regard Mr. Berwick as a man of character?"

O'Flaherty hesitated. The conversation was taking a strange turn, but he made up his mind to tell her the truth as far as he saw it. "I think," he said deliberately, "that it is very difficult for a man of great ability to be also a man of flawless character. He is probably tempted in a thousand ways which pass the less gifted nature by; on the other hand, his fate is much more in his own control. Berwick has come very well out of ordeals partly brought about by his own desire to succeed. Take his rather singular marriage."—the speaker looked straight before him—"Of course I well remember that episode in his life. Men marry every day for money, but Berwick conducted himself with propriety and dignity under extremely trying circumstances."

"Did you ever see her?"—there was a painful catch in Barbara's voice—"she was a friend, was she not, of Miss Berwick?"

"Hardly a friend—rather a worshipping acquaintance. No, I never saw Mrs. James Berwick. She was rather an invalid both before and after the marriage. I think she did a very wrong thing by her husband—one that may even yet have evil consequences. You are doubtless aware that in the event of Berwick's making a second marriage he loses the immense fortune his wife left to him."

"That, then, was what Miss Berwick meant when she said he could never marry." Barbara seemed to be speaking to herself, but the words fell on O'Flaherty's ear with an unpleasing significance. His mind made a sudden leap. Could Arabella be planning—oh! what a horrible suspicion concerning the woman he had once loved! But it came back again and again during the hour which followed. Had he not himself thought Miss Berwick was doing all in her power to throw her brother and Mrs. Rebell together?

He went on speaking, as if impelled to say what he really thought. "Well, such a thing as that is enough to test a man's character. From being a poor man, practically dependent on his uncle, Berwick became the owner of almost unlimited money, to the possession of which, however, was attached a clause which meant that in his case none of the normal conditions of a man's life could be fulfilled—no wife, no child, friendship with women perpetually open, as I know Berwick's more than once has been, to misconstruction."

"And yet other men—?" Barbara looked at him deprecatingly, "You yourself, Mr. O'Flaherty"—then she cried, "Forgive me! I have no right to say that to you!"

"Nay," he said, "I give you for the moment every right to say, to ask, what you like! I have no wife, no child, no home, Mrs. Rebell, because the woman I loved rejected me; and also because, though I have tried to like other women, I have failed. You see, it was not that I had made a mistake, such as men make every day, for she loved me too—that makes all the difference. She was in a different position to my own; I was very poor, and there was the further bar of my religion, even of my nationality"—he spoke with a certain difficulty. "At the time she acted as she thought best for both our sakes. But, whatever my personal experiences or motives for remaining unmarried may be, I have no doubt,—no doubt at all,—as to the general question. To my mind, James Berwick's friends must regret that he has never, apparently, been tempted to make the great sacrifice; and for my part, I hope the day will come when he will meet with a woman for whom he will think his fortune well lost, whom he will long to make his wife in a sense that the poor creature he married never was, and in whom he will see the future mother of his children." He paused, then added in a low voice, "In no other tie can such a man as he find permanent solace and satisfaction. If report speaks truly, he has more than once tried an alternative experiment."

He dared not look at her. They walked on in absolute silence.

At last she spoke, "Please say nothing of our walk round by Chancton Priory." And when, some hours later, there came a letter from Doctor McKirdy declaring that Madame Sampiero was not well, and longed for Mrs. Rebell's presence, Daniel O'Flaherty thought he understood. A pang of miserable self-reproach struck his heart and conscience. What right had he to have put this woman to the torture—to take on himself the part of Providence?

After they had all seen Barbara off, after he had noted her very quiet but determined rejection of Berwick's company on the way to Chancton Priory, Daniel O'Flaherty was in no mood to go for the walk to which Miss Berwick had been looking forward all that afternoon.

CHAPTER XVII.

"Look in my face: my name is Might-have-been,
And I am also called No-more, Too-late, Farewell."

DANTE GABRIEL ROSSETTI.

THE days following Barbara's return to Chancton Priory went slowly by, and she received no sign, no word from Berwick. She had felt quite sure that he would come—if not that same evening of her leaving Fletchings, then the next morning; if not in the morning, then in the afternoon.

During those days she went through every phase of feeling. She learnt the lesson most human beings learn at some time of their lives—how to listen without appearing to do so for the sounds denoting arrival, how to hunger for the sound of a voice which to the listener brings happiness, however indifferently these same accents fall on the ears of others. She schooled herself not to flinch when the days went by bringing no successor to that letter in which Berwick had promised her so much more than she had ever asked of him.

Even in the midst of her restless self-questioning and unhappiness, she was touched and pleased at the gladness with which she had been welcomed home again by Madame Sampiero, and even by Doctor McKirdy. It seemed strange that neither of them spoke of the man who now so wholly occupied her thoughts; no one, with the exception perhaps of his old nurse, noted Berwick's absence, or seemed to find it untoward. Barbara had at first been nervously afraid that Madame Sampiero would make some allusion to the few moments they had spent together that Sunday morning, that she would perhaps ask her what had induced her eager wish to leave Fletchings; but no such word was said, and Barbara could not even discover whether Doctor McKirdy was aware that her sudden return to the Priory had been entirely voluntary.

And then, as the short winter days seemed to drag themselves along, Mrs. Rebell, almost in spite of herself, again began to see a great deal of Oliver Boringdon. There was something in his matter-of-fact eagerness for her society which soothed her sore heart; her manner to him became very gracious, more what it had been before Berwick had come into her life; and again she found herself taking the young man's part with Madame Sampiero and the old Scotchman. Boringdon soon felt as happy as it was in his nature to be. He told himself he had been a jealous fool, for Barbara spoke very little of her visit to Fletchings, and not at all of Berwick; perhaps she had seen him when there at a disadvantage.

As Oliver happened to know, Berwick had left Sussex; he was now in London, and doubtless they would none of them see anything of him till Easter. The young man took the trouble to go down to the Grange and tell Mrs. Kemp that he had been mistaken in that matter of which he had spoken to her. He begged her, rather shamefacedly, to forget what he had said. Lucy's mother heard him in silence, but she did not repeat her call on Mrs. Rebell. So it was that during those days which were so full of dull wretchedness and suspense to Barbara Rebell, Oliver Boringdon also went through a mental crisis of his own, the upshot of which was that he wrote a long and explicit letter to Andrew Johnstone.

They were both men to whom ambiguous situations were utterly alien. Boringdon told himself that Johnstone might not understand, or might understand and not approve, his personal reason for interference; but Johnstone would certainly agree that Mrs. Rebell's present position was intolerable from every point of view, and that some effort should be made to set her legally free from such a man as was this Pedro Rebell. Once Barbara was free,—Oliver thrust back the leaping rapture of the thought—

After much deliberation he had added, as a postscript: "I have no objection to your showing this letter to Grace."

Doctor McKirdy watched Mrs. Rebell very narrowly during these same early December days, and as he did so he became full of wrath against James Berwick. He and Madame Sampiero had few secrets from one another. The old Scotchman had heard of Barbara's sudden Sunday morning appearance at the Priory, and of her appeal—was it for protection against herself? He made up his mind that she and Berwick must have had, if not a quarrel, then one of those encounters which leave deeper marks on the combatants than mere quarrels are apt to do.

More than once the rough old fellow was strongly tempted to say to her: "If you wish to make yourself ill, you are just going the way to do it!" but Mrs. Rebell's determination to go on as usual, to allow no one to divine the state of her mind, aroused his unwilling admiration, nay more, his sympathy. He had known, so he told himself, what it was to feel as Barbara felt now, but in his case jealousy, an agony of jealousy, had been added to his other torments, and shame too for the futility of it all.

Nine days after Barbara had left Fletchings she received a letter from Berwick. It bore the London postmark, but was dated the evening of the day they had parted,—of that day when she had successfully eluded his desire, his determination, to see her alone.

A certain savagery of anger, hurt pride, over-mastering passion breathed in the few lines of the short note which began abruptly, "I have no wish to force my presence on you," and ended "Under the circumstances perhaps it were better that we should not meet for a while." Something had been added, and then erased; most women would have tried to find out what that hasty scrawl concealed, but if it hid some kinder sentiment the writer, before despatching his missive, had repented, and to Barbara the fact that he did not wish her to read what he had added was enough to prevent her trying to do so.

With deep trouble and self-reproach she told herself that perhaps she had been wrong in taking to flight—nay, more, that she had surely owed Berwick an explanation. No wonder he was hurt and angry! And he would never know, that was the pity of it, that it was of herself she had been afraid—

Then those about her suddenly began to tell Mrs. Rebell that which would have made such a difference before the arrival of Berwick's letter. "I suppose you know that James Berwick is in London? He was sent for suddenly," and Boringdon mentioned the name of the statesman who had been Prime Minister when Berwick held office.

"Has he been gone long?"—Barbara's voice sounded indifferent.

"Yes, he seems to have had a wire on a Sunday, on the day you came back from Fletchings."

And Boringdon had never told her this all-important fact! Barbara felt a sudden secret resentment against the young man. So it had lain with him to spare her those days of utter wretchedness; of perpetually waiting for one whom she believed to be in the near neighbourhood; nay more, those moments of sick anxiety, for at times she had feared that Berwick might be ill, physically unable to leave Fletchings or Chillingworth. But this most unreasonable resentment against Oliver she kept in her own heart.

The next to speak to her of Berwick had been Mrs. Turke. "So our Mr. Berwick's in London? But he'll be back soon, for he hasn't taken Dean with him. Sometimes months go by without our seeing the dear lad, and then all in a minute he's here again. That's the way with gentlemen; you never know when you have 'em!" And she had given Barbara a quick, meaning look, as if the remark had a double application.

Then came a day, the 8th of December, which Mrs. Rebell became aware was not like other days. For the first time since she had been at the Priory Madame Sampiero inquired as to the day of the month. Doctor McKirdy was more odd, more abrupt even than usual, and she saw him turn Boringdon unceremoniously from the door with the snarling intimation that Madame Sampiero did not wish to-day to be troubled with business matters. Mrs. Turke also was more mysterious, less talkative than usual; she went about her own quarters sighing and muttering to herself.

A sudden suspicion came into Barbara's heart; could it be that James Berwick was coming back, that they expected him to-day, and that none of them liked to tell her? If so, how wise of McKirdy to have sent away Oliver Boringdon! But then cold reason declared that if such was indeed the case, to make so great a mystery of the matter would be an insult to her, surely the last thing that any of them, with the exception perhaps of the old housekeeper, would dare to do?

Still, when at last, late in the morning, she was sent for by Doctor McKirdy, and informed curtly that someone was waiting for her in the grass walk, she made no doubt of who it could be. In her passion of relief, in her desire to bear herself well, to return, if it might be possible, to the old ideal terms on which she and

Berwick had been before he had been seized with what she to herself now characterised as a passing madness, Barbara hardly noticed how moved, how unlike himself the old Scotchman seemed to be, and how, again and again, he opened his lips as if to tell her something which native prudence thrust back into his heart.

So great, so overwhelming was Barbara's disappointment when she saw that the man leaning on the iron gate leading to the now leafless rosery was Lord Bosworth, and not James Berwick, that she had much ado to prevent herself from bursting into tears. But she saw the massive figure before she herself was seen, and so was able to make a determined effort to conceal both her bitter deception, and also her great surprise at finding him there.

"As you are doubtless aware," Lord Bosworth began abruptly, "I come here three or four times a year, and McKirdy is good enough to arrange that on those occasions I can visit my child's grave without fear of interruption. I ventured to ask that you might be told that I wished to see you here, because I have a request to make you—"

He hesitated, and with eyes cast down began tracing with the heavy stick he bore in his hand imaginary geometrical patterns on the turf.

"If my daughter Julia had lived, she would have been seventeen to-day, and so it seemed to me—perhaps I was wrong—to be a good opportunity to make another effort to soften Barbara's heart." He put his hand on Mrs. Rebell's shoulder, and smiled rather strangely as he quickly added, "You understand? I mean my own poor Barbara's heart, not that of this kind young Barbara, who I am hoping will intercede for me, on whom I am counting to help me in this matter. I do not know how far I should be justified in letting her know what is undoubtedly the truth, namely, that I have not very long to live. McKirdy absolutely refuses to tell her; but perhaps, if she knew this fact, it would alter her feeling, and make her more willing to consider the question of—of—our marriage."

And then, as Barbara started and looked at him attentively, he went on slowly, and with a quiet dignity which moved his listener deeply: "Of course you know our story? Sometimes I think there is no one in the whole world who does not know it. There were years, especially after the birth of our little Julia, when I think I may say we both had marriage on the brain. And then, when at last Barbara was free, when Napoleone Sampiero"—his face contracted when he uttered the name—"was dead, she would not hear of it. She seemed to think—perhaps at the time it was natural she should do so—that the death of our poor child had been a judgment on us both. But now, after all these years, I think she might do as I ask. I even think—perhaps you might put that to her—that she owes me something. No husband was ever more devoted to a wife than I have been to her. Now, and Heaven knows how many years it is since we last met, I think of her constantly. She is there!—there!" He struck his breast, then went on more calmly: "My niece knows my wishes, there would be no trouble with her; and as for my nephew, James Berwick, you know how attached he has always been to Barbara. Why, I'm told he's much more here now than he is at Chillingworth!"

He turned abruptly, and they walked slowly, side by side, down the broad grass path till there came a spot where it became merged in the road under the beeches. Here he stopped her.

"You are surely not going to walk back all the way alone!" she cried, for she saw with emotion that he looked older even in the few days which had elapsed since he had bade her good-bye at Fletchings.

"No, the carriage is waiting for me down there. I only walked up through the park. Then I have your promise to speak to Madame Sampiero?" he held her hand, and looked down with peculiar earnestness into her face. As she bent her head, he added, "You'll let me have word when you can? Of course, if she's still of the same mind, I'll not trouble her." He walked on, and then turned suddenly back and grasped Barbara's hand once more. "Better not use the health argument," he said, "doctors do make mistakes—an old friend of mine married his cook on, as he thought, his death-bed, and then got quite well again!" He smiled at her rather deprecatingly, "I know my cause is in good hands," and she watched him walk with heavy, deliberate steps down the leaf-strewn way.

For the first time Barbara drew the parallel those about her had so often drawn. Was James Berwick capable of such constancy, of such long devotion as his uncle had shown? Something whispered yes; but even if so, how would that affect her, how would that make her conduct less reprehensible, were she ever to fall short of what had been her own mother's standard?

Before her interview with Lord Bosworth, it had seemed to Barbara that she constantly spent long hours alone with her god-mother; but, after that memorable eighth of December, she felt as if those about Madame Sampiero had entered into a conspiracy to prevent her being ever left alone with her god-mother for more than a very few moments at a time. Doctor McKirdy suddenly decided to have his house repapered, and he accordingly moved himself bodily over to the Priory, where Barbara could not complain of his constant presence in "Madam's" room, for he always found something to amuse or interest his patient.

Twice he spoke to Barbara of Lord Bosworth, each time with strange bitterness and dislike. "No doubt his lordship was after seeing Madam?" and, as Barbara hesitated: "Fine I knew it!—but he might just as well go and kill her outright. I've had to tell him so again and again"—

Barbara kept her own counsel, but she could not resist the question, "Then he comes often?"

"Often?—that he does not! He's never been one to put himself out, he's far too high! He just sends for me over to Fletchings, and I just go, though I've felt more than once minded to tell him that I'm not his servant. Madam's determined that he shall never see her as she is now, and who can blame her? Not I, certainly! Besides, he hasn't a bit of right to insist on such a thing." And he looked fiercely at Barbara as he spoke, as if daring her to contradict him.

"I think he has a right," she said in a low tone—then with more courage, "Of course he has a right, Doctor McKirdy! I'm sure if my god-mother could see Lord Bosworth, could hear him——" her voice broke, and she bit her lip, sorry at having said so much.

But the interview with Madame Sampiero's old friend, and the little encounters with Doctor McKirdy, did Barbara good. They forced her to think of something else than of herself, of another man than James Berwick; and at last she made up her mind that she would tell her god-mother she wished to speak to her without this dread of constant, futile interruption. At once her wish was granted, for the paralysed mistress of the Priory could always ensure privacy when she chose.

But, alas for Barbara, the result of the painful talk was not what she had perhaps been vain enough to think herself capable of achieving on behalf of Lord Bosworth: indeed, for a moment she had been really frightened, on the point of calling Doctor McKirdy, so terrible, so physically injurious had been Madame Sampiero's agitation.

"I cannot see him! He must not see me in this state—he should not ask it of me." Such, Mrs. Rebell had divined, were the words her god-mother struggled over and over again to utter. "Marriage?"—a lightning flash of horror, revolt, bitter sarcasm, had illumined for a moment the paralysed woman's face. Then, softening, she had added words signifying that she was not angry, that she forgave—Barbara!

Very sadly, with a heart full of pain at the disappointment she knew she was about to inflict, Mrs. Rebell wrote to Lord Bosworth. She softened the refusal she had to convey by telling, with tenderness and simplicity, how much the man to whom she was writing seemed to be ever in her god-mother's thoughts, how often Madame Sampiero spoke of him, how eagerly she had cross-questioned her god-daughter as to the days Barbara had spent at Fletchings and her conversations with her host.

Mrs. Rebell wrote this difficult letter in the drawing-room, sitting at the beautiful bureau which had been the gift of the man to whom she was writing, and which even now contained hundreds of his letters. Suddenly, and while she was hesitating as to how she should sign herself, James Berwick walked, unannounced, into the room, coming so quietly that for a moment he stood looking at Barbara before she herself became aware that he was there. So had Barbara looked, on that first evening he had seen her; but then he had been outside the window and gazing at the woman bending over the bureau with cool, critical eyes.

Now, he was aware of nothing, save that the hunger of his eyes was appeased, and that he had come to eat humble pie and make his peace, for in his case that prescription which is said to be so excellent for lovers—absence—had only made him feel, more than he had done before, that he could not and would not live without her.

An hour later Berwick was gone, as Barbara believed in all sincerity, for ever. He knew better, but even he felt inclined to try another dose of that absence, of that absorption in the business that he loved, to compel forgetfulness. It was clear—so he told himself when rushing back to Chillingworth through the December night air—it was clear that what this woman wanted was a stone image, not a man, for her friend!

For a while, perhaps for half the time he had been with her, standing by the mantel-piece while she sat two or three yards off, there had been a truce of God. Berwick had thought out a certain line of action, and he tried to be, as some hidden instinct told him she wished to see him, once more the tender, self-less, sexless friend. He even brought his lips to mutter something like a prayer for forgiveness, and the tears came into her eyes as with uplifted hand she checked the words. Poor Barbara! She was so divinely happy, for his mere presence satisfied her heart. She had never known him quite so gentle, quite so submissive, as to-day. So glad had she been to see him that for a moment she had felt tempted to show him how welcome he was! But he had chosen,—and she was deeply grateful to him for this—to behave as if he had only parted from her the day before. Fletchings, all that happened there, was to be as if it had not been—as if the scene in the music gallery had been blotted out from their memories.

Then came an allusion on his part to his forthcoming visit to Scotland, and to the invitation which he knew his sister had been at some pains to procure for Mrs. Rebell, and which Barbara would receive the next morning.

"I cannot accept it; it is very kind of Miss Berwick, but how could I leave my god-mother again so soon?"

"Is that the only reason?" he said, and she heard with beating heart the under-current of anger, of suppressed feeling in his voice. "If so, I am sure I can make it all right. It would only be ten days, and Madame Sampiero would like you to meet the people who will be there. But perhaps"—he came nearer and stood glowering down at her—"perhaps that is not your only reason!"

And Barbara, looking up at him with beseeching eyes, shook her head.

"Do you mean"—Berwick spoke so quietly that his tone deceived her, and made her think him in amicable agreement with herself—"Do you mean that you do not wish to find yourself again under the same roof with me? Did what happened at Fletchings make that difference?"

She hesitated most painfully. "I have been very unhappy," she whispered at last, "I know we have both regretted——"

"By God, I have regretted nothing—excepting your coldness!" He grasped her hands not over-gently, and the look came into his eyes which had come there in the music room at Fletchings. "Do you wish us to go back to coldly-measured friendship?" Then he bent down and gathered her into his arms, even now not daring to kiss her. "Tell me," he said with sudden gentleness, "am I—am I—disagreeable to you, my dearest? I shall not be angry if you say yes." And Barbara, lying trembling, and as he thought inertly, unresponsively, in his arms, found the courage to answer, "I do care—but not as you wish me to do. Why cannot we go back to where we were?"

On hearing the whispered words he quickly released her, and, turning, made his way to the door. Barbara, for an agonised moment, nearly called out to him to come back and learn from her arms—her lips—how untrue were the words which were driving him away.

But in a moment, or so it seemed to her, he had thrust her from him and had gone, hastening down the great hall, and out through the porch into the air.

By the morning she had taught herself to think it was better he should never come back, for never would she find the strength to send him away again as she had done last night.

CHAPTER XVIII.

"Nay, but the maddest gambler throws his heart."

George Meredith.

"L'orgueil, remède souverain, qui n'est pas à l'usage des âmes tendres."

Stendhal.

The pretty Breton legend setting forth that, during the night, angels take sanctuary from evil spirits in the neighbourhood of sleeping maidens, often came to Mrs. Kemp's mind when she said good-night to Lucy. There was something very virginal, very peaceful and bright, in the girl's room, of which the window overlooked the paddock of the Grange, the walled kitchen garden of the Priory, and beyond that a splendid stretch of meadow land and beechwood.

Small low-shelved mahogany bookshelves, put together at a time of the world's history when women's hands were considered too fragile and delicate to hold heavy volumes, made squares of dark colour against the blue walls. Lucy Kemp had always been a reader, both as child and as girl. Here were all her old books, from that familiar and yet rather ill-assorted trio, "The Fairchild Family," "The Swiss Family Robinson," and "The Little Duke," to "Queechy," "Wives and Daughters," and "The Heir of Redclyffe," for their owner's upbringing had been essentially old-fashioned.

Lucy lay back in the dreamless sleep of girlhood. It was a cold January morning, and the embers of last night's fire still slumbered in the grate. Suddenly there broke on the intense stillness the rhythmical sound of pebbles being thrown with careful, sure aim against the window, open some inches from the top. The sleeper stirred uneasily, but she slept on till a small stone, aimed higher than most of those which had preceded it, fell into the room. Then Lucy Kemp woke with a great start and sat up in bed listening.

Yes, there could be no doubt about it, someone was standing in the paddock below trying to attract her attention! She got up, wrapped something round her, and then lifted the window-sash. In the dim light she saw a man standing just below, and Boringdon's hoarse, quick tones floated up to her.

"Lucy—Miss Kemp! Would you ask your mother if she could come to the Priory as soon as possible? There's been an accident there—a fire—and I fear Mrs. Rebell has been badly burnt."

His voice filled Lucy with varying feelings—joy that he had instinctively turned to the Grange for help, horror and concern at what he had come to tell.

"Mother's away," she cried in a troubled tone. "She and father have gone over to Berechurch for three nights. Should I be of any use? I shouldn't be a moment getting ready."

In less than ten minutes she joined him, and together they hastened through a seldom opened door giving access from the garden of the Grange into the Priory Park. Soon Oliver was hurrying her up the path, walking so quickly that she could scarcely keep up with him, towards the great silent mass of building the top windows of which, those which lay half hidden by the Tudor stone balcony, were now strangely lit up, forming a coronal of light to the house beneath.

"What happened?" she asked breathlessly.

"It's impossible to say what happened," Boringdon spoke in sharp preoccupied tones, "Mrs. Rebell seems to have been reading in bed and to have set fire to a curtain. She behaved, as she always does, with great good sense, and she and McGregor—heaven knows how—managed to put out the flames; not, however, before the fire had spread into the sitting-room next her bedroom. McKirdy, it seems, has always insisted that there should be buckets of water ready on every landing." Oliver would have scorned to defraud his enemy of his due. "When the whole thing was over, then they all—that stupid old Mrs. Turke and the maids—saw that she was badly burnt!"

The speaker's voice altered; he paused for a moment, and then continued, "They sent for McKirdy, who, as bad luck would have it, went back to his own house last week, and found him away, for he's been helping that Scotch doctor at Halnakeham with a bad case. Then they came on to me. Even now they're like a pack of frightened sheep! Madame Sampiero knows nothing of what has happened, and Mrs. Rebell is extremely anxious that her god-mother should not be agitated—why, she actually wanted to go down herself to tell her that everything was all right."

Lucy listened in silence. How Oliver cared, how dreadfully he cared! was the thought which would thrust itself into the girl's mind. "Is Mrs. Rebell very badly hurt?" she asked. "Oh! I wish that mother was here. Have you sent for another doctor?"

"I don't know how far she is hurt," he muttered, "her arm and shoulder, some of her hair—" then, more firmly, "No, she won't let me send for anyone but McKirdy. Besides, by the time we could get a man over from Halnakeham, he would certainly be back. But it will be everything to her to have you there, if only to keep order among the frightened, hysterical women."

Lucy had never before been inside Chancton Priory; and now, filled though she was by very varying emotions, she yet gazed about her, when passing through into the great hall, with feelings of deep interest and curiosity: it looked vast, cavernous, awe-inspiring in the early morning light.

A moment later they were hastening up the corner staircase. At the first landing, they were stopped by Madame Sampiero's French maid, who put a claw-like hand on Boringdon's arm—"Do come in and see my mistress, Sir. She divines something, and we cannot calm her."

Boringdon hesitated, then he turned to Lucy.

"I must go," he said, "I promised I would. You go on straight upstairs, as far as you can go; once there you will be sure to find someone to show you the way to the room where we have put Mrs. Rebell." And the girl went on alone, groping her way up the dark, to her they seemed the interminable, stairs.

An amazing figure—Mrs. Turke in *déshabillé*—awaited Lucy on the top landing, and greeted her with considerable circumstance.

"The young lady from the Grange, I do declare! A sad day for your first visit to the Priory, missy! But la, never mind. I've often seen you, you and your dear papa, and I read all about him in a book I've got. What a brave gentleman! But reading about it gave me the shivers, that it did—I would like to see that Victoria Cross of his! So Mr. Boringdon thinks you may be of use to Mrs. Rebell? Well, miss, I'll take you in to her. But she's made us all go away and leave her—she says she'd rather be alone to wait for the doctor."

Mrs. Turke preceded Lucy down the passage, and finally opened the door of a pretty, old-fashioned bedroom; the girl went in timidly and then gave a sigh of relief; the woman whom Oliver Boringdon had described as having been "badly burnt" was sitting up in a large armchair. She was wrapped in some kind of ample white dressing-gown, and a large piece of wadding had been clumsily attached to her left arm, concealing the left side of her face and hair.

Mrs. Rebell's eyes were fixed eagerly on the door through which Lucy had just come in. She did not show any surprise at seeing the girl, but at once began talking to her eagerly; and as she did so Lucy saw that she was shivering, for the room was very cold. A fire was laid in the grate, but evidently no one had thought of lighting it. Three candles, placed on the narrow mantel-piece, threw a bright light on as much of Barbara's face as Lucy could see. Her cheeks were red, her dark eyes bright, with excitement.

"It is kind of you to have come," she said. "Mr. Boringdon told me he would fetch your mother. I suppose Doctor McKirdy will be here soon? Has Mr. Boringdon gone to fetch him?"

"No," Lucy looked at her doubtfully; was it possible that anyone who looked as Mrs. Rebell did now, so excited, so—so strangely beautiful, could be really hurt, in pain? "He has gone to tell Madame Sampiero that all danger is over, that there is nothing more to fear."

A look of great anxiety crossed Barbara's face. "My god-mother is very brave. I do not think she will give much thought to the fire, but I hope he will tell her that I am not really hurt. Perhaps, after Doctor McKirdy has come, I can go down, and show her that there is really nothing the matter."

As she spoke, she winced. "Are you much hurt?" asked Lucy in a low voice, and her shrinking eyes again glanced at the sheet of wadding which wholly concealed Mrs. Rebell's arm, left breast, and one side of her head.

Barbara looked at her rather piteously. "I don't know," she said; "It hurt dreadfully at first, but now I feel nothing, only a slight pricking sensation." She repeated, "It hurt dreadfully till they fetched Mr. Boringdon, and then he found—I don't know where or how—the oil and wadding, which he made poor old Mrs. Turke put on. He was so good and kind!" She smiled at the girl, a friendly smile, and the look in her eyes brought a burning blush to Lucy's cheeks.

There was a pause; then Lucy, having taken off her hat and jacket, lighted the fire.

"Miss Kemp," Barbara's voice sank to a whisper, "I want you to do something for me. That fire which you have so kindly lighted has made me think of it. Will you go into my room, two doors from here, and bring me a packet of letters you will find in my dressing-table drawer? The drawer is locked, but the key is in my purse. When you have brought it, I want you to burn the letters, here, before me," and as Lucy was turning to obey her, she added, "Take one of the candles. Mr. Boringdon said the two rooms were to be left exactly as they are, and everything must be dripping with water, and in fearful confusion."

Lucy never forgot her little expedition down the dark passage, and the strange scene which met her eyes in the two rooms which had evidently been, till that night, as neat, as delicately clean, as was her own at the Grange. Well was it for poor Barbara that she had so few personal treasures. But the dressing-table had escaped injury save from the water, which in the bedroom had actually done more harm than the fire.

When she got back into the room where Mrs. Rebell was sitting, it seemed to Lucy that Barbara had changed in the short interval—that she looked, not well, as she had done when Lucy had first seen her half an hour before, but very, very ill. The colour now lay in patches on her cheek, and she watched with growing feverishness the burning of the few letters, from each of which, as she put it in the bright crackling fire, Lucy averted her eyes, a fact which Mrs. Rebell, in spite of her increasing dizziness and pain, saw and was grateful for.

"Miss Kemp," the speaker's voice was very low, "come here, close to me. Someone may come in, and I am feeling so strange— —Perhaps I may forget what I want to tell you. You know Mr. Berwick?" Lucy was kneeling down by the arm-chair, and Barbara put her right hand on the girl's slight shoulder—"But of course you do, I was forgetting the ball— —Why, he danced with you. If I die, only if I die, promise me— —" an agonised look came into the dark eyes—

"I promise," said Lucy steadily; "only if you die— —"

"If I die, you are to tell him that I cared as he wished me to care,—that when I sent him away, and in the letters I have written to him since, I said what was not true— —"

Lucy felt the burning hand laid on her shoulder press more heavily: "No one else must ever know, but you promise that you will tell him— —"

"I promise," said Lucy again. "I will tell him exactly what you have told me, and no one else shall ever know."

A slight noise made her look round. Doctor McKirdy stood in the doorway. He was bare-headed, but he still wore the great coat in which he had driven from Halnakeham. He was pale, his plain face set in a watchful, alert grimace, as his eyes took in every detail of the scene, of the room before him.

Barbara gave a cry—or was it a moan?—of relief. He turned and slipped the bolt in the door. "Time for talking secrets will come next week," then he took off his great coat, washed his hands—with a gruff word of commendation at the fact that there were water, soap, a towel, in what had been a disused room—turned up his sleeves, and bade Lucy stand aside.

"Now," he said, quickly, "would ye rather go away, Miss Lucy? If yes, there's the door!"

"Can I help you?" Lucy was very pale; she felt sick, a little faint.

"If ye were ye're mother, I should say *yes*——"

"Then I'll stay," said Lucy.

"'Twould be an ill thing if such a brave pair had produced a chicken-livered lass, eh?"

He did not speak again till everything there was to see had been seen, till everything there was to do had been done; it seemed a very long business to Lucy, and by the time the doctor had finished tears were rolling down her face. How could she have thought that perhaps Mrs. Rebell was not much hurt after all? "Now ye're just to have a good sip of that brandy ye've been giving Mrs. Rebell. I'm well pleased with ye both!" And when Lucy shook her head, he gave her such a look that she hastened to obey him, and suddenly felt a flash of sympathy for drunkards. How wonderful that a few spoonfuls of this horrid stuff should check her wish to cry, and make her feel sensible again!

As Doctor McKirdy unceremoniously signified that he could dispense with her presence, as he unlocked the door for her to pass through, something in Lucy's face made him follow her, unwillingly, into the passage. "What is it?" he said sharply.

"Oh, Doctor McKirdy! Do you think she will die?"

"Die? Are ye mad, my poor lass? There's no question of such a thing. She's more likely to die o' cold than anything else! Now go downstairs and send your fine friend Mr. Boringdon and McGregor this way. We've got to move her to the Queen's Room. There have been big fires there all this week—regard for the furniture, the apple of Mrs. Turke's eye, I said they were to get it ready—but we shall have a business getting her down there."

The long, painful progress down the winding staircase was safely over. Barbara was comfortably settled in the great square canopied bed, where, if tradition could be believed, Queen Elizabeth and her less magnificent successor had both, at intervals of fifty years, reposed. Madame Sampiero's Scotch attendant was installed as nurse, and there was nothing left for Lucy Kemp to do but to go home to her solitary breakfast at the Grange. Boringdon, after having done his part, and a very useful one, in lifting and carrying Mrs. Rebell down the two flights, had retreated into the broad corridor, and was walking up and down waiting—he himself hardly knew for what.

But Doctor McKirdy had quite made up his mind as to the next thing to be done. "Now then, you must just take Miss Kemp home again, and I charge you to see that she has a good breakfast! Take her down through the Park. The village will be a buzzing wasps' nest by this time; half of them seem to think—so Mrs. Turke's just told me—that we're all burnt to cinders! You just stay with the poor lass as long as you can, and don't let Miss Vipen or any other havering woman get at her to be asking her useless questions. If I want you I'll send to the Grange."

And so it was to Doctor McKirdy that Lucy owed the happy, peaceful hours spent by her that morning. Boringdon had dreaded the going back to the Cottage, to his mother's excited questionings and reflections, to her annoyance that he had gone to the Grange, rather than to her, for help. He knew he would have to tell her everything. She was not a woman from whom it was possible to conceal very much, and in the long run she always got at the truth, but just now it was much to be able to put off his return home.

Dear Lucy! How good, how sensible, how *quiet* she had been! She stumbled over the porch flag-stone, and he drew her arm through his. So together they walked down to the Grange. Oliver had never before breakfasted with the Kemps; how comfortable, how homely everything was! The eggs and bacon seemed crisper and fresher, also better, than those ever eaten at the Cottage; the tea poured out by Lucy was certainly infinitely nicer—not for a moment would Oliver have admitted that this was owing to the fact of its being a shilling a pound dearer than that made by his mother!

Each tacitly agreed not to speak of all that had just happened at the Priory. They talked of all sorts of other things. Lucy heard with startled interest that Oliver was thinking very seriously of giving up his land agency, and of going back, if it were in any way possible, to London. What had become the great central desire of his life must never be mentioned to any human being, not even to his dear friend Lucy, till its realisation was possible—legally possible. But even to talk of his plans, as he was now doing, was a comfort; his present listener, unlike his mother, always seemed to understand his point of view, and to realise why he had altered his mind without his being compelled to go into tiresome explanations.

After to-day Lucy and Mrs. Rebell would surely become friends. Even within the last few days Barbara had said to him, "I should like to see more of Miss Kemp. It was a pity she and her mother called when I was away." He liked to think of these two in juxtaposition. If the thought of life without Barbara was intolerable, not indeed to be considered,—once she was free from that West Indian brute, his great love must, in the long run, win return,—the thought of existence with no Lucy Kemp as friend was distinctly painful. He, Barbara, and Lucy, would all be happy; and then, not yet, but in some years to come, for she was still so young, his and Barbara's friend would marry some good honest fellow—not Laxton, no, but such a man as he himself had been till Mrs. Rebell came to the Priory, one to whom Lucy's fortune would be useful in promoting a public career.

At last, about twelve, he reluctantly rose, and Lucy went with him to the door. Suddenly it struck him that she looked very tired, "Lucy," he exclaimed—they had just said good-bye, but he still held her hand—"promise me that you will rest all this afternoon. Perhaps you would be wiser to go to bed, and then no one—not even Miss Vipen—can come and trouble you!" He spoke with his usual friendly—one of those near and dear to Lucy would have described it as priggish—air of authority. She drew away her hand, and laughed nervously,—but he again repeated, "Please promise me that you will have a good rest."

"I promise," said Lucy.

"I promise"—Lucy, sleeping restlessly through the winter afternoon and evening, found herself repeating the two words again and again. What had she promised? That she would rest. Well, she was fulfilling that promise. As soon as Oliver had left her, she had gone up, full of measureless lassitude, to bed. Then she would wake with a start to hear Mrs. Rebell's imploring voice, "Promise—if I die—" and then, "No one must know—"

How would Mr. Berwick take the piteous message? Lucy had always felt afraid of him, but she had promised—

Then came the comforting recollection of Doctor McKirdy's gruff whisper. Oh no, poor Mrs. Rebell was not going to die, and she, Lucy, would never have to redeem her promise. But if Mrs. Rebell cared for Mr. Berwick, would not Oliver be unhappy?

And Lucy, sitting up in bed, pushed her fair hair off her hot forehead. The whole thing seemed so unreal! Barbara Rebell was not free to care for anyone. Of course there were horrid women in the world who cared for other people than their own husbands, though Lucy had never met any of them, but she knew they existed. But those were the sort of women who rouged and were "fast"—not gentle, kindly souls like poor brave Mrs. Rebell.

General and Mrs. Kemp, paying a short visit to Anglo-Indian friends who had taken a house in the neighbourhood, little knew the physical and mental ordeal to which their absence had exposed their darling.

Three days had gone by since the fire. Doctor McKirdy was quite honest in telling Madame Sampiero that he was pleased and astonished at the progress Barbara had made, and yet the paralysed woman felt that her old friend was keeping something back.

"What is it?" she muttered. "You are not telling me everything, McKirdy!"

And so he spoke out: "When a human being has gone through such an experience as that of the other night, what we doctors have to fear, quite as much as the actual injury,—which in this case, as I tell you, is not so very bad, after all,—is shock." He paused, and his listener made him feel, in some subtle fashion, that she could have well spared this preamble. "Now, the surprising thing about Mrs. Rebell is that she is *not* suffering from shock! Her mind is so full of something else, perhaps 'twould be more honest to say of someone else, that she has no thought to spare for that horrid experience of hers. She is concerned, very much so, about her appearance," the old Scotchman's eyes twinkled. "There she's as much the woman as any of them! But she has good nights—better nights, so she confesses, than she had before the fire. There she lies thinking, not of flames mind you, but of—well, you know of whom she's thinking! She's wondering if any of us have written and told Jamie of the affair; she's asking herself how he'll take it, whether he'll be hurrying back, whether, if he does come, she'll be informed of it. Then there's Boringdon's fashing himself to bits, wondering how long it will be before he is allowed to see her, trying to get news of her in devious ways, even coming to me when all else fails! Mrs. Kemp's lass is the only sensible one among 'em. I've been thinking of getting her to come and sit with Mrs. Rebell for a bit, 'twould just distract her mind— —"

So it was that Lucy Kemp received a note from Doctor McKirdy asking her to be good enough to come and see Mrs. Rebell, and Mrs. Kemp was struck with the eagerness with which the girl obeyed the call.

Lucy's parents had found her still tired and listless when they came back, cutting short their visit as soon as they heard the news of the fire, and the part their daughter had played; but with the coming of the old doctor's summons all Lucy's tiredness had gone—"If you will come up after you have had your tea," so ran the note, "you might sit with her an hour. I have ascertained that she would like to see you."

CHAPTER XIX.

"Il n'y a rien de doux comme le retour de joie qui suit le renoncement de la joie, rien de vif, de profond, de charmant, comme l'enchantement du désenchanté."

Oliver Boringdon held in his hand the West Indian letter which he knew was an answer to the one he had written to his brother-in-law rather more than a month before. For nearly a week he had made it his business to be always at home when the postman called, and this had required on his part a certain amount of contrivance which was intensely disagreeable to his straightforward nature. He had missed but one post—that which had come on the morning of the fire at Chancton Priory.

Three days had gone by since then, but his nerves were still quivering, not yet wholly under his own control, and to such a man as Boringdon this sensation was not only unpleasant, but something to be ashamed of. The hand holding the large square envelope, addressed in the neat clear writing of Andrew Johnstone, shook so that the letter fell, still unopened, on the gravel at Oliver's feet. He stooped and picked it up, then turned into the garden and so through a large meadow which led ultimately to the edge of the downs, at this time of the year generally deserted. Not till he was actually there, with no possibility of sudden interruption, did he break the seal of his brother-in-law's thick letter.

At once he saw with quick disappointment that what had so weighted the envelope was one of his sister Grace's long letters; her husband's note only consisted of a few lines:—

"Grace insists on your being told more than I feel we are justified in telling. Still, I believe her information is substantially correct. There would be very serious difficulties in the way of what you suggest. By next mail you shall know more."

For a moment he felt full of unreasoning anger against Johnstone. He had asked a perfectly plain question—namely, whether it would not be possible for Mrs. Rebell to obtain a divorce from the man of whom Grace had given so terrible an account; and in answer to that question his brother-in-law merely referred him to Grace and spoke of "serious difficulties"! Well, whatever these were, they must be surmounted. Oliver had already made up his mind to resign his post of agent to the Chancton estate, and he would use his little remaining capital in going out to Santa Maria, there to do what lay in his power to set Barbara free. Again he glanced at Johnstone's laconic note, and between the lines he read considerable disapproval of himself. He set his teeth and turned to the sheets of paper covered with Grace's large handwriting.

Then, in a moment, there leapt to his eyes a sentence which brought with it such a rush of uncontrollable relief that the sensation seemed akin to pain,—and yet he felt a species of horror that this was so, for the words which altered his whole outlook on life were these:—

"My darling Oliver, Pedro Rebell is dying."

What matter if Grace went on to qualify that first statement considerably,—to confess that she only knew of the wretched man's condition from a not very trustworthy source, but that before next mail Andrew would go over himself, "though he does not like the idea of doing so," to see if the report was well founded? "Andrew says," she went on, "that of course it will be his duty to try and keep him alive."

Boringdon beat the turf viciously with his stick, and then felt bitterly ashamed of himself.

Only one passage in his sister's letter gave definite information—

"Is it not odd that a place where they send consumptive people from home should have so many native cases? Pedro Rebell treats himself in the most idiotic manner—he is being actually attended by a witch doctor! I am more glad than I can say that poor Barbara got safe away before he became suddenly worse. Andrew confesses that he knew the man was very ill when we moved her here, but he said nothing, so like him, because he thought that if Barbara knew she simply wouldn't leave the plantation——"

Again Oliver turned to Johnstone's note—"still, I believe that her information is substantially correct;" it was curious how immensely that one dry cautious sentence enhanced the value of Grace's long letter.

Boringdon walked slowly back into the village by the lovely lane—lovely even in its present leafless bareness—down which Doctor McKirdy had accompanied Mrs. Rebell the first morning of her stay at the Priory three months ago. Oliver recalled that first meeting; it had taken place just where he was now walking, where the lane emerged on the open down. He remembered his annoyance when Berwick had stared so fixedly at the old Scotchman's companion.

James Berwick! The evocation of his friend's peculiar, masterful personality was not pleasant. But a slight, rather grim smile, came over Boringdon's lips. The moment Mrs. Rebell became a widow, she would be labelled "dangerous" in the eyes of James and Arabella Berwick. Oliver had known something of the Louise Marshall episode, and, without for a moment instituting any real comparison between the two cases, his mind unconsciously drew the old moral, "The burnt child dreads the fire." If it became advisable, but he did not think it at all likely that it would, he would certainly tell Berwick the news contained in Grace's letter.

When passing the Priory gates, he met Lucy Kemp. "Mrs. Rebell must be much better," she said gladly, "for Doctor McKirdy has asked me to go and sit with her for an hour." Oliver turned and went with her up to the porch of the great house, lingered a moment to receive the latest good but colourless bulletin, and then walked down to the estate office.

He had not been there many moments when a carriage dashed furiously up the steep village street, the horses galloping past the window of the room in which Boringdon sat writing.

Doctor McKirdy was waiting in the hall, and, as Lucy came forward rather timidly, he looked at her not very pleasantly. "You've been a long while," he said crossly, "a very long while, and who was it came with you to the door? But I won't trouble ye to answer me, for I heard the voice—I've heard it more than once this day. I doubt that ye ever were told, Miss Lucy, of the bachelors' club to which Rabbie Burns belonged as a youth. Membership was only conferred on the spark who could prove his allegiance to more than one lass. Your friend Mr. Oliver Boringdon would ha' been very eligible, I'm thinking!"

"I don't think you have any right to say such a thing, Doctor McKirdy!"

"Toots! Toots!" The doctor felt like a lion confronted with an angry lamb; he saw he had gone too far. Bless us, what a spirit the girl had! He rather liked her for it. "This way," he said, more amiably; "not so far up as the other morning, eh? When you're with her, you just chatter about the things ladies like to talk about—just light nonsense, you know. No going back to the fire, mind! She doesn't trouble her head much about it, and I don't want her to begin."

He opened a door, and Lucy walked through into the beautiful room where Barbara now lay, in the immense canopied bed, her left shoulder and arm outlined by a wicker cage-like arrangement. Her hair was concealed by a white hood, Léonie's handiwork, and, as Lucy drew near, she lifted her free hand off the embroidered coverlet, and laid it on that of the girl.

Doctor McKirdy stood by. "Well, I'll tell old Jean she needn't disturb you for a bit, and now I'll be going home. You'll see me after supper." He nodded his head, but Barbara, still holding Lucy's gloved hand, was speaking. "You won't forget the *Scotsman*——" in her eagerness she moved, and in doing so she suddenly winced.

"Never fear it! But the one we want to see won't be here till to-morrow afternoon—the meeting was only last night." He spoke in a very gentle voice, and then walked quickly to the door.

"Sit down just there, behind the leaf of the screen, and then I can see you. I'm afraid I gave you a great fright the other night? How good you were to me! Doctor McKirdy tells me that it might have been much worse, and that I shall be all right in a few weeks——"

Suddenly Barbara lifted her head a little,—"Miss Kemp! Lucy! What is the matter?"

"Nothing—nothing at all! Doctor McKirdy made a remark that annoyed me. It is stupid of me to mind." Poor Lucy tried to smile, but her lips quivered; she repeated, "It really was nothing, but you know how odd he is, and—and rude, sometimes?"

The sound of a carriage coming quickly up through the trees, and then being driven more carefully round the broad sweep of lawn, and so to the space before the porch, put an end to a moment of rather painful silence. Then the bell pealed loudly through the house—a vigorous peal. "Someone coming to inquire how you are," suggested Lucy diffidently, but Barbara made no answer, she was listening intently. Would McGregor never answer that insistent summons? At last they heard the front door being opened, and then quickly shut again. Now the carriage was driving away, quite slowly, in very different fashion from that of its arrival.

Barbara closed her eyes, absurdly disappointed. What reason had she to suppose that Berwick would hasten back as soon as he heard of the great danger she had been in? And even if something in her heart assured her that in this matter her instinct was not at fault, who would have conveyed the news to him? Not Oliver Boringdon, not Doctor McKirdy? Poor Barbara was very ignorant of the geography of her own country, but she knew that Scotland was a long way off, and the most important of the meetings he had gone there to attend had taken place only the night before.

But hark! there came a sound of quick muffled footsteps down the short corridor. A knock at the door, and Berwick was in the room—Berwick, haggard, sunken-eyed, bearing on his face, now ravaged with contending feelings, a look of utter physical fatigue. For a moment he stood hesitating. McGregor had told him that Miss Kemp was with Mrs. Rebell, but, as he looked round with a quick searching look, the room seemed to him to hold only Barbara—he saw nothing but Barbara's little head lying propped up on a large pillow, her eyes, her lips smiling at him with an odd look of deprecating tenderness, as if his being there was the most natural thing in the world, and yet as if she understood the dreadful night and day he had gone through, and felt grieved to think he was so tired.

Very slowly, still held by her eyes, he came forward, and as he sank on his knees, and laid his cheek on the hand stretched out on the coverlet, he saw with shuddering pain by what her other hand and arm were concealed, and he broke into hard, difficult sobs.

Lucy got up, and almost ran to the door,—she felt a passion of sympathy and pity for them both. Then she waited in the corridor, wondering what she ought to do—what Barbara would wish her to do. But that point, as generally happens in this world, was settled for her. Doctor McKirdy suddenly loomed in front of her, and even before she saw him, as the staircase creaked under his heavy footsteps, Lucy heard him muttering something to himself.

"Then he's in there, eh? And they've sent you out here?"

"Nothing of the sort!" said Lucy briefly: "I came out without being sent."

"Well, now, you must just go in again, and I'll follow. A fine thing it would be for the jabbering folk of Chancton to learn of these crazy comings and goings!" And, as Lucy made no haste to obey him, he added sharply, "Now you just knock and open the door and walk right in. We don't want old Jean to be the one to disturb them, eh?"

Lucy knocked, and opened the door with hesitating fingers. What she then saw was James Berwick quietly engaged in putting some coal on the fire; as the girl and Doctor McKirdy came in, he did not look round, but went on mechanically picking up the little lumps and putting them noiselessly into the grate.

"Well now, you've had two visitors, that's quite enough for one day,"—the doctor spoke very gently. "Here's Miss Kemp come to say good-bye, and Mr. Berwick no doubt will do himself the pleasure of taking her to the Grange, for it's a very dark night." He added in an aside, "I'm always finding you cavaliers, eh, Miss Lucy?"

Berwick came forward: "Yes, of course I will! By the way, I'm staying here to-night, so will you dine with me, McKirdy?"

"Well, no, I don't think I will. By the way, I'll be staying here too, and you'll do well to have your dinner in your bed, I'm thinking." He followed Barbara's two visitors to the door: "I can't make out how you ever did it, man, if it's true the meeting didn't break up till after twelve——"

For the first time Berwick laughed. "Come," he said, "where are your wits? Specials, of course—and if we hadn't had a stupid, an inexcusable delay at Crewe, I should have been here hours ago!"

And then, without again looking at Barbara, he followed Lucy out into the corridor, and down into the hall.

"Just one moment, Miss Kemp. I must put on my boots. I took them off before coming upstairs."

"But I can go home alone perfectly well."

"No, indeed! I should like to take you. Mrs. Rebell has been telling me how good you were to her the other night."

And not another word was said by him or by Lucy till they exchanged a brief good-night at the Grange gate.

The Priory and its inmates settled down to a long period of quietude. With the possible exception of Lucy Kemp and Oliver Boringdon—who both called there daily—little or nothing was known in the village save that Mrs. Rebell was slowly, very slowly, getting better. No Chancton gossip could discover exactly how much she had been injured, and even Mrs. Boringdon could learn nothing definite from her son.

At last there came a day when the mistress of Chancton Cottage thought she would make a little experiment. "Is it true that Mrs. Rebell is now allowed to be downstairs?"

"Yes."

"Then you are seeing her, I suppose?"

"Yes, sometimes, for a little while."

"Parliament met last week, didn't it?" The question sounded rather irrelevant.

Oliver looked up: "Yes, mother, of course—on the fifteenth."

"Then Mr. Berwick won't be able to be here so much. Miss Vipen tells me that the village people all think he must be in love with Mrs. Rebell!"

Mrs. Boringdon's words had an effect very different from what she had intended them to have. They drew from her son neither assent nor denial, but they confirmed and made real to him certain facts from which he had shrunk, and which he had tried to persuade himself did not exist. For five long weeks he had been alive to the knowledge that Berwick was continually with Barbara—in fact, that he was with her whenever he chose to be, excepting during those few moments when he, Boringdon, was grudgingly allowed to have a few minutes' talk, generally in the presence of some third person, with the invalid. The state of things at the Priory had made the young man so wretched, so indignant, that more than once he had felt tempted to attack Doctor McKirdy. What did they all mean by allowing James Berwick to behave as if he were Mrs. Rebell's brother instead of a mere acquaintance?

And so Mrs. Boringdon's words spurred her son to do that which he had hoped would not be necessary. They showed him that the time had come for a clear explanation between himself and Berwick. He told himself that the latter would probably be surprised to learn how his constant visits to the Priory were regarded; still, the matter could not be to him one of vital concern, and when once the man who had been for so many years his friend told him how matters stood, he would surely leave Chancton.

Boringdon thought he knew only too well James Berwick's peculiar moral code; certain things he might be trusted not to do. Thus, Oliver had heard him speak with condemnation of the type of man who makes love to a happily-married woman, or who takes advantage of his amatory science to poach on an intimate's preserves. Surely he would withdraw from this strange sentimental friendship with Barbara Rebell the moment it was made clear to him that she would soon be free,—free to be wooed and won by any honest man, and, as a matter of fact, already loved by Boringdon, his friend of so many years' standing? Accordingly, after a day or two of painful hesitation, Oliver wrote a note, more formal in its wording than usual, and asked Berwick for an appointment.

He received his answer—life is full of such ironies—in Mrs. Rebell's presence, on the day when she was allowed to take her first drive in the little French brougham, which, as Boringdon noted with jealous eyes, had been sent over for her use from Chillingworth. Oliver happened to come up to the porch of the Priory as Berwick was actually settling her and the grim Scotchwoman, Jean, into the carriage. Barbara was flushed and smiling—a happy light in her eyes. "I'm so sorry to be going out just now," she cried, "Will you come to tea this afternoon, Mr. Boringdon? Miss Kemp is coming, and I shall be down in the Blue drawing-room for the first time. To-day is a day of first times!"

Then Berwick turned round: "I didn't answer your note because I thought I should almost certainly be seeing you to-day. Would you like to come over to Chillingworth this evening? Come to dinner, and we can have a talk afterwards——"

But Boringdon answered quickly: "Thanks, I won't come to dinner, I'll turn up about nine."

And now Berwick sat waiting for Boringdon in the room where he had spent the rest of the night after his drive with Barbara from Halnakeham Castle.

He was in that delightful state of mind which comes so rarely to thinking mortals,—when the thinker wishes to look neither backwards nor forwards. It was worth while to have gone through all he had gone through, to have won such weeks as had been his! Nay more, he was in the mood to tell himself that he would be content were life to go on as it was now for ever and a day, were his relations with Mrs. Rebell to remain as close, as tender—ay, even as platonic—as they had been during that strange period of her convalescence. With what emotion, with what sympathy she had described to him her interview with Lord Bosworth; there had been such complete comprehension of his attitude, such keen distress that Madame Sampiero had repulsed him!

But, deep in Berwick's heart, something told him that Barbara's attitude to him and to their joint future was changing, and that she was in very truth on the eve of surrender. Nature, so he assured himself to-night had triumphed over convention, and, as a still voice also whispered, proved stronger than conscience. Berwick's own conscience was not ill at ease, but he experienced many phases of feeling, and went through many moods.

Lately he had asked himself boldly whether there was any real reason why he and Barbara should not repeat, in happier fashion, the example set them by the two beings for whom they both had so sincere and—yes, it might be said, reverent—an affection? Those two, Lord Bosworth and Madame Sampiero, had shown that it was possible to be grandly faithful to a tie unsanctioned by law, unsanctified by religious faith. Already Berwick's love for Barbara had purified and elevated his nature; surely together they might use his vast fortune to better purpose than he had done alone, for he had long ago discovered how tender, how charitable were all her impulses. Then, again, he would acknowledge to himself, with something like impatient amazement, that he loved Barbara too well, too intimately, to ask her to do violence to her sensitive, rather scrupulous conscience. She could scarcely be more his own than he felt her to be now.

Of the man for whom he was now waiting, Berwick had long ago ceased to be jealous. He felt ashamed to remember that he had ever been so; nay, he now understood from Barbara that Boringdon liked Lucy Kemp. Was she not just the sort of girl whom he would have expected such a man as Oliver to choose for a wife? As to Barbara Rebell, of course Boringdon had liked to be with her,—had been perhaps, if all the truth were known, caught for a moment by her charm, as who could help being? But Berwick was not in a mood to waste much thought on such speculations, and no presentiment of what Oliver was coming to say to him to-night shadowed his exquisite content, or his satisfaction with himself, with the woman he loved, and with the whole of this delightful world.

In fact, he thought he knew quite well why Boringdon wished to see him. The head of the public department in which Oliver had begun his suddenly interrupted career as a member of the Civil Service, had lately said to Berwick, "So your friend Boringdon wants to come back to us? I think in his case an exception might be made!" And Berwick had done what was in his power to gratify the other's rather inexplicable wish to get once more into official harness. The Chancton experiment had evidently been a mistake. Boringdon had not possessed the qualities necessary for such a post as that of land agent to Madame Sampiero; he had not understood, or, if he had understood, he had not chosen to take, his friend's hint to keep on the right side of old McKirdy. Well, it couldn't be helped! Of course Oliver must feel the telling of his news rather awkward, but he, Berwick, would meet him half way, and make it clear that, though he was personally sorry Boringdon was leaving Chancton, he thoroughly understood his reasons for doing so, and, what was more, sympathised with them.

As it struck nine from the various clocks which had been a special hobby of the man who had built Chillingworth, Boringdon walked in, and his first abrupt words confirmed Berwick's belief concerning the subject of their coming conversation: "I am leaving Chancton, and I felt that I ought to tell you my determination before speaking to Madame Sampiero. There seems a chance of my getting back to the old shop!"

Berwick nodded his head; he pushed a large box of cigars across the table which stood between them. "I know," he said, "I met Kingdon last week, and by a word he let fall I gathered that you were thinking of doing this. Well, of course I'm sorry, but I know you've done your best, and after all no one could have foreseen how difficult the position would be! I suppose they will have to go back to the unsatisfactory plan with McKirdy." But at the back of the speaker's mind was the thought that, if he was as much at the Priory as he hoped to be, he might himself be able to look into things rather more—

Neither man spoke again for a few moments; then Boringdon got up, and stood with his back to the fire, "But that," he said, "is not all I have come to say to you. I am really taking this step because it is my intention"—he hesitated, and Berwick perceived that a peculiarly dogged expression had come over the dark, rather narrow face,—"I wish to tell you that it is my intention," repeated Oliver, "to ask Mrs. Rebell to become my wife."

His host looked up at him with frank astonishment, and a good deal of concern. "But, my dear fellow," he began rather hurriedly, "is it possible that you don't know?——"

"I know everything." Boringdon raised his voice, then went on more calmly, "But I do not suppose that you yourself, Berwick, are aware that Mrs. Rebell's husband is dying, that there is every chance that in a few months, or perhaps in a few weeks, she will be a widow—free, that is, to accept an offer of marriage."

In one sense Boringdon had certainly succeeded in his object. More than he was ever destined to know, his words, his revelation, had brought the man before him sharp up to his bearings. James Berwick was both amazed and discomfited by this unexpected piece of news, and for the moment it made him very ill at ease.

He had been playing with a tortoiseshell paper knife; suddenly it snapped in two, and, with an oath, he threw the pieces down on the table and got up from the chair in which he had been lying back.

"Are you quite sure of your information?" he said slowly. "It's ill waiting for dead men's shoes." Then he felt ashamed of what he had just said, and he added, more to give himself time for thought than anything else: "Have you any reason to suppose that Mrs. Rebell— —?" Then he stopped abruptly, realising that he had been betrayed into making a remark which to Boringdon must seem an outrage.

But the other had not apparently taken it in that sense. "No, I have no reason to suppose that Mrs. Rebell has ever thought of such a thing. I think far too well of her to suppose it for a moment," Oliver was speaking very deliberately. "I received the news of the man's state within a very few days of the fire at the Priory, and it has since been confirmed. He has, it seems, some kind of bad chest disease, accelerated, I fancy, by drink. As yet she knows nothing of it. Perhaps I ought to add that I have no reason to suppose that she will accept the offer I mean to make her as soon as a decent interval of time has elapsed. But, on the other hand, I should like to assure you that if she refuses me I intend to go on asking her. Nothing, short of her marriage to someone else, will make me give her up." He repeated, and as he did so Boringdon fixed his eyes on his friend with a peculiar, and what Berwick felt to be a terrible, look: "Nothing—you understand me, Berwick—nothing but her *marriage* to another man."

The speaker of these strange words took a step forward. For a moment the two stood opposite one another. The man Barbara loved was a brave man, but he quailed before the other's eyes. "I have now told you what I came to say. Of late you seem to have become very intimate with Mrs. Rebell, and I wish to warn you that the day may come when I shall require your good offices. Good-night,"—and without offering to shake hands with Berwick, Boringdon turned on his heel and left the room.

CHAPTER XX.

"Shall I to Honour or to Love give way?

For, as bright day, with black approach of night,
Contending makes a doubtful puzzling light,
So does my Honour and my Love together
Puzzle me so I can decide on neither."

SPENSER.

As time went on, as harsh winter turned into soft spring, Boringdon tried to assure himself that his conversation with Berwick had achieved all that he had hoped.

James Berwick was certainly less often at the Priory, but this was doubtless owing in a measure to the fact that he had to be constantly in London, attending to his Parliamentary duties. Even now he was far more frequently at Chancton than he had been the year before, and Oliver was still jealous, sometimes intolerably so, for some subtle instinct told him that he was on a very different footing with Mrs. Rebell from that on which she stood with Berwick. As to his own relation with the man with whom his intimacy had once been so close, it had become, since their conversation, that of mere formal acquaintance. Mrs. Boringdon felt sure there had been a quarrel, but she was afraid to ask, so taciturn, so unapproachable, had her son become.

Oliver had one subject of consolation. To the amazement of those about her, with the exception perhaps of Doctor McKirdy, the paralysed mistress of the Priory now caused herself to be moved down each day to the Blue drawing-room, and this, as Boringdon of course realised, made it very difficult for James Berwick, when at Chancton, to see much of Mrs. Rebell alone.

And Barbara? To her, as to Berwick, the weeks which had immediately followed the fire had been a time of deep content and tranquil happiness. She was well aware that there must come a day of painful reckoning; but, unlike Berwick, she put off the evil moment of making up her mind as to what form that reckoning would take.

She looked back with a kind of shrinking horror to the mental struggle she had gone through before the accident which had so wholly changed all the circumstances of her life. Those days when she believed that Berwick would never return to her were ill to remember. Then had come the fire, followed by hours of physical pain and terror of death, but now she looked back on those hours with positive gratitude, for they had surely brought an experience nothing else could have given her.

At once, with a resistless, quiet determination which had constrained those about Barbara into acquiescence, Berwick had established his right to be with her. The putting on of the coal—that act of service on the first evening—had been, so Doctor McKirdy later told himself with a twist of his thin lips, symbolic of what was to be his attitude to the Queen's Room and its present inmate. Berwick soon came and went as freely as if he had been the invalid's twin brother, or he a father, and Barbara his sick child,—with, however, the one significant exception that both he and she refrained wholly from caress.

The old Scotchman won a deep and an abiding place in the hearts of the two over whom he threw, during these days, the ample mantle of his eccentricity and masterful disposition. He moved over to the Priory, occupying a room close to Berwick's, and in some odd fashion he made each member of the large household believe that it was by his order and wish that Berwick was so often with his patient, concerning the extent of whose injury many legends grew, for she was only tended by Scotch Jean, French Léonie, Doctor McKirdy, and—James Berwick. And so it was that, as often happens with regard to events which none could have foretold, and which would have been described before they occurred as clearly impossible, what went on excited, at any rate within the Priory, no comment.

The strange situation which had arisen did not pass wholly without outside remark. Lucy Kemp at first came daily—indeed, sometimes twice a day—to sit with Barbara and to read to her; and though at those times Berwick kept out of the Queen's Room, there came a moment in Barbara's illness when she perceived, with a sad feeling of humiliation, that Lucy's visits were being curtailed, also that she never came to the Priory unaccompanied.

To the girl herself her father's sudden stern objection to her daily visits to Mrs. Rebell had been inexplicable,—even more so her mother's refusal to discuss the question. Then a word said before her by Mrs. Boringdon, a question put to Oliver as to James Berwick's prolonged stay at Chancton, had partly opened Lucy's eyes.

"Do you dislike my going to see Mrs. Rebell because Mr. Berwick is there?"

With some hesitation Mrs. Kemp answered her: "Yes, my dear, that is the reason your father does not wish you to go to the Priory so often."

And then Lucy had turned and asked one of those questions, difficult to answer truthfully to one who, even if in her parents' eyes a child, was yet a woman grown: "Mother, I want to ask you something. Is it very wrong, always wrong, for a woman to like another man better than she likes her husband? How can she help it if the man to whom she is married is such a man as Mr. Pedro Rebell seems to be?"

But Mrs. Kemp answered with unwonted decision and sharpness: "There is a moment—there is always a moment—when the matter is in a woman's own hands and conscience. And in any case, Lucy, two wrongs don't make a right!"

And with this the girl had to be content, but the question made Mrs. Kemp more than ever determined to discontinue her daughter's growing intimacy with poor Barbara. First Oliver Boringdon, and then James Berwick,—this Mrs. Rebell must indeed be an unfit friend for her little Lucy!

To Madame Sampiero, who lay at the other end of the corridor out of which opened the Queen's Room, the doctor would sometimes declare, "I've little mind for the part I am playing." But when she answered, with perplexity and fear in her large blue eyes, "Why then do you play it?" he would content himself with shrugging his shoulders, and muttering between his teeth, "Because I'm a sentimental old fool!"

But, whatever the reason, so well had Doctor McKirdy managed the extraordinary situation, that not till Mrs. Rebell was promoted to getting up and coming downstairs, did the long hours spent by Berwick in her company provoke the kind of gossip which had finally reached the ears of Mrs. Boringdon. Even then what was repeated had been said in jest. Was it likely, so the humble gossips of Chancton would have declared, that such a gentleman as Mr. Berwick would fancy a lady who was by all accounts half burnt to a cinder!

When Madame Sampiero had suddenly made up her mind to be moved downstairs, Barbara knew that the old Scotchman and her god-mother had entered into a conspiracy to put an end to what she considered her innocent, if peculiar, intimacy with James Berwick. There took place in her heart a silent, but none the less strong, movement of passionate revolt,—she thought this attempt to check their friendship the more cruel inasmuch as Berwick had to be away a good deal and could only now and again snatch a day from London. Still, it was then, not perhaps till then, that Mrs. Rebell began to foresee the logical outcome of the situation into which she had allowed herself to drift.

Every day came his letters,—nearly always more than one together, by each of the two daily posts,—but he never asked her—significant omission—to answer them, for had she done so, all Chancton must have known of the correspondence. And yet all the world might have seen the letters Barbara cherished, and on which her heart lived from day to day; they were a diary of the writer's doings, a history of what was going on in the House, such brief, intimate notes as many a politician writes daily to his wife.

A woman is always quicker to perceive certain danger-signals than is a man. Barbara was aware of the change of attitude in Doctor McKirdy and in Madame Sampiero long before Berwick noticed it. That these two could threaten or destroy his intimacy with Mrs. Rebell had never occurred to him as being possible. On the other hand, he had resented deeply Boringdon's interference, and, as far as was possible, he put out of his mind what had been undoubtedly intended as a threat. The reminder that Pedro Rebell lived had been an outrage; that Barbara's husband was mortal, nay, on the eve of death, a piece of information which Berwick could have well spared. For the present he was content, as was apparently Barbara, to let things drift on as they were.

But there came a day when, after a long afternoon spent by them both in Madame Sampiero's company, Berwick asked Barbara with sudden deep irritation,

"Why is it that we never seem to be alone together? I have hardly spoken to you since I have been here! Is it impossible for you to leave Madame Sampiero? Is there no room in the whole of this great house where we can talk together in peace? I have a thousand things to say to you!"

They were on their way to the dining-room, there to be respectfully chaperoned by McGregor, and Barbara had no answer ready. Suddenly looking into her downcast face, he understood the unspoken answer to his imperious questioning, and his eyes flashed wroth. And yet what could he do? He could not, nay, he would not, ask her to stoop to any kind of deception, to make secret assignations outside the house. On the other hand, he no longer felt "on honour" as regarded the woman he loved; even less was he bound to consider the feelings of Madame Sampiero.

So it came to pass that Berwick was less often at the Priory; his letters to Barbara altered in tone, and became those of an ardent, of an impatient lover. Sometimes Barbara wondered whether he possessed secret means of his own for knowing all that went on at the Priory, and of obtaining news of its inmates. Occasionally she would be surprised, even amused, at his apparent knowledge of little incidents which occurred during his absences. The source of his information, if it was as she suspected, must of course be Mrs. Turke! Mrs. Rebell felt a little afraid of the old woman, of her far-seeing, twinkling eyes, and of her sly hilarity of manner; she kept as much as possible out of the housekeeper's way.

To Boringdon, who came with pertinacious regularity, Barbara gave scarcely any thought, save perhaps to wonder why Lucy Kemp was so fond of him. In old days, when he had talked to her of politics, and of things in which she had begun to take a new and keen interest, she had liked to listen to him; but now he seemed tongue-tied when in her presence, and she perceived that he was no longer on good terms with James Berwick.

With Madame Sampiero, Barbara's relations also seemed to have become less affectionate, less intimate, than before the fire, and this troubled them both. Mrs. Rebell knew herself to be the subject of anxious thought on the part of her god-mother; for what other reason than that of protecting her from some imaginary danger had Madame Sampiero altered the habits of dignified seclusion to which she had remained rigidly faithful for so many years? She did not see—or was it that she saw only too well—the force of her own past example on such a nature as that of her god-daughter? But it was too late now to try and separate Barbara Rebell from the one human being who made life worth living, and sometimes the younger woman longed to tell her so.

At last there came a break in the monotony of a life which was beginning to tell on Barbara's health and nerves. At the end of one of Berwick's short, unsatisfactory visits, he mentioned that he would not be able to come down again for another two or three weeks.

And when he was gone, after a cold, estranged farewell, uttered perforce in the presence of Madame Sampiero, Barbara turned her face away to hide her tears.

Almost at once her god-mother asked her, "Would you not like to go away, with Léonie, to Paris for a few days?" She caught with feverish relief at the proposal; it was good, it was more than kind, of Marraine to suggest so delightful a plan! But she would prefer, honestly so, to go alone, not to take the old French servant whom in her heart she well knew the paralysed woman could ill spare. It would have been a great pleasure to Barbara to have had the company of Lucy Kemp, but she had not dared suggest it, being afraid of a refusal. If she could not have Lucy for a companion, she felt she would rather go alone. And Madame Sampiero had at last consented to this modification of her plan,—a plan which had not met with Doctor McKirdy's approval, but as to which his old friend, as was usually the case, got her own way.

And now had come the last night but one before Mrs. Rebell's departure. She felt excited and pleased at the thought of the little holiday. Berwick had evidently been told as soon as the household knew of her coming journey, and yet, when writing, he had only once alluded to it, and she had felt rather hurt, for to herself it was a matter of much moment. This journey would be, in a sense, a pilgrimage; Barbara meant to go to some of the places, within easy reach of Paris, where she and her parents had spent most of their exile. During the last few days she had passed much time in discussion with Doctor McKirdy as to what she was to see, and in helping him to draw up a little plan of the places she was to go to,—Versailles, St. Germains, Fontainebleau, with all of which she had cherished associations! The moments went by so quickly that, for the first time for many weeks, Barbara thought but little of Berwick, and of her own strange relation to him.

Now she was on her way to bed. She would have only two more nights in the Queen's Room, for she had herself insisted that a humbler apartment, but still one on the same floor as that of Madame Sampiero, should be found for her, and the change was to take place on her return. She looked round the beautiful room which had become to her a place of so many memories, and as she did so a shadow came over her face. Would she ever again be as happy as she had been in this room, so simply, childishly content as during those days when she had lain on the great canopied bed, while those about her ministered to her slightest wish—when she had been the spoiled darling of Doctor McKirdy, of the grim Scotch nurse, and last, not least, of James Berwick?

There came a knock at the door—a hesitating, low knock, very unlike that of Jean or Léonie. Barbara suddenly felt an odd pang of fear: "Come in," she cried loudly,—what, after all, had she to be afraid of?

There was a pause, and then Mrs. Turke, resplendent in the bright yellow gown in which Barbara Rebell had first seen her, advanced tip-toeing into the room. "Hush, Ma'am—I don't want anyone to hear us! Will you be pleased to come down at once to my parlour? There's someone there been waiting such a time, and most anxious to see you—!"

Barbara seemed in no hurry to follow the old woman; a look of suffering, of humiliation, came over her face. Must she and Berwick stoop to this?

But Mrs. Turke was in an agony of impatience. "He's got to go back this very night!" she whispered, and the jovial, sly look faded from her rubicund face. "He's walked all the way from Halnakeham, that he has, in the pouring rain, and he's wet through, that he is! Am I to tell him that you won't come down then?" and she pretended to edge towards the still open door.

"No," said Barbara irresolutely, "of course I am coming down—"

Mrs. Turke's account of Berwick's long walk in the rain had done its work, and yet shame of a very keen quality almost blotted out Mrs. Rebell's joy at the thought of seeing him, and of seeing him—the first time for weeks—without fear of interruption.

As she went quickly down, following Mrs. Turke's ample person, and so through the stone corridors of what had been the mediæval monastery, Barbara's heart softened strangely. Had he not made this hurried journey to bid her good-bye, God-speed? And she had thought he did not care—

Mrs. Turke knew her place far too well to risk being present at the meeting in her parlour. She stopped at the foot of the short flight of stairs leading up to her own bedroom and Berwick's old nursery, but Barbara clung to the fat, ring-laden hand: "Do come, Mrs. Turke,—I am sure Mr. Berwick will want to see you——"

"Bless you, *no*, Ma'am, that he won't! Why, I declare your hand's burning! There's nothing to be afraid of, he's a most reasonable gentleman, he wouldn't hurt a hair of your pretty head!"

And then, rather to the old housekeeper's surprise, Mrs. Rebell suddenly let go her hand, and walked forward, alone, down the passage.

When she reached the door of the room to which she was bound, she stopped irresolutely. But Berwick had been listening; he flung open the door, and as she crossed the threshold he bent forward and took her hands in a tight grip.

Barbara said nothing, but she looked at him rather sadly, and as she did so she perceived that he was dressed in a rough shooting suit she had often seen him wear the autumn before. She understood, without a word, that it was worn to-night as a half disguise,—he wished no one to know of this secret visit to the Priory,—and again a feeling of shame, of humiliation, swept over her. And yet how glad she was to see him, how infinitely dear he had become to her!

Suddenly she felt herself being drawn,—nay driven,—into the shelter of his arms. His lips trembled on her closed eyelids, were pressed on the slight scar left by the burn on her forehead, and then swiftly sought and found her soft quivering mouth——. But even then Berwick was very gentle with her, taking care to bruise neither the soul nor the body of the creature who was now, at last, completely subject to his will.

Barbara tried to withdraw herself from his arms, but he still held her to him with a passion of mute feeling in his eyes; and then, while looking down at her strangely, as if wishing to see into her very heart, he suddenly exclaimed "Barbara, this can't go on! What is to happen to you and to me? As long as they left us alone I was content—ah no, not content, but submissive. But now? Do you think it is pleasant for me to do what I have had to do to-night,—to come here like a thief? While I was waiting for you, I told myself that doubtless you would refuse to come down. I had no right to ask you to come to me. It is I—I—who should always come to you——"

He had released her, and drawn himself away. Now he was speaking with a tired bitterness which frightened her, and in a moment the desire to soothe, to comfort him, drove out from her every thought of self. "Of course I came down,—I will always come when you want me," she smiled at him with a look of shy, wistful tenderness.

"Will you? Always? Is that true? Oh! Barbara, if I could only believe you mean those words, I could find courage to ask you—to say to you——"

"What do you want to say to me?" Her voice sank to a whisper; then, seized with a sudden rush of love, of pity, of self-abnegation, she added, "Nay, I will tell you! You have come to ask of me what Lord Bosworth must once have come to ask of Madame Sampiero, and, like her, I will say, yes,—" she covered her face with her hands.

And then she listened, very quietly, while Berwick told her, with broken words of passionate gratitude and endearment, of the plan which he had scarcely dared to believe he would have courage to propose. She knew he had a house, an old hunting lodge built by Louis XIII., on the edge of the Forest of St. Germains. It was a curious solitary pavilion, bought by his father as a very young man, and dear to Berwick and his sister as having been the scene,—the speaker's accents became more deeply tender,—of their parents' honeymoon. Within a drive of this enchanting spot was the little town of Poissy, where the mail train could be made to stop and where, the day after to-morrow, he would be waiting—

Barbara sat listening. She had raised her head and was staring straight before her. Berwick looked at her with entreating eyes—"It is close to Paris! Besides, they know you will be moving about."

"It is not that," she spoke with difficulty, hardly knowing why she felt so torn by conflicting feelings of shame and pain. Perhaps it was only because the evocation of St. Germains brought the presence of her mother before her.

She tried to tell herself that she had known that this would—nay, must—happen. The battle had been fought and lost before to-night. During the long solitary days Barbara had just lived through, she had acknowledged that she could not give up Berwick,—rather than that they must inevitably come to do what Lord Bosworth and Madame Sampiero had done. And yet this discussion, the unfolding of this plan, filled her with humiliation and misery. "When I come back," she said, looking at him, for the first time straight in the eyes, "I shall have to tell my god-mother—and—and Doctor McKirdy the truth."

"You will do what you wish. We shall both do exactly what you think right, my dearest!" Berwick could hardly believe in his own amazing good fortune, and yet he also felt ill at ease. "Barbara," he said suddenly, "before I go—and I ought to be going now, for I shall cross to France to-morrow—I want to tell you something——"

"Something else?" there was a tone of appeal in her voice.

"Yes, it will not take long. Perhaps I ought to have begun by doing so. Some time ago Oliver Boringdon made me a curious confidence. He told me that, were you ever free to marry, he meant to make you an offer, and if you refused,—he was good enough to intimate that he thought this quite possible,—to go on doing so at intervals unless you became the wife of another man!"

Barbara looked at him, and then began to laugh helplessly, though the words had jarred on her horribly. "Oliver Boringdon? You can't have understood; how dared he say such a thing—about me?" and the tears ran down her cheeks.

"Nay, he was right, perhaps, to say what he did. In any case I am sure you ought to know—it was my duty to tell you."

"But why?" cried Barbara. "Why?"

"A sop," he said with sudden sharpness, "to my own conscience."

But conscience proved an unappeased, upbraiding companion during James Berwick's four-mile walk to Halnakeham station.

CHAPTER XXI.

"They have most power to hurt us whom we love;
We lay our sleeping lives within their arms."

Beaumont and Fletcher.

A short avenue of chestnut trees, now in their scented glory of rose-pink blossom, hid the square red-brick hunting lodge, still known by its pre-Revolution name of Le Pavillon du Dauphin, from the broad solitary roadway skirting the Forest of St. Germains. Under this avenue James Berwick, his hands clasped behind him, his eyes bent on the ground, was walking up and down the morning of the day he was expecting Barbara to join him.

It was seven o'clock—not early, according to French hours, for now and again the heavy wheels of a market cart, the jingling of the tiny bells hung on to the blue worsted-covered harness, the neighing of the horses, would break on his ear, and serve to remind him that he was in France—in the land where, if long tradition speaks truly, the thing that he was about to do would find many more honest apologists than in his own; in France which had given, close to this very spot, so magnificent a hospitality to his own Stuart ancestors. All about him lay the deep, mysterious, unbroken calm of the great forest; every trace of last summer's merrymakers—if, indeed, such people ever made their way to this, the further edge of the wooded peninsula,—had been completely obliterated. What more enchanting spot could be found in the wide world to form the setting of what he believed would be a life-long romance?

Like most men, he had always seen something offensive, almost grotesque, in the preliminaries now usual to conventional marriage. Heavens! what a lack of imagination had the modern bride and bridegroom! Especially in England—especially in his own class. Here the mating birds, amid awakening spring, would sing his own and Barbara's epithalamium.

And yet Berwick was not happy, as he had thought to be, to-day. Again and again during the long wakeful night he had just passed he had caught himself wondering whether his uncle, at the beginning of his long intimacy with Madame Sampiero, had felt such scruples as these which now tormented him. If so, they had soon vanished; Lord Bosworth, during many years, had been supremely content with life, and all that life brought him.

Perhaps he, Berwick, was made of more scrupulous stuff. To-day he had to face the fact that in his cup of honey there was a drop of exceeding bitterness. The knowledge that Boringdon might be mistaken,—that Barbara might, after all, never be free,—made the matter scarcely more tolerable. Oliver had so spoken that at the time his words had carried conviction. Berwick asked himself why he had not told her the whole truth, and then let her be the judge as to what they should do. He had always been aware that there were the two streaks in his character—the two Stuart streaks—that of extreme nobility, and that which makes a man capable of acts of inexplicable betrayal.

In vain he tried to persuade himself that now was too late to change. Human nature has its limits; in a few hours Barbara would be here, and with quickening pulses he tried to think only of the immediate future. Later on, there would—there must—come inevitable pain and difficulty; they would have to face the reproachful gaze of Madame Sampiero, the undoubted disapproval of Lord Bosworth, and yet whose example were he and Barbara now about to follow?

The present was his own, no one—no one, that is, but himself—could deprive him of to-day's completed joy; and yet he would have given much to hasten the march of the lagging hours, to sleep, to dream the time away. Perhaps, when he was in the actual presence of the woman he loved with a depth of feeling which, to a certain extent, purified and rendered selfless his longing for her, he would find courage to tell her the whole of what Boringdon had said—

This concession to his conscience lightened his heart, and he looked with leisurely and pleased gaze at the finely proportioned building—a miniature replica of what the central portion of the Palace of Versailles must have looked like in the days of Louis XIII. No wonder the curious, stately little pavilion had caught the fancy of his father—that whimsical, unfortunate Charles Berwick, whose son thought of him far oftener than he had ever done as a younger man. The Pavilion du Dauphin, put up for sale in one of France's many political convulsions, had only cost its English purchaser twenty thousand francs; and now each year Berwick received an offer from the French Government to buy the place back at five times that sum! He always refused this offer, and yet he came there but seldom, sometimes in the autumn for a few days, occasionally, perhaps once in two or three years, with Arabella. Since the death of his own mother, no woman save James Berwick's sister had enjoyed the rare charm of the old hunting lodge.

The building was not fitted for ordinary life. It consisted of two vast central rooms,—that above the central hall being little more than a loft,—out of which opened smaller apartments, each and all bearing traces of the prodigal wealth and luxurious fancy of that fermier général into whose acquisitive hands the place had drifted for a while during the last half of the eighteenth century. It was he, doubtless, who had added the painted ceilings, the panels which Berwick's father believed had been painted by Nattier, and which, if this were so, would have made the Pavilion du Dauphin a bargain even at the price which Berwick yearly refused for it.

When Arabella was there, the brother and sister managed very well without English servants, done for, and that most adequately, by an old garde de chasse, Jean Lecerf, and his wife, whom Berwick paid generously for looking after the property during the winter months of the year.

This old couple,—with the solitary exception of Lord Bosworth, who rarely alluded to his younger brother,—were the only people who ever spoke to Berwick and his sister of their parents. Those eccentric parents, whose marriage had been in itself a wilful, innocent romance, culminating in a runaway wedding, had spent five summers here, bringing with them, after the first year, their baby daughter. The stories the Lecerfs had to tell of that time lost nothing in the telling!

Mère Lecerf—a name generic of the soil in that part of Northern France—knew very little of her present employer, saving the agreeable fact that he must be very rich. She was quite unaware that he was a widower, and she had accepted with apparent satisfaction, and quaintly expressed felicitations, the story he had seen fit to tell her within an hour of his arrival the day before—namely that he was now married, and that his wife was coming to join him for a few days!

Berwick would have preferred to make no such explanation, but something had to be said, and, after all, would not he henceforth regard Barbara Rebell as in very truth his honoured, his cherished wife?

He walked from the outside air into the spacious room, into which the morning sun was streaming through the one immense window which gave on to a steep clearing, now carpeted with the vivid delicate green of lily-of-the-valley leaves. One of the qualities which had most delighted him in Barbara during the early days of their acquaintance had been her perception of, and delight in, natural beauty. How charmed she would be with this place! How the child which had awakened in her would revel in the strangeness of a dwelling-place which so little resembled the ordinary conventional house!

Groups of fair shepherdesses, each attended by her faithful swain, smiled down from the pale grisaille walls, but close to the deep chimney,—indeed, fixed inside, above the wooden seat—was a reminder of an age more austere, more creative than that of Nattier. This was a framed sheet of parchment—a contemporary copy of Plantin's curious sonnet, "Le Bonheur de ce Monde," whose *naif* philosophy of life has found echoes in many worthy hearts since it was first composed by the greatest of Flemish printers.

"Avoir une maison, commode, propre, et belle,
Un jardin tapissé d'espaliers odorans,
Des fruits, d'excellent vin, peu de train, peu d'enfants,
Posséder seul sans bruit une femme fidèle.

"N'avoir dettes, amour, ni procès, ni querelle,
Ni de partage à faire avecque ses parens,
Se contenter de peu, n'espérer rien des
Grands, Régler tous ses desseins sur un juste modèle.

"Vivre avecque franchise et sans ambition,
S'adonner sans scrupule à la dévotion,
Domter ses passions, les rendre obéissantes.

"Conserver l'esprit libre et le jugement fort,

Dire son Chapelet en cultivant ses entes,
C'est attendre chez soi bien doucement la mort."

With the exception, perhaps, of three or four lines, Berwick now found himself in unexpected agreement with old Plantin's analysis of human happiness.

And Barbara? Ah! she undoubtedly would agree with almost every word of it; he caught himself wondering whether the position he had won, and which he owed in a measure,—perhaps in a very great measure,—to his wife's fortune, would be really forfeited, were he to become again a comparatively poor man. Berwick had by no means forgotten what it was to be straitened in means; and he realised that want of substantial wealth had been a great bar even to Lord Bosworth. Still, oddly enough, the thought of giving up his wealth for the sake of Barbara was beginning to appeal to his imagination. He went so far as to tell himself that, had he come across her as a girl, he would of course have married her, and forfeited his large income without a regret.

So it was that, during the long solitary spring day, spent by him almost wholly in the forest, Berwick experienced many phases of acute and varying feeling, most of which tended to war with the course to which he was being inexorably driven by his sense of honour rather than by his conscience.

But for Boringdon's revelation as to Pedro Rebell's state, Berwick's conscience would have been at ease. So much he had the honesty to admit. Apart from that one point which so intimately involved his honour, he was without scruple, and that although he loved Barbara the more for being, as he well knew she was, scrupulous, and, as he thought, conscience-ridden. Nothing, so he told himself again and again during those hours of fierce battle, could alter the fact that she belonged to him in that special sense which is, as concerns a man and a woman, the outcome of certain emotional experiences only possible between two natures which are drawn to one another by an over-mastering instinct.

In the days that followed the fire at Chancton Priory, there had arisen, between Berwick and Barbara, a deep, wordless intimacy and communion, which at the time had had the effect of making him divine what was in her mind, with a clearness which had struck those about them as being actually uncanny. And yet it was then, during those days, that Berwick had sworn to himself that his love was pure and selfless in its essence. As she had lain there, her hand quivering when it felt his touch, every gross element of his nature had become fused and refined in the clear flame of his passion. It had been during these exquisite, to him sacred moments, that he had told himself that on these terms of spiritual closeness and fusion he would be content to remain.

But alas! that mood had quickly changed; and the interview with Boringdon had reawakened the violent primeval instinct which had slumbered,—only slumbered,—during the illness of Barbara. The knowledge that another man loved her, with an ordinary, natural love by no means free from that element of physical attraction which Berwick himself had been striving, not unsuccessfully, to control in his own heart, had had a curious effect upon him. His soul, ay, and something much less spiritual and more tangible than his soul, rushed down from Heaven to earth, and he began to allow himself, when in the company of the woman he loved, certain experiments, slight, almost gossamer in texture, but which he would afterwards recall with a strange mingling of shame and rapture, for they proved him master of that most delicate and sensitive of human instruments, a pure and passionate heart.

The wide solitary glades carpeted with flowers, the chestnut groves, skirting the great avenue of firs, which is one of the glories of the Forest,—everything to-day seemed to minister to his passion, to bring Barbara Rebell vividly before him. Coming on a bank from whose mossy surface sprang high, delicately tinted wind-flowers, Berwick was suddenly haunted by a physical memory—that of Barbara's movement of surrender two days before. Again he felt her soft quivering mouth yielding itself to his lips, and, still so feeling, he suddenly bent down and put these lips, now sanctified, to the cool petals of a windflower. Was it a sure instinct which warned him that Barbara's love for him, even if it contained every element the natural man seeks to find in his mate, was so far governed by conscience that she would never be really content and unashamed so long as they were outside the law? More, if Boringdon were right, if Pedro Rebell were indeed dying, and Barbara became in time James Berwick's wife, would she ever forget, would she ever cease to feel a pang of pain and remorse in, the fact of this episode, and of the confession which would—which must—follow after? He had to ask himself whether he was prepared to cast so dark a shadow over the picture of these days, these hours, which her mind would carry into all the future years of their lives.

More difficult, because far more subtle and unanswerable, was the knowledge that Boringdon might after all have been wrong, and that Barbara might never be free. In that case, so Berwick with fierce determination told himself, he would be fool indeed to retard the decisive step which would resolve what had already become, both to him and to Barbara, if the truth were to be faced honestly, an intolerable situation.

But in his heart Berwick knew well that Oliver Boringdon had spoken the truth. Even now, to-day, release might have come, and Barbara might be a free woman. Slowly, painfully, as he fought and debated the question with himself, he became aware that only one course was compatible with his own self-respect.

A secret misgiving, a hidden, unmentionable dread, which would have troubled, perhaps with reason, many a man in Berwick's position, was spared this man. He knew that he need have no fear that Barbara would misunderstand, or question, even in her heart of hearts, his sacrifice. It would not be now, but later, that she would suffer,—when they went back to their old humiliating position at Chancton, as lovers unacknowledged, separated, watched.

And so, at last, the outcome of the struggle which saw him go through so many different moments of revolt and sharp temptation, was that Berwick brought himself to envisage that immediate renunciation, which seemed so much more difficult to face than did the further, if less poignant, sacrifice which still lay in the distant future, when, to make Barbara his wife, he would give up so much that had hitherto, or so he had thought, made life worth living.

Slowly he made his way back to the Pavilion du Dauphin, there to set himself grimly to do all that was possible to make his decision, if not irrevocable, then most difficult of revocation. Mère Lecerf was abruptly told that as her master must leave the hunting lodge that night she must arrange to come and sleep there, in order that "Madame" should not be alone in the solitary building. But that, as Berwick well knew, was by no means enough, for Mère Lecerf would acquiesce in any change of plan with joyful alacrity.

So it was that six o'clock saw him passing into the Pavilion Henri IV., the famous hostelry which terminates the long Terrace of St. Germains. There he was well known, and could, in his present mood, have well spared the delight with which his orders were received, as also the few sentences in which the landlady's young daughter aired her English. "But how so! Of course! The most beautiful of our rooms shall be ready for Monsieur's occupation. Perhaps for three nights? La, la! What a short sojourn! A carriage now, at once? Another one to be at the Pavilion du Dauphin this evening? But yes, certainly!"

Barbara, stepping down from the high French railway carriage, looked about her with a strange shrinking and fear in her dark eyes. From the moment she had left the boat she had been reminded, and that intolerably, of another journey taken, not alone,—on the day of her marriage to Pedro Rebell. The last few months seemed obliterated, and Berwick for the moment forgotten. She was haunted by two very different presences,—that of her mother, and that of the West Indian planter, whose physical nearness, which had ever, from their marriage day onward, filled her with agonised revolt and terror, she seemed now to feel as she had not felt it for years, for he had soon tired of his victim. Had it not been that thoughts of Madame Sampiero, and of the duty she owed to the paralysed woman, restrained her, she would have been tempted to open the railway carriage door and step out into the rushing wind, and so end, for ever, the conflict in her mind.

There are women, more women than men, who are born to follow the straight way,—to whom crooked paths are full of unknown terrors. Such a woman was Barbara Rebell. And yet the sight of Berwick,—Berwick, pale indeed, but quiet, self-possessed and smiling, as they advanced towards each other across the primitive little station,—brought comfort, and even security, to her heart. It was so clearly impossible that he would wish to work her any ill—

No other passenger had got out at Poissy, and the station-master, who knew the owner of the Pavillon du Dauphin, looked with curiosity at the man and woman now going towards one another. The information given to Mère Lecerf had already reached him, "Cold types, these English!" but he cheered up when he saw Berwick suddenly bend down and kiss each of the traveller's pale cheeks, in French husbandly fashion. "Salut Monsieur! Salut Madame!" the familiar accents fell sweetly on Barbara's ear as she walked through to the town square, where a victoria was waiting to take them to the Pavillon du Dauphin.

As she sat, silent by his side, Berwick took her hand in his. Again and again he opened his lips to speak, to tell her of his decision. But something seemed to hold him back from doing so now. Later, when they were alone, would be time enough.

And Barbara? Still full of vague, unsubstantial fears, she yet felt free—absolutely free—from the presence which had journeyed by her side. Berwick now stood between herself and Pedro Rebell, but, during the long silent drive up the steep road leading from the valley to the forest plateau, Barbara's mother seemed to stand sentinel between herself and Berwick.

At last they were alone,—alone in the shadow-filled hall where the beams of the May moon, slanting in through the wide, curtainless window, warred with the light thrown by the lamp still standing on the table where they had sat at supper half an hour before.

As she heard the door shut behind Madame Lecerf, Barbara had risen and gone over to the friendly glow of the fire. She was now sitting, rather rigidly upright, on the wooden bench which formed a kind of inglenook within the stone fireplace. Just above her head hung the faded gilt frame containing Plantin's sonnet; her hands were clasped loosely over her knees, and she was looking straight into the heart of the burning peat.

Berwick, himself in shadow, watched her in tense silence; there was something enigmatical, and to him rather fearful, in her stillness,—in some ways he felt her more remote from himself than he had ever felt her to be since the night they had first met.

When driving from Poissy, he had taken her hand, and she had let it rest in his; but only for one brief moment, during the last two hours, had the woman he loved shown any sign of emotion. This was when, as they sat at table, the old French woman serving them had said, in answer to some question: "Mais oui, Madame Berwick!" and Barbara's face had suddenly become flooded with colour.

At last she looked round from the fire, and sought to see where her companion was sitting. Berwick thought the gesture beckoned; he leapt up and came forward with a certain eagerness, and, standing before her, smiled down into her serious eyes.

Suddenly she put out her hand and touched his sleeve. "Won't you sit down," she said, "here, by me?"

He obeyed, and she felt his arm slowly gathering her to him, while he, on his side, became aware that she first shrank back, and then gradually yielded to his embrace. Nay more, she suddenly laid her cheek against his lips with a curious childish abandonment, but he knew there was something wanting,—something which had been there during the moment that their souls, as well as their bodies, had rushed together the last,—the only time, till now,—that he had held her in his arms.

She made a slight, an ineffectual effort to disengage herself as she asked in a low voice: "Why did your servant call me that? Call me, I mean, by your name?"

"Because," he answered, rather huskily, "because I told her that you were my wife. I hope that name is what all will call you some day."

Barbara's lips trembled. "No," she said very slowly, "I do not think that will ever happen. God will not let me be so happy. I have not deserved it." Yet even as she said the words, he felt, with quick, overmastering emotion, that she was surrendering herself, in spirit as well as in body, and that she came willingly.

He turned and caught her more closely to him.

"Listen," he said hoarsely, "listen while I say something to you that perhaps I ought to have said before, earlier, to-night."

Then, rather suddenly, he withdrew his arms from about the slight rounded figure enfolded in them. The utterance of what he had made up his mind must now be said had become immeasurably more difficult during the last few moments. He asked himself, with rough self-reproach and self-contempt, why he had so delayed, why he had allowed her to come here to be so wholly at his mercy, and he—yes, he—at hers? He got up and walked slowly to the other side of the great room, and came back, even more slowly, to where Barbara was sitting.

There he knelt down by her.

"Barbara," he said, "be kind to me! Help me! My pure angel, what does your heart tell you would be to-night the greatest proof of my love—of my adoration of you?"

And then the most amazing, and, to the man looking up at her with burning eyes the most moving, change came over the face bent down to his. Barbara had understood. But she said nothing,—only slipped down and put her arms, a wholly voluntary movement of caress, round him, in a strange speechless passion of gratitude and tenderness.

"Ah, Barbara," he said, "you have made me know you too well. You have allowed me to see too clearly into your heart not to know that I was a brute to ask you to do this thing,—to do that which I knew you believed to be wrong." And, as she pressed more closely to him, her tears wetting his face, he went on: "But I promise,—I swear,—I will never ask it of you again. We will go on as we did,—as we found ourselves able to do,—after the fire."

"But will not that make you unhappy?" Her lips scarcely moved as she whispered the words, looking into his strained face with sad, beseeching eyes.

"Yes," he said, rather shortly, "if I thought it impossible, or even improbable, that you would become my wife, it would make me very unhappy, but that, or so I believe, is not impossible, not even improbable. Ah, Barbara, must I tell you,—do you wish me to tell you,—everything?"

She looked up at him with a sudden fear and perplexity. What did he mean, what was it he had heard and wished to keep from her? But she would trust him, trust him to the end, and so, "No," she whispered, "tell me nothing you would ever regret having told me. I am quite content, nay, more than content, with your goodness to your poor Barbara."

An hour later Berwick was driving away from the Pavillon du Dauphin, not to the station as Mère Lecerf believed, but to St. Germains, within easy, tantalising distance of the woman he had just left,—a very tearful, a very radiant, a most adoring, and alas! a most adorable Barbara.

Looking out with absent eyes across the great moonlit plain to his left, Berwick thought over the strange little scene which had taken place. He hardly knew what he had said,—in any case far less than he had meant. Not a word, for instance, of what Boringdon had told him,—how could he have spoilt, with the image of death, such an evening as had just been theirs? Heavens! how strangely Barbara had altered, even before that whispered assurance that he would never, never ask her to do that which she thought wrong.

When he had first brought her into the Pavilion, there had been something tragic, as well as touching, in her still submissiveness of manner. But afterwards—ah, afterwards!—he had been privileged to see a side of her nature—ardent, yet spiritual, passionate, yet pure,—which he felt that he alone had the power to awaken, which had manifested itself only for him. How happy each had been in the feeling of nearness to the other, in the knowledge that they were at last free from watching, even if kindly, eyes, and listening ears,—what happiness they promised each other for the morrow! They would give themselves, so Berwick told Barbara, three days in this sylvan fairy land, and then he would take her to Paris, and go himself back to England.

Barbara Rebell never knew that those three days, of to her unalloyed bliss, held dark hours for her companion--hours when he cursed himself for a quixotic fool. But, even in the midst of that strange experience, Berwick was able to write in all honesty to his sister, the only human being to whom he confided the fact that he was in France,—might she not already have learnt it from some less trustworthy source?—certain cryptic words, to which she could then attach no meaning: "One word more. I wish to remind you that appearances are deceitful, and also to tell you that I have at last found that it is possible to be good, to be happy, and also to have a good time."

CHAPTER XXII.

"There are moments struck from midnights!"

ROBERT BROWNING.

WITHIN a week of her return to Chancton Priory, Barbara heard of Pedro Rebell's serious condition. A short, dry note from Andrew Johnstone conveyed to her the fact that he was dying, and that, whether he lived a few weeks or a few months longer was in his own hands,—a question, however, only of time, and of a short time.

Berwick had judged truly the woman he had grown to love with so intimate an understanding and sympathy. The news of approaching release let loose in Barbara's mind a flood of agonising memories, which crowded out for a while everything else. During the long years she had endured every humiliation such a man as Pedro Rebell could inflict on so proud, and so sensitive a human being as herself, she had never foreseen this way of escape. He had ever seemed instinct with a rather malignant vitality, and the young,—Barbara had remained in some ways very young after her marriage,—are not apt to take death into their calculations.

For some days she told none of those about her of the astounding news she had received from Santa Maria, but the two in whose thoughts she dwelt constantly divined her knowledge. It quickened Boringdon's desire to leave Chancton, and, with that self-delusion to which men who love are so often prone, in Mrs. Rebell's new coldness of manner to himself, he saw hope. Not so James Berwick,—he, judging more truly, was seized with a great fear lest Barbara should think it her duty to go back to Santa Maria. Rather than that, so he told himself during those days of strain and waiting for the confidence which she withheld, he would go himself,—men have gone stranger pilgrimages on behalf of their beloveds.

At last he told her that he knew what was so deeply troubling her. "And you are thinking," he said quietly, "that perhaps you ought to go back and look after him till the end? Is not that so?"

Barbara looked at him very piteously,—they were walking under the beeches, and, having wandered off the path, were now utterly alone. But, before she could speak, he again opened his lips: "If such action is necessary, if you do not think he will be well cared for by those about him, I will go for you."

"You?" Barbara's dark eyes dilated with sudden fear—"Oh! no, not you!——"

"Indeed, you could trust me to do all that was possible. You do not think, surely, that your actual presence would be welcome to him?" The words were uttered very quietly, but, as he asked the apparently indifferent question, Berwick clenched the stick he held with a nervous movement.

"No, I should not be personally welcome." Barbara spoke in a low voice, almost in a whisper; she felt it impossible to make those confidences regarding her life with Pedro Rebell which another woman would, perhaps, in her place, have been eager to make. And yet she longed to convey to Berwick how short-lived on his part had been the sudden attraction which had led this half-Spaniard to behave, in those sad weeks just before and after her father's death, so as to bring her to believe that marriage with him was the only way out of a difficult and undignified situation; how little, when once he was married to her, the man who was now dying had taken her into his scheming, vicious life.

But now she could say nothing of all this. And yet those few words with Berwick comforted her, and made her see more clearly, even gave her courage to telegraph to the Johnstones,—only to receive the decided answer that all that could be done was being done, and that her coming, from every point of view, was undesirable.

Then, and not till then, did Mrs. Rebell tell her god-mother the news which meant so much to her, indeed to them both.

Madame Sampiero made but one comment—"James Berwick must have known this before you went to France!"

Barbara bent forward to hear the quickly muttered words. The suggestion surprised her, perhaps troubled her a little. She hesitated,—but surely such knowledge could not have reached him before it reached herself, and so, "No—I do not think so," she said.

"Ah! well, I do think so——"

Madame Sampiero said no other word, but when her mind—that shrewd, acute mind, as keenly able to weigh actions and to judge those about her as ever it had been—pondered the confession Barbara had made to her immediately on her return from France, her heart grew very tender to James Berwick. She realised, what one who had been a better woman than herself would perhaps not have understood so well, the force of the temptation which must have assailed the man who loved Barbara with so jealous and instinctive a passion. At last, too, Madame Sampiero understood the riddle of Oliver Boringdon's sudden resignation of the conduct of her business. It must have been from him that Berwick had learnt that Mrs. Rebell was on the eve of becoming a free woman. But not even to Doctor McKirdy did the paralysed mistress of the Priory say what was in her mind; the old Scotchman divined that her view as to the danger of the relation of her god-daughter and Berwick had altered, and that the change had come about because of some confidence—or was it confession?—made by Barbara within a few hours of her return from Paris. Only Madame Sampiero,—and, long afterwards, Arabella Berwick,—ever knew of those three days spent by Berwick and Barbara at St. Germains.

The one person in Chancton, to whom Boringdon made any explanation concerning his resignation of the post he had now held for nearly two years, was Lucy Kemp. His mother told her many acquaintances that the public office her son had left to enter Parliament had found it quite impossible to carry on its portion of the nation's work without him, and that a very great inducement had been held out to him to persuade him to go back! But of these confidences of Mrs. Boringdon's he was happily ignorant, and to Lucy alone Oliver felt a longing to justify the future as well as the present.

Shortly, baldly, making no excuse for himself, unconsciously trusting to her sympathy, and to the instinctive understanding she had always shown where he and his feelings were concerned, he told her the truth, adding in conclusion: "You, now knowing her as you did not know her before the fire, can understand my—— " he hesitated, then brought the words out with a certain effort,—"my love for her. I shall wait a year; I should not insult her by coming any sooner. I do not expect to be listened to—at first. She has suffered——" Again he stopped abruptly, then went on: "Lucy, do you think it strange that I should tell you all this?" And, as she shook her head, he added: "Lately she has seemed to avoid me,—that is, since her return from France, in fact since I know that my brother-in-law's letter must have reached her."

A sharp temptation assailed Lucy Kemp. Would it be so very wrong to break her promise to Mrs. Rebell,—that promise given so solemnly the night of the fire? Could she not say a word, only a word, indicating that he was making a terrible mistake? What hope could there be for Oliver Boringdon if Barbara loved James Berwick? But the girl fought down the longing, and Boringdon's next words showed her that perhaps he knew or guessed more than she had thought possible.

"Perhaps you have heard,—I know my mother has done so,—foolish gossip concerning Mrs. Rebell and James Berwick, but I can assure you that there is no truth in it. Berwick's financial condition makes it impossible that he should think of marriage." And, as something in Lucy's look or manner made him aware that she also had heard of, perhaps had noticed, the constant presence of Berwick at the Priory, Oliver bit his lip and went on, rather hurriedly: "I am not excusing him. I think his assumption of friendship with Mrs. Rebell has been regrettable. But, Lucy, I spoke to him about it, and though in doing so I lost his friendship, I am quite sure that it made a difference, and that it caused him to realise the harm he might be doing. In a country neighbourhood such as this, a man cannot be too careful." Oliver delivered himself of this maxim with considerable energy.

He seemed to be about to add something, then changed his mind. One further word, however, he did say:

"I wonder if you would let me write to you sometimes, and if Mrs. Kemp would mind your sometimes writing to me? In any case I hope my mother will hear from you."

And then, for a short space of time, a deep calm settled over Chancton. Berwick, who was staying at Fletchings, came almost daily, spending, 'tis true, long hours in Barbara's company, but treating her, during that strange interval of waiting, with a silent, unmaterial tenderness which moved and rather surprised those about them.

Barbara and her god-mother were in the Blue drawing-room, spending there, not unhappily, a solitary evening. Spring had suddenly become summer. It was so hot that the younger woman, when coming back from the dining-room, had left the doors deliberately wide open, but no sound came from the great hall and upper stories of the Priory.

Madame Sampiero preferred the twilight, and the two candles, placed far behind her couch, left her own still face and quivering lips in shadow, while casting a not unkindly light on her companion.

Barbara had been fanning the paralysed woman, but during the last few moments she had let the fan fall idly on her knee, and she was looking down with a look of gravity, almost of suffering, on her face. She was thinking, as she so often did think in these days, of Pedro Rebell, wondering if she ought to have gone back to Santa Maria as soon as she received Andrew Johnstone's letter. Had she believed that her presence would bring pleasure or consolation to the man who, she was told, was so soon to die, she might have found the strength to go to him,—her mother would have said that in any case her duty was to be there,—but then her mother had never come across, had never imagined—thank God that it was so!—such a man as her daughter had married. And so little does even the tenderest and most intelligent love bridge the gulf between any two of us, that Madame Sampiero, taking note of the downcast eyes, thought Barbara absorbed in some happy vision of dreams come true.

A good and noble deed, even if it takes the unusual form of supreme personal self-abnegation, often has a far-reaching effect, concealed, and that for ever, from the doer. How amazed James Berwick would have been to learn that one result of his renunciation had been to broaden, to sweeten Madame Sampiero's whole view of human nature! She realised, far more than Barbara Rebell could possibly do, the kind of heroism such conduct as that of Berwick had implied in such a nature as his, and she understood and foresaw its logical consequence—the altering, the reshaping in a material form, of the whole of his future life and career.

Sometimes, when gazing at her god-daughter with those penetrating blue eyes which had always been her greatest beauty, and which remained, in a peculiar pathetic sense, the windows of her soul and the interpreters of her inmost heart, the mistress of Chancton Priory wondered if Barbara was aware of what James Berwick had done, and of what he evidently meant to do, for her sake.

To-night these thoughts were specially present to Madame Sampiero; slowly, but very surely, she also was making up her mind to what would be, on her part, an act of supreme self-humiliation and renunciation.

"Barbara," she said, in the hoarse muffled tone of which the understanding was sometimes so difficult—"listen—" Mrs. Rebell started violently, the two words broke the silence which seemed to brood over the vast house. "I have determined to receive Julian—Lord Bosworth. You will prepare him"—she paused a moment, then concluded more indistinctly, "for the sight he is to see."

"But, Marraine, it is *you* he loves, and not—not——" Mrs. Rebell's voice was choked by tears. She slipped down on her knees, and laid her two hands on Madame Sampiero's stiff fingers, while she looked imploringly up into the still face.

Suddenly, as she knelt there, a slight sound fell on Barbara's ears; she knew it at once as that of the door, leading from the great hall to the vestibule, being quietly closed from the inside. A moment later there came the rhythmical thud of heavy footsteps making their way, under the music gallery, across to the staircase. A vague feeling of fear possessed the kneeling listener. Into her mind there flashed the thought that whoever had come in must have walked across the lawn very softly, also that the footfalls striking so distinctly on her ear were unfamiliar.

Then, in a moment, an amazing, and, to Barbara Rebell, a very awful thing took place. The stiff fingers she held so firmly slipped from her grasp, she felt a sudden sensation of void, and, looking up, she saw Madame Sampiero, drawn to her full height, standing by the empty couch. A moment later the tall figure was moving with steady swiftness towards the door which stood open at the other end of the long room—Barbara sprang up, and rushed forward; she was just in time to put her arms round her god-mother as Madame Sampiero suddenly swayed—wavered—

There was a moment of tense silence, for outside in the hall the heavy footsteps had stayed their progress—

"It is Julian." Madame Sampiero spoke quite distinctly, but she was leaning heavily, heavily, on her companion, and Barbara could feel the violent trembling of her emaciated body. "He used to come—in that way—long ago—He thinks I am upstairs. You must go and find him—"

To Barbara, looking back, as she often did look back during her later life, to that night, three things, in their due sequence, stood out clearly—the terrifying sight of the paralysed woman walking with such firm swift steps down the long room; the slow and fearful progress back to the couch; and then, her own fruitless, baffling search through the upper stories of the Priory—a search interrupted at intervals by the far-away, but oh! how clear and insistent voice, crying out "Barbara!" "Barbara!" a cry which, again and again, brought the seeker hurrying down, but with never a word of having found him whom she sought.

Doctor McKirdy, coming in as he always did come each evening, was the only human being to whom Mrs. Rebell ever told what had occurred; and she was indifferent to the knowledge that he discredited her statement as to how far Madame Sampiero had walked before she, Barbara, had caught the swaying figure in her arms. Would she herself have believed the story, had it been told her? No, for nothing could have convinced her of its truth but the evidence of her own eyes.

As was his way when what he judged to be serious illness or disturbance was in question, the old Scotchman was very silent, intent at first only on soothing his patient, and on having her transported upstairs as quickly and as quietly as possible. At last Barbara heard the words, "I promise ye most solemnly I will look mysel', but no doubt he's away by now, slipt out somehow"—uttered in the gentle voice he only kept for the woman to whom he was speaking, and which he rarely used even to her. And so, when Madame Sampiero was finally left with Jean—Jean, whose stern countenance showed no quiver of curiosity or surprise, though she must have known well enough that something very unusual had happened—Mrs. Rebell followed Doctor McKirdy downstairs.

"Then you do think it really was Lord Bosworth?" she asked rather eagerly.

"Indeed I do not!" he turned on her fiercely, "I just think it was nobody but your fancy!"

Barbara felt foolishly vexed.

"But, Doctor McKirdy, some man undoubtedly came in, and walked across the hall. We both heard him, quite distinctly."

"And of whom were ye thinking,—ay, and may-be talking,—when ye both heard this mysterious person?"

It was a random shot, but Barbara reddened and remained silent.

Doctor McKirdy, however, did not pursue his advantage. "Look ye here," he said, not unkindly, "try and get that notion out of her head, even if ye can't out of yours. If I thought he had come, that it was he"—he clenched his hands, "'Twould be a dastardly thing to do after what I've told him of her state! But, Mrs. Barbara, believe me, 'twas all fancy,"—he looked at her with an odd twisted smile, "I'll tell you something I've never told. Years ago, just after Madam's bad illness, I went away, more fool I, for what they call a change. Well, wherever I went they followed me—she and little Julia, as much there before me as you are now! 'Twas vain to reason with myself. Julia, poor bairn, was dead—who should know it as well as I?—and Madam lay stretched out here. And yet—well, since then I've known that seeing is not all believing. Once I got back,—to her, to them,—I laid their wraiths."

Barbara shuddered. "Then you are not going to look any more? I quite admit that whoever came in is probably gone away by now."

"Of course I'll make a round of the place. D'ye think I'd break my word in that fashion?"

Together they made a long and fruitless search through the vast old house, and up to the last moment Barbara thought it possible they might find someone in hiding, some poor foot-sore sailor tramp, may-be, who had wandered in, little knowing of the trouble he was bringing—but the long search yielded nothing.

"Are ye satisfied *now*?" Doctor McKirdy held up the hooded candle, and turned the light on her flushed, excited face.

"Yes!—no!—I mean that of course I know now there is no one in the house, but someone, a man, certainly came in."

For long hours Barbara lay awake, listening with beating heart for any unwonted sound, but none broke across the May night, and she fell asleep as the birds woke singing.

At eight in the morning Léonie brought her a note just arrived from Fletchings: "Dearest,—Your kind heart will be grieved to learn that my uncle died, quite suddenly, last evening. I nearly came over, then thought it wisest to wait till the morning. Better perhaps make McKirdy break it to her."

CHAPTER XXIII.

"O sovereign power of love! O grief! O balm!"

A WHOLE year had gone by, and it had been, so Chancton village and the whole neighbourhood agreed, the dullest and longest twelve months the place had ever known. What events had happened had all been of a disturbing or lugubrious character, and even Miss Vipen confessed that there had been really nothing pleasant to talk about!

The Cottage was again empty, for Oliver Boringdon and his mother had gone, and their departure, especially that of Mrs. Boringdon, had certainly been viewed with sincere regret. She was such an agreeable, pleasant person, and the village people on their side had soon regretted Oliver's just dealings, which compared most commendably with the favouritism and uncertain behaviour of Doctor McKirdy, who now, as before Mr. Boringdon's brief tenure of the land agency, acted as go-between to the tenants and Madame Sampiero.

Another occurrence, which had certainly played its part in bringing about the general dulness and flatness that seemed to hang over the place as a pall, had been the death, from sudden heart failure, of Lord Bosworth. The owner of Fletchings had been for many years the great man of the neighbourhood; his had been the popular presence at all the local functions he could be persuaded to attend, and there had been a constant stream of distinguished and noteworthy folk to and from his country house. Even those who only saw Lord Bosworth's distinguished guests being conveyed to and from the station, shared in the gratification afforded by their presence. The only day which stood out in the recollection of both gentle and simple was that of Lord Bosworth's funeral; quite a number of really famous people had come down from London to be present.

Then had followed many pleasant discussions, in Miss Vipen's drawing-room and elsewhere, concerning the late peer's will. Lord Bosworth had left everything that could be left away from his heir to the latter's sister, and this of course was as it should be. But there had been a few curious bequests; a considerable legacy, for instance, to Madame Sampiero's old housekeeper, Mrs. Turke; the dead man's watch and chain, a set of pearl studs, and a valuable snuff-box which had been given to him by the Emperor of the French, actually became the property of Doctor McKirdy, who—so said popular rumour—had begun by declining the legacy, and then, in deference to Madame Sampiero's wish, had accepted it! All agreed that it had been very generous of her to interest herself in the matter, for strange, very strange, to say, her name was not mentioned at all in the will! Oddest of all, in the opinion of the neighbourhood, was the bequest to Mrs. Rebell of the portrait of the child, described as that of "My daughter Julia"; but the picture still hung in what had been Lord Bosworth's study at Fletchings. There was a crumb of comfort inasmuch as the little estate had not been sold. Perhaps the new Lord Bosworth, to whom such an insignificant possession could be of but little account, intended to present it to his sister, Miss Berwick.

The fact that all the Priory servants had been put into mourning had given most people subject for remark, and had rather scandalised everybody; it seemed to dot the i's and cross the t's of the now forgotten scandal. Indeed, the more charitable were inclined to think that the servants' mourning was really worn because of the death of Mrs. Rebell's husband, which had become known at Chancton two days after that of Lord Bosworth,—a fact which had prevented its attracting as much attention and comment as perhaps the event deserved.

It had been noted, however, with a good deal of concern, that Mrs. Rebell did not wear proper widow's weeds; true, she made her widowhood the excuse for living a life of even greater seclusion than she had done before, and she wore black, but no one—so those interested in the matter declared—would take her for a newly-made widow.

Yet another thing which had certainly contributed to the dulness of the neighbourhood had been the absence, the whole summer and autumn through, of the new Lord Bosworth,—for this of course had meant the shutting up of Chillingworth. After making an ineffectual, and, so most of the people belonging to that part of the world thought, a very ridiculous attempt to assert his right to go on sitting in the House of Commons, he had started "in a huff" for a tour round the world. But he wrote, so said report, very regularly to Madame Sampiero, and to his old nurse, Mrs. Turke. He had also sent to various humble folk in Chancton wonderful presents; no one connected with Chillingworth had been forgotten, not even Dean's new baby,—to whom, by the way, Dean's master had acted, being of course represented by proxy, as god-father.

Now, however, the neighbourhood was waking up a little; for one thing the wanderer was home again, having hurried back to be present at the distribution of the Liberal loaves and fishes,—strange though it seemed that a peer should continue to be a Radical, especially such an immensely wealthy peer as was the new Lord Bosworth.

With only one group of people might time be said to have stood quite still. These were General and Mrs. Kemp and their daughter Lucy. But Lucy was certainly less bright—perhaps one ought to say duller—than she used to be. On the other hand, she had become very intimate with Mrs. Rebell; they were constantly together, and people could not help wondering what the latter saw in Lucy Kemp.

It was the third of April. Miss Vipen prided herself upon remembering dates; the anniversaries of birthdays, of weddings, of deaths, lingered in her well-stored mind, and she also kept a little book in which she noted such things. To-day was to be long remembered by her, for, having most fortunately had occasion to go across to the post office just after luncheon, she had seen, lying on the counter, a telegram containing a most extraordinary and unexpected piece of news.

Miss Vipen regarded telegrams as more or less public property, and she had met the flustered postmaster's eye,—an eye she had known absolutely from its infancy,—with a look of triumphant confidence. Then, by amazing good luck, while on the way back to her own house, she had come across Mrs. Sampson, the rector's wife, and from her had won ample, overwhelming confirmation, of the most interesting event which had happened in the neighbourhood for years and years!

It was a delightful spring day and Miss Vipen decided that, instead of waiting calmly at home until her usual circle gathered about her at tea time, she would make a number of calls, ensuring a warm welcome at each house by the amazing and secret tidings she would be able to bring. Mrs. Sampson was still bound to silence, and only the fact that Miss Vipen was already acquainted with the morning's happenings had made the rector's wife reluctantly complete, and as it were, round off, the story.

Miss Vipen's first call was at Chancton Grange. Since General Kemp had behaved so strangely some two years before, turning on his heel and leaving her drawing-room before he had even said how do you do, she had scarcely ever crossed Mrs. Kemp's threshold. But to-day an unwonted feeling of kindness made her aware that the important piece of gossip she came to bring would make her welcome to at least one of the Grange's inmates, and to the one whom she liked best, for she had always been, so she assured herself to-day, rather fond of Lucy. Poor Lucy, wasting her youth in thinking of a man who would certainly never think of her, and yet with whom, so Miss Vipen understood, her parents very wrongly allowed her to correspond!

The old lady was naturally delighted to find the inmates of the Grange all at home, and all three sitting together in the room into which she was shown. Both the General and his wife made what they flattered themselves was a perfectly successful attempt to conceal their surprise at seeing Miss Vipen, but they were not long left in doubt as to why she had come, for she plunged at once into the matter, looking sharply from her host to her hostess, and from Mrs. Kemp to Lucy, as she exclaimed, "I suppose that you have not heard the great news? You have no idea of what took place this morning? Here, in Chancton Church?"

But General and Mrs. Kemp shook their heads, but their daughter began to look, or so Miss Vipen thought, rather guilty.

"Well, there was a wedding at our church this morning! But you will never guess,—I defy any of you to guess,—who was the bride and who the bridegroom!"

Then the speaker saw with satisfaction that General Kemp gave a sudden anxious glance at Lucy. "The lady has not lost much time," continued Miss Vipen, "for her husband has only been dead four or five months. Now can you guess who it is?"

But Lucy broke the awkward silence. "Just ten months, Miss Vipen—Mrs. Rebell became a widow early in June——"

"Well, no matter, but can you guess the name of the happy man? Of course one could give *two* guesses— —"

But alas! Miss Vipen was denied her great wish to be the first to tell the delightful piece of news, for, while she was enjoying Mrs. Kemp's obvious discomfort, Lucy again spoke, and in a sharp voice very unlike her own,

"Why, Mr. Berwick—I mean Lord Bosworth, of course! Who else could it be?" Then she looked rather deprecatingly at her parents: "I could not say anything about it, because it was told me only yesterday, as a great, a very great, secret."

"And do you know," continued Miss Vipen in a rather discomfited tone, "who were the witnesses?"

"No," said Lucy, "that I do not."

"Doctor McKirdy for Lord Bosworth, and Daniel O'Flaherty, that Home Ruling barrister who is mixed up in so many queer cases, for Mrs. Rebell! I can tell you another most extraordinary thing. She was actually married in a white dress—not a veil of course, but a white gown and a hat. And who else do you think were there? Mrs. Turke—it's the first time to my knowledge that she's been in that church for years—the Scotchwoman, Jean, the French maid Léonie, and the butler McGregor! Mrs. Turke wore a pale blue watered silk dress and a pink bonnet; she cried, it seems, so loudly that Mr. Sampson became quite confused— —"

"And Miss Berwick?" said Lucy quietly, "was she not there too?"

"Yes, of course; I was forgetting Miss Berwick. Well, this must be a sad day for her—after all her striving and scheming for her brother! No wonder he kept Fletchings, for I suppose they will have to live there now," Miss Vipen spoke with deep and sincere commiseration. "What a change for *him* after Chillingworth! He becomes a pauper—for a peer, for a Cabinet Minister, an absolute pauper! They are going to France this afternoon for the honeymoon, but they are to be back soon."

When Miss Vipen had been seen safely out of the gate by General Kemp, he came back to find his wife alone. Lucy had gone up to her room.

"I suppose you expected this, Mary?"

"Yes—no"—Mrs. Kemp had an odd look on her face—"and yet I always liked Mr. Berwick from the very little I saw of him. But I confess I never thought this would happen. Indeed, I was afraid, Tom,—there is no harm in saying so now,—I was afraid that in time Oliver Boringdon would obtain what seemed to be the desire of his heart— —"

"Afraid?" cried the General, "Nothing could have pleased me better, excepting that I should have been sorry for Mrs. Rebell! I suppose that now you are quite delighted, Mary, at the thought that Boringdon will again begin haunting Lucy. It is not by my good will that you have allowed them to write to one another."

Poor Mrs. Kemp! She had no answer ready. During the last year she had learnt what hatred was, for she had hated Oliver Boringdon with all the strength of her strong nature; not only had he left Chancton taking Lucy's heart with him, but he had made no effort to free himself of the unwanted possession. Nay, more, almost at once a regular correspondence had begun between the two, and though Lucy was not unwilling that her mother should see his letters, Mrs. Kemp did not find much to console her in them.

And now? The mother realised that she must make haste to transform her feeling towards Oliver Boringdon into something akin to liking. As a beginning she now went up to Lucy's room, her heart yearning over the girl, but with no words prepared. Perhaps now her child would come back to her—the last year had been a long, sad year to Mrs. Kemp.

Lucy was sitting idly by the rosewood davenport. There were traces of tears on her face. "Mother!" she said, "Oh, mother!" Then she took Mrs. Kemp's hand and laid her cheek against it. In a very different tone she added, "I felt rather ashamed at not telling you yesterday. Barbara would not have minded your knowing, but Lord Bosworth was anxious that no one should be told."

"Is that why you are crying?" asked Mrs. Kemp in a low voice.

"No, no, of course not! I am afraid—Oh! mother! do you think it will make *him* very unhappy?"

"For a little while," said Mrs. Kemp drily, "he will fancy himself so, and then he will begin to wonder whether, after all, she was quite worthy of him!"

"Don't say that—don't think so unkindly of him!" Lucy stood up, she put her hand through her mother's arm, "Do you think people ever leave off caring, when they have once cared—so much?"

"Lucy," said Mrs. Kemp, "have you ever wondered why your father and I married so late? You know we were engaged—first—when I was only nineteen——"

"Because you were too poor!" cried Lucy quickly, "because father was in India!" and then, as her mother looked at her quite silently, the girl added, with a kind of cry, "Oh! mother! what do you mean?"

"I mean,—I do not think that now he would be unwilling that you should know, my darling,—that a woman came between us. Someone not so good, not so innocent as Barbara Rebell,—for I do think that in this matter she was quite innocent, Lucy."

"But father always liked you best, mother? How could he help it?"

"No," said Mrs. Kemp, "there was a time when he did not like me best. There were years when he loved the other woman, and I was—well, horribly unhappy. And yet, you see, he came back to me,—I fought through,—and you, my dear one, will fight through, please God, to be as happy a woman as your mother has been ever since you have known her."

THE END.

Lector House believes that a society develops through a two-fold approach of continuous learning and adaptation, which is derived from the study of classic literary works spread across the historic timeline of literature records. Therefore, we aim at reviving, repairing and redeveloping all those inaccessible or damaged but historically as well as culturally important literature across subjects so that the future generations may have an opportunity to study and learn from past works to embark upon a journey of creating a better future.

This book is a result of an effort made by Lector House towards making a contribution to the preservation and repair of original ancient works which might hold historical significance to the approach of continuous learning across subjects.

HAPPY READING & LEARNING!

LECTOR HOUSE LLP
E-MAIL: lectorpublishing@gmail.com

Lightning Source UK Ltd.
Milton Keynes UK
UKHW010842141220
375205UK00002B/221